ABOUT THE AUTHOR

...es Lackey is one of the most brilliant and pop-
...ing fantasy authors writing today. Adept at
...d high fantasy, she is best known for her
...ar books, which comprise a duology (*The
...nd* and *Oathbreakers*), three trilogies (*The Last
...Mage: Magic's Pawn, Magic's Promise* and
...Price; The Heralds of Valdemar: Arrows of the
...Arrow's Flight* and *Arrow's Fall*; and *The Mage
...Winds of Fate, Winds of Change* and *Winds of
...d one novel, *By the Sword*. She collaborated
...dré Norton on *The Elvenbane*. She is a prolific
...writer and a born storyteller whose diverse
...coming to be appreciated by an ever-growing
... She lives in Tulsa, Oklahoma, with her hus-
...e artist Larry Dixon.

MAGIC'S PRICE

BOOK THREE OF
THE LAST HERALD-MAGE

MERCEDES LACKEY

A ROC BOOK

ROC

Published by the Penguin Group
Penguin Books Ltd, 27 Wrights Lane, London W8 5TZ, England
Penguin Books USA Inc., 375 Hudson Street, New York, New York 10014, USA
Penguin Books Australia Ltd, Ringwood, Victoria, Australia
Penguin Books Canada Ltd, 10 Alcorn Avenue, Toronto, Ontario, Canada M4V 3B2
Penguin Books (NZ) Ltd, 182–190 Wairau Road, Auckland 10, New Zealand

Penguin Books Ltd, Registered Offices: Harmondsworth, Middlesex, England

First published in the USA by Daw Books, Inc., New York, 1990
First published in Great Britain by Roc, 1992
10 9 8 7 6 5 4 3 2 1

 Roc is a trademark of Penguin Books Ltd

Printed in England by Clays Ltd, St Ives plc

To
Russell Galen
Judith Louvis and Sally Paduch
and everyone who dreams of wearing Whites

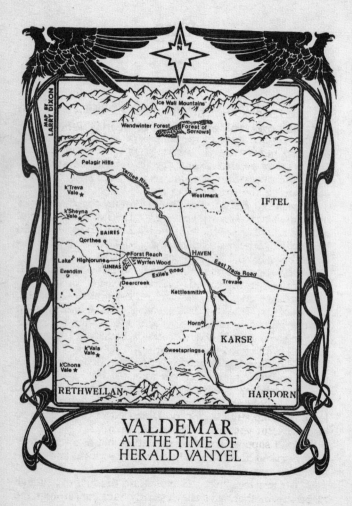

VALDEMAR
AT THE TIME OF
HERALD VANYEL

One

Sweat ran down Herald Vanyel's back, and his ankle hurt a little—he hadn't twisted it, quite, when he'd slipped on the wooden floor of the salle back at the beginning of this bout, but it was still bothering him five exchanges later.

A point of weakness, and one he'd better be aware of, because his opponent was watching for such signs of weakness, sure as the sun rose.

He watched his adversary's eyes within the shadows of his helm. *Watch the eyes*, he remembered Jervis saying, over and over. *The eyes will tell you what the hands won't.* So he studied those half-hidden eyes, and tried to hide his entire body behind the quillons of his blade.

The eyes warned him, narrowing and glancing to the left just before Tantras moved. Vanyel was ready for him.

Experience told him, just before their blades touched, that this would be the last exchange. He lunged toward Tantras instead of retreating as Tran was obviously expecting, engaged and bound the other's blade, and disarmed him, all in the space of a breath.

The practice blade clattered onto the floor as Tantras shook his now-empty hand, swearing.

"Stung, did it?" Vanyel said. He straightened, and pulled at the tie holding his hair out of his eyes, letting it fall loose in damp strands. "Sorry. Didn't mean to get quite so vigorous. But *you* are out of shape, Tran."

"I don't suppose you'd accept getting old as an excuse?" Tantras asked hopefully, as he took off his gloves and examined the abused fingers.

Vanyel snorted. "Not a chance. Bard Breda is old enough to be my mother, and she regularly runs me around the salle. You are woefully out of condition."

The other Herald pulled off his helm, and laughed rue-

7

fully. "You're right. Being Seneschal's Herald may be high in status, but it's low in exercise."

"Spar with my nephew Medren," Vanyel replied. "If you think *I'm* fast, you should see him. That'll keep you in shape." He unbuckled his practice gambeson while he spoke, leaving it in a pile of other equipment that needed cleaning up against the wall of the salle.

"I'll do that." Tantras was slower in freeing himself from the heavier armor he wore. "The gods know I may need to face somebody using that cut-and-run style of yours some day, so I might as well get used to fights that are half race and half combat. And *entirely* unorthodox."

"That's me, unorthodox to the core." Vanyel racked his practice sword and headed for the door of the salle. "Thanks for the workout, Tran. After this morning, I needed it."

The cool air hit his sweaty skin as he opened the door; it felt wonderful. So good, in fact, that between his reluctance to return to the Palace and the fresh crispness of the early morning, he decided to take a roundabout way back to his room. One that would take him away from people. One that would, for a moment perhaps, take his mind off things as well as his bout with Tantras had.

He headed for the paths to the Palace gardens.

Full-throated birdsong spiraled up into the empty sky. Vanyel let his thoughts drift away, following the warbling notes, leaving every weighty problem behind him until his mind was as empty as the air above—

:*Van, wake up! Your feet are soaked!*: Yfandes' mindvoice sounded rather aggrieved. :*And you're chilling yourself. You're going to catch a cold.*:

Herald-Mage Vanyel blinked, and stared down at the dew-laden grass of the neglected garden. He couldn't actually see his feet, hidden as they were by the long, dank, dead grass—but he could feel them, now that 'Fandes had called his attention back to reality. He'd come out here wearing his soft suede indoor boots—they'd been perfect for sparring with Tran, but now—

:*They are undoubtedly ruined,*: she said acidly.

She sounded so like his aunt, Herald-Mage Savil, that he had to smile. "Won't be the first pair of boots I've ruined, sweetheart," he replied mildly. His feet *were* very wet. And very cold. A week ago it wouldn't have been dew out here, it would have been frost. But Spring was well on the way now; the grass was greening under the dead growth of last year, there were young leaves unfolding on every branch, and a few of the earliest songbirds had begun to invade the garden. Vanyel had been watching and listening to a pair of them, rival male yellowthroats, square off in a duel of melody.

:Probably not the last article of clothing you'll ruin, either,: she said with resignation. *:You've come a long way from the vain little peacock I Chose.:*

"That vain little peacock you Chose would still have been in bed." He yawned. "I think he was the more sensible one. This hour of the day is positively unholy."

The sun was barely above the horizon, and most of the Palace inhabitants were still sleeping the sleep of the exhausted, if not the just. This half-wild garden was the only one within the Palace grounds with its eastern side unblocked by buildings or walls, and the thin, clear sunlight poured across it, making every tender leaf and grass blade glow. Tradition claimed this patch of earth and its maze of hedges and bowers to be the Queen's Garden—which was the reason for its current state of neglect. There was no Queen in Valdemar now, and the King's lifebonded had more urgent cares than tending pleasure gardens.

An old man, a gardener by his earth-stained apron, emerged from one of the nearby doors of the Palace and limped up the path toward Vanyel. The Herald stepped to one side to let him pass and gave him a friendly enough nod of greeting, but the old man completely ignored him; muttering something under his breath as he brushed by.

His goal, evidently, was a rosevine-covered shed a few feet away; he vanished inside it for a moment, emerged with a hoe, and began methodically cultivating the nearest flowerbed with it. Van might as well have been a spirit for all the attention the old man gave him.

Vanyel watched him for a moment more, then turned and walked slowly back toward the Palace. "Did it ever occur to you, love," he said to the empty air, "that you and I and the entire Palace could vanish overnight, and people like that old man would never miss us?"

:Except that we wouldn't be trampling his flowers anymore,: Yfandes replied. *:It was a bad morning, wasn't it.:*

A statement, not a question. Yfandes had been present in the back of Vanyel's mind during the whole Privy Council session.

"One of Randi's worst yet. That's why I was taking my frustration out with Tran." Vanyel kicked at an inoffensive weed growing up through the cobbles of the path. "And Randi's got some important things to take care of this afternoon. Formal audiences, for one—ambassadorial receptions. *I* won't do, not this time. It has to be the King, they're insisting on it. Sometimes I wish I didn't have to be so politic, and could knock a few diplomatic heads together. Tashir, bless his generous young heart, handled things a bit better with his lot."

Another gardener appeared, and looked at Vanyel oddly as he passed. Van suppressed the urge to call him back and explain. *He must be new; he'll learn soon enough about Heralds talking to thin air.*

:What did Tashir do with his envoys? I was talking to Ariel's Darvena while you were dealing with them. You know, I still can't believe your brother Mekeal produced a child sensitive enough to be Chosen.:

"Neither can I. But then, illogic runs in the family, I guess. As for Tashir; his envoys have been ordered to accept me as the voice of the King—" Vanyel explained. "The trouble's with the territories he annexed on Lake Evendim. This lot from the Lake District is touchy as hell, and being received by anyone less than Randi is going to be a mortal affront."

:Where did you pick that tidbit up?:

"Last night. After you decided that stallion from up North had a gorgeous—"

:Nose,: Yfandes interrupted primly. *:He had a perfectly lovely nose. And you and Joshe were boring me to tears with your treasury accounts.:*

"Poor Joshe."

He meant that. *Less than a year in the office, and trying to do the work of twenty. And wishing with all his soul he was back as somebody's assistant. And unfortunately, Tran knows less about the position then he does.*

:He's not comfortable as Seneschal.:

"In the black, love. He's young, and he's nervous, and he wanted somebody else to go over his figures before he presents them to the Council." Vanyel sighed. "The gods know Randi can't. He'll be lucky to make it through this afternoon."

:Esten will help. He'll do anything for Randi.:

"I know that, but—'Fandes, the pain-sharing a Companion can do and the strength a Companion can lend just aren't enough anymore. And it's time we all admitted what we know. Randi's too sick for anything we know to cure—" Vanyel took a deep breath to steady his churning insides. "—and the very best we can hope for is to find some way to ease his pain so he can function when he has to. And hope we can get Treven trained soon in case we can't."

:Get Treven trained in time, you mean,: Yfandes replied glumly. *:Because we're running out of it. I hate this, Van. We can't do anything, the Healers can't do anything—Randale is just dying by inches, and none of us can do anything about it!:*

"Except watch," Van replied with bitterness. "He gets a little worse every day, and not only can't we stop it, we don't even know why! I mean, there are some things not even the Healers can cure, but we don't even know what this illness that's killing Randi *is*—is it inheritable? Could Treven have it, too? Randi didn't show signs until his mid-twenties, and Trev is only seventeen. We could be facing the same situation we have now in another ten or fifteen years."

Unbidden thoughts lurked at the back of his mind. *A good thing Jisa isn't in the line of succession, or people would be asking that about her, too. And how could I explain why she's in no danger without opening a much bigger trouble-box than any of us care to deal with? Especially her. She takes on too much. It's bad enough just being fifteen and the King's daughter. To have to deal with the rest of this—thank the gods there are some difficulties I can spare her.*

He stared down at the overgrown path as he walked, so deep in thought that Yfandes tactfully withdrew from contact. There were some things, or so she had told him, that even a Companion felt uncomfortable about eavesdropping on.

He walked slowly through the neglected garden. He took the winding path back to the door from the Palace, setting his feet down with exaggerated care, putting off his return to the confines of the building as long as he could. But his troubles had a tendency to pursue him beyond the walls.

"Uncle Van?" a breathless young female voice called from behind him. He heard the ache in the familiar voice, the unshed tears; he turned and opened his arms, and Jisa ran into them.

She didn't say anything; she didn't have to. He knew what brought her out here; the same problems that had driven him out into the unkempt maze of the deserted garden. She'd been with her mother and father all morning, right beside Van, doing what she could to ease Randale's pain and boost Shavri's strength.

Van stroked her long, unbound hair, and let her sob into his shoulder. He hadn't known she was behind him—

Ordinarily that would have worried him. But not since it was Jisa. She was very good at shielding; so good, in fact, that she could render herself invisible to his Othersense. That was no small protection to her—since if she could hide her presence from *him*, she could certainly hide it from enemies.

Vanyel was tied to every other Herald alive, and was able to sense *them* whenever he chose, but since Jisa wasn't a Herald, he wouldn't "know" where she was unless he was deliberately "Looking" for her.

Jisa had not yet been Chosen, which Vanyel thought all to the good. To his way of thinking, she didn't need to be. As an Empath she was getting full Healer's training, and Van and his aunt Savil were instructing her exactly as they would have a newly-Chosen Herald. If people wondered why the child of two full Heralds wasn't yet Chosen when every Companion at Haven loved her and treated her as one of their own, let them continue to wonder. Vanyel was one of the few who knew the reason. Jisa hadn't been Chosen because her Companion would be Taver, and Taver was the Companion to the King's Own, Jisa's mother Shavri. So Jisa and Taver would not bond until Shavri was dead.

Not an event anyone cared to rush.

None of them, not Randale, Shavri nor Vanyel, were ready for even the Heraldic Circle to know *why* she hadn't been Chosen. Jisa knew—Vanyel had told her—but she seldom said anything about it, and Van didn't push her. The child had more than enough to cope with as it was.

Being an Empath and living in the household of your dying parent—

It was one thing to know that someone you loved was going to die; to share Randale's pain as Jisa did must be as bad as any torture Van could think of.

Small wonder she came to Vanyel and cried on his shoulder. The greater wonder was that she didn't do so more often.

He insinuated a tiny thread of thought into her mind as he stroked her tangled, sable-brown hair. Not to comfort; there was no comfort in this situation. Just something to let her know she wasn't alone. *:I know, sweetling. I know. I'd give my sight to take this from you.:*

She turned her red-eyed, tear-smudged face toward his. *:Sometimes I think I can't bear it anymore; I'll kill something or go mad. Except that there's nothing to kill, and going mad wouldn't change anything.:*

He smoothed the hair away from her face with both hands, cupped her chin in one hand, and met her hazel eyes with his own. *:You are much too practical for me, sweetling. I doubt that either of those considerations would hold me for a second in your place.:* He pretended to think for a moment. *:I believe, on the whole, I'd choose to go mad. Killing something is so very messy if you want it to be satisfying. And how would I get the blood out of my Whites?:*

She giggled a little, diverted. He smiled back at her, and blotted the tears from her eyes and cheeks with a handkerchief he pulled from the cuff of one sleeve. *:You'll manage as you always do, dearest. By taking things one day at a time, and coming to me or Trev when you can't bear it all on your own shoulders.:*

She sniffled, and rubbed her nose with her knuckle. He pulled her hand away with a mock-disapproving frown and handed her his handkerchief. *:Stop that, little girl. I've told you a hundred times not go out without a handkerchief. What will people think, to see the King's daughter wiping her nose on her sleeve?:*

:That she's a barbarian, I suppose,: Jisa replied, taking it with a sigh.

:I swear, I'll have your women sew scratchy silver braid on all your sleeves to keep you from misusing them.: He frowned again, and she smiled.

:Now wouldn't that be a pretty picture? Sewing silver braid

on my clothing would be like putting lace on a horseblanket.: Jisa dressed plainly, as soberly as a priestly novice, except when coerced into something more elaborate by her mother. Take now; she was in an ordinary brown tunic and full homespun breeches that would not have been out-of-place on one of the Holderkin beyond the Karsite Border.

:Jisa, Jisa,: he sighed, and shook his head. Her eyes lit, and her pretty, triangular face became prettier with the mischief behind them. There were times he suspected her of dressing so plainly just to annoy him a little. *:Any other girl your age in your position would have a closet full of fine clothing. My mother's maids dress better than you do!:*

Mindspeech with Jisa was easier than talking aloud; she'd been a Mindspeaker since she was six and use of Mindspeech was literally second-nature to her. On the other hand, that made it very difficult to keep things from her. . . .

:Then no one will ever guess you *are my father, will they?:* she replied impudently. *:Perhaps you should be grateful to me, Father-Peacock.:*

He tugged a lock of hair. *:Mind your manners, girl. I get more than sufficient back-chat from Yfandes; I don't need it from you. Feeling any better?:*

She rubbed her right eye with the back of her hand, ignoring the handkerchief she held in it. *:A bit,:* she admitted.

:Then why don't you go find Trev? He's probably looking for you.: Van chuckled. Everyone who knew them knew that the two had been inseparable from the moment Treven stepped onto the Palace grounds. That pleased most of the Circle and Court—except those young ladies of the Court who cherished an infatuation with the handsome young Herald. Treven was a finely-honed, blond copy of his distant cousin Herald Tantras, one with all of Tran's defects—not that there were many—corrected. He had half the girls of the Court trailing languidly after him.

And he was Jisa's, utterly and completely. His loyalty was without question—and no one among the Gifted had any doubts as to his love for her.

Sometimes that worried Van; not that they were so strongly attracted to each other, but because Treven was likely to have to make an alliance-marriage, just the way his grandmother, Queen Elspeth, had.

It would never be a marriage in more than name, Vanyel
was certain of that. There were conditions in Treven's case
that his grandmother and cousin had not ever needed to
consider. Elspeth had not been a Mindspeaker; Randi
wasn't much of one. No one but another Herald with that
particular Gift could guess how distasteful it would be for
a powerful Mindspeaker like Trev to make love to someone
who was not only mind-blocked, but a total stranger. Probably a frightened, unhappy stranger.

*One wonders how any Mindspeaking Monarch could be
anything but chaste. . . .*

Yet the Monarchs of Valdemar had done their duty
before, and likely would do so again. Probably Trev would
have to, as well. Yes, it was heartrending, but it was a fact
of life. Heralds did a lot of things they didn't always like.
As far as that went, for the good of Valdemar, *Vanyel* could
and would have bedded anyone or anything.

In fact, he had done something of the sort, though it
hadn't been exactly disagreeable; Van had fathered Jisa
with poor, dear Shavri, when Randale proved to be sterile—
even though his *preference* was, then and now, for his own
sex. . . .

Shaych, they called it now—from the *Tayledras* word
shay'a'chern, though only a handful of people in all of Valdemar knew that. Though openly shaych, he'd given Shavri
a child because Randale couldn't, and because she'd wanted
one so desperately—Randi needed his lifebonded stable and
whole, and the need for a child had been tearing her apart.

And her pregnancy had stilled any rumors that Randale
might not be capable of fathering a child, which kept the
channels open for proposals of alliance-marriages to *him*, at
least until his illness became too severe to hide.

But because Randale had needed to keep those lines
open—and because Shavri was terrified of even the *idea* of
ruling—he'd never married his lifebonded. So when it
became evident that Randale was desperately ill, and that
the Companions "inexplicably" were not going to Choose
Jisa, Randale's collateral lines had been searched for a suitable candidate.

Treven was the only possible choice at that point; he'd
been Chosen two years ago, he was a Mindspeaker as powerful as Vanyel. He understood the principles of govern-
ing—at least so far as they applied to his own parents'

Border-barony, since he'd been acting as his father's right-hand man since he was nine.

Jisa had loved him from the moment he'd crossed the threshold of the Palace. It wasn't obligatory for the King's Own to be in love with her monarch, but Vanyel was of the opinion that it helped. . . .

Except that it makes things awfully complicated.

:She's not a child anymore,: Yfandes reminded him. At that point he really *looked* at her, and saw the body of a young woman defining the shape of what had been shapeless before this year.

:Let's not borrow trouble before we have to,: he thought back at his Companion, avoiding the topic.

Jisa looked back at him with those too-old, too-wise eyes. *:Trev's waiting for me; he sent me to you. Sometimes he knows what I need before I do.:*

He released her, and stepped back a pace. *:Think you still need me?:*

She shook her head, and pulled her hair back over her shoulders. *:No, I think I'll be all right, now. I don't know how you do it, Father—how you manage to be so strong for all of us. I'll go back in now, but if you need me for anything—:*

He shook his head, and she smiled weakly, then turned and threaded her way across the overgrown flowerbeds, taking the most direct route back, the route he had avoided.

Soaking *her* shoes. And not caring in the least.

:Like father, like daughter,: Yfandes snorted.

:Shut up, horse,: Van retorted absently.

His own thoughts followed his daughter. *It's a life-bonding, the thing between her and Trev. I'm positive. The way she's always aware of him, and Trev of her . . . in a way that's not a bad thing. She's going to need all the emotional help she can get when Randi dies, and she surely won't get it from Shavri. Shavri is going to be in too much pain herself to help Jisa—assuming Shavri lives a candlemark beyond Randi. . . .*

But the problems . . . gods above and below! Is she old enough to understand what Trev is going to have to do—that the good of Valdemar may—will—take precedence over her happiness? How can any fifteen-year-old understand that? Especially with her heart and soul so bound up with his?

But—she was old enough to understand about me. . . .

How well Vanyel remembered. . . .

* * *

. . . .the provisions of the exclusion to be as follows. . . .

"Uncle Van?"

Vanyel had looked up from the proposed new treaty with Hardorn. He had the odd feeling that there was something hidden in the numerous clauses and subclauses, something that could cause a lot of trouble for Valdemar. He wasn't the only one—the Seneschal was uneasy, and so were any Heralds with the Gift of ForeSight that so much as entered the same room with it.

So he'd been burning candles long into the night, searching for the catch, trying to ferret out the problem and amend it before premonition became reality.

He'd taken the infernal thing back to his own room where he could study it in peace. It was past the hour when even the most pleasure-loving courtier had sought his or her bed; it was long past the hour when Jisa should have been in hers. Yet there she stood, wrapped in a robe three sizes too big for her, half-in, half-out of his doorway.

"Jisa?" he'd said, blinking at her, as he tried to pull his thoughts out of the maze of "whereases" and "party of the first parts." "Jisa, what are you doing still awake?"

"It's Papa," she'd said simply. She moved out of the doorway and into the light. Her eyes were dark-circled and red-rimmed. "I can't do anything, but I can't sleep, either."

He'd held out his arms to her, and she'd come to him, drooping into his embrace like an exhausted bird into its nest.

:Uncle Van—: She'd Mindtouched him immediately, and he could sense thoughts seething behind the ones she Sent. *:Uncle Van, it's not just Papa. I have a question. And I don't know if you're going to like it or not, but I have to ask you, because—because I need to know the answer.:*

He'd smoothed her hair back off her forehead. *:I've never lied to you, and I've never put you off, sweetling,:* he'd replied. *:Even when you asked uncomfortable questions. Go ahead.:*

She took a deep breath and shook off his hands. *:Papa isn't my real father, is he? You* are.*:*

He'd had less of a shock from mage-lightning. And he'd answered without thinking. *:I—yes—but—:*

She'd thrown her arms around his neck and clung to him, not saying anything, simply radiating relief.

Relief—and an odd, subdued joy.

He blinked again, and touched her mind, tentatively.
:*Sweetling? Do*—:

:*I'm glad,*: she said. And let him fully into her mind. He
saw her fears—that she would become sick, as Randale had.
Her puzzlement at some odd things she'd overheard her
mother say—and the strange evasions Shavri had given
instead of replies. The frustration when she sensed she
wasn't being told the truth. The bewilderment as she tried
to fathom questions that became mystery. And the love she
had for *him*. A love she now felt free to offer him, like a
gift.

Perhaps it was that last that surprised him the most. :*You
don't mind?*: he asked, incredulously. He could hardly
believe it. Like many youngsters in adolescence, she'd been
a little touchy around him of late. He'd assumed that it was
because she felt uncomfortable around him—and in truth,
he'd expected it. Jisa knew what he was, that he was shaych,
and what that meant, at least insofar as understanding that
he preferred men as close companions. Neither he nor her
parents had seen any point in trying to hide that from her;
she'd always been a precocious child, as evidenced by *this*
little surprise. :*You really don't mind?*: he repeated, dazed.

"Why should I *mind?*" she asked aloud, and hugged him
harder. "Just—tell me why? Why isn't Papa my father—
and why is it you?"

So he had, as simply and clearly as he could. She might
have been barely over twelve, but she'd taken in his words
with the understanding of someone much older.

She left him amazed.

She'd finally gone off to her bed—but had sent him back
to his treaty both bewildered and flattered, that she admired
him so very much. . . .

And loved him so very much.

She still loved him, admired him, and trusted him; sometimes she trusted him more than her "parents." Certainly
she confided more in him than in Shavri.

He shook his head a little, and continued down the cob-
bled path that would lead him eventually to the door out
of the garden. *Poor Jisa. Shavri leans on her as if she were
an adult—depends on her for so much—it hardly seems fair.*

Then again, maybe I should envy the little minx. I still can't get my parents to think of me as an adult.

All too soon he came to the end of the path. Buried in a tangle of hedges and vines was the chipped, green-painted door. He opened it, and stepped into the darkened hallway of the Queen's suite.

The rooms were just as neglected as the garden had been; dark, full of dusty furniture, and with a faint ghost of Elspeth's violet perfume still hanging in the air. Shavri had never felt comfortable here, and Randale had deemed it politic (after much discussion) to leave this suite empty as a sign that he *might* take a Queen.

That "might" had been hard-won from Randi—because although Shavri was both his King's Own and his lifebonded love, his advisors (Vanyel among them) had managed to convince him that he should at least *appear* to be free to make an alliance and seal it with a wedding.

Shavri had seen the need, but Randale had been rebellious, even angry with them. But after hours of argument, even he could not deny the fact that Valdemar's safety would be ill-served if he acted to please only himself. It was a lesson Trev was going to have to learn all too soon.

Fortunately Shavri—lovely, quiet Shavri—had backed them with all the will in her slender body. And that was considerable, for she was a full and powerful Healer as well as being a Herald. Herald-Mages were rare; before Taver Chose Shavri, Valdemar had never seen a Herald-Healer. Van hoped the need would never arise for there to be another.

Vanyel eased through the rooms with a sense, as always, that he was disturbing something. Dust motes hung in the sunbeams that shone through places where the curtains had parted. Despite that hint of perfume, there was no sense of "presence"—it was rather as though what he was disturbing were the rooms themselves rather than something inhabiting them. There were several places in the Palace like that; places where it seemed as if the walls themselves were alive. . . .

Taver had Chosen Shavri when Lancir had died—just before Elspeth herself had passed. The Heralds had been puzzled; they hadn't known why a Healer should be Chosen, though most assumed it was for lack of a more suitable candidate, or simply because Shavri and Randale were life-

bonded. Only later, when Shavri couldn't seem to conceive
for all her trying, did *she* suspect that the reason for Taver's
taking her was that something was wrong with Randi.

And only *much* later did they all learn that her suspicion
was correct.

At that point, wild horses couldn't have dragged her to
the altar to marry Randale. If there was one thing Shavri
didn't want, it was the responsibility of rule.

Vanyel eased open one side of the heavy double door to
the main corridor, and shut it behind him. His own responsibilities settled over him like a too-weighty cloak. He
straightened his back, squared his shoulders, and set off
down the stone-floored hall toward his own quarters in the
Heralds' Wing.

Shavri was, if truth were to be told, entirely unsuited to
ruling. *I guess we should be just as pleased that she doesn't
want Consort status,* Vanyel thought, nodding to an early-
rising courtier, one already clad in peacock-bright, elaborately embellished Court garb. *For her own sake, and Jisa's
sake, I think she made the right decision. I know she didn't
want Jisa forced into the position of Heir, and really, this
was the only way to keep that from happening. She can't be
sure that Jisa wouldn't be Chosen if the Companions thought
it necessary. And if she were Chosen and rightborn—*

*But Jisa's legally a bastard and can't inherit, and not being
Chosen makes her doubly safe.*

The stone floor gave way to wood; the "Old Palace" to
the New. Vanyel ran over the plans for the day in his mind;
first *his* audience with Tashir's people, then a session with
the Privy Council, then with the Heraldic Circle. Then the
audiences with Randale and the Lake District envoys. Shavri would be there, of course; Randale needed her Gift and
her strength. She spent it all on him, which left her no time
or energy for any of the normal duties of the King's Own.
No matter; Vanyel took those—and even if she'd had the
strength to spare, Shavri had not been very skilled at those
tasks. . . .

:Shavri was abysmal at those tasks,: Yfandes said tartly.
*:The only reason she wasn't a total failure was that she relied
on Taver and on you to tell her what to do and say.:*

Vanyel stopped long enough to have a few words with
one of Joshe's aides, an older girl-page with a solemn face,

his mind only vaguely on what he was saying to the girl.
:'Fandes, that isn't kind.:

*:Maybe. But it's true. The only thing she showed any real
talent in was managing Randi and in knowing where her
skills weren't up to the job. If Shavri'd let Randale go
through with wedding her,* she'd *be next in line even before
Jisa, and that would be a disaster.:*

Vanyel wanted to be able to refute her, but he couldn't.
Shavri *wasn't* a ruler; she wasn't even a Herald except in
having Taver. Vanyel did most of her work, from playing
ambassador with full plenipotentiary powers, to creating
and signing minor legal changes into effect. From being
First in the Circle to being First in the Council, to being
Northern Guardian of the Web; he did it all. He even took
Randale's place in the Council in the King's absence.

:That's most of the time, now,: Yfandes observed sadly.

Van got the answer he wanted out of the child, despite
his distraction. She smoothed her tunic nervously, plainly
anxious to be gone, and Vanyel obliged her. He was still
analyzing the overtones of his conversation with Jisa. *:We've
got a new problem. Did you pick up what I did from Jisa?:*
he asked, hurrying his steps toward his room. His feet were
beginning to ache with the cold, and the wet leather had
begun to chafe his ankles.

*:About the real reason why she came to cry on your shoul-
der? The one she doesn't want to think about? It was too
cloudy for me to read.:*

Vanyel sensed someone in his room as he neared it, but
it was a familiar presence, though one without the "feel"
of a Herald, so he didn't bother to identify his visitor. *:Sha-
vri,:* he said grimly. *:It's what she's picking up from her
mother. Jisa knows Randi's doomed; she's coming to grips
with that. What she can't handle is that Shavri's getting more
desperate by the moment, more afraid of being left alone.
Jisa's afraid that when Randi leaves us—her mother will
follow.:*

He felt Yfandes jerk her head up in surprise. *:She's a
Healer!:* the Companion exclaimed. *:She can't—she
wouldn't—:*

:Don't count on it, dearheart,: Vanyel answered, one hand
on the door latch. *:Even I can't tell you what she'll do. I
don't think she'd actively suicide on us—but she* is *a Healer.
She knows enough about the way that the body works to kill*

herself through lacking the will to live. And that's what Jisa's afraid she'll do; just pine away on us. And the worst of it is, I think she'd right.:

He pushed the door to his spare quarters open; it was full of light and air, but not much else. Just a bed, a low, square table, a few floor-pillows, a wardrobe, and a couch.

On the couch was his visitor—and despite his worries, Vanyel felt his mouth stretching in a real smile.

"Medren!" he exclaimed, as the lanky, brown-haired young Bard-trainee rose and reached across the table to embrace him. "Lord and Lady, nephew, I think you get taller every week! I'm sorry about not being able to get to your recital, but—"

Medren shook long hair out of his warm brown eyes, and smiled. "Tripes, it isn't my first, and it isn't going to be my last. That's not what I came after you for, anyway."

"No?" Vanyel settled himself down in his favorite chair, and raised an inquiring eyebrow. "What brings you, then?"

Medren resumed his seat, leaning forward over the table, his eyes locking with Van's. "Something a hell of a lot more important than a stupid recital. Van, I think I have something that can help the King."

Two

Vanyel closed the door behind him, balanced with one hand still on the door handle, and reached down to pull one of his boots off. "What exactly do you mean?" he asked, examining it, and deciding that it was going to survive the soaking after all. "Forgive me if I sound skeptical, Medren, but I've heard that particular phrase dozens of times in the past few years, and in the end nothing anyone tried made any difference. I'm sure you mean well—"

Medren perched in a chair beside the window, with not only his expression but his entire body betraying how tense he was. The curtains fluttered in a sudden gust of breeze, wrapping themselves over his arm. He pushed them away with an impatient grimace. "That's why I waited so long, I really thought about this for a while before I decided to talk to you," Medren told him earnestly. "You've had every Healer, herbalist, and so-called 'physician' in the Kingdom in and out of here—I wasn't going to come to you unless it wasn't just me who was sure we had something."

Vanyel pulled off his other boot, and regarded his nephew dubiously. He'd never known Medren to go overboard—but there had been so many times when a new treatment had sounded promising and had achieved nothing. . . . Medren's judgment was unlikely to be better than anyone else's.

Still—there was always the chance. There was little doubt that in Medren Van was dealing with a rational adult now, not an overly impressionable boy. Medren had grown taller in the years since Vanyel had sent him off to Bardic Collegium, and even though he hadn't put on any bulk at all he was obviously at full growth. He actually looked like a pared-down, thin version of his father, Vanyel's brother Mekeal. Except for one small detail—he had his mother Melenna's sweet, doelike eyes.

*He must be just about ready to finish Journeyman's status
at least,* Vanyel realized with a start. *He might even be due
for Full Bard rank. Ye holy stars, he must be nearly twenty!*

The curtains flapped, and Medren pushed them away
again. "You know I wouldn't bring you anything trivial or
untried. I know better, and anyway, I've got my ranking to
think of. I'm one master-work away from Full Bard," he
finished, confirming Vanyel's startled assessment. He
combed his fingers restlessly through his long hair. "I can't
start my career by getting a reputation for chasing wild
geese. I've had Breda check this for me, and she's confirmed it. It seems my roommate, Stefen, has a Wild Talent.
He can sing pain away."

Van had made his way to the side of the bed by the end
of this speech; he sat down on it rather abruptly, and stared
at his young cousin. "He can—what?"

"He sings pain away." Medren shrugged, and the cloth
of his red-brown tunic strained over his shoulders. "We
don't know how, we only know he can. Found it out when
I had that foul case of marsh-fever and a head like an over-
ripe pumpkin."

Vanyel grimaced in sympathy; he'd had a dose of that
fever himself, and knew the miserable head and bone aches
it brought with it.

"Stef didn't know I was in the room; came in and started
practicing. I started to open my mouth to chase him out, I
figured that was the *last* thing I needed, but after the first
two notes *I couldn't feel any headache.* Point of fact, I fell
asleep." Medren leaned forward, and his words tumbled out
as he tried to tell Vanyel everything at once. "I woke up
when he finished, he was putting his gittern away, and the
headache was coming back. Managed to gabble something
out before he got away from me, and we tried it again.
Damned if I didn't fall asleep again."

"That could have been those awful herbal teas the Healers seem to set such store by," Vanyel reminded him. "They
put *me* to sleep—"

"Put you to sleep, sure, but they don't do much about
the head. Besides, we thought of that. Got at Breda when
I cured up, told her, got her to agree to play victim next
time she had one of her dazzle-headaches, and it worked
for her, too." He took a deep breath, and looked at Vanyel
expectantly.

"It did?" Vanyel was impressed despite his skepticism. Breda, as someone with the Bardic Gift, wasn't easily influenced by the illusions a strong Gift could weave. Besides, so far as he knew, nothing short of a dangerous concoction of wheat-smut could ease the pain of one of her dazzle-headaches.

Medren spread his hands. "Damned if I know how he does it, Van. But Stef's had a way of surprising us over at Bardic about once a week. Only eighteen, and *he's* about to make Full Bard. Just may beat me to it. Anyway, you were telling me how Randale hates to take those pain-drugs because they make him muddled—"

"But can't endure more than an hour without them, yes, I remember." Vanyel threw the abused boots in the corner and leaned forward on his bed, crossing his arms. "I take it you think we can use this Stefen instead of the drugs? I'm not sure that would work, Medren—the reason Randi hates the drugs is that his concentration goes to pieces under them. How can he do anything and listen to your friend at the same time?"

Medren swatted the curtains away again, jumped to his feet and began pacing restlessly, keeping his eyes on Vanyel. "That's the whole beauty of it—this Wild Talent of his seems to work whether you're consciously listening or not! Honest, Van, I thought this out—I mean, if it would work when Breda and I were *asleep,* it should work under any circumstances."

Vanyel stood up, slowly. This Wild Talent of Stefen's might not help—but then again, it might. It was worth trying. These days anything was worth trying. . . .

And they had tried anything and everything once the Healers had confessed themselves baffled. Hot springs, mud baths, diets that varied from little more than leaves and raw grains to nothing but raw meat. There had been no signs of a cure, no signs of improvement, just increasing pain and a steadily growing weakness. Nothing had helped Randale in the last year, not even for a candlemark. Nothing but the debilitating, mind-numbing drugs that Randi hated.

"Let's go talk to Breda," Van said abruptly, kneeling and fishing his outdoor boots out from under the bed. He looked up to catch Medren's elated grin. "Don't get excited," he warned. "I know you're convinced, but this may be nothing more than pain-sharing, and Randi's past the point where that's at all effective." He stood up, boots in hand, and pulled them on over his damp stockings. "But as you pointed out, it's worth trying. Astera knows we've tried stranger things."

Medren kept pace with his uncle easily, despite Vanyel's longer legs and ground-devouring strides. After all, *he* had just spent his Journeyman period completely afoot, in the wild northlands, where villages were weeks apart. *Fortunately it was also the shortest Journeyman trial in the history of the Collegium,* he reflected wryly, recalling his aching feet, sore back, and the nights he spent half-frozen in his little tent-shelter. *And it wasn't even winter yet! Three months up there gave me enough material for a hundred songs. Although so far half of them seem to be about poor souls freezing to death—*

Medren watched his uncle out of the corner of his eye, trying to gauge his feelings, but he couldn't tell what Van was thinking. In that, as in any number of things, Vanyel hadn't changed much in the past few years, though he had altered subtly from the uncle Medren had first encountered.

Gotten quieter, more focused inside himself. Doesn't even talk to anybody about himself anymore, not even Savil. Medren frowned a little. *Uncle Van isn't doing himself any favors, isolating himself like that.*

Vanyel had the kind of fine-boned, ascetic face that aged well, with no sign of wrinkling except around the eyes and a permanent worry-line between his brows. His once-black hair was thickly streaked with white, but that wasn't from age, that was from working magic with what he and his aunt, Herald-Mage Savil, called "nodes." Medren had gathered from Vanyel's complicated explanations that these node-things were collecting points for magical energy—and that they were infernally hard to deal with.

For whatever reason, the silver-streaked hair, when combined with the ageless face and a body that would have been the envy of most of Medren's peers, made Vanyel's appearance confusing—even to those who knew him. Young-old, and hard to categorize.

Add eyes the color of burnished silver, eyes that seemed to look right through a person, and you had the single most striking Herald in Whites. . . .

Medren frowned again. *And the least approachable.*

His nephew guessed that Vanyel had been purposefully learning how to control his expressions completely in the same way a Bard could. Probably for some of the same reasons. Not even a flicker of eyelid gave his thoughts away; over the past couple of years control had become complete. Even Medren, who knew him about as well as anyone, never knew what was running through his mind unless Van wanted him to know.

Vanyel was as beautiful as a statue carved from the finest alabaster by the hand of a master. But thanks to that absolute control, he was also about as remote and chill as that same statue.

Which is the way he wants it, Medren sighed. *Or at least, that's what he says. "I can't afford hostages," he says. "I can't let anyone close enough to be used against me." He doesn't even like having people know that he and I are as friendly as we are—and we're related. He thinks it makes me a target. . . .*

There actually had been at least one close scrape, toward the end of the Tashir affair. Medren hadn't realized how close that scrape had been until long after, in his third year at Bardic. And in some ways, Van was absolutely right, in that he couldn't afford close emotional relationships. If he'd been the marble statue he resembled, his isolation would likely have been a good thing.

But he wasn't. He was a living human being, and one who would not admit that he was desperately lonely.

To the lowest hells with that. If he doesn't find somebody he can at least talk to besides Savil, he's going to go mad in white linen one of these days. He's keeping everyone else sane, but who can he go to?

Nobody, that's who. Medren gritted his teeth. *Well, we'll see about that, uncle. If you can resist Stef, you're a candidate for the Order of Saint Thiera the Immaculate.*

They left the Palace itself, and followed a graveled path toward the separate building housing the Bardic Collegium; a three-storied, gray stone edifice. The first floor held classrooms, the second, the rooms of such Bards as taught here, and the third, the rooms of the apprentices and Journeymen about to be made Masters. There were only two of the latter, himself and Stefen. Some might have objected to being roomed with Stef, for the younger boy was shaych, and made no bones about it—but not Medren.

Not with Vanyel for an uncle, Medren reflected, with tolerant amusement. *Not that Stef's anything like Van. If uncle's a candidate for the Order of Saint Thiera, Stef's a candidate for the Order of the Brothers of Perpetual Indulgence! No wonder he writes good lovesongs; he's certainly had enough experience!*

One of the brown-tunicked Bardic apprentices passed them, laboring under a burden of four or five instruments. They stepped off the path long enough to let her pass; her eyes widened at the sight of Vanyel, and she swallowed and sketched a kind of salute as they passed by her. Van didn't notice, but Medren did; he winked at her and returned it.

Medren had gotten Stef as a roommate before this, back when he was an apprentice. *That was surely an experience! I'm not sure which was stranger for me; Stef as he arrived, or Stef once he figured out what he was.* Medren mentally shook his head. *What a country-bred innocent I was!*

Stef had arrived at the Collegium in the care of Bard Lynnell; barely ten, and frightened half to death. He had no idea what was going on, or why this strange woman had plucked him off his street corner and carried him off. Lynnell wasn't terribly good with children, and she hadn't bothered to explain much to young Stefen. That had been left to Medren, the only apprentice at the time who had no roommate.

And first I had to explain that this wasn't a bordello. He'd thought Lynn was a procurer.

Lynnell had heard the boy singing on the street corner, attracting good crowds despite being accompanied only by an unskilled hag with a bodhran. While the Bard had no talent for taking care of children, she *was* both skilled and graced with the Bardic Gift herself. She had recognized Stefen's Gift with the first notes she heard. And she knew what would happen if that child was left unprotected much longer—some accident would befall him, he could be sold to a whoremaster, some illness left untreated could ruin his voice for life—there were a thousand endings to this child's story, and few of them happy.

Until Lynnell had entered it, anyway. *One thing about Lynn; she goes straight for what she wants so fast that most people are left gaping after her as she rides out of sight.*

She'd made enough inquiries to ascertain that the crude old woman playing the drum and collecting the coins was *not* Stef's mother, nor any kind of relative. That was all it took for her to be on the sunny side of legality; once that was established, she had invoked Bardic Immunity and kidnapped him.

Then dumped him on me. Medren smiled. *Glad she did. He may have gotten me into trouble, but it was generally fun trouble.*

There were some who opined that Stefen's preference for his own sex stemmed from some experience with that nasty old harridan that was so appalling he'd totally repressed the memory. Privately Medren thought that was unlikely. So far as he was able to determine, she'd never laid a finger on Stefen except for an occasional hard shaking, or a slap now and then.

From everything Stef said, when she was sober, she knew where her money was coming from. She wasn't cruel, just crude, and not too bright. So long as her little songbird kept singing, she wasn't going to do anything to upset him.

He held the door to the Bardic Collegium open for his uncle, and followed closely on his heels.

All that Stef had suffered from was neglect, physical and emotional. The emotional neglect was quickly remedied by every adult female in the Collegium, who found the half-starved, big-eyed child irresistible.

Stef's spirits certainly revived quickly enough once he discovered the attention was genuine—and also learned he was to share the (relative) luxuries of the Bardic Collegium.

Like a roof over his head every night, u real bed, all he could eat whenever he wanted it, Medren thought, following Vanyel up the narrow staircase to the second floor. *Poor little lad. Whatever his keeper had been spending the money on, it certainly wasn't high living. Drugs, maybe. The gods know Stef's death on anybody he catches playing with them.*

Bard Breda's rooms were right by the staircase; Collegium lore had it that she'd picked that suite just so she could humiliate apprentices she caught sneaking in late at night.

The *fact* was that she had chosen those rooms because she was something of an Empath and something of a chirugeon; she'd gotten early herbalist training before her Gift was discovered. Bardic apprentices tended to get themselves in trouble with alarming regularity. Sometimes that trouble ended in black eyes—and occasionally in worse. Breda's

minor Talents had come to the rescue of more than one
wayward apprentice since the day she'd settled in to teach.

Like every other female in the place, she'd taken a liking
to Stef, which was just as well. Once Stef had reached the
age of thirteen his preferences were well established—and
his frail build combined with those preferences got him into
more fights than the rest of the apprentices combined.
Breda had patched Stefen up so many times she declared
that she was considering having the Healers assign him to
one of *their* apprentices as a permanent case study.

Vanyel paused outside the worn wooden door, and
knocked lightly.

"Come," Breda replied, her deep voice still as smooth as
cream despite her age, and steadier than the Palace founda-
tions. Vanyel pushed the door ajar, and let them both into
the dim cool of Breda's quarters.

Medren often suspected that Breda was at least half owl.
She was never awake before noon, she stayed alert until the
unholiest hours of the dawn, and she kept the curtains
drawn in her rooms no matter what time of day or night it
was. Of course, that could have been at least in part because
she was subject to those terrible headaches, during which
the least amount of light was painful . . . still, walking into
her quarters was like walking into a cave.

Medren peered around, trying to see her in the gloom,
blinking as his eyes became accustomed to it. He heard
a chuckle, rich and throaty. "By the window. I do read
occasionally."

Medren realized then that what he'd taken for an empty
chair did in fact have the Bard in it; he'd been fooled by
the shadows cast by the high back. "Hullo, Van," the
elderly Bard continued serenely. "Come to verify your
scapegrace nephew's tale, hmm?"

"Something like that," Vanyel admitted, finding another
chair and easing himself down into it. "You must admit that
most of the rumors of cures we've chased lately have been
mist-maidens."

Medren groped for a chair for himself; winced as the legs
scraped discordantly against the floor, and dropped down
onto its hard wooden seat.

"Sad, but true," Breda admitted. "I must tell you,
though, I was completely skeptical, myself. I'm difficult to
deceive at the best of times; when I have one of my spells

I really don't have much thought for anything but the pain. And that youngling *dealt* with the pain. I've no idea how, but he did it."

"So I take it you're in favor of this little experiement?" Medren thought Van sounded relieved, but he couldn't be sure.

A faint movement from the shadows in the chair signaled what might have been a shrug. "What have we got to lose? The boy can't hurt anyone with that Wild Talent, so the very worst that could happen is that the King will have one of our better young Journeymen providing appropriately soothing background music for the audiences. He'll have to have *someone* there entertaining in any case—someone with the Gift, to keep those ambassadors in a good mood. No reason why it can't be Stefen. The boy's amazingly good; very deft, so deft that even most Gifted Bards don't notice he's soothing them."

"No reason at all," Vanyel agreed. "Especially if he's that good. Can he do both at once?"

"Can you Mindspeak with 'Fandes and spellcast at the same time?" Breda countered.

"If the spell is familiar enough." Vanyel pondered. "But I don't know, he's not very experienced, is he? Medren told me he's still a Journeyman."

"He may not be experienced, but he's a damned remarkable boy," Breda replied, with an edge to her voice. "You ought to pay a bit more attention to what's going on under your nose, Van, the lad's been the talk of the Collegium for the past couple of years. That's why we kept him *here* for his Journeyman period instead of sending him out. The boy's got all *three* Bardic requirements, Van, not just two. The Gift, the ability to perform, and the creative Talent to compose. Three of his ballads are in the common repertory already, and he's not out of Journeyman status."

Vanyel coughed. "I stand rebuked," he replied, a hint of humor in his voice. "Well, let's give this Stefen a chance. Do you want to tell him, or shall I?"

Breda laughed. "You. I'd just gotten comfortable when you two sailed in. And at my age, one finds stairs more than a little daunting."

Vanyel rose, and Medren scrambled to join him. "You're just lazy, that's all," he mocked gently. "You can outdance,

outfight, outdrink, and outlast people half your age when
you choose."

"That's as may be," Breda replied as Vanyel turned toward
the door, her own voice just as mocking. "But right now I
don't choose. Let me know how things work out, youngling."

Medren felt a hand between his shoulderblades propelling
him out the door and into the corridor. "Just for that,"
Vanyel said over his shoulder as he closed the door, "I think
I'll see that someone tells you—some time next week."

A pungent expletive emerged, muffled, through the door.
Medren hadn't known Breda knew *that* particular phrase
. . . though anatomically impossible, it certainly would have
been interesting to watch if she'd decided to put his uncle
in that particular position. . . .

Stephen—or rather, Stefen's appearance—came as something of a surprise to Van. Vanyel had been expecting something entirely different—a youngster like Medren, but
perhaps a little plainer, a little taller. At some point he'd
formed a vague notion that people gifted with extraordinary
abilities tended to look perfectly ordinary.

Stefen was far from ordinary—

Van hung back when they'd gotten to the room Medren
shared with the boy, prompted by the feeling that Stefen
might be uneasy in his presence. Stef had just been leaving,
in fact. Medren intercepted him right at the door, and
Vanyel had lingered in an alcove while Medren explained
to the boy what they wanted of him. That gave Van ample
opportunity to study the musician while the youngster
remained unaware of the Herald's scrutiny.

Vanyel's first impression was of fragility. Stefen was
slight; had he been a girl, he'd have been called "delicate."
He was a little shorter than Vanyel, and as slim. That didn't
matter, though—Vanyel could tell that Stef's appearance
was as deceptive as his own. Stefen was fine-boned, yes,
but there was muscle over that bone; tough, wiry muscle.

I wouldn't care to take him on in a street fight, Van
observed, eyes half-closed as he studied the boy. *Something
tells me he'd win.*

Dark auburn hair crowned a triangular face; one composed, at first impression, of a pair of bottomless hazel eyes,
high cheekbones, and the most stubborn chin Van had ever
seen.

*He looks like a demented angel, like that painting in the
High Temple of the Spirit of Truth. The one that convinced
me that knowing too much truth will drive you mad. . . .*
Vanyel watched carefully as Stef listened to Medren's plans.
Once or twice, the boy nodded, and some of that wavy hair
fell into his eyes. He brushed it out of the way absently, all
his attention given to his roommate.

He was tense; that was understandable. Vanyel was very
glad that he had chosen to keep himself out of the way
now. The boy was under quite enough pressure without the
added stress of Herald Vanyel's presence. Van was quite
well aware how much he overawed most of the people he
came into contact with—that gardener this morning was the
exception. Most folk reacted the way that young Bardic
apprentice had on the way over here—the kind of mix of
fear and worship that made her try to bow to him despite
having both arms full, and despite custom that decreed otherwise. Heralds were not supposed to be "special." Rank was
not supposed to matter except inside Circle and Council.

Rules, apparently, did not apply to Herald-Mage Vanyel
Ashkevron.

Well, that's neither here nor there, he thought, watching
the young Journeyman-Bard carefully. *:'Fandes, what do
you think of this youngster?:*

He felt her looking out of his eyes, and felt her approval
before she voiced it. *:I like him, Van. He'll give you everything he has, without holding back. He has a very powerful
Bardic Gift, and he does indeed have a secondary Gift as
well that is nearly as powerful. It's something like MindHea-
ling, but very specific. I can't tell you any more than that
until I See it in action.:*

For the first time that day, Vanyel allowed his hope to
rise a little. *:Then you think this might work?:*

:I don't know any more than you do,: she replied, *:But
the boy has something unusual, and I think you'd be a fool
not to give him all he needs to wield it.:*

Van blinked. *:Huh. Well, right now, the only other thing
I can give him is to stay out of the way. I don't want to
frighten him into freezing by having The Great Herald-Mage
Vanyel Demonsbane descend on him.:*

:The Great Herald-Mage indeed,: she snorted. *:Sounds
like someone I know may not fit his hats before too long.:*

Medren opened the door to their room and waved Stefen

inside. He looked back over his shoulder at Van, who just nodded at him. The boy was doing just fine; so long as Stefen got to the Throne Room in time for the audiences, Vanyel didn't see any reason to interfere in the way things were going. He turned and headed back down the hallway to the stairs.

:I won't fit my hats, hmm?: he replied as he descended the stairs. *:Isn't that interesting. I was just thinking that it's been too long since the last time you and I went over the advanced endurance course together. Who was it I overheard boasting about the times she used to make over the course?:*

If she'd been human, she'd have spluttered. *:Van! That was a long time ago! The trainees are going to be out on the course at this time of the day—I'm going to look like an out-of-shape old bag of bones in front of them!:*

Vanyel chuckled, and pushed open the door to the outside with one hand. *:And who was it who told me she could run those trainees into the ground?:*

He hadn't known Yfandes knew that particular curse. He wondered if she'd learned it from Breda.

Stefen sagged bonelessly into the room's single comfortable chair, and stared at a discolored spot on the plastered wall.

This was what I wanted, right? That's why I let Medren talk me into trying that trick on Breda. I used to "cure" old Berte's hangovers by singing them away—I was sure I could do the same for what ailed Medren and Breda. And that would get me what I needed, since I knew damn well he has connections up into the Court. I knew he'd get me in to see if I could help the King. This is the only way I could think of to get Court favor, and get it honestly. Now, I know I can help King Randale. What I can do is better for him than his taking a lot of drugs. It'll be a fair exchange. So why am I so nervous about this?

He couldn't stand sitting there idle; he reached automatically for the gittern he kept, strung and tuned, beside the chair. It was one of his first student instruments—worn and shabby, a comforting old friend. He ran his fingers over the strings, in the finger exercises every Bard practiced every day of his life, rain or shine, well or ill.

He'd known about this trick of his, this knack of "singing pain away" for a long time—he'd had it forced on him, for

all practical purposes, by the old woman who had cared for
him for as long as he could remember. It was either sing
her pain away, or put up with her uncertain temper and
trust he could get out of her reach when she was suffering
a "morning after."

Old Berte wasn't his mother—but he couldn't remember
anyone who might have been his mother. There had only
been Berte. Those memories were vivid, and edged with
a constant hunger that was physical and emotional. Berte
teaching him to beg before he could even walk. Berte making false sores of flour-paste and cow's blood, so that he
looked ill. Berte binding up one of his legs so that he had
to hobble with the help of a crutch.

The hours of sitting beside her on a street corner, learning
to cry on cue.

Then the day when one of the other beggars brought out
a tin whistle, and Stef had begun to sing along, in a thin,
clear soprano—and when he'd finished, there was a crowd
about the three of them, a crowd that tossed more coppers
into Berte's cracked wooden bowl than he'd ever seen in
his short life.

*I looked up, and I saw the expression on her face, and I
knew I'd never have to limp around on a crutch again.*

He closed his eyes, and let his fingers walk into the next
set of exercises. *Berte bought us both a real supper of
cooked food from a food stall at the market. Fresh food, not
stale, not crumbs and leavings—and we shared a pallet and
a blanket that she bought from a ragman that night. That
was the best day of my life.*

It remained the best day of his life for a long while, for
once she had a steady source of income, Berte returned to
the pleasures that had made her a beggar in the first place.
Liquor, and the drug called "dreamerie."

*She drank and drugged away every copper we made. At
least I didn't have to spend half of every night trying to run
the cramps out of my legs,* he thought, forcing the muscles
in his shoulders to relax while he continued to play. *Things
were a little better. I could take care of her hangovers—
enough so that we could get out every morning. I was hungry, but I wasn't quite as hungry as when we'd just been
begging for a living. The worse she got, the easier it was to
hide a coin or two, and once she was gone into her dreams,
I could sneak out and buy something to eat. But I kept won-*

dering when she was going to run afoul of whoever it was
that sold her the drugs—how long it would be before the
craving got too much and she sold me the way she'd sold
her own children. An involuntary shudder made both his
hands tremble on the strings. *I was sure that was what had
happened when Lynnell grabbed me that night.*

It had been late; Berte had just sunk into snoring oblivion, and Stef had eased out between the loose boards at the
back of their tenement room, a couple of coppers clutched
in his fist. He had intended to head straight for Inn Row
where he knew he could buy a bowl of soup and all the
bread he could eat for those two coppers—but someone had
been waiting for him. A woman, tall, and sweet-smelling,
dressed all in scarlet.

She'd grabbed his arm as he rounded the corner, and
there had been two uniformed Guardsmen with her. Terror
had branded her words into his memory.

"Come with me, boy. You belong to Valdemar now."

He hadn't the faintest idea what she'd meant. He hadn't
known that "Valdemar" was the name of the kingdom
where he lived. He hadn't even known he lived in a Kingdom! All he'd ever known was the town; he'd never even
been outside its walls. He'd thought this "Valdemar" was a
person, and that Berte had either sold him or traded him
away.

*I was in terror—too frightened to object, too petrified to
even talk. I kept wondering who this "Valdemar" was, and
whether it was a he or a she—* He smiled at the next set of
memories. *Poor Lynn. When she finally figured out what I
thought she'd bought me for, she blushed as red as her tunic.*

She'd done her best to try and convince him otherwise,
but he really didn't believe her. He really didn't believe any
of it until a week or two after he'd been brought to the
Collegium, tested, and confirmed in his Gifts.

*It was really Medren that convinced me. Bless him. Bless
Breda for putting us together. He was a complete country
bumpkin, and I was an ignorant piece of street scum, and
together we managed to muddle through. If he was just
shaych, he'd have been perfect. He wasn't even jealous when
he found out I had all three Gifts, too, and in a greater
measure than he did. . . .*

It took two of what were commonly called "the Bardic
Gifts" to ensure entry into Bardic Collegium as a Bardic

apprentice rather than a simple minstrel. The first of those two were the most common: the ability to compose music, often referred to as the "Creative Gift," and the unique combination of skills and aptitudes that comprised the "Gift of Musicianship." The third was more along the lines of the Gift of Healing or one of the Heraldic Gifts—and that was simply called the "Bardic Gift."

It seemed to be related to projective Empathy; a person born with it had the ability to manipulate the moods of his audience through music. Some of the Bards of legend had been reputed to be able to *control* their listeners with their songs.

Stef had all three Gifts, just as Lynnell had suspected. Medren, who until Stefen had arrived had been the star apprentice, also had all three, but not to the extent Stef did.

Take the Creative Gift, for instance. Medren cheerfully admitted that he could no more compose anything more complicated than a simple ballad than he could walk on water. Or Musicianship; there were few even among the Master Bards that were Stef's peers in skill on his chosen instruments. In sober truth, there were few who even played as many instruments as he did. Although his favorite by far was the twelve-stringed gittern, he played virtually every string and percussion instrument known to exist, and even a few wind instruments, like the shepherd's pipes.

But it was Stefan's Bardic Gift that was the most impressive. Even before he had revealed his ability to come between the listener and his pain, the Master Bards had marveled at the strength of his Gift. Untrained, he could easily hold an audience of more than twenty; and when he exerted himself they would be deaf and blind to anything other than himself and his music.

Anybody but Medren would have been jealous. He just felt sorry for me, because I was alone. Stefen smiled, and modulated the last exercise into a lullaby. *There I was, the cygnet among the chicks, and instead of trying to peck me to bits like anyone else would have, he decided I needed a protector. Life would have been a lot harder without him. He kept me from making a lot of enemies. . . .*

He hadn't known until much later that a number of the sharp-tongued boys who initially closed their ranks against the stranger were children of high-ranking nobles, or were nobles in their own right. When he would have gone after them in the straight-forward "fight-or-be-beaten" manner of the streets, Medren had kept him from losing his head.

He helped me to at least get them to accept me. And I may need them. I certainly couldn't afford to have any of them holding grudges. He sighed and racked his instrument. *That's my only hope; court favor. And it's a damned good thing Medren kept me from losing it before I even had a chance at it. Being a Bard is better than being a beggar, but it's still a risky profession to be in, with no real security. A Healer can always rely on the Temple to care for him if something happens to him, and if a Herald ends up hurt or ill—Havens, most of them end up dead—there are always places for them* here, *at the Palace. But a Bard has only himself to rely on. If he loses his voice, or the use of his hands. . . .*

The harsh reality was that Stefen had come from the streets, and if something happened to him, the streets were likely where he'd end. Unless he built himself some kind of secure future.

Otherwise—

No. He got up, and stared for a moment out his window, at the Palace, the heart of all his hopes. *No. I'll do it. I'll make my own luck. I swear I won't go back to that. I won't end up like Berte.*

He gazed at the Palace for a moment more, then picked up the case holding his good gittern, squared his shoulders, and headed for the door.

So now "Valdemar" needs me, after all. That should work. I serve Valdemar, and we both get what we need. He nodded to himself, and closed the door behind him. *Fair enough.*

Three

"Are you going to be all right?" Vanyel asked in an undertone. Then he thought savagely in the next instant, *Of course he isn't going to be all right, you fool.* The King was as pale as paper, thin to transparency, with pain-lines permanently etched about his mouth and eyes. Under any other circumstances, Vanyel would have ordered him back to his bed; beads of sweat stood out all over his forehead with the effort of walking as far as the Audience Chamber, and Vanyel didn't have to exert his Empathy to know how much pain his joints were causing him. Vanyel would have traded away years of his life to give the King a few moments' respite from that agony. But he allowed none of this to show as he settled the colorless wraith that was King Randale into the heavily-padded shelter of his throne.

"I'll be fine," Randale replied, managing a strained smile. "Really, Van, you worry too much." But he couldn't restrain a gasp of pain as he slipped a little and hit his arm against the side of the throne.

Vanyel cursed his own clumsiness, and did his best not to clutch at Randale's fragile arms, as he caught Randale before he could fall and lowered the King carefully the rest of the way down into his seat. *Another bruise the size of my hand, and he doesn't need ten more where my fingers were.*

"Really, Van," Randale repeated with patently false cheer, once he'd been settled as comfortably as possible. "You worry too much." Vanyel stepped back a pace, ready to aid in any way he could, but sensing the King's irritability at his own weakness and helplessness. *He also doesn't need to be reminded of how little he can do anymore.*

The slight noise of the chamber's side door opening and shutting caught Randale's attention. He craned his head around a little to see who it was, as young Stefen entered the Audience Chamber, put down a stool, and began setting up near the throne.

"Is that a new Bard?" he asked with more real interest than he'd shown in anything all day. "I don't remember seeing that youngster in Court, and I'd surely remember that head of hair! He looks like a forest fire at sunset."

:Should I tell him, 'Fandes?:

:No,: came the immediate reply. *:It would be cruel to raise his hopes. Stefen is either going to be able to help him, or not. And if not, better that the King simply enjoy the music, as best he can.:*

Vanyel sighed. Yfandes could be coldly pragmatic at the oddest times. "Breda sent him over," Van temporized. "She says he's very good, and you can probably use him with this particular lot of hardheads."

"Gifted, hmm?" Randale looked genuinely interested.

"Quite remarkably, according to Breda." Vanyel coughed. "I gather she caught something in the wind about the Lake District lot, and sent him over specially. I understand he's to concentrate on something soothing."

Randale actually chuckled. "Breda is a very wise woman. Remind me to thank her."

At that moment, the delegation from the Lake District arrived, a knot of brightly-clad figures beside the door, who waited impatiently for the Seneschal to announce them. Vanyel stepped back to his place behind the throne and to Randale's left, while Shavri stepped forward to her position as King's Own at his right.

Please, he sent up a silent plea, *just let him get through this audience.*

Shavri nodded to the young Journeyman Bard, and Stefan began to play as the delegation formed themselves into a line and approached the throne.

Stefen fought down the urge to stare at the King, and concentrated on his tuning instead. Each brief glance at Randale that he stole appalled him more than the one before it. Only the thin gold band holding his lank hair back, and the deference everyone gave this man, convinced him that the man on—or rather, *in*—the throne was Valdemar's King. There were two other Heralds on the dais, one on either side of the throne; a dusky woman, and a man Stefen couldn't see because the woman was in his line-of-sight. Either one of them was a more kingly figure than Randale.

He'd known that Randale was sick, of course—that was no secret, and hadn't been for as long as Stefen had *been* in Haven. But he hadn't known just how sick Randale was; after all, apprentice and Journeymen Bards hardly were of sufficient rank to join the Court, especially not bastards like Medren and gutter rats like himself. The Bards didn't gossip about the King, at least not where their students could hear them. And Stef had never believed more than a quarter of what the townsfolk and nobly-born students would tell the presumptive Bards. He'd imagined that Randale would look ill; thin and pale, perhaps, since his illness was obviously serious. He'd never thought that the King could actually be dying.

Randale looked like a ghost; from colorless hair to skeletal features to corpse-pale complexion, if Stef had come upon this man in a darkened hallway, he'd have believed all the tales of spirits haunting the Palace. That the King wore Heraldic Whites didn't help matters; they only emphasized his pallor.

Stefen was stunned. He couldn't have imagined that the King was in *that* bad a state. It didn't seem possible; Kings weren't supposed to die in the ways ordinary mortals did. When Kings were ill, the Healers were supposed to take heroic measures, and cure them. Kings weren't supposed to have pain so much a part of their lives that every movement was hesitant, tremulous.

Kings were supposed to be able to command miracles.

Except this one can't. This one can't even command his own body to leave him in peace. . . .

There was something so heroic about this man, this King—sitting there despite the fact that he obviously belonged in bed, doing his job in spite of the fact that he was suffering—Stefen wanted to *do* something for him, to protect him. For the first time in his life, Stefen found himself wanting to help someone for no reason other than that the person needed the help.

And for a moment he was confused.

But I am *getting something out of this,* he reminded himself. *Notice at Court. Maybe even the King's favor, if I really do well. Come on, Stef, you know what's at stake here; settle down and do your work. If he needs your help, that's all the more reason that he'll be grateful when he gets it.*

There was a stir among the group of people beside the door, and they began to sort themselves out and move toward the throne. Stefen looked back to the three on the dais for instructions, and the dark-haired woman with the sorrowful eyes nodded at him purposefully.

Taking that as a signal, he began to play, dividing his power as he'd been instructed. The greater part went to King Randale. Once that was established, the remainder went toward the approaching delegates, soothing their fears, their suspicions—and they *were* suspicious, he could read that in their attitudes, just as he'd been taught. Bards weren't Thoughtsensers, but the kind of instruction they had in reading movement and expression sometimes made it seem that they were. It was plain to Stef that this lot thought Randale had been playing some kind of political game with them, calculatedly insulting them by making them wait for their audience.

Look, you fools, he thought at them, surprising himself with his anger at their attitude. *See what he's going through? He wasn't putting you off, the man's in agony; every moment he spends with you he's paying for in pain.*

He tried to put some of that behind his music, and it worked. He saw the mistrust in their hard, closed faces fade; watched the expressions turn to shock and bewilderment, then faint shame.

He allowed himself a moment of triumph before turning his attention back to the King.

He hadn't quite known what to expect from Randale in the way of an indication that he was doing some good. He had known he would manage *something* in the way of relief for the King; he had been completely confident of that. But how much—and whether there would be any outward sign—

It was the woman's reaction that surprised him the most. She clutched at the other Herald's arm, her expression astonished and incredulous. Randale simply looked—well, better. He sat up straighter, there was a bit more alertness in the set of his head and shoulders, and he moved with more freedom than he had before.

But then Stefen caught a glimpse of his face.

Breda had been transfigured when his Gift had taken away the pain of her dazzle-headache; Medren had revived when it had eased the misery of the fever—but those reactions compared to the relief Randale showed now—well, there simply was no comparison.

Only at that moment did Stefen realize how the King must have been living with this pain as a constant companion, day and night, with no hope of surcease.

He couldn't bear to bring that relief to an end, not after seeing that. So even when the audience concluded, he played on, allowing himself to drift into a trance-state in which there was nothing but the music and the flowing of the power through him—all of it directed to Randale now. A cynical little voice in the back of his mind wondered at that; wondered why he was so affected by this man and why he was giving so much of himself with no promise of reward.

He ignored that thought; though he might have heeded it an hour ago, now it seemed petty and ugly, not sensible and realistic.

Besides, it really wasn't important anymore. All that was important was the music, and the places it was reaching.

There was only the flow of melody, no real thought at all. This was the world he really lived for once he'd discovered it, the little universe woven entirely of music. This was where he belonged, and nothing could touch him here; not hunger, not pain, not loneliness.

He closed his eyes, and let the music take him deeper into that world than he had ever gone before.

Something brushed against Stefen's wandering thoughts; a presence, where no one had ever intruded until now. *What?* he thought, and his fingers faltered for a moment.

That slight hesitation broke the spell he had woven about himself, and suddenly *he* was in pain, real pain, and not some echo from Randale. His fingers ached with weariness, threatening cramps—the tips burned in a way that told him he'd played for much longer than he should have. . . .

In fact, when he opened his eyes, slowly, then pulled fingers that felt flayed off the strings and looked at his chording hand, the reddened and slightly swollen skin told him of blisters beneath the callus.

Blisters that are really going to hurt in a moment.

But that wasn't what had broken his trance; there was someone standing near enough to him to have intruded on his trance, but not so near as to loom over him.

He felt himself flushing; why, he wasn't quite sure. It wasn't quite embarrassment, it was more confusion than anything else. He glanced up from his mangled hand at whoever it was that was standing beside him.

The Audience Chamber had been nearly empty when he'd lost himself in his music—now it was filled to overflowing. But it wasn't the crowd that had broken his entrancement; it was that single person.

The other Herald, the one he hadn't been able to see clearly because the woman had been in the way. And *now* Stefen knew him, knew exactly who he was. Long, silvered black hair, the face every women in the Court sighed over, silver eyes that seemed to look straight into the heart—there was no mistaking *this* Herald for any other. This was Herald-Mage Vanyel Ashkevron. *Demonsbane*, they called him sometimes, or *Firelord*, or *Shadowstalker*.

There were a hundred names for him, and twice as many tales about him, ballads about him; he was probably *the* most sung-about Herald alive.

Stefen knew every song, and he knew things about Vanyel that were *not* in the ballads. For one thing, he knew that Vanyel's reputation of being a lone wolf was well-founded; he'd held himself aloof from non-Heralds for years, and even those he called "friend" were scarcely more than casual acquaintances.

He had no lovers—not even the rumor of a lover for as long as Stef had been at the Collegium. *So the ladies set their wits to catch him, each one hoping she'll be the one to capture his fancy, to break through that shell of ice.*

Stef would have felt sorry for them if the situation hadn't been so ridiculous. The ladies were doomed to sigh in vain over Vanyel; their hopes could never bear fruit. He knew what they didn't—thanks to the fact that Vanyel might just as well have taken a vow of celibacy, and that the few older Heralds who knew him from his younger days were not inclined to gossip. Because of Medren, Stef was well aware that Vanyel, like Stef himself, was shaych. And that his current state of solitude was not due to a lack of capability or desire.

It was due to fear, according to Medren. Fear that being close to Vanyel would put prospective partners in danger. Fear that others he cared for could be used against him.

The past seemed to have proved Vanyel right, in some

ways. Certainly the Herald had not had a great deal of good luck in his emotional life. . . .

Especially with Tylendel.

Stef knew all about Tylendel, the Herald-trainee no one talked about—at least not willingly. They'd talk about his *Companion*, but they'd avoid mentioning his name, if they could. "Gala repudiated her Chosen," they'd say—

As if by mentioning Tylendel's name, his mistake would rub off on them.

There were no songs and few people were willing to discuss the deceased young trainee, even though that repudiation had led to Vanyel's coming into his powers in the first place.

People knew that Herald Vanyel had been Tylendel's closest friend—and some even remembered that they'd been lovers—but it sometimes seemed to Stefen that despite that, they wanted to forget that Tylendel had ever existed.

That struck him as unfair, somehow. The whole tragic mess had been directly responsible for Vanyel becoming the most respected and powerful Herald-Mage in the Circle—and from what Stefen had learned, Tylendel hadn't been *sane* when he'd pursued revenge at the cost of all else. The Companions knew that; they'd rung the Death Bell for him. That was why he'd been buried with full honors, *despite* the repudiation, which told Stef that *someone* thought he'd have been worth his Whites if he hadn't gone over the edge.

Someone besides Vanyel. Stefen was one of the few outside of the Heraldic Circle who knew that doomed Tylendel had been Vanyel's very first lover—and according to Medren, his lifebonded, and only love.

And Medren should know, seeing that Vanyel is his uncle, Stefen thought, staring stupidly into those incredible silver eyes. This was the closest by far he'd ever been to the famous Herald-Mage, though he'd secretly worshiped Vanyel and daydreamed about him for—well, years.

Medren had offered an introduction, but Stef just couldn't scrape up the courage. Certainly Medren was Stef's friend, and certainly Medren was Vanyel's favorite nephew—but the Herald himself was as far from Stef's reach as a beggar child from a star.

Still, he could dream.

In all those daydreams, Stefen imagined himself doing something wonderful—writing a ballad that would bring

tears to the eyes of everyone who heard it, perhaps, or
performing some vague but important service for the
Crown. He had pictured himself being presented to the
Court, then being formally introduced to Herald Vanyel.
He'd invented a hundred witty things to say, something to
make the Herald laugh, or simply to entertain him. And
from there the daydreams had always led to Vanyel's seeking out his company—and finally courting him. Because,
thanks to Medren's gossip, Stefen was very well aware that
before the Herald-Mage had gotten so bound up in assuming most of the duties rightfully belonging to the King's
Own—and before he'd decided that his attentions could
prove dangerous to those around him—Vanyel hadn't been
at all celibate.

Now the moment was here; Herald-Mage Vanyel was
within arm's reach, and looking at him with both gratitude
and concern. Now was the time to say or do something
clever—

The music limped to a faltering conclusion as Stefen
stared back at his idol, unable to think of a single word,
clever, or otherwise.

Vanyel pivoted and strode back over to the dais, while
Stefen's ears burned with chagrin.

*I had my chance. I had it. I should have said something,
anything, dammit! Why couldn't I say anything? Oh, ye
mothering gods, how can I be such a gap-faced idiot?*

The King was talking with someone in Healer's Greens;
this looked like more of an interview than an audience—
though judging by the way they were leaning toward each
other and the intensity of their concentration, there was no
doubt that it was an important exchange. While Stefen sat
dumbly, berating himself for being such a dolt, the Herald-
Mage interrupted the earnest colloquy with a whispered
comment.

Both Randale and the Healer turned their heads in his
direction, and Stefen suddenly found himself the focus of
every eye in the Audience Chamber.

He felt his face growing hot, a sure sign that he was
blushing. He wanted to look away, to hide his embarrassment, but he didn't dare. He knew that if he did, he'd look
like a child, and a bigger fool than he already was. Instead
he raised his chin a little, and politely ignored the scrutiny

of everyone in the room, and kept his eyes fixed on the King.

Randale smiled; it was an unexpected smile, and Stefen smiled hesitantly back. It was easy enough to be cocky among his own peers, but between Vanyel's attentions, and then the King's, Stef was getting very flustered.

He struggled to keep himself from dropping his eyes—the King's smile spread a little wider, then he turned away. He said something to Vanyel, something too quiet to overhear.

Then people were suddenly clearing out of the chamber—

Stefen blinked. *I guess the audience must be over.* In the bustle over the getting the King out of his throne and on his feet, everyone seemed to have forgotten that Stef existed. He took a deep breath, and began to pack up his things. In one way he was relieved that he was no longer the center of attention, but in another, he was a little annoyed. After all, he'd just played his hands bloody for Randale's benefit—he'd be a week recovering, at least. If it hadn't been for him, there wouldn't have *been* a session of Court this afternoon.

Thank you, Stefen. You're very welcome, your Majesty. Think nothing of it. All in a day's—

Movement at the edge of his vision made him look up. Herald Vanyel was walking back toward him.

He looked back down at his gittern, and at the leather traveling case. His hands were shaking, which didn't make it any easier to get it into the tight leather case—and didn't make him look any more confident, either. He hastily fumbled the buckles into place, his heart pounding somewhere in the vicinity of his throat. *I'm jumping to conclusions,* he thought, stacking his music and putting it back into the carrier. *He's not coming toward me. He doesn't know me, he has more important people to worry about. He's really going to talk to somebody behind me before they leave. He's—*

"Here," said a soft, deep voice, as his music carrier vanished from his hand, "Let me help you with that."

Stefen looked up into the clouded silver of Vanyel's eyes, and forgot to breathe.

He couldn't break the eye contact; it was Vanyel who looked away, glancing down at Stefen's chording hand. The Herald's mouth tightened, and he made an odd little sound

of something that sounded suspiciously like a reaction to
pain.

Stefen reminded himself that blue was not his best color,
and got his lungs to work again.

Then his lungs stopped working for a second time, as the
Herald took his elbow as if he were a friend, and urged him
onto his feet.

Vanyel looked back over his shoulder at the milling
crowd, now clustered about the departing monarch, and his
lips curled in a half smile. "No one is going to miss either
of us," the Herald said. "Would you mind if I did something
about those fingers?"

"Uh, no—" Stefen managed; at least he thought that was
what he choked out. It must have sounded right, since
Vanyel steered him deftly out of the room and toward the
Heralds' Wing.

Stefen immediately stopped being able to think; he
couldn't even manage a ghost of a coherent thought.

Vanyel took the young Bard's music carrier and gittern
away from him, and gave the youngster a nudge toward the
side door. He refused to let Stefen carry anything; the boy's
fingers were a mess. He chided himself for not having
noticed sooner.

*For that matter, if I'd thought about how he'd been playing
without a break, I'd have realized that no one, not even a
Master Bard, can play all damned afternoon and not suffer
damage.* He tightened his jaw. *The boy must have been in
some kind of a trance, otherwise he'd have been in agony.*

He guided the youngster through the door to his quarters,
thanking whatever deities happened to be watching that no
one seemed to have noticed their exit from the Audience
Chamber together, and that there was no one in the halls
that would have noticed the two of them on the way there.
*The last thing I need is for this poor boy to end up with his
reputation ruined,* he thought wryly, pushing Stefen down
into the couch near the door, and putting his instrument
and music case on the floor next to him.

The youngster blinked at him dazedly, confirming Vanyel's guess that he'd put himself in a trance-state. *It's just as
well; once he starts to feel those fingers—*

Well, that was why Vanyel had brought the boy here;
there was a cure for the injury. Two, actually, one of them

residing in his traveling kit. Vanyel had become perforce
something of an herbalist over the years—all too often he,
or someone he was with, had been hurt with no Healer in
reach. *He* had a touch of Healing Gift, but not reliable, and
not enough to Heal anything serious. So he'd learned other
ways of keeping himself and those around him alive. He
kept a full medical kit with him at all times, even now,
though here at the Palace he was unlikely to have to use it.

He found it, after a moment of rummaging, under the
bed. He knew the shape of the jar he wanted, and fished
it out without having to empty the entire kit out on his bed.
A roll of soft bandage followed, and Vanyel returned to the
boy's side with both in his hands.

A distinctive, sharp-spicy scent rose from the jar as soon
as he opened it. "Cinnamon and marigold," he told the
boy, and took the most maltreated hand in his to spread
the salve on the ridged and swollen fingertips, feeling the
heat of inflammation as he began his doctoring. "Numbs
and heals, and it's good for the muscle cramps you'd be
having if you hadn't played your fingers past *that* point. I'm
surprised you have any skin left."

The boy smiled shyly but didn't say anything. Vanyel
massaged the salve into the undamaged areas of the boy's
hands and spread it gently on the blistered fingertips. With
the care the raw skin merited, he wrapped each finger in a
cushion of bandage, then closed his eyes and invoked the
tiny spark of Healing talent *he* had along with his Empathy.
He couldn't do much, but at least he could reduce the
inflammation and numb some of the pain that the salve
wouldn't touch.

But when he opened his eyes again, he was dismayed by
the expression on the boy's face. Pure adoration. Unadul-
terated hero-worship. As plain as the condition of the boy's
fingers, and just as disturbing.

It was bad enough when he saw it in the eyes of pages
and Herald-trainees, or even younger Heralds. It made him
uncomfortable to see it in the pages, and sick to see it from
the Heralds.

He couldn't avoid it, so he'd learned to cope with it. He
could distance himself from it when it was someone he
didn't know, and wouldn't have to spend any amount of
time with.

I can't leave it like this, he decided, feeling his guts knot a little. *I'll be working with him constantly, seeing him in Court—I can't allow him to go on thinking I'm some kind of godling.*

"So," he said lightly, as he put the boy's hand down. "According to my nephew, you're the best thing to come out of Bardic in an age." He raised an eyebrow and half-smiled. "Though if you don't show a little more sense, you'll play the ends of your fingers off next time, and *then* where will you be?"

"I suppose I could—uh—learn to play with my feet," the boy ventured. "Then I could *always* get a job at Fair-time, in the freak tent."

Van laughed, as much from surprise that the boy had managed a retort as at the joke. *There's more to this lad than I thought!* "Well, that's true enough—but I'd rather you just learned to pace yourself a bit better. I'll wager you haven't eaten yet, either."

Stefen looked guilty enough to convince him even before the boy shook his head.

Vanyel snorted. "Gods. Why is it that anyone under twenty seems convinced he can live on air and sunshine?"

"Maybe because anyone under fifteen is convinced he has to eat his weight twice a day," Stefen retorted, his eyes starting to sparkle. "So once you hit sixteen you realize you've stored up enough to live on your fat until you're thirty."

"Fat?" Vanyel widened his eyes in mock dismay. "You'd fade away to nothing overnight! Well, rank does have its privileges, and I'm going to invoke one of mine—" He reached for the bell-rope to summon a servant, then stopped with his hand around it. "—unless you'd rather go back to Bardic and get a meal there?"

"Me?" Stefen shook his head the awe-struck look back on his face. "Havens, no! But why would you want to—I mean, I'm just—"

"You're the first person I've had to talk music with in an age," Vanyel replied, stretching the truth just a trifle. "And for one thing, I'd like to know where you got that odd fingering for the D-minor diminished chord—"

He rang the bell as he spoke; a page answered so quickly Vanyel was startled. He sent the child off after provisions as Stefen attempted to demonstrate with his bandaged hand.

When the page returned a few moments later, laden with

food and wine, they were deep in a discussion of whether or not the tradition was true that the "Tandere Cycle" had been created by the same Bard as "Blood Bound." Once into the heated argument (Vanyel arguing "for," based on some eccentricities in the lyrics, Stefen just as vehemently "against" because of the patterns of the melodies) the boy settled and began treating him as he would anyone else. Vanyel relaxed, and began to enjoy himself. Stefen was certainly good company—in some ways, very much older than his chronological age, and certainly able to hold his own in an argument. This was the first chance he'd had in weeks to simply sit back and *talk* with someone about something that had nothing whatsoever to do with politics, Randale, or a crisis.

The page had brought two bottles of wine with the meal; it was only when Vanyel was pouring the last of the second bottle into both their glasses that he realized how late it was—

And how strong that wine had been.

He blinked, and the candle flames blurred and wavered, and not from a draft.

I think maybe I've had a little too much— Vanyel forced his eyes to focus, and licked his lips. Stefen had curled up in the corner of the overstuffed couch with his legs tucked under him; his eyes had the soft, slightly dazed stare of someone who is drunk, knows it, and is trying *very* hard to keep everyone else from noticing.

Vanyel glanced up at the time-candle; well past midnight, and both of them probably too drunk to stand, much less walk.

Certainly Stefen couldn't. Even as Vanyel looked back at him, he set his goblet down with exaggerated care—on the thin air *beside* the table.

In no way is he going to be able to walk back to his room, Vanyel thought, nobly choking down the laugh that threatened to burst from his throat, and fumbling for a handful of napkins, as Stefen swore in language that was quite enough to take the varnish off the table, and snatched at the fallen goblet. *Even if he got as far as the Collegium building, he'd probably fall down the stairs and break his neck.*

He mopped at the wine before it could soak into the

wood of the floor, Stefen on his knees beside him, alternately swearing and begging Van's pardon.

*Seriously, if I send him back to his room, he'll get hurt
on the way, I just know it. Maybe all he'd get would be a
bruising, but he really* could *break his neck.*

Stefen sat back on his heels, hands full of wet, stained
napkins, and looked about helplessly for someplace to put
them—some place where they wouldn't ruin anything else.

Vanyel solved his dilemma by taking the cloths away from
him and pitching them into a hamper beside the wardrobe.
He took no little pride in the fact that although *he* was just
as drunk as Stefen, he managed to get the wadded cloths
into the basket.

*Aside from the fact that I like this youngster, there's the
fact that he's proven himself valuable—after his performance
this afternoon, I'd say that he's far too valuable to risk.* Van
sat back on his own heels and thought for a moment. He
allowed his shields to soften a little, and did a quick "look"
through the Palace. *None of the servants are awake. There's
nobody I'd trust to see the lad safely over to his quarters
except myself. And right now, I wouldn't trust me! I can still
think, but I know damn well I can't walk without weaving.*

He became aware, painfully aware, that Stefen was looking at him with an intense and unmistakable hunger.

He flushed, and tried not to look in the boy's eyes.
*Damn. Damn, damn, damn. If I let him stay—it is not fair,
dammit! He's too young. He can't possibly know what he
wants. He thinks he wants me, and maybe he does, right
now. But in the morning? That's another thing altogether.*

He Felt Stefen's gaze, like hot sunshine against his skin,
Felt the youngster willing him to look up.

And stubbornly resisted. The boy was too young; less
than half *his* age.

And the boy was infernally attractive. . . .
Damn it all, it's not fair. . . .

Stephen could hardly believe it. He was in Herald Vanyel's private quarters; the door was shut and they were quite
alone together. He'd finally managed to redeem himself, at
least in his own eyes, for looking like such an idiot. In fact,
it looked like he'd impressed Vanyel once or twice in the
discussion—at least, up until he'd spilled the wine.

And even then, he could tell that Vanyel was attracted;

he sensed it in the way the Herald was carefully looking to one side or the other, but never directly at him, and in the way Vanyel was avoiding even an accidental touch.

Yet Vanyel wouldn't *do* anything!

What's the matter with him? Stefen asked himself, afroth with frustration. *Or is it me? No, it can't be me. Or is it? Maybe he's not sure of me. Maybe he's not sure of himself. . . .*

The wine was going to Stefen's head with a vengeance, making him bolder than he might otherwise have been. So when Vanyel reached blindly for his own goblet on the table beside them, Stefen reached for it, too, and their hands closed on the stem at the same time. Stefen's hand was atop Vanyel's—and as Vanyel's startled gaze met his own, he tightened his hand on the Herald's.

Vanyel's ears grew hot, and his hands cold. He couldn't look away from Stefen's eyes, startled and tempted by the bold invitation he read there.

No, dammit. No. Boy, child, *you don't know what you're asking for.*

In all his life, Vanyel had never been so tempted to throw over everything he'd pledged to himself and just do what he wanted, so very badly, to do.

Not that there hadn't been seduction attempts before this; his enemies frequently knew what his tastes were, and where his preferences lay. And all too often the vehicle of temptation had been someone like this—a young, seemingly innocent boy. Sometimes, in fact, it *was* an innocent. But in all cases, Vanyel had been able to detect the hidden trap and avoid the bait.

And there had been encounters that *looked* like seduction attempts. Young, impressionable children, overwhelmed by his reputation and perfectly willing to give him everything he wanted from them.

And that's what's going on here, he told himself fiercely, the back of his neck hot, his hand beneath Stefen's icy. *That's all that's going on. I swore by everything I consider holy that I was never going to take advantage of my rank and fame to seduce anyone, anyone at all, much less impressionable children who have no notion of what they're getting into. No. It hasn't happened before, and I'm not going to permit it to happen now.*

He rose to his feet, perforce bringing Stefen up with him. Once on his feet he took advantage of Stefen's momentary confusion to put the goblet down. The boy's hand slid from his reluctantly, and Vanyel endured a flash of dizziness that had nothing at all to do with the wine they'd been drinking.

"Come on, lad," he said cheerfully, casually. "You're in no shape to walk back to your bed, and I'm in no shape to see that you get there in one piece. So you'll have to make do with mine tonight."

He reached for the boy's shoulder before the young Bard could figure out what he was up to, and turned him about to face the bed. He gave the boy a gentle shove, and Stefen was so thoroughly intoxicated that he stumbled right to the enormous bedstead and only saved himself from falling by grabbing the footboard.

"Sorry," Vanyel replied sincerely. "I guess I'm a bit farther gone than I thought; I can usually judge my shoves better than that!"

Stefen started to strip off his tunic, and turned to stare as Vanyel walked slowly and carefully to the storage chest and removed his bedroll.

"What are you doing?" the youngster asked, bewildered.

"You're my guest," Vanyel said quietly, busying himself with untying the cords holding the bedroll together. "I can do without my bed for one night."

The young Bard sat heavily down on the side of the bed, looking completely deflated. "But—where are you going to sleep?" he asked, as if he didn't quite believe what he was hearing.

"The floor, of course," Vanyel replied, unrolling the parcel, and looking up to grin at the boy's perplexed expression. "It won't be the first time. In fact, I've slept in places a lot less comfortable than this floor."

"But—"

"Good night, Stefen," Vanyel interrupted, using his Gift to douse all the lights except the night-candle in the headboard of the bed because he didn't trust his hands to snuff them without an accident. He stripped off his own tunic and his boots and socks, but decided against removing anything else. His virtuous resistance might not survive another onslaught of temptation, particularly if *he* wasn't clothed. "Don't bother to get up when I do—the hours I keep are positively unholy, and no one sane would put up with them."

"But—"

"Good *night,* Stefen," Vanyel said firmly, crawling in and turning his back on the room.

He kept his eyes tightly shut and all his shields up; after a while, he heard a long-suffering sigh; then the sound of boots hitting the floor, and cloth following. Then the faint sounds of someone settling into a strange bed, and the night-candle went out.

"Good night, Vanyel," came from the darkness. "I appreciate this."

You'll appreciate me more in the morning, Vanyel thought ironically. *And I hope you leave before there're too many people in the corridor, or you'll end up with people thinking you* are *shaych.*

But—"Good night, Stefen," he replied. "You're welcome to stay as long as you like." He smiled into the darkness. "In fact, you're welcome any time. Consider yourself my adoptive nephew if you like."

And chew on that for a while, lad, Vanyel thought as he turned over and stated at the embers of the dying fire. *I have the feeling that in the morning, you'll thank me for it.*

Four

*H*ard surface beneath him. Too even to be dirt, too warm *to be stone. Where?*

Van woke, as he always did, all at once, with no transition from sleep to full awareness. And since he was not where he *expected* to be, he held himself very still, waiting for memory to catch up with the rest of him.

A slight headache between his eyebrows gave him the clue he needed to sort himself out. *Of course. I'm sleeping—virtuously—alone. On the floor. With a hangover. Because there's a Bard who's altogether too beautiful and too young in my bed. And I'll bet he doesn't wake up with a hangover.*

He heard Yfandes laughing in the back of his mind. *:Poor, suffering child. I shall certainly nominate you for sainthood.:*

Van opened his eyes, and the first morning light stabbed through them and straight into his brain. *:Shut up, horse.:* He groaned and closed his eyes tightly.

:No you don't,: Yfandes said sweetly. *:You have an appointment. With Lissandra, Kilchas, Tran, and your aunt. Remember?:*

He stifled another groan, and opened his eyes again. The sunlight was no dimmer. *:Now that you've reminded me, yes. I have done stupider things in my life than get drunk the night before a major spellcasting, I'm sure, but right now I can't recall any.:*

:I can,: Yfandes replied too promptly.

He knew better than to reply. In the state he was in now, she'd be a constant step ahead of him. *Some day,* he vowed to himself, *I'm going to find out how to make a Companion drunk, and when* she *wakes up, I'll be waiting.*

So there was nothing for it but to crawl out of his bedroll, aching in every limb from a night on the hard floor, to stare resentfully at the youngster who'd usurped his bed. Stefen lay sprawled across the entire width of the bed, a beatific half-smile on his face, and deaf, dumb and blind to the world. Dark red hair fanned across the pillow—*Van's* pillow—not the least tangled with restless tossing, as Van's was. No dark circles under Stefen's eyes—oh, no. The young Bard slept like an innocent child.

Vanyel snarled silently, snatched up his towels and a clean uniform, and headed for the bathing room.

The room was very quiet this early in the morning, and every sound he made echoed from the white-tiled walls. He might well have been the only person alive in the Palace; he couldn't hear anything at all but the noise *he* made. After plunging his head under cold water, then following that torture with a hot bath, he was much more inclined to face the world without biting something. In fact, he actually felt up to breakfast, of sorts; perhaps a little bread and a great deal of herb tea.

Stefen was still blissfully asleep, no doubt, which made Van's room off limits. Well, it was probably too early for any of the servants to be awake.

He dressed quickly, shivering a little as the chill morning air hit his wet skin, and headed down the deserted hallways to the kitchen, where he found two cooks hard at work. They were pulling hot loaves from the ovens, anonymous in their floured brown tunics and trousers, their hair caught up under caps. They gave him startled looks—it probably wasn't too often that a Herald wandered into *their* purview—but they gave him a pot of tea and a bit of warm bread when he asked them for it, and he took both up to the library.

The Palace library was a good place to settle; the fire was still banked from last night, and a little bit of work had it crackling cheerfully under new logs, filling the empty silence. Vanyel chose a comfortable chair near it, his mug of tea on the hearthstone beside him, and nibbled at his bread while watching the flames and basking in the heat. The last of the headache faded under the gentle soothing warmth of the tea. Yfandes, having sensed, no doubt, that he had reached the limits of his patience, had remained wisely silent.

:Are you up to this?: she asked, when his ill-humor had turned to rueful contemplation of his own stupidity. *:It won't hurt to put it off another day, or even two.:*

He leaned back in his chair and tested all the channels of his mind and powers. *:Oh, I think so, No harm done, other than to my temper. Sorry I snapped.:*

She sent no real thoughts in reply to that, just affection. He closed everything down and thought about the planned session. They would be working magic of the highest order, something so complicated that no one had ever tried it before.

If he'd had any choice, Vanyel wouldn't be doing it now—but the ranks of the Herald-Mages had thinned so much that there was no one to replace any of the four Guardians should something happen to one of them. There were no spare Herald-Mages anymore. The Web, the watch-spell that kept the Heralds informed of danger, required four experienced and powerful mages to make it work; a Guardian of the Web was effectively tied to Haven—not physically, but psychically—as long as he or she was a Guardian. One fourth of the Guardians' energy and time were devoted to powering and monitoring the Web.

Van intended to change all that.

He had been gradually augmenting a mage-node underneath Haven for the past several years. He was no *Tayledras*, but he was Hawkbrother-trained; creating a new node probably would have been beyond him, but feeding new energy-flows into an existing node wasn't. He intended to power the new Web-spell with that node, and he intended to replace the Guardians with *all* the Heralds of Valdemar, Mage-Gifted or no.

And lastly, he intended to set the new Web-spell to do more than watch Valdemar; he intended to make it part of Valdemar's defenses, albeit a subtle part.

He was going to summon *vrondi*, the little air-elementals used in the Truth Spell, and summon them in greater numbers than anyone ever had before. Then he was going to "purpose" them; set them to watching for disturbances in the fabric of mage-energy that lay over Valdemar, disturbances that would signal the presence of a mage at work.

No one but a mage would feel their scrutiny. It would be as if there was something constantly tapping the mage's shoulder at irregular intervals, asking who he was.

And if the mage in question was not a Herald, it would report his presence to the nearest Herald-Mage.

This was just the initial plan; if this worked, Vanyel

intended to elaborate his protections, using other elementals besides *vrondi*, to keep Valdemar as free as he could from hostile magics. He wasn't quite certain where to draw the line just yet, though. For now, it would probably be enough for every mage in Valdemar to sense he was being watched; it would likely drive a would-be enemy right out of his mind.

Well, sitting there thinking about it wasn't going to get anything accomplished.

Vanyel rose reluctantly from his chair, left his napkin stuffed into his mug on the hearth, and left the comforting warmth of the library for the chilly silence of the stone-floored corridors.

He headed straight for the Work Room; the old, shielded chamber in the heart of the Palace that had been used for apprentice Herald-Mages to practice their skills under the eyes of their teachers. But there were no apprentices here now, and every Herald-Mage stationed in Haven had his or her own private workrooms that would serve for training if any new youngsters with the Mage-Gift were Chosen.

Now the heavily shielded room could serve another purpose; to become the Heart of the new Web.

Tantras was already waiting for him when he arrived, arranging the furniture Vanyel had ordered. A new oil lamp hung from a chain in the center of the room. Directly beneath it was a circular table with a depression in the middle. Around it stood four high-backed, curved benches. Over in one corner, Tran was wrestling a heavy chair into place, putting it as far from the table as possible.

The older Herald looked up as Van closed the door behind him, raked graying hair out of his eyes with one hand, and smiled.

"Ready?" Vanyel asked, taking his seat, and putting his mage-focus, a large, irregular piece of polished tiger-eye, in the depression in the center. He hadn't been able to find a piece of unflawed amber big enough to use as a Web-focus, and fire-opals were too fragile to use in the Web. Fortunately when he'd replaced Jaysen as Guardian, he'd learned that he worked as well with Jaysen's tiger-eye as with opal and amber; flawless tiger-eye was *much* easier to find.

Vanyel looked back over his shoulder at his friend. "About as ready as I'm ever likely to be," Tantras replied, shrugging his shoulders. "This is the first time I've ever been involved with one of these high-level set-spells of yours. First time I've ever worked with *one* Adept, much less two."

"Nervous?" Vanyel raised an eyebrow at him. "I wouldn't blame you. We've never tried anything like this before."

"Me? Nervous? When you're playing with something that could fry my mind like a breakfast egg?" Tran laughed. "Of course I'm nervous. But I trust you. I think."

"Thanks for the vote of confidence—" Van began, when the door behind him opened and the other three Herald-Mages entered in a chattering knot.

The chattering subsided as they took their places around the table; Savil directly across from Van in the West, Kilchas in the South, Lissandra in the North.

Savil hadn't changed much in the last ten years; lean and spare as an aged greyhound, she moved stiffly, and seldom left Haven anymore. Her hair was pure silver, but it had been that color since she was in her early forties. Working with node-magic was the cause, the powerful energies bleached hair and eyes to silver and blue, and the more one worked with it, the sooner one went entirely silver. She placed her mage-focus, a perfect, unflawed natural crystal of rose-quartz, opposite the tiger-eye. She pursed her lips and contemplated the arrangement, then adjusted her stone until one side of the crystal was just touching the tiger-eye before she sat down. She smiled briefly at Vanyel, then her blue eyes darkened as she began opening up her own channels. Her face lost expression as she concentrated. What wrinkles she had were clustered around her eyes and mouth; there was nothing about her that told her true age, which was just shy of eighty.

On the other hand, Kilchas looked far older than Savil, although in reality he was twenty years younger. A wizened, shriveled old tree of a man, he had more wrinkles than a dried apple, hair like a tangle of gray wire and a smile that could call an answering grin from just about anyone. At the moment, that smile was nowhere in evidence. He set his focus-stone touching Vanyel's and Savil's. A piece of translucent, apple-green jade, he'd had it carved into the shape of a pyramid. He fussed with it a moment until its position satisfied him. Then he took his seat and lowered his eyelids to concentrate, frowning a little, and his eyes were lost in his creased and weathered face.

Lissandra was the most senior of the Guardians, despite being younger than Vanyel. She had been a Guardian for much longer even than Savil. She had assumed the Northern quadrant along with her Whites, and although she was not quite Adept status, she wasn't far from it. Outside of her duties as a Herald-Mage, she specialized in alchemy, in poisons and their antidotes. Taller than many men, and brown of hair, eyes and skin, her movements were deliberate, and yet oddly birdlike. She had always reminded Vanyel of a stalking marsh-heron.

Like a heron, she wasted no motion; she dropped her half-globe of obsidian in precisely the right place, and sat down in her chair, planting her elbows on the table and steepling her fingers in front of her face.

Tantras settled gingerly in his chair in the corner as Vanyel reached for the lamp, dimming it until everything outside the table was hardly more than a dim shadow. He reached into his belt pouch and felt for the final stone he'd selected for this spell; a single flawless quartz-crystal, perfectly formed, unkeyed, and as colorless as pure water.

And I must have gone through five hundred-weight of quartz to find it.

He closed his hand around it, a sharp-edged lump wrapped carefully in silk to insulate it, and brought it out into the light. The silk fell away from it as he placed it atop the other four, and it glowed with light refracted through all its facets.

Lissandra nodded her approval, Kilchas' eyes widened, and Savil smiled.

"I take it that we are ready?" Vanyel asked. He didn't need their nods; as he lowered all of his barriers and brought them into rapport with him, he Felt their assent.

Now he closed his eyes, the better to concentrate on bringing them all completely into rapport with himself and each other. He'd worked with Savil so many times that he and his aunt joined together with the firm clasp of long-time dancing partners.

:Or lovers,: she teased, catching the essence of the fleeting thought.

He smiled. *:You're not my type, dearest aunt. Besides, you'd wear me out.:*

He reached for Kilchas next, half expecting a certain reticence, given that Van was shaych—but there was nothing of the sort.

:I'm too old to be bothered by inconsequentials, boy,: came the acrid reply, strong and clear. *:You don't spend most of your life in other peoples' heads without losing every prejudice you ever had.:*

Kilchas' mind meshed easily enough with theirs—not surprising, really, given that he was the best Mindspeaker in the Circle—but Vanyel found it very hard to match the vibrations of his magic. The old man was powerful, but his control was crude, which was why he had never gotten to Adept status; he was much like a sculptor used to working with an axe instead of a chisel. Every time Van thought he had their shields matched, the old man would Reach toward him impatiently, or his shields would react to the presence of alien power, and the protections would flare, which had the effect of knocking the meld of Van and his aunt away.

Vanyel opened his eyes, clenching his teeth in frustration, and saw Kilchas shaking his head. "Sorry about that, lad," he said gruffly. "I'm better at blasting things apart than putting them together. And I'm 'fraid some things have gotten instinctive."

"Would you object to having me or Savil match everything *for* you?" Vanyel asked, unclenching his fists and twisting his head to loosen his tensed shoulder muscles.

"You mean—you take over?" Kilchas frowned. "I thought Heralds didn't do that. Isn't that the protocol?"

"Well, yes and no," Savil replied, massaging her temples with her fingertips. "Yes, that's the protocol, but the protocol was never meant for Mindspeaking Adepts, especially not with the strong Gifts my nephew and I have. Van and I can get in there, show you what to do, then get out again without leaving anything of ourselves behind. Occasionally rules *were* made to be broken."

"You're sure?" Kilchas said doubtfully. "I don't want to find myself not knowing if an odd thought is a bit of one of you, left over from this spellcasting, or someone trying to squeak past my shielding."

"I'm positive," Van told him. "it's how the *Tayledras* trained me. One of them would take over, walk me through something, then get out and expect me to imitate them."

Kilchas sighed, and placed both his palms flat on the

tabletop. "All right, then. Savil, by preference, Van. You're
the one directing this little fireworks show—I'd rather you
had your mind on that, and not distracted with one old
man's wavering controls."

"Good enough." Vanyel nodded, relieved that it was
nothing more personal than that; Kilchas' reasoning made
excellent sense. "Let's try this again."

This time he waited, watching, for his aunt to take over
Kilchas' mage-powers and bring them into harmony with
her own, putting into place a much finer level of control
than he had learned on his own. Not to fault Kilchas—for
all that his hobby was the peaceable one of astronomy, he'd
been primarily an offensive combat mage. He hadn't had
much time to learn the kind of control Van and Savil had,
nor had he any reason.

:*So we take a shortcut,*: Yfandes said softly. :*There's nothing wrong with a shortcut. I wish this were going faster,
though.*:

:*So do I, love,*: Van replied, watching the edges of Kilchas' shields for the moment when the fluctuations ended,
since that would signal Savil's success. :*I take it that the
others are impatient?*:

:*Kilchas' Rohan is petrified,*: she said frankly. :*He's afraid
Kilchas isn't up to this. Lissandra's Shonsea just wants it
over; she's not happy about this, but she's confident that
Lissandra can handle her part.*:

:*I don't blame her for being unhappy. I want it over, too.
I'm not going to be worth much when we finish this job.*:
Suddenly Kilchas' shields stopped pulsing, and the color
smoothed to an even yellow-gold. :*Tell her it won't be long
now.*:

He Reached out again to his aunt, and let her bring *him*
into the meld, to avoid disturbing Kilchas' fragile control.
Then, before the delicate balance could fall apart, he and
Savil flung lines of power to Lissandra.

The fourth Guardian was used to working with Savil; she
had been waiting for them, and with the smooth timing of
a professional acrobat, caught them, and drew herself into
the meld. Vanyel had, in the not-too-distant past, had more
than one dislocated joint; the *snap* as Lissandra locked herself into place was a physical sensation very like having a
bone put back in the socket. And once she was there, the
meld stabilized; a ring instead of an arc. Vanyel breathed a

sigh of relief, and Yfandes took that as the signal to bring the Companions into the meld.

They were to be the foundation, the anchoring point, so that none of them would be caught up in the currents of mage-power Vanyel would be using and find themselves lost. Kilchas and Lissandra would be contributing their powers and their presence, and Savil her expertise in handling *vrondi,* but most of this would be up to Vanyel.

Vanyel had worked this entire procedure out with the *Tayledras* Adepts of k'Treva, taking several years to research and test his ideas. The Hawkbrothers Moondance and Starwind, and their foster-son Brightstar were the ones that had helped him the most. No one knew node-magic like the *Tayledras* did; they were bred in and of it, and those that were Mage-Gifted handled it from the time their Gifts first began to manifest, which could be as young as eight or nine. And among the k'Treva clan, those three were the unrivaled masters of their calling.

In point of fact, it had been the spell that another master of an unidentified *Tayledras* clan had left behind in Lineas long ago, the one that bound Tashir's family to the protection of the heart-stone there, that had given Van the idea for this in the first place. In that case, the compulsions set by the spell had been relatively simple; guard the heart-stone, discourage the use of magic, keep the stone and the power it tapped out of the hands of unscrupulous mages. While *Tayledras* normally drained any area they abandoned of magic, they had left the heart-stone in what would become the capital of Lineas because the stone had been bound into another spell meant to Heal a mage-caused fault-line. That spell would take centuries to complete, and meanwhile, only magic was keeping the fault stable. If that magic were to be drained, the devastation caused by the resulting earthquake would be extensive, carrying even into Valdemar. Tashir's family had been selected precisely because they had *no* Mage-Gift and little talent with Mind-magic; although this would ensure that none of them would succumb to the temptation to use the magic, that meant that the creators of the spell had very little to work with.

Vanyel had all of the Heralds, and all their varied Gifts, to integrate into his spell. So what he planned to do was infinitely more complicated, though the results would be equally beneficial.

First things first, he told himself. *Get a good shield up
around the four of us. If anything goes wrong, I don't want
Tran caught in the backlash.*

The shield was the tightest he'd ever built, and when he
was finished, the other three Guardians tested it for possible
leaks and weak points. Ironically, of the five of them, it
was Tantras, who sat *outside* that shield, who would be in
the most danger if anything got loose. The Work Room
itself was shielded, and so securely that even sounds from
without came through the walls muffled, when they penetrated at all. Each of them had their own personal shields;
that, in part, was what had been the cause of the difficulty
Van had in melding with Kilchas—those shields *never* came
down, and it was difficult to match shields one to another
so that the power would flow between mages without inter-
ruption or interference. If the energy Van planned to call up
got away from him, he and the others would be protected by
their personal shields. The Work Room shields would protect those beyond the doors, but Tran would be caught in
between the two. And since he wasn't a mage, he had none
of his own. Van had spent many hours manufacturing protections for him, but they'd never been tested to destruction
and he had no idea how much they would really take.

:He knows that,: Yfandes reminded him, *:And he agreed.
Life is a risk; our lives ten times the risk.:*

Somehow that only made Vanyel feel guiltier.

But he had no choice; his decision to go ahead was based
entirely on Valdemar's need. The problem was that the
Mage-Gift had always been rare, and the troubles following
Elspeth's passing had resulted in the deaths of more Herald-
Mages than could be replaced. It had been appallingly clear
to Vanyel after the death of Herald-Mage Jaysen that there
weren't going to be enough Guardian-candidates to take
over the vacant seat in the Web in the event of another
death. Yet the Web was Valdemar's only means of antici-
pating danger before it crossed the Border. Heralds with no
Mage-Gift, but with very powerful Gifts of Mindspeech or
FarSight, had been tested in the seats; the Web-spell
wouldn't work for them because it was powered by a Mage's
own personal energies, and there was no way for a Herald
without the Mage-Gift to supply that energy.

What Vanyel proposed was to modify that spell.

For the first time since his Gifts had been awakened, he

dropped all but the last of his shields. Every mage ever
born could establish a "line" to the mind of another with
whom he had shared magic—but Vanyel had a line to every
living Herald in Valdemar, by virtue of their being Heralds.
When his shields were down, he found himself part of a
vast network linking all the Heralds together. As delicate
as a snowflake, as intricate as the finest lacework, the
strands of power that bound them all were deep-laid, but
strong. They pulsed with life, as if someone had joined
every star in the night sky to every other star, linking them
with faint strands of spun-crystal light. It was beautiful.
He'd suspected this network existed from the glimpses he'd
caught when following his lines to other Heralds, but this
was the first time Vanyel had ever Seen the whole of it.
Through his mind, the others Saw the same.

:*Amazing,*: Kilchas said at last. :*Why has no one ever
spoken of this before?*:

:*Probably because unless your Gift is very strong, you
can't detect it since the actual linkage is through the Companions,*: Vanyel replied. :*We share magic with the Heralds
without the Mage-Gift through the Companions. That's the
other reason I wanted them in the meld; I can See this without them, but with them, I can also manipulate it.*:

:*This must be what King Valdemar first saw when he created the Web.*: Savil's mind-voice was subdued.

:*Except that things were a lot less complicated in his day,*:
Vanyel said dryly. :*Let's get to this before we lose the meld.*:

:*Or we get bored with your chatter and find something
more interesting,*: Yfandes Mindspoke him alone.

:*One more comment like that, and I'll replace you with
one of the* Tayledras *birds,*: Vanyel retorted. Before 'Fandes
had a chance to respond, Savil had begun invoking the
Web, and Van's attention was fully take up with the task
at hand.

As each Guardian responded, his or her focus-stone came
alive with power. When Lissandra completed her response,
the four stones were glowing softly, as brightly as the lamp
flame above them, and the quartz crystal that topped them
was refracting their light in little spots of rainbow all over
the room.

Now Vanyel closed his eyes and Saw the Web overlaying
the network lacing the entire Kingdom. There were secondary lines of power wisping out from the Web, as if the spell-

structure was trying to make full contact with the entire
body of Heralds, and yet lacked the power and direction to
do so.

That was exactly what Moondance had surmised; the
spell-structure was capable of linking all Heralds, but was
incomplete and underpowered.

There was no way of knowing if King Valdemar had
intended that, or not. Somehow the idea of legendary Valdemar being incapable of completing such a spell did not
make Vanyel feel any easier.

If he couldn't, how in Havens can we?

Never mind; he was already committed, and it was too
late to back out now. He Reached for the assemblage of
focus-stones in the center of the table; Felt a sudden flare
of heat/light/pressure as he melded with all five of them,
then stabbed his power deep into the earth below Haven,
to the ancient node there, a node he and Savil had reawak-
ened. It was *very* deep, and hard to sense, but now that it
was active it was one of the most powerful he'd ever used.

Finding it was like plunging into the heart of the sun; too
overwhelming to be painful—it was beyond pain—and it
threatened to burn him away from himself. It was easy to
be lost in a node, and that was why the Companions were
in this meld—after the first breathless, mind-numbing contact he Felt them anchoring him, reminding him of where
and what he was.

It took him a moment to lean on their strength and steady
himself, to catch his breath. Then he took hold of the heart
of the node, braced himself, and Pulled—

This was something no one outside of the *Tayledras* clans
had ever attempted. Vanyel was going to create a heart-
stone. A small one, but nevertheless, a true heart-stone.

*He was fire, he was riven earth, he was molten rock. He
was raging water and lightning. He was ancient and new-
born. He was, with no memory, and no anchor. No identity.
Then something prodded him. A name. Yfandes. He . . .
remembered. . . .*

With memory came sensation. He was agony.

*He Pulled, though his nerves screamed and his heart raced,
overburdened. He Pulled, though it felt as though he was
pulling himself apart.*

*Slowly, reluctantly, the power swelled, then settled again
at his command.*

He Reached again, this time for the Web, and brought it into contact with the raw power of the node—

Contact wasn't enough.

He entered the Web itself; Reached from inside it with mental hands that were burned and raw, and with the melded will of the four Guardians and their Companions, forced it to match magics with the raw node-power and take it in—

And with the very last of his strength, keyed it.

The Web flared; from the heart of it, he Saw and Felt the power surging through it, opening up new connections, casting new lines, until the Web was no longer distinguishable from the fainter, but more extensive network he'd seen before.

He cast himself free from the new heart-stone, and sent delicate tendrils of thought along the new force-lines of the Web. And wanted to shout with joy at what he found, for the spell had taken full effect.

From this moment on, all Heralds were now one with Valdemar, and all were bound into the Web in whatever way their Gifts could best serve. When danger threatened, the FarSeers would know "where," the ForeSeers would know "when," and every Herald needed to handle the danger would find himself aware of the peril and its location.

At that moment, Vanyel Felt the Companions withdraw themselves from the meld.

For a moment, he panicked—until he Saw that the new Web was still in place, still intact.

Damn. I'd hoped—but they're still laws unto themselves, he thought ruefully. *They were apart from the Web before—and it looks like they've decided it's going to stay that way. Too bad; we could have used them to make up for Heralds with weak Gifts. And since every human magic I've seen has always left them unaffected, I was hoping they might have conferred that immunity on us. Companions have never done more than aid their Chosen, but it would have been nice if this time had been an exception.*

At least his original intentions were holding; the new Web was powered by the magic of the node, and only augmented by the Heralds instead of depending entirely on them. When the call came, those without more pressing emergencies would leave everything to meet greater threats to Valdemar.

Now for the addition to the Web protections. . . .

He dropped out of the meld, for this was something he had to handle alone. He stilled himself, isolated himself from every outside sensation, then brought Savil in closer. Together, they reached out to the *vrondi* and Called—

One came immediately; then a dozen, then a hundred. And still they Called, until the air elementals pressed around them on all sides, thousands of the creatures—

It was a good thing they didn't really exist on the same plane of reality where his body slumped in the Work Room, or he and everyone in it would have been smothered.

He Reached again, much more carefully this time, and created a new line to the Web and the power it fed upon. And showed it to the assembled *vrondi*, as Savil told them wordlessly that this power would be theirs for the taking—

—they surged forward, hungrily—

:—*if,*: said Savil, holding the line a bit out of their reach.

:*If?*: The word echoed from *vrondi* to *vrondi*, ripples of hunger/doubt/hunger. :*If? If?*:

They withdrew a little, and contemplated both of them. Finally they responded.

:*What?*:

Vanyel showed them, as Savil held the line. To earn the power, all they need do, would be to watch for mages. Always watch for mages. And let them know they were being watched.

They swirled about him, about Savil, thousands of blue eyes in little mist-clouds. :*All?*: they asked, in a chorus of mind-voices.

:*That's all,*: he replied, feeling the strength of his own power starting to fade. :*Watch. Let them know you watch.*:

The *vrondi* swirled around him, thinking it over. Then, just when he was beginning to worry—

:*YES!*: they cried, and seized on the line of power—and vanished.

And he let go of Savil, of the meld, and let himself fall.

"Gods," Kilchas moaned.

Vanyel raised his head from the table, where he'd slumped forward. "My sentiments exactly." Kilchas was half-lying on the table with his hands over his head, fingers tangled in his gray mane.

"I think," Lissandra said, pronouncing the words with

care, "That I am going to sleep for a week. Did your thing with the *vrondi* work?"

"They took it," Vanyel replied, staring at the single globe of iridescent crystal in the center of the table where the grouping of five stones had been. "Every mage inside the borders of Valdemar is going to know he's being watched. That's going to make him uncomfortable if he doesn't belong here, or he's up to no good. The deeper inside Valdemar, the more *vrondi* he'll attract, and the worse he'll feel."

"And he'll have to shield pretty heavily to avoid detection," Savil added, leaning into the back of her chair and letting it support all her weight. "The *vrondi* are quite sensitive to mage-energy. And they're curious as all hell; I suspect wild ones will start joining our bound ones in watching out for mages just for the amusement factor."

"That's good—as far as it goes." Lissandra reached out and touched the globe in the center with an expression of bemusement. "But it doesn't let *us* know we have mages working on our territory, not unless you can get the *vrondi* to tell us."

"I do have some other plans," Vanyel admitted. "I'd like to get the *vrondi* to react to strange mages with alarm—and since they're now bound into the Web, that in itself would feed back to the Heralds. But I haven't got that part worked out yet. I don't want them to react that way to Herald-Mages, for one thing, and for another, I'm not sure the *vrondi* are capable of telling mages apart."

"Neither am I," Savil said dubiously. "Seems to me it's enough to let mages know they're being watched. If you're guilty, that alone is enough to make you jumpy."

Kilchas had managed to stand up while they were talking; he reached for the globe and tried to pick it up. His expression of surprise when he couldn't made Vanyel chuckle weakly.

"That's a heart-stone now," he said apologetically. "It's fused to the table, and the table is fused to the stone of the Palace and the bedrock beneath it."

"Oh," Kilchas replied, sitting down with a *thump*. Vanyel banished the shields, then turned to the only person in the room who hadn't yet spoken a single word.

Van leaned against the back of his chair, and faced Tantras. "Well?" he asked.

Tran nodded. "It's there, all right. There's something *there* that wasn't a part of of me before—"

"What about the trouble-spots?" Vanyel asked.

The other Herald closed his eyes, and frowned with concentration. "I'm trying to think of a map," he said, finally. "I'm working my way around the Border. It's like Reading an object; I get a kind of sick feeling when I come up on some place where there're problems. I'll bet it would be even more accurate if I had a real map."

Vanyel sighed, and slumped his shoulders, allowing his exhaustion to catch up with him. "Then we did it."

"I never doubted it," Savil retorted.

:Nor I,: said the familiar voice in his head.

"Then it's time for me to go fall on my nose; I think I've earned it." Vanyel got to his feet, feeling every joint ache. "I think all of us have earned it."

"Aye to that." Lissandra copied him; Kilchas levered himself up with the aid of the table, and Savil needed Tantras' help to get her onto her feet. Vanyel headed for the door and pulled it open, leaving the others to take care of themselves. Right now all he could think about was his bed—and how badly he needed it.

He walked wearily down the corridor leading out of the Old Palace and toward his quarters, doing his best not to stagger. He was so tired that it would probably look as if he was drunk, and that wouldn't do the Heraldic reputation any good. . . .

:Oh, I don't know,: Yfandes chuckled. *:You might get more invitations to parties that way.:*

:I might. But would they be parties I'd want to attend?:

:Probably not,: she acknowledged.

It didn't occur to him until he was most of the way to the Herald's Wing that his bed might not be unoccupied. . . .

But it was; he pulled his door open to find his room empty, the bed made, and no sign of his visitor anywhere. Evidently the servants had already cleaned and tidied his quarters; there was nothing out of the ordinary about the room.

He clung to the doorframe, surprised by his own disappointment that the young Bard hadn't at least stayed long enough to make some arrangements to get together again.

This time with a little less wine. . . .

That disappointment made no sense; he'd only met the

boy last night. And he couldn't *afford* close friends; he'd told himself that over and over.

Anybody you let close is liable to become a target or a hostage, he repeated to himself for the thousandth time. *You can't afford friends, fool. You should be grateful that the boy came to his senses. You can talk to him safely in Court. You know very well that after yesterday you're going to be seeing him there every day. That should certainly be enough. He had no idea what he was offering you last night; it was the wine and his hero-worship talking. You're too old, and he's too young.*

But his bed, when he threw himself into it, seemed very cold, and very empty.

Five

A door closed, somewhere nearby. Stefen stretched, only half-awake, and when his right hand *didn't* hit the wall, he woke up entirely with a start of surprise. He found himself staring at a portion of wood paneling, rather than plaster-covered stone. It was an entirely unfamiliar wall.

Therefore, he wasn't in his own bed.

Well, that wasn't too terribly unusual. Over the course of the past couple of years, he'd woken up in any number of beds, with a wide variety of partners. What was unusual was that this morning he was quite alone, and every sign indicated he'd gone to sleep that way. He rubbed his eyes, and turned over, and blinked at the room beyond the bedcurtains. There on the floor, like a mute reproach, was a rumpled bedroll.

Looks like I did go to bed alone. Damn.

A pile of discarded clothing, unmistakably Heraldic Whites, lay beside the bedroll.

So it wasn't a dream. Stefen sat up, and ran his right hand through his tangled hair. *I really did end up in Herald Vanyel's room last night. And if he slept* there *and I slept* here—Stefen frowned. *He's shaych. I certainly made an advance toward him. He was attracted. What went wrong?*

Stef unwound the blankets from around himself, and slid out of Vanyel's bed. On the table beside the chairs on the opposite side of the room were the remains of last night's supper, and two empty bottles of wine. *I wasn't that drunk; I know what I did. It should have worked. Why didn't it? He* was *certainly drunk enough not to be shy. Should I have been more aggressive?*

He reached down to the floor, picked up his tunic and pulled it over his head. His boots seemed to have vanished, but he thought he remembered taking them off early in the evening. He found the footgear after a bit of searching, where they'd been pushed under one of the chairs, and sat down on the floor to pull them on, his bandaged left hand making him a little awkward.

No, I think being aggressive would have repelled him. I read him right, dammit!

Another thought occurred to him, then, and he stopped with his left foot halfway in the boot. *But what if he wasn't reading me right? What if he thinks I'm just some kind of bedazzled child? Ye gods, little does he know—*

Stef started to smile at that thought, when another thought sobered him.

But if he knew—or if he finds out, what would he think then?

That was a disturbing notion indeed. *I haven't exactly been discreet. Or terribly discriminating.* He felt himself blushing with—shame? It certainly felt like it. *I was just enjoying myself. I never hurt anybody. I didn't think it mattered.*

But maybe to somebody like Vanyel, who had never had more than a handful of lovers in his life, it might matter. And before last night, Stef would have shrugged that kind of reaction off, and gone on to someone else.

Before last night, it wouldn't have mattered. But something had happened last night, something that made what Vanyel thought very important to Stefen.

Maybe that's it. Maybe it's that he's heard about me, heard about the way I've been living, and—

But that didn't make any sense either. Vanyel hadn't been repelled, or at least, he hadn't shown any sign of it. He'd just put Stefen to bed—alone, like a child, or like his nephew—and left him to sleep his drunk off. And had himself gone to some duty or other this morning, without a single word of reproach.

Stef stood up, collected his gittern and music case from where they were propped beside the door, and slipped out into the hallway, still completely at a loss for what to think.

All I know is, it's a good thing nobody knows I slept alone last night, or my reputation would be ruined.

There were no less than four messages waiting for him when he reached the room he shared with Medren. Fortunately, his friend wasn't in; he didn't want to face the older Journeyman until he could think of a reasonable excuse for what *hadn't* happened. There were times when Medren could be worse than the village matchmaker.

And he didn't even want to look at all those messages until after he was clean and fed.

The first was easily taken care of in the student's bathing room; the youngsters were all in class at this hour, and the bathing room deserted. The second was even easier; he'd learned when he was a student himself that his slight frame and a wistful expression could coax food out of the cooks no matter how busy they were. Thus fortified, he went back to his room to discover that the messages had spawned two more in his absence.

He sat down on his bed to read them. Four of the six messages were from Healers; one from the Dean of Healer's Collegium, two from Randale's personal physicians, and one—astonishingly—from Lady Shavri herself.

They all began much alike; with variations on the same theme. Effusive, but obviously genuine gratitude, assurance that he had done more for the King's comfort than he could guess. The Dean asked obliquely if he would be willing to allow the Healers to study him; the King's attending Healers hinted at requests to attach him directly to the Court. Shavri's note said, bluntly, "I intend to do everything I can to see that you are well rewarded for the services you performed for Randale. As King's Own, I will be consulting with the Dean of your Collegium and the head of the Bardic Circle. If you are willing to continue to serve Randale, Journeyman Stefen, I will do my best for you."

Stef held the last message in his bandaged hand, and contemplated it with amazement and elation.

Last night I thought they'd forgotten I existed. Vanyel was the only one who seemed to care that I'd played my hand raw for them. But this—

Then his keen sense of reality intruded. Shavri hadn't promised anything specific. The others had only been interested in finding out if he'd work with them, and while their gratitude was nice, it didn't put any silver in his pocket or grant him a permanent position. There were two more messages, and one was from the Dean of the Bardic Collegium. There was no telling what they held.

You spent too much time with Vanyel, Stef, he told himself. *All that altruism is catching.*

The fourth was from Medren; letting him know that his

roommate was taking a week to travel up north of the city
with a couple of full Bards for a Spring Fair. "I want to try
out some new songs, pick up some others," the note concluded. "Sorry about running off like this, but I didn't get
much notice. Hope things work out for you."

An oblique and discreet hint if ever I heard one, Stef
thought cynically. *Obviously he noticed I didn't come back
to the room last night, and I'll bet he's wondering if it was
his uncle I was with. Unless somebody already told him.*
Stefen sighed. *Horseturds, I hope not. If nobody knows, I'll
have a chance to make something up to satisfy his curiosity
between then and now.*

That left the message from the Dean of the Collegium;
Stefen weighed it in his hand and wished he could tell if it
was good or bad news before he opened it. But he couldn't,
and there was no point in putting it off further.

He broke the seal, hesitated a moment further, and
unfolded the thick vellum.

*Sealed, and written on brand new vellum, not a scrap of
palimpsest. Very official—which means either very good, or
very bad.*

He skimmed through the formal greeting, then stopped
cold as his eyes took in the next words, but his mind refused
to grasp them.

*". . . at the second noon bell, the Bardic Circle will meet
to consider your status and disposition. Please hold yourself
ready to receive our judgment.*

What did I do? he thought wildly. *I only just made Journeyman—they can't be meaning to jump me to Master! But—
why would they demote me? What could I have possibly
done that was that bad? Unless they just found something
out about my past. . . .*

That could be it; not something he'd *done,* but something
he *was.* The lost heir to some title or other? No, not likely;
that sort of thing only happened in apprentice-ballads. But
there were other things that might cause the Circle to have
to demote him, at least temporarily. If his family ran to
inheritable insanity, for instance; they'd want to make sure
he wasn't going to run mad with a cleaver before they
restored his rank. Or if he'd been pledged to wed in
infancy—

Now *there* was a horrid thought. In that case the only
thing that would save him would be Apprentice-rank;

apprentices were not permitted marriage. And galling as it would be to be demoted, it would be a lot worse to find himself shackled to some pudgy baker's daughter with a face like her father's unbaked loaves. But being demoted would give the Bardic Collegium all the time they needed to get him free of the pledge or simply outwait the would-be spouse, delaying and delaying until the parents gave up and fobbed her off on someone else.

Or until they found out about his sexual preferences. Even in Valdemar most fathers would sooner see their daughters married to a gaffer, a drunkard, or a *goat* than to someone who was shaych.

For one thing, they'd never get any grandchildren out of me, Stef thought grimly. *And as long as I'm an anonymous apprentice, there's no status or money to be gained by forcing a marriage through anyway.*

That seemed the likeliest—*far* likelier than that the Circle would convene to elevate an eighteen-year-old barely three months a Journeyman to Master rank.

Well, there was only one way to find out; get himself down to the Council Hall and wait there for the answer.

But first he'd better make himself presentable. He flung himself into the chest holding his clothing in a search for *one* set of Bardic Scarlets that wasn't much the worse for hard wearing.

Waiting was the hardest thing in the world for Stefen. And he found himself waiting for candlemarks outside the Council chamber.

He did not wait graciously. The single, hard wooden chair was a torture to sit in, so he opted for one of the benches (meant for hopeful tradesmen) instead. He managed to stay put rather than pacing the length and breadth of the ante-room, but he didn't sit quietly. He fidgeted, rubbing at the bandages on his fingers, tapping one foot—fortunately there was no one else in the room, or they might have been driven to desperate measures by his fretting.

Finally, with scarcely half a candlemark left until the bell signaling supper, the door opened, and Bard Breda beckoned him inside.

He jumped to his feet and obeyed, his stomach in knots, his right hand clenched tightly on his bandaged left.

The Council Chamber, the heart of Bardic Collegium,

was not particularly large. In fact, there was just barely
room for him to stand facing the members of the Bardic
Council once the door was closed.

The Council consisted of seven members, including his
escort, Breda. She took her place at the end of the square
marble-topped table around which they were gathered.
There was an untidy scattering of papers in front of the
Chief Councillor, Bard Dellar.

The Councillor looked *nothing* like a Bard, which sometimes led to some awkward moments; set slightly askew in
a face much like a lumpy potato were a nose that resembled
a knot on that potato, separating a mouth so wide Dellar
could eat an entire loaf of bread in one bite, and a pair of
bright, black eyes that would have well suited a raven.

"Well," Dellar said, his mouth stretching even wider in
a caricature of a grin. "You've certainly been the cause of
much excitement this morning. And no end of trouble, I
might add."

Stefen licked his lips, and decided not to say anything.
Dellar looked friendly and quite affable, so the trouble
couldn't have been that bad. . . .

"Cheer up, Stefen," Breda chuckled, cocking her head to
one side. "You're not at fault. What caused all the problems
was that we were trying to satisfy everyone without hurting
anyone's feelings. Making you a Master and assigning you
directly to Randale was bound to put someone out unless
we did it carefully."

"Making me—*what?*" Stefen gulped. Dellar laughed at
the look on his face.

"We're making you a full Bard, lad. Shavri was most
insistent on that." The chief Councillor smiled again, and
Stef managed to smile back. Dellar picked up the papers in
front of him, and shuffled them into a ragged pile. "She
doesn't want a valuable young man like you gallivanting
about the countryside, getting yourself in scrapes—"

"Nonsense, Dell," Breda cut him off with an imperious
wave of her hand, and pointed an emphatic finger at Stefen.
"What Shavri did or didn't want wouldn't have mattered a
pin if you weren't also one of the brightest and best apprentices we've had in Bardic in—I don't know—ages, at any
rate. We don't make exceptions because someone with rank
pressures us, Stefen. We *do* make them when someone is
worthy of them. You are. You have no need to prove your-

self out in the world, and your unique Gift makes you double valuable, to us, and to the Crown."

She gave Dellar a challenging look; he just shrugged and chuckled. "She's put it in a nutshell, lad. We need to keep you here for the King's sake, and the only way to do that is to assign you to King Randale permanently. The only way to give you the rank to rate *that* kind of assignment is for you to be a Master Bard. But there's a problem—"

"I can see that, sir," Stef replied, regaining his composure. "It's not the way things are supposed to be done. There's likely to be some bad feelings."

"That is an understatement," one of the others said dryly, examining her chording hand with care. "Bards are only human. There's more than a few that will want your privates for pulling this plum. About half of that lot will be sure you slept your way to it. And unless we can do something to head that jealousy off, gossip will dog your footsteps, and make both your job and your life infinitely harder. Need I remind you that we're dealing with Bards here, and experts with words? Before they're through, that risque reputation of yours will be the stuff of tavern-songs and stories from here to Hardorn."

Stefan felt his face getting hot.

"That's been the problem, lad," Dellar shrugged. "And this is where we had to make some compromises. So now I'll have to give you the bad news. You'll be assigned as the King's personal Bard, but it will be on the basic stipend. Bare expenses, just like now. No privileges, and your quarters will be your old room right here, rather than something plusher at the Palace. We'll have Medren move out so it's private, but that's the best we can do for you."

Stef nodded, and hid his disappointment. He was *still* going to be the youngest Master Bard in the history of the Collegium. He *still* had royal favor, and he would be in the Court, in everyone's eye, where he had the chance to earn rewards on the side. "I can understand that, sir," he said, trying to sound as if he was taking all this in stride. "If it looks like I'm not getting special treatment—if, in fact, it's pretty obvious that the only reason I've been made Master is so I can serve the King directly—well, nobody who's that ambitious is going to envy me a position with no special considerations attached."

"Exactly." Dellar nodded with satisfaction and folded his

hands on top of his papers. "I'd hoped you would see it that way. You'll also be working with the Healers, of course. They're mad to know how it is you do what you do, and to see if it's possible for them to duplicate it."

Stefen sighed. That would mean more time taken out of his day, and less that he could spend getting some attention where it could do him some long-term good. He'd seen Randale now, and just how ill the King really was; he wouldn't last more than a few years, at best, and *then* where would Stefen be?

Out, probably. If nobody needs that pain-killing Gift of mine. And having nowhere else to go, unless I make myself into a desirable possession.

"Yes, sir," he replied with resignation he did his best to conceal.

Still, the Healers can't take up all my time. What I really need to find out is where the ladies of the Court congregate, since there isn't any Queen. The married ones, that is. The young ones won't have any influence—no, what I need is a gaggle of bored, middle-aged women, young enough to be flattered, old enough not to take it seriously. Ones I can be a diversion for. . . .

He realized suddenly that Bard Dellar was still talking, and he'd lost the last couple of sentences. And what had caught his attention was a name.

"—Herald Vanyel," Dellar concluded, and Stef cursed himself for his inattention. Now he had no idea at all what it was Vanyel had said or done or was supposed to do, nor what it could possibly have to do with himself. "Well, I think that about covers everything, lad. Think you're up to this?"

"I hope so, sir," Stefen said fervently.

"Very well, then; report to Court about midmorning, just as you did yesterday. Herald Vanyel will instruct you when you get there."

So, Vanyel's to be my keeper, hmm? Stefen bowed to the members of the Bardic Council, and smiled to himself as he left the room. *Well. Things are beginning to look promising.*

Despite the precautions, there was still jealousy. Stef found himself being ignored, and even snubbed, by several of the full Bards—mostly those who were passing through Haven on the way to somewhere else, but it still happened.

It wasn't the first time he'd been snubbed, though, and it probably wouldn't be the last. The Bards that stayed any length of time soon noticed that he wasn't getting better treatment than an ordinary Journeyman, and the ice thawed a little.

But only a little. They were still remote, and didn't encourage him to socialize. Stef was not at all happy about the way they were acting, and it didn't help that he had something of a guilty conscience over his rapid advancement. Making the jump from Journeyman to Master was much more than a matter of talent, no matter what the Council said; it was also a matter of experience.

Experience Stef didn't have. He wasn't that much different from Medren on that score. Nevertheless, here he was, jumped over the heads of his year-mates, and even those *older* than he was, getting shoved into the midst of the High Court—

The side of him that calculated everything rubbed its hands in glee, but the rest of him was having second and third thoughts, and serious misgivings. The way some of the other full Bards were treating him just seemed to be a confirmation of those misgivings.

And the Healers were beginning to get on his nerves. They wanted to monopolize every free moment of his time, studying him, and he had no chance during that first week to make any of the Court contacts he had intended to.

In fact, for the first time he was *using* that Gift of his every time he sang, and by the end of the day he was exhausted. If he wasn't singing for Randale's benefit, he was demonstrating for the Healers. If he'd had any time to think, he might well have told them, one and all, to chuck their Master Bardship and quit the place. But he was so tired at day's end that he just fell into bed and slept like a dead thing, and telling the Council to go take a long hike never occurred to him.

Maddeningly, he seldom saw much of Vanyel either, and every attempt to get the Herald's amatory attention fell absolutely flat.

Every time he pressed his attentions, the Herald seemed to become—nervous. He could *not* figure out what the problem was. Vanyel would *start* to respond, but then would pull back inside himself, and a mask would drop down over his face.

If he'd had the energy left, he'd have strangled something in frustration.

That was the way matters stood when Medren returned from his little expedition.

Stefen stared at himself in the mirror, then made a face at himself. "You," he said accusingly, pointing a finger at his thin, disheveled other self, "are an idiot."

"I'll second that," said Medren, popping up behind him, startling Stef so much that he yelped and threw himself sideways into the wall.

While he gasped for breath and tried to get his heart to stop pounding, Medren thumped his back. "Good gods, Stef," his friend said apologetically, "What in the seventh hell's made you so jumpy?"

"No—nothing," Stef managed.

"Huh," Medren replied skeptically. "Probably the same 'nothing' that made you call yourself an idiot. So how's it feel to be a Master Bard?" When Stef didn't immediately answer, Medren held him at arm's length and scrutinized him carefully. "If it feels like you look, I think I'll stay a Journeyman. Don't you ever sleep?" A sly smile crept over Medren's face. "Or is somebody keeping you up all night?"

Stefen groaned and covered his eyes. "Kernos' codpiece, *don't* remind me. My bed is as you see it. Virtuously empty."

"Since when have you and virtue been nodding acquaintances?" Medren gibed.

"Since just before you left," Stef replied, deciding on impulse to tell his friend the exact truth.

"That's odd." Medren let go of his shoulders and moved back a step. "I would have thought that you and Uncle Van would have hit it off—"

Stef bit off a curse. "Since when—you've been—what do you—"

"I set you up," Medren said casually. "The opportunity was there, and I grabbed it—I knew Van would try anything to help the King, and I know you think he hung the moon. I figured neither one of you would be able to resist the other. Gods know I'd been *trying* to get you two in the same place at the same time for over a year. So—" Now he paused, and frowned. "So what went wrong?"

"*I* don't know," Stef groaned, and turned away, flinging

himself down in a chair. "I can't think anymore. I've tried every ploy that's ever worked before, and I just can't imagine why they aren't succeeding now. The Healers are working me to death, and Herald Vanyel keeps sidestepping me like a skittish horse. I'd scream, if I could find the energy."

"Tell the Healers to go chase their shadows," Medren ordered gruffly. "Horseturds, Stef, you're exercising a *Gift*; that takes power, physical energy, and you're using yours up faster than you can replace it! No wonder you're tired!"

"I am?" This was news to Stefen. He'd always just assumed using his Gift was a lot like breathing. You just *did* it. And he said as much.

Medren snorted. "Good gods, doesn't *anybody* in this place think? I guess not, or the Healers wouldn't be stretching you to your limits. Or else nobody's ever figured the Bardic Gift was like any other. I promise you, it is; using your Gift *does* take energy and you've been burning yours up too fast. If the blasted Healers want to study you any more, tell them that. Then tell them that from now on they can just wedge themselves into a corner behind the throne and study you from there. Idiots. Honestly, Stef, Healers can be so damned focused; give them half a chance and they'll kill you trying to figure out how you're put together."

Stefen laughed, his sense of humor rapidly being restored. "That's why I was telling myself I was an idiot. I was letting them run me into the ground, but I couldn't think of a way to get them to stop. They can be damned persuasive, you know."

"Oh, I know." Medren took the other chair and sprawled in it gracelessly. "I know. Heralds are the same way; they don't seem to think ordinary folks need something besides work, work, and more work. I've watched Uncle Van drive himself into the ground a score of times. Once or twice, it's been *me* that had to go pound on him and make him rest. And speaking of Uncle Van, that brings me right back to the question I started with: what went wrong? You still haven't really told me anything. Take it from the beginning."

Stefen gave in, and related the whole tale, his frustration increasing with every word. Medren listened carefully, his eyes darkening with thought. "Hmm. I guess—"

His voice trailed off, and Stef snapped his fingers to get his attention. "You guess *what*?"

"I guess he's gotten really shy," Medren replied with a shrug. "It's the only thing I can think of to explain the way he's acting. That and this obsession he has about not letting anyone get close to him because they'll become a target."

Stefen felt a cold finger of fear run suddenly down his back. "He's not wrong," he told his friend solemnly, trying *not* to think of some of the things he'd seen as a street beggar. How during "wars" between street gangs or thief cadres, it was the lovers and the offspring who became the targets—and the victims—more often than not. And it was pretty evident from the Border news that a war between the nations and a war between gangs had that much in common. "It's a lot more effective to strike at an emotional target than a physical one."

Medren shook his head. "Oh, come on, Stef! You're in the heart of Valdemar! Who's going to be able to touch you here? That's even assuming Van *is* right, which I'm not willing to grant."

"I don't know," Stefen replied, still shivering from that odd touch of fear. "I just don't know."

"Then snap out of this mood of yours," Medren demanded. "Give over, and let's see if we can't think of a way to bring Uncle Van to bay."

Stefen had to laugh. "You talk about him as if he was some kind of wild animal."

Medren grinned. "Well, this is a hunt, isn't it? You're either going to have to coax him, or ambush him. Take your pick."

At that moment, one of the legion of Healers that had been plaguing Stefen appeared like a green bird of ill-omen in the doorway. "Excuse me, Bard Stefen," the bearded, swarthy man began, "but—"

"No," Stef interrupted.

"The Healer blinked. "What?"

"I said, 'no.' I won't excuse you." Stefen stood, and faced the Healer with his hands spread. "Look at me—I look like a shadow. You people have been wearing me to death. I'm tired of it, and I'm not going to do anything more today."

The Healer looked incensed. "What do you mean by that?" he snapped, bristling. "What do you mean, we've been 'wearing you to death'? We haven't been—"

"I meant just what I said," Stef said coolly. "I've been using a *Gift*, Healer. That takes energy. And I don't have any left."

Now the Healer *did* look closely at him, focusing first on the dark rings under his eyes, then looking oddly *through* him, and the man's weathered face reflected alarm. "Great good gods," he said softly. "We never intended—"

"Probably not, but you've been wearing me to a thread." Stefen sat down again, feigning more weariness than he actually felt. The guilt on the Healer's face gave him no end of pleasure. "In fact," he continued, drooping a little, "if you *don't* let me alone, I fear I will have nothing for the King. . . ."

He sighed, and rested his head on the back of the chair as if it had grown too heavy to hold up. Through half-closed eyes he watched the Healer pale and grow agitated.

"We can't—I mean, King Randale's needs come first, of course," the man stammered. "I'll speak to—I'll see that you aren't disturbed any more today, Bard Stefen—"

"I don't know," Stefen said weakly. "I hope that will be enough, but I'm so tired—"

Out of the corner of his eye he saw Medren with his fist shoved into his mouth, strangling on his own laughter.

"Never mind, Bard," the Healer said, strangling on his own words. "We'll do something about all this—I—"

And with that, he turned and fled. Medren doubled up in silent laughter, and Stefen preened, feeling enormously pleased with himself.

"I really *am* tired, you know," he said with a grin, when Medren began to wheeze. "I honestly am."

"Lord and Lady!" the Journeyman gasped. "I know but—good gods, you should go on the stage!" He clasped the back of his hand to his forehead, and swooned theatrically across the back of his chair. "Oh la, good sir, I do believe I shall fai—"

The pillow caught Medren squarely in the face.

All right, Stefen thought, carefully putting his gittern back in its case. *I've left you alone except for simple politeness for three days, Herald Vanyel. Let's see if you respond to being ignored.* He began tightening the buckles holding the case closed. *I've never known anyone yet who could deal with* that.

He suppressed a smile as he caught Vanyel making his way through the crowd, obviously coming in Stef's direction. *Looks like you won't be the first to be the exception to the rule.*

"Bard Stefen?" Vanyel's voice was very low, with a note of hesitancy in it.

Stefen looked up, and smiled. He didn't have to feign the hint of shyness that crept into the smile; Vanyel *still* affected him that way. "I can't get used to that," he confessed, surprising himself with the words. "People calling me Bard Stefen, I mean. I keep looking around to see who you're talking to."

Vanyel smiled, and Stefen's throat tightened. "I know what you mean," he said. "If it hadn't been that I spent the winter with the Hawkbrothers and had gotten used to wearing white, I would have spent half every morning for the first couple of months trying to figure out whose Whites had gotten into my wardrobe."

Do I—no, I don't think so. Every time I've tried to touch him, he's started to respond, then pulled back. Let's keep things casual, and see if that works.

"I sometimes wish I've never gotten Scarlets," Stef said, instead of trying to touch Vanyel's hand. "I never have any time for myself anymore. And I don't recognize myself anymore when I look in the mirror. I *used* to know how to have fun. . . ."

Vanyel relaxed just the tiniest bit, and Stefen felt a surge of satisfaction. *Finally, finally, I'm reading him right.*

The crowd was almost gone now, and Stefen wondered fleetingly what business had been transacted this time. He wouldn't know unless someone told him.

"You did a good day's work, Bard Stefen," Vanyel said, as if reading his mind. "Randi was able to judge three inter-family disputes that have been getting worse for the past year or more. I'll make you an offer, Stefen—*if* you promise not to get so intoxicated you can't navigate across the grounds." Vanyel smiled, teasingly. "We'll have dinner in my quarters, and you can show me those bar-chords you promised to demonstrate the night you played your fingers to bits."

I did? I don't remember promising that. For a moment Stefen was startled, because he thought he remembered everything about that evening. Then he suppressed a smile.

Clever, Herald Vanyel. A nice, innocent excuse. And you might even believe it. Well, I'll take it.

"I don't make a habit of getting falling-down drunk, Herald," he replied, with a grin to take the sting out of the words. "And since the food is *much* better at the Palace, I'll accept that offer."

"You mean you're only interested in the food?" Vanyel laughed. "I suppose my conversation hasn't much impressed you."

He's a lot more relaxed. I think Medren's right, I'm either going to have to coax him or ambush him, and in either case I'm going to have to keep things very casual or I'll scare him off again. Damn. Stefen stood up and slung his gittern case over one shoulder before replying.

"Actually, I *am* much more interested in someone who'll talk to me," he said. "I'm not exactly the most popular Bard in the Collegium right now."

Vangel grimaced. "Because of being advanced so quickly?"

Stefen nodded, and picked up his music carrier. "I had only just made Journeyman, and a lot of Bards resent my being jumped up like I was. A lot of the apprentices and Journeymen do, too. I can't say as I blame them too much, but I'm getting tired of being treated like a leper."

He fell into step beside Vanyel, and the two of them left through the side door.

"At least the Council's put it about that the whole promotion was at Herald Shavri's request," he continued. "That makes it a little more palatable, at least to some of the older ones. And the younger Bards can't claim I earned it in bed—that's one blessing, however small."

Vanyel raised one eyebrow at that last statement, but didn't comment. "I got something of the same treatment, though not for too long," the Herald told him. "Since it was Savil that gave me my Whites, there was an awful lot of suspicion of nepotism, or sympathy because of 'Lendel. . . ."

The Herald's expression grew remote and saddened for a moment, then he shook his head. "Well, fortunately, Heralds being what they are, that didn't last too long. Especially not after Savil got herself hurt, and I cleaned out that nest of hedge-wizards up north. I pretty much proved then and there that I'd *earned* my Whites."

"I'm afraid I won't be able to do anything that spectacular," Stef replied, lightly. "It's not in the nature of the job for a Bard to do anything particularly constructive."

Instead of laughing, the Herald gave Stefen a peculiar, sideways look. "I think you underestimate both yourself and the potential power of your office, Stefen," he said.

Stefen laughed. "Oh, come now! You don't really expect me to agree with that old cliche that music can change the world, do you?"

"Things usually become cliched precisely because there's a grain of truth in them," was the surprising answer. "And—well, never mind. I expect you're right."

They had reached the Herald's Wing, that bright, wood-paneled extension of the Old Palace. Vanyel's room was one of the first beyond the double doors that separated the wing from the rest of the Palace. Vanyel held one of the doors open for Stef, then stepped gracefully around him and got the door to his own room open.

Stefen put his burdens down just inside the door, and arched his back in a stretch. "Brightest Havens—" he groaned. "—I feel as stiff as an old bellows. I bet I even creak."

"You're too young to creak," Vanyel chuckled, and pulled the bell-rope to summon a servant. "I don't suppose you play hinds and hounds, do you?"

Stefen widened his eyes, and assumed a patently false expression of naivete. "Why, no, Herald Vanyel—but I'd love to learn."

Vanyel laughed out loud. "Oh, no—you don't fool me with that old trick! You've probably been playing for years."

"Since I could talk," Stef admitted. "Can't blame me for trying."

"Since I might have done the same to you, I suppose I can't." Vanyel gestured at the board set up on the table. "Red or white?"

"Red," Stef replied happily. "And since *you're* the strategist, you can spot me a courser."

Stefen moved his gaze-hound into what he thought was a secure position, and watched with dismay as Vanyel captured it with a lowly courser. Then, to add insult to injury, the Herald maneuvered that same courser into the promotion square and exchanged it for a year-stag.

"Damn!" he exclaimed, seeing his pack in imminent danger of being driven off, and taking steps to retrench his forces. The "hind" side of hounds and hinds was supposed to be the weaker, which was why the better player took it. It was usually considered a good game if the play ended in statemate.

Vanyel beat him about half the time.

It looked as though this game was going to end in defeat too. Three moves later, and Stef surveyed the board in amazement, unable to see any way out. Vanyel's herd had trapped his pack, and there was no way out.

"I yield," he conceded. "I don't know how you do it. You always take the hinds, and I can count the number of times I've won on one hand."

Vanyel replaced the carved pieces in their box with thoughtful care. "I have a distinct advantage," he said, after a long pause. "Until Randi got so sick that Shavri was spending all her time keeping him going, I helped guard the Karsite Border. I have a lot of experience in taking on situations with unfavorable odds."

"Ah," Stef replied, unable to think of anything else to say. He watched Vanyel's hands, admiring their strength and grace, and tried not to think about how much he wanted those hands to be touching something other than game pieces.

Ever since he'd stopped pursuing Van and started keeping things strictly on the level of "friendship," he'd found himself spending most evenings with Herald. He was learning an enormous amount, and not just about hinds and hounds. Economics, politics, the things Vanyel had experienced over the years—it was fascinating, if frustrating. Being so near Vanyel, and yet not daring to court him, overtly or otherwise—Stef had never dreamed he possessed such patience.

This was an entirely new experience; wanting someone and being unable to gratify that desire.

It was a nerve-wracking experience, yet it was not completely unpleasant. He was coming to know Vanyel, the *real* Vanyel, far better than anyone else except Herald Savil. That was not a suspicion; he'd had the fact confirmed more than once, by letting some tidbit of information slip in conversations with Medren. And Medren would give him a star-

tled look that told Stefen that once again, he'd been told
something Vanyel had never confided to anyone else.

He knew Van better than he'd ever known any lover.
And for all this knowledge, the Herald was still a mystery.
He was no closer to grasping what music Vanyel moved to
than he had been when this all began.

Which made him think of something else to say after all.

"Van?" he ventured. "You hated it out there—but you
sound as if you wish you were back on the Border."

Vanyel turned those silver eyes on him and stared at him
for a moment. "I suppose I did," he said, finally. "I suppose
in a way I do. Partially because it would mean that Randi
was in good enough health that Shavri could take her own
duties up again—"

Stef shook his head. "There was more to it than that. It
sounded like you *wanted* to be out there."

Vanyel looked away, and put the last of the pieces in
their padded niches. "Well, it's rather hard to explain. It's
miserable out there on the lines, you're constantly hungry,
wet, cold, afraid, in danger—but I was doing some good."

"You're doing good here," Stefen pointed out.

Vanyel shook his head. "It's not the same. Any reasonably adept diplomat could do what I'm doing now. Any
combination of Heralds could supply the same talents and
Gifts. The only reason it's me is Randi's need and Randi's
whims. I keep having the feeling that I could be doing a lot
more good if I was elsewhere."

Stefen sprawled back in his chair, studying the Herald
carefully. "I don't understand it," he said at last. "I don't
understand you Heralds at all. You're constantly putting
yourselves in danger, and for what? For the sake of people
who don't even know you're doing it, much less that you're
doing it for them, and who couldn't point you out in a
crowd if their lives depended on it. Why, Van?"

That earned him another strange stare from the Herald,
one that went on so long that Stef began to think he'd really
said something wrong this time. "Van—what's the matter?
Did I—"

Vanyel seemed to come out of a kind of trance, and
blinked at him. "No, it's quite all right, Stef. It's just—this
is like an echo from the past. I remember having exactly
this same conversation with 'Lendel—except it was *me* asking 'Why?' and him trying to tell me the reasons." Vanyel

looked off at some vague point over Stefen's head. "I didn't understand his reasons then, and you probably won't understand mine now, but I'll try to explain. It has to do with a duty to myself as much as anything else. I have these abilities. Most other people don't. I have a duty to *use* them, because I have a duty to myself to be the kind of person I would want to have as a—a friend. If I don't use my abilities, I'm not only failing people who depend on me, I'm failing myself. Am I making sense?"

"Not really," Stefen confessed.

Vanyel sighed. "Just say that it's a need to help—could you *not* sing and play? Well, I can't *not* help. Not anymore, anyway. And it doesn't matter if anyone knows what I'm doing or not; I know, and I know I'm doing my best. And because of what I'm doing, things are better for other people. Sometimes a great many other people."

"This is loyalty, right?" Stefen hazarded.

"Only in being loyal to people in general, and not any one land. I could no more have let those farmers in Hardorn be enslaved than I could have our own people." Vanyel leaned forward earnestly. "Don't you see, Stef? It's not that I'm serving Valdemar, it's that I'm helping to preserve the kind of people who leave the world better than they found it, and trying to stop the ones who take instead of giving."

"You sound like one of those *Tayledras*—"

"I am. Moondance himself has said so more than once. Their priority is for the land, and mine is for the people— but that's at least in part because the land is so damaged where they live." Vanyel smiled a little. "I wish you could see them, Stef. You'd want to write a thousand songs about them."

"If they're so wonderful, why are people afraid of them?" Stefen asked. "And why aren't you and Savil?"

Vanyel laughed at that. "Let me tell you about the first time I ever worked with Moondance—"

The story was almost enough to make Stefen forget his frustration.

Six

"Damn!" Medren swore, pounding the arm of his chair. "This is *stupid*! I swear to you, my uncle is about to drive me mad!"

The windows to Stefen's room were open to the summer evening, and Medren was trying to keep his voice down to prevent everybody in the neighborhood from being privy to their plight. Stef evidently didn't *care* who overheard them.

"About to drive *you* mad?" Stefen's voice cracked, and Medren winced in sympathy. Stef was pulling at his hair, totally unaware that he was doing so, and looked about ready to climb the walls. He shifted position so often that his chair was doing a little dance around the room, a thumblength at a time.

"I know, I know, it's a lot worse for you. I'm just frustrated. You're—" Medren paused, unable to think of a delicate way to put it."

"I'm *celibate*, that's what I am!" Stefen growled, lurching to his feet and beginning to pace restlessly. "I'm *worse* than celibate. I'm fixated. It's not just that Vanyel isn't cooperating, it's that I don't *want* anyone else anymore, and the better I know him, the worse it gets!" He stopped dead in his tracks, suddenly, and stared out the window for a moment. "I'm never happier than when I'm around him. I sometimes wonder how long I'm going to be able to stand this. There are times when I can't think of anything but him."

Medren stared at his friend, wondering if Stefen had really listened to himself just now. Because what he'd just described was the classic reaction of a lifebonded. . . .

Stef and Uncle Van? No. Not possible; not when Van has already been lifebonded once. . . . Or is it? Is there a rule somewhere that lifebondings can only happen once in a lifetime, even if you lose your bondmate?

92

A lifebonding would certainly explain a great deal of Stef's behavior. Medren had long ago given up on trying to second-guess his uncle. Vanyel was far too adept at hiding what he felt, even from himself.

"So, what have we tried so far?" Medren said aloud. Stef at least stopped pacing long enough to push his hair out of his eyes and count up all the schemes they'd concocted on his fingers.

"We tried getting him drunk again. He didn't cooperate. We tried that trip to the hot springs. That *almost* worked, except that we got company right when it looked like he was going to break down and do something. We tried every variation on my hurting myself and him having to help me, and all I got were bruises in some fascinating places." Stefen gritted his teeth. "We tried my asking him for a massage for my shoulder muscles. He referred me to a Healer. The only thing we haven't tried is catching him asleep and tying him up."

"Don't even *think* about that!" Medren said hastily. "Listen, first of all, you *won't* catch him asleep, and secondly, even if you did—you wouldn't want to be standing there if he mistook you for an enemy."

Like the last time he was home, when that idiot with the petition tried to tackle him in the bath. Medren shuddered. *I know Grandfather said he needed to replace the bathhouse—but that wasn't the best way to get it torn down.*

"He wouldn't hurt me," Stefen said with absolute certainty.

"Don't bet on that," Medren replied, grimly. "Especially if he doesn't know it's you. I've seen what he can do, and you wouldn't want to stand in the way of it. If he wants to level something or someone, he will, and anything in between him and what he wants to flatten is going to wind up just as flat as his target."

"No," Stef denied vehemently. "No—I swear to you, I know it. No matter what, he wouldn't hurt me."

Medren just shook his head and hoped Stef would never have to test that particular faith. "All right," he said after a moment's thought. "What about this—"

Vanyel closed his weary eyes for a moment, and thought longingly, selfishly, of rest, of peace, of a chance to enjoy the bright summer day.

But there was no peace for Valdemar, and hence, no rest for Herald Vanyel.

:Take a break tonight, Van,: Yfandes advised him. *:You haven't had young Stefen over for the past three evenings. And I think you can afford to let the Seneschal and the Lord Marshal hash this one out without you.:*

At least the news out of Karse was something other than a disaster, for a change.

"So there's no doubt of it?" he asked the messenger. "The Karsites have declared the use of magic anathema?"

The dust-covered messenger nodded. It was hard to tell much about her, other than the fact that she was not a Herald. Road grime had left her pretty much a uniform gray-brown from head to toe. "There's more to it than that, m'lord," she said. "They're outlawing everyone even suspected of having mage-craft. Just before I left, the first of the lucky ones came straggling across the Border. I didn't have time to collect much of their tales, but there's another messenger coming along behind me who'll have the whole of it."

"Lucky ones?" said the Seneschal, puzzled. "Lucky for us, perhaps, but since when has it been lucky for enemy mages to fall into our hands?"

"Aye, it wouldn't seem that way, but 'tis," she replied, wiping the back of her hand across her forehead, and leaving a paler smear through the dirt and sweat. "The ones we got are the lucky ones. They're the ones that 'scaped the hunters. They're burning and hanging over there, whoever they can catch. 'Tis a bit of a holy crusade, it seems. Like some kind of plague, all of a sudden half of Karse wants to murder the Gifted."

"Good gods." The Seneschal ran his hand over his closed eyes. "It sounds insane—"

"How did it start?" the Lord Marshall asked bluntly. "or do you know?"

The messenger nodded. "Lord Vanyel's turning those demons back on Karse ten years ago was the start of it, but the real motivator seems to be from the priesthood."

"The *priesthood*?" Healer Liam exclaimed, sitting up straight. "Which priesthood?"

"Sunlord Vkanda," the messenger replied. "And there's not enough news yet to tell if it's only the one priest, or the whole lot of them."

At that moment, a servant appeared with wine. The messenger took it and gulped it down gratefully. Lord Marshall Reven leaned forward over the table when she'd finished, his lean face intent, his spare body betraying how tense he was.

"What else can you tell us?" he asked. "Any fragment of information will help."

The messenger leaned back in her chair. "Quite a bit, actually," she said. "I'm trained by one of your Heralds. The one that started this crusade's a nameless lad of maybe twenty or so; calls himself The Prophet. No one knows much else about him, 'cept that he started on that there was a curse on the land, on account of them using mages. That was a bit less than a month ago. Next thing you know, the countryside's afire, and Karse's got more'n enough troubles to make 'em pull back every trooper they had on the Border. That was how matters stood a week ago when I left; gods only know what's going on in there now."

"Have we heard from any of our operatives in Karse itself?" the Seneschal asked Vanyel.

The Herald shook his head. "Not yet."

He was worried for those operatives—there were at least three of them, one Mindspeaking Herald among them—but his chief reaction was relief. *I cannot believe that we pulled the last of the mages out less than a year ago. There is no one in there now who should be suspected of magery. . . .*

"You say this situation is causing some civil disorder?" Archpriest Everet had a knack for understatement, but he was serious enough. His close-cropped, winter-white hair was far too short to fidget with, so he fingered his earlobe worriedly instead. Beneath his bland exterior, Vanyel sensed he was deeply concerned.

Not surprising; while it might look as if this was unalloyed good news for Valdemar, that fact that it was a religious crusade meant the possibility of it spilling over the Border. There were several houses of the Sunlord within the borders of Valdemar. If they joined their fellows in this holy war against mages, not only would the Archpriest be responsible for their actions, he would be obligated to see to it that they were stopped.

Which is about all he's thinking of. He doesn't see how much chaos this could cause the entire country. If the followers of the Sunlord move against Heralds—

*Some of us are mages; they might also count all Gifts as
"magic."*

*And we have the backing of other religious orders. If the
Heralds were attacked, those orders might move before the
Crown and Archpriest could. What would happen if the acolytes of Kernos decided to take matters into their own hands
and fight back on the mages' behalf? After all, the order is
primarily martial . . . fighting monks and the like. And they
favor the Heralds.*

The situation, if it crossed the Border, could be as damag-
ing to Valdemar as to Karse.

"The Sunlord's the Karsite official state religion," the
messenger reminded them. "If this Prophet has the backing
of the priesthood, then he's got the backing of the Crown.
When I left, that was what things looked like—but there's
a fair number of people with a bit of magery in their blood,
and a-plenty of hedge-wizards and herb-witches that do the
common folk a fair amount of good. Not everybody can
find a Healer when they need one; when the big magics are
flyin' about, the lords tend to forget about the little ones
that bring the rain and protect the crops. So not everybody
is taking well to this holy crusade."

"I would suggest a series of personal visits to our own
enclaves of the Sunlord, my lord Everet," Vanyel said
mildly. "I suspect your presence will make cooler heads
prevail, especially if you point out that this so-called
'Prophet' seems to be operating on nothing more than his
charisma and his own word that he speaks for the Sunlord
Vkanda."

Everet nodded, his mouth tight. "They owe their estab-
lishments to His Majesty's tolerance," he replied. "I shall
be at pains to point that out."

"I'll assure him that you're already working on the potential problem," Vanyel told him, glancing at the empty
throne. *Barring a miracle, Randi will never use that seat
again. I wonder if we should have it taken out? It's certainly
depressing to have it there.*

The Seneschal dismissed the messenger, who got stiffly to
her feet, bowed, and limped out. "Well," Seneschal Arved
said, once the door had closed behind her, "I think we have
a Situation."

The Lord Marshal nodded. "If it stays within the Karse
Border, this situation can only benefit us."

"If." Vanyel shook his head. "There's no guarantee of that."

:And what about later?: Yfandes prompted. *:After this crusade is over?:*

:Good point.: "We use magic openly in Valdemar, sanctioned and supported by the Crown," Van continued. "If this crusade doesn't burn itself out, if in fact *it* is sanctioned by the Karsite Crown, where does that leave us?"

"The deadliest of enemies," Everet answered grimly. "It will be worse than before; it will become a holy war."

Arved groaned, and closed his eyes for a moment. "You're right," he said, finally. "You're absolutely right. And if that situation occurs, there's nothing we can do to stop it."

"What we need now is information," Vanyel told them. "And that's my department. I'll get on it. *Whatever* happens, we'll have a respite from Karsite incursions for a couple of weeks while they get their own house in order. We should use that respite to our own advantage."

"Good," Arved said, shaking back his tawny hair. "Let's take this in manageable chunks. Herald Vanyel, you get us that information, and find out what the King wants us to do with refugees. We'll see what we can do to use this involuntary truce. Tomorrow we'll put together plans to cover all the contingencies we can think of. Everet—"

"I'll be making myself conspicuous in the Vkanda enclaves," the Archpriest said, rising from his seat. "You'll have to go on without me. I think I'd better leave as soon as I can pack."

:He's going to be out of here within two candlemarks,: Yfandes said. *:He travels light.:*

"Lord Everet, I'll have a document from Randale for you before you leave, authorizing you to take whatever actions you think necessary with the followers of Vkanda," Vanyel said. "Please don't leave without it."

Everet paused in midturn, and half-smiled. "Thank you, Herald. I would have gone charging off trusting in my office and so-called 'sanctity,' forgetting that neither apply to the Guard."

"Nor some highborn," the Lord Marshal reminded him. "And unless I miss my guess, there'll be one or two of those among the Sunlord's followers."

"Gentlemen, the Archpriest and I will get to our duties,

and we'll leave you to work on this in our absence," Vanyel
told them. He and Everet pushed their chairs aside and left
the Council Chamber, going in opposite directions once
they reached the door.

Randi first, then get in touch with Kera. . . . he thought,
then Mindsent, *:'Fandes, can you boost me that far?:* knowing she'd been watching his surface thoughts.

*:If not, we can at least reach someone stationed near the
Border to relay.:* She sounded quite confident, and Van
relaxed a little. *:We'll have inside information shortly. And
don't worry about Kera—thanks to that new Web we wove,
if she was in trouble, we'd know. One of us would, anyway.:*

:Thanks, love.: He'd reached the door to Randale's quarters, and was such a familiar sight to the guards that one of
them had already pushed the door open for him.

He thanked the man with a nod, and slipped inside.

Most of the time Randale was cold, so the room was as
hot as a desert, with a fire in the fireplace despite the fact
that it was full summer. The King lay on a day-bed beside
the fire, bundled up in a blanket, Shavri on a stool beside
him; he looked exhausted, but the pain lines about his
mouth and eyes were mercifully few.

Those eyes were closed, but he wasn't sleeping. Vanyel
saw his lids flutter a little the moment before he spoke.
"So," he said quietly. "What's sent you flying out of the
Council Chamber this time? Good news, or bad?"

"Wish I could tell you," Vanyel replied, dropping down
beside the bed, and putting one hand on Shavri's shoulder.
She brushed her cheek briefly against it, but didn't let go
of Randale's hand. Van touched her dark, gypsy-tumble of
curls for a moment, then turned his full attention back to
the King. "We just got a messenger from the Border and
the Karsites have just confirmed my belief that they're all
completely mad."

He outlined the situation as quickly as he could, while
Randale listened, with his eyes still closed. The King had
long ago shaved off his beard, saying it no longer hid anything and made him look like the business end of a mop,
he'd grown so thin. That was the day he'd finally acknowledged his illness, and the fact that he was never going to
recover from it; the day Van had been reassigned permanently and indefinitely to the Palace.

All of Randale that could be seen, under the swathings

of blankets, were his head and hands. Both were emaciated
and colorless; even Randale's hair was an indeterminate
shade of brown. Herald Joshe, who was something of an
artist, had remarked sadly that the King was like an under-
painting, all bones and shadows.

But there was nothing wrong with his mind, and he dem-
onstrated that he'd inherited his grandmother's good sense.

"Rethwellan," he said, after listening to Vanyel. "They
have mages in their bloodline; if Karse starts an anti-mage
campaign, they'll be in as much danger as we. Get Arved
to draft up some letters to Queen Lythiaren, feeling her out
and offering alliance." He paused a moment. "Tell him to
word those carefully; she doesn't entirely trust me right now
after that mess with the Amarites."

"It wasn't your fault," Vanyel protested, as Shavri
stroked her lifebonded's forehead. Randale opened his eyes
and smiled slightly.

"I know that, but she can't admit it," he replied. "Have
we got a 'limited powers' declaration around here somewhere? You'll need one for Everet."

"I think so," Vanyel answered, and got to his feet. After
a moment of checking through the various drawers, he
found what he was looking for—a pre-inscribed document
assigning limited powers of the Crown, with blanks for the
person and the circumstances. There was always pen, ink,
and blotter waiting on the desk; in another moment Vanyel
had filled in the appropriate blank spaces.

"Good, let me see it." Randale read it carefully, as he
always did. "Your usual thorough and lawyerlike job,
Van." He looked up at Vanyel, and smiled. "I hope you
brought the pen with you."

"I did." Vanyel laid the bottom of the document over a
book and held both so that Randale could initial the appropriate line. Blowing on the ink to dry it more quickly, he
took the paper over to the desk and affixed the Seal of
the Monarch. "What about the mages coming across the
Border?" he asked over his shoulder.

"Unhindered passage via guarded trade-road into Rethwellan," Randale told him. "But I don't want to offer them
sanctuary. This would be a good opportunity for Karse to
get an agent into Valdemar. We can't know which are
blameless, which are hirelings, and which are spies. Send
them on, unless one of them happens to get Chosen."

"Not likely." Vanyel left the paper where it was, and returned to Randale's side. "How has today been?"

"Shavri's beginning to understand what it is that young Bard of yours actually does," Randale replied. "She's able to do a bit more for me. But yesterday was bad, I'd rather not give audiences today, because I don't think I can get past the door right now. No strength left."

Vanyel touched his shoulder; Randale sighed, and covered Vanyel's hand with his own. "Then don't try," Van said quietly. "Anything more I should do about Karse?"

"Get us inside information, then get our Herald operatives out of there," Randale replied. "Then send a few non-Gifted agents to deliver aid to the rest, then insinuate themselves into the trouble. And let's get moving on the Rethwellan situation."

By this time, the corners of his mouth were tight and pinched, and he was very pale. Vanyel felt a lump rising in his throat. Randale was proving a better King than anyone had ever expected; the weaker he became, the more he seemed to rise to the challenge. As his body set tighter physical limits on what he could do, his mind roved, keeping track of all of the tangles inside Valdemar and out.

Vanyel swallowed the lump that caught in his throat every time he looked at Randale. "Anything else?" he asked. "There's a lot of matters pending."

Randale closed his eyes and leaned back into the pillows. "Compromise in the Lendori situation by offering them the contract for the Guard mules if they'll cede the water rights to Balderston. Their animals are good enough, if priced a little high. The Evendim lot has their own militia; feel them out and see if they might be willing to spare us some men. Tell Lord Preatur that if he doesn't either take that little mink he calls his daughter and marry her off or send her back home, I'll find a husband for her; she's got half my Guard officers at dagger's point with each other. That's all."

"That's enough." Vanyel touched one finger to Randale's hot forehead, and exerted his own small Healing ability. Shavri had told him that every tiny bit helped some. "Rest, Randi."

"I'll do my best," the King whispered, and Vanyel took himself out before he started weeping.

Pages and acolytes were flying about Everet's rooms like leaves in a storm, while Everet stood in the middle of the chaos and directed it calmly. Vanyel dodged a running child and handed Everet the document.

Everet read it through as carefully as Randale had. "Excellent. Enough authority to cow just about anyone I might need to." He intercepted one of the acolytes and directed the young man to pack the document with the rest of his papers. "Thank you, Herald. Let's hope I don't need to use it."

"Fervently," Vanyel replied, and returned briefly to the Council Chamber to give the Seneschal the rest of King Randale's orders.

Sunlight on the water blinded him a moment. :*I feel like the Fair Maid of Bredesmere, waiting for her lover,:* 'Fandes Mindsent.

Vanyel squinted against the light, then waved to her; she was standing on the Field side of the bridge spanning the river separating the Palace grounds from Companion's Field. :*Well, you're all in white,:* he teased as he approached the bridge. :*And there's the River for you to get thrown into.:*

:*Just* try *it, my lad,:* she reared a little, and danced in place, the long grass muffling the sound of her hooves. :*We'll see who throws who in!:*

:*Thank you, I'd rather not.:* He ran the last few steps over the echoing bridge, and took her silken head in both his hands. "You're beautiful today, love," he said aloud.

:*Huh.:* She snorted, and shook his hands off. :*You say that every day.:* But he could tell by the way she arched her neck that she was pleased.

:*That's because you* are *beautiful every day,:* he replied.

:*Flatterer.:* she said, tossing her silver waterfall of a mane. Since they weren't in combat situations anymore, she'd told him to let it and her tail grow, and both were as long and full as a Companion's in an illuminated manuscript.

"It isn't flattery when it's true," he told her honestly. "I wish I had more time to spend with you."

Her blue eyes darkened with love. :*I do, too. A plague on reality! I just want to* be *with you, not have to work!:*

He laughed. "Now you're as lazy as I used to be! Come along, love, and let's get ourselves settled so we can make a stab at reaching Kera."

At one time there had been a grove of ancient pine trees

near the bridge—the grove that had been destroyed when
Herald-trainee Tylendel had lost control of his Gift in the
shock following his twin brother's death. There was nothing
there now except grass, a few seedlings and a couple of
trees that had escaped the destruction. The dead trees had
long since been cut up and used for firewood.

Since that night had been the start of the train of events
that led to Tylendel's suicide, it would have been logical for
Vanyel to shun the spot, but logic didn't seem to play a
very large part in Vanyel's life. He still found the place
peaceful, protective, and he and Yfandes often went there
when they needed to work together.

There was a little hollow in the center of what had been
the grove; Yfandes folded her legs under her and settled
down there in the long grass. There wasn't so much as a
breath of wind to stir the tips of the grass blades. Vanyel
lowered himself down beside her, and braced his back
against her side. The warm afternoon sun flowed over both
of them.

"Ready?" he asked.

:When you are.: she replied.

He closed his eyes, and slid into full rapport with her; it
was even easier with her than with Savil. He waited for a
moment while they settled around each other, then Reached
for Kera.

She couldn't know when someone was going to try to
contact her, but Kera *had* to realize that they were going
to do so eventually. Vanyel was counting on that, on the
receptivity. He'd worked with Kera before this, so he knew
her well enough to find her immediately *if* he could reach
that far.

He strained to Hear her; to sort her out of the distant
whispers on the Border of Karse. Most of those mind-voices
were strident with anger; a few were full of panic. It was
by the lack of both those traits that he identified Kera; that,
and the carefully crafted shields about her. Savil's work,
and beautiful, like a faceted crystal.

He stretched—it was like trying to touch something just
barely within his grasp; the tips of his "fingers" brushed the
edge of it. *:Kera.:* He offered his identification to her
shields, which parted briefly and silently.

:Who?: came the thought; then incredulity. *:Vanyel?:*
She knew where he was and the kind of strain it was to

reach her. Hard on that incredulity came the information he needed; exactly what was going on over in Karse, everything Kara knew about the Prophet, and that he was, indeed, backed by the full force of the Karsite Crown and the priesthood of the Sunlord.

:Get out of there,: Vanyel urged. *:Go over White Foal Pass if you have to, or get out through Rethwellan, but leave. Warn the others you're leaving if you can. With a Companion around you, however disguised, you're the most likely to be uncovered.:*

Fear, and complete agreement. Evidently she'd had some close calls already.

:Go,: she told him, courage layered over the fear. *:I've got my plans, I was just waiting for contact.:*

He released her, and dropped into clamoring darkness.

When he opened his eyes again, the last of a glorious scarlet sunset was fading from the clouds. Crickets sang in the grass near his knee, and he shivered with cold.

Not a physical cold, but the cold of depletion. Yfandes nudged him with her nose. *:I got it all, and I passed it on to Joshe's Kimbry, and Joshe passed it to the Seneschal.:*

"Good, 'Fandes," he coughed, leaning on her warm strength. "Thank you."

:I never suspected you had that kind of reach. You outdistanced me.:

"I did?" He rubbed his eyes with a knuckle. "Well, I don't know what to say."

:I do,: she replied, humor in her mind-voice, *:You're going to have a reaction-headache in a few more breaths. I suggest you stop by Randale's Healers on the way to your room.:*

"I'll do that." He got to his knees, then lurched to his feet. She scrambled up next to him, glowing in the blue dusk.

:Have you forgotten you'd invited young Stefen to your room tonight?:

"Oh, gods. I had." He was torn, truly torn. He was weary, but—dammit, he wanted the Bard's company.

:He wants yours just as badly,: Yfandes said, with no emotion coloring in her mind-voice at all.

"Oh, 'Fandes, he's just infatuated," Vanyel protested. "It'll wear off. If I told him to leave me alone—assuming I wanted to, which I don't—it would just make him that much more determined to throw himself in my way."

:I think it's more than infatuation,: she responded, and he thought he caught overtones of approval when she thought about the Bard. *:I think he really cares a great deal about you.:*

"Well, I care about him—which is precisely why I'm going to keep this relationship within the bounds of friendship." Vanyel tested his legs, and found them capable of taking him back to the Palace, though the threatened reaction-headache was just beginning to throb in his temples. "He doesn't need to ruin his life by flinging himself at me." He stroked her neck. "Goodnight, sweetling. And thank you."

:My privilege and pleasure,: she said fondly.

He began the trek back to the Palace, dusk thickening around him, his head throbbing in time with his steps. *Friendship. Oh, certainly. Havens, Van,* he chided himself. *You know very well that you're just looking for excuses to see more of Stef.*

Now, finally, a breeze blew up; a stiff one, that made the branches bend a little. He had warmed up quite a bit just from the long walk, but although the cool air felt good against his forehead, it made him shiver. *Well, there's no harm in it, except to me. I'm certainly exercising all my self-control. . . .*

The depth of his attraction to the Bard bothered him, and not only because he felt the lad was still pursuing him out of hero-worship. As night fell around him and the lights of the Palace began to appear in the windows, he realized that over the past few weeks he had become more and more confused about his relationship with Stefen. Stars appeared long before he reached the doors to the Palace gardens, and he looked up at them, wishing he could find an answer in their patterns.

I don't understand this at all. I want to care for him so much—too much. It feels like I'm betraying 'Lendel's memory.

He turned away from the night sky and pulled open the door, blinking at the light from the lantern set just inside it.

He entered the hall, and closed the door behind him. *Great good gods, the boy should be glad I'm not 'Lendel,* he thought, with a hint of returning humor. *'Lendel would have cheerfully tumbled the lad into bed long before this. Gods, I need that headache tea—*

Evidently the gods thought otherwise, for at that moment, a page waiting in the hallway spotted him, and ran to meet him.

"Herald Vanyel," the child panted. "The King wants you! Jisa's done something horrible!"

The child couldn't tell him much; just that Jisa had come to Randale's suite with Treven and a stranger. There had been some shouting, and the page had been called in from the hall. Randale had collapsed onto his couch, Shavri and Jisa were pale as death, and Shavri had sent the page off in search of Vanyel.

An odd gathering waited for him in Randale's suite; The King and Shavri, Jisa and young Treven, the Seneschal, Joshe, and a stranger in the robes of a priest of Astera. And a veritable swarm of servants and Guards. By this time, Vanyel was ready to hear almost anything; a tale of theft, murder, drunkenness—but not what Jisa flatly told him, with a rebellious lift of her chin.

"Married?" he choked, looking from Jisa to Treven and back again. "You've gotten *married?* How? Who in the Havens' name would dare?"

"I did, Herald Vanyel." The stranger said; not cowed, as Vanyel would have expected, but defiantly. As he raised his head, the cowl of his robe fell back, taking his face out of the shadows. It was no one Vanyel knew, and not a young man. Middle-aged, or older; that was Van's guess. Old enough not to have been tricked into this.

"I wasn't tricked," the priest continued, as if he had read Vanyel's thought. "I knew who they were; they told me. No one specifically forbade them to marry, and it seemed to me that there was no reason to deny them that status."

"No reason—" Vanyel couldn't get anything else out.

"The vows are completely legal and binding," Joshe said apologetically. "The only way they could be broken would be if either of them wanted a divorcement."

Treven put his arm around Jisa, and the girl took his hand in hers. Both of them stared at Vanyel with rebellion in their eyes; rebellion, and a little fear.

Randale chose that moment to turn a shade lighter and

gasp. Shavri was at his side in an instant; and in the next, had him taken out of the room into their private quarters.

"No reason," Vanyel repeated in disbelief. "What about Treven's duty to Valdemar? What are we going to do now, if the only way out of a problem is an alliance-marriage?"

He addressed the priest, but it was Treven who replied. "I thought about that, Herald Vanyel," he said. "I thought about it quite a long time. Then I did some careful check-ing—and unless you plan to have me turn shaych, there isn't anyone who could possibly suit as a marriage candidate, not even in Karse—unless there's some barbarian chieftain's daughter up north that nobody knows about. Of the unwedded, most are past childbearing, and the rest are infants. Of the wedded who might *possibly* lose their hus-bands in the next five years, most are bound with contracts that keep them tied to their spouse's land, and the rest are the designated regents for their minor children." Despite his relatively mild tone, Treven's expression boded no good for anyone who got in his way. "I didn't see any reason to deny ourselves happiness when we *know* that we're lifebonded."

"Happiness?" Shavri's voice sounded unusually shrill. "You talk about happiness, *here?*" She stood in the door-way, clutching a fold of her robe just below her throat. "You've put my daughter right back in the line of succes-sion, you young fool! Do you have any idea how long and hard I fought to keep her *out* of that position? You've seen what the Crown has done to Randi, both of you—Treven, how can you possibly want that kind of pain for Jisa?"

:Shavri doesn't want the Crown, so she thinks her daughter shouldn't, either,: Yfandes observed. *:Your objection is rational, but hers is entirely emotional.:*

Jisa ignored her mother's impassioned speech, turning to Vanyel and the Seneschal. "If there's pain, I'm prepared to deal with it," she said calmly, addressing them and not her mother. "I don't blame Mother for not wanting the Crown—she doesn't want that kind of responsibility, she doesn't like being a leader, and she isn't any good at it. She says that the Crown means pain, and it does, for her—but—my lords, I'm *not* Mother! Why should she make my decisions *for* me?"

The priest nodded a little, and Shavri's face went white.

"Mother—" now Jisa turned toward her, pleading. "Mother, I'm sorry, but we're two different people, you and I. I am a leader, I have been all my life, you've said so yourself. I'm not afraid of power, but I respect it, and the responsibility it brings. There's another factor here; Treven will be the King—I'll be his partner. We will be sharing the power, the responsibility, and yes, the pain. It will be different for us. Can't you see that?"

Shavri shook her head, unable to speak; then turned and fled back into the shelter of her room.

Arved was red-faced with anger. "Who gave you the authority to take it upon yourself to decide who and what was a suitable contract?" he snarled at Treven. The young man paled, but stood his ground.

"Two things, sir," he replied steadily. "The fact that Jisa and I are lifebonded, and the fact that a marriage with anyone except my lifebonded would be a marriage in name only, and a travesty of holy vows."

"In my opinion," put in the priest, "that would be blasphemy. A perversion of a rite meant to sanctify. Lifebonding is a rare and sacred thing, and should be treated with reverence. It is one thing to remain unwedded so as to give the appearance of being available, provided it is done for the safety of the realm. It seems to me, however, that to force a young person into an entirely unsuitable marriage when he is already lifebonded is—well, a grave sin."

Arved stared at the priest, then looked helplessly at Vanyel, and threw up his hands. "It's done," he said. "It can't be undone, and I'm not the one to beat a dead dog in hopes of him getting up and running to the hunt."

Joshe just shrugged.

Shavri had fled the room, Randale had collapsed—the Seneschal and his Herald had abrogated their responsibility. It was going to be left to Van to make the decision.

He ground his teeth in frustration, but there really was very little choice. As the Seneschal had pointed out, the thing was accomplished, and there would be no profit in trying to fight it further.

"Done is done," he said with resignation, ignoring Jisa's squeal of joy. "But I hope you realize you two have saddled me with the hard part."

"Hard part?" Treven asked.

"Yes," he replied. "Trying to convince the rest of the world that you haven't made a mistake, when *I'm* not sure of it myself.

Seven

"**I** . . . thought you'd be pleased," Jisa said sullenly. "You know how we feel about each other. I thought *you* would understand."

Vanyel counted to ten, and sighted on a point just above Jisa's head. They weren't alone; the priest was trying to talk Shavri around, Treven hovered right at Jisa's elbow, and there were at least half a dozen servants in the room. It wouldn't do to strangle her.

The only blessing was that Arved and Joshe were gone, which meant two less edgy tempers in a room full of tension.

"Whatever gave you the idea that I'd be pleased?" he asked. "And why should I understand?"

"Because you were willing to defy everything and everyone to have Tylendel," she replied, maddeningly. "You *know* what it's like to be lifebonded!" :*Father,*: she continued in Mindspeech, :*We've done everything else anyone ever asked of us. Why should we have to give up each other? And why can't you see our side of it?*:

He wanted to argue that *her* case was entirely different—that Tylendel was only an ordinary Herald-Mage trainee, that neither he nor 'Lendel was the Heir to the Throne—

But he couldn't. They were young and in love, and so it was useless to bring logic into the argument.

:*I can't understand why Treven's Companion didn't stop him.*: he replied, irritated by her relative calm.

:*Father, Eren not only didn't stop him, she helped us. She's the one that found Father Owain for us.*: She couldn't have kept the triumph out of her mind-voice, and she didn't even try.

"She *what*?" Vanyel exclaimed aloud. One of the servants picking up the clutter nearly jumped a foot, then glared out of the corner of his eye at them.

"Bloody, 'Eralds," he muttered, just loud enough for Van to hear. "Standin' around *thinkin'* at each other . . . still can't get used to it."

"Eren helped us," Jisa persisted. "Ask Yfandes."

"I will," he told her grimly. *:'Fandes, what do you know about all this?:*

:Everything,: she replied.

:And you didn't stop them? You didn't even tell me?: He couldn't believe what he was hearing.

:Of course we didn't stop them,: she said sharply. *:We approve. You would, too, if you'd take a minute to think with your head and your heart. What else would you have? Jisa will make a fine Consort, better than anyone else your stuffy Council would have picked for Treven. The boy is entirely right; there are no female offspring of a suitable age among any of the neutrals, and why should he make an alliance-marriage with someone who's already an ally? If you'd have him hang about for years without wedding Jisa, I think you're a fool.:*

:But Randi—: he began.

:Randale's case is entirely different; for a start, there is— or was—a Karsite princess only a year older, and the Queen of Rethwellan is exactly his age. Before his illness became a problem, there was always the potential for an alliance-wedding.:

He was too taken aback to reply for a moment, and when he finally managed to recover, one of the pages appeared at his elbow, looking anxious.

"M'lord Herald?" the child said nervously. "M'lord, the King is doing poorly. The Healers said to tell you he was in pain and refusing to take anything and that you'd know what to do."

"Go fetch Bard Stefen," Vanyel told the boy instantly. "If he's not in his own rooms, check mine." He ignored the raised eyebrows as Shavri turned away from the priest and rounded on Jisa and Treven.

"*Now* see what you've done—" the distraught Herald-Healer began, her hair a wild tangle around her face, her eyes red-rimmed. "You've made him worse, your own father! I—"

Vanyel put a hand on her arm and restrained her, projecting calm at her. "Shavri, dearheart, in all honesty you can't say that. Randi goes in cycles, you know that—and you know he was about due for an attack. You can't say that's Jisa's fault—"

"But she brought it on!" Shavri exclaimed. "She made it worse!"

"You don't know that," Vanyel began, when the page reappeared with Stefen in tow.

The Bard strolled right up to the tense knot of people, ignoring the page's frantic tugs on his sleeve. He bowed slightly to Treven, and took Jisa's limp hand and kissed it. "Congratulations," he said, as Shavri went rigid and Vanyel silently recited every curse he knew. "I think you did the right thing. I *know* you'll be happy."

He finally responded to the page's efforts, and turned toward the door to the private rooms. But before he could take more than a step, Shavri seized him by the elbow to stop him. "Wait!" she snapped. "Where did you hear this?"

He looked down at her hand, still clutching his elbow, then up at her face. "It's all over the Palace, milady Herald," he replied mildly, and looked down at her hand again.

She let go of him and pulled away, and clenched her hands in the folds of her robe. "Then there's no way we can hide this."

"I would say not, milady," Stefen replied. "By this time tomorrow it'll be all over the Kingdom."

He winked at Treven as Shavri turned back to the priest. To Van's amazement and anger, Treven winked back.

:You didn't—: he Mindsent to Jisa.

The anger in his eyes was met by matching anger in hers. *:Of course we did. The first thing we did was tell the servants and two of the biggest gossips in the Court, one of whom is Stef.:*

:Why?: he asked, anger amplifying his mind-voice so that she flinched. *:Why? To make your mother a laughingstock?:*

:No!: she flared back. *:To keep you and her from finding some way to annul what we did! We thought that the more people that knew about it, the less you'd be able to cover it up.:*

:The Companions spread it about, too,: Yfandes said, complacently. *:I was told by Liam's Orser just as you found out.:*

"Dear gods," he groaned. "It's a conspiracy of fools!"

Jisa looked hurt: Yfandes gave a disgusted mental snort and blocked him out.

Stefen stepped back a pace and straightened his back, taking on a dignity far beyond his years. "You can call it what you like, Herald Vanyel," he said stiffly, "and you can think what you like. But a good many people think that these two did exactly the right thing, and I'm one of them."

And with that, he turned on his heel, and followed the frantic page to the doorway at the back of the room.

As the priest nodded in satisfaction and took Shavri's arm, Vanyel threw up his hands in a gesture of defeat, and left before his tattered temper and dignity could entirely go to shreds.

As the Seneschal had pointed out, it was done, and couldn't be undone. In the week following, Shavri forgave her daughter, Jisa reconciled with Vanyel—but the Council was unlikely to accept the situation any time soon. As Stefen remarked sagely, in one of the few moments he had to spare away from Randale's side, "They'd gotten used to having a pair of pretty little puppets that danced whenever they pulled the strings. But the puppets just came alive and cut the strings—and they don't have any control anymore. Younglings grow up, Van—and when they do, it generally annoys *somebody*. Do you want a potential King and Queen, or a couple of rag dolls? If you want the King and Queen, you'd better get used to those two thinking for themselves, because that's what they're going to have to do."

Vanyel hadn't expected that much sense out of Stefen— though why he should have been surprised by it after all their long talks made him wonder how well *he* was thinking. The young Bard was showing his mettle in the crisis; not only easing Randale's pain for candlemarks at a time, but soothing Shavri's distress and bringing about her reconciliation with Jisa and Treven. That left Van free to deal with Council, Court, and outKingdom; making decisions in Randale's name, or waiting for one of the King's coherent spells and getting the decrees from him. The two of them worked like two halves of a complicated, beautifully engineered machine, and Vanyel wondered daily how he had gotten along without Stefen's presence and talents before this. The Bard seemed always to be at the right place, at the right time, using his Gift in exactly the right way, but that wasn't all he did. He made himself indispensable in a hundred little

ways; seeing that no one forgot important papers, that pages
were on hand to fetch and carry, and that Shavri and Randale were *never* left alone except with each other. He had
food and drink sent in to Council meetings; saw to it that
ambassadors felt themselves treated as the most important
envoys Valdemar had ever harbored.

If it hadn't been for Stefen, Vanyel would never have
survived that week.

As it was, by the time the crisis was over, both of them
looked like identical frayed threads.

And that was when the second shoe dropped.

Vanyel opened the door to his room, and stared in surprise at Stefen. The Bard was draped over "his" chair, head
thrown back, obviously asleep. As Vanyel closed the door,
the slight noise woke Stefen, who raised his head and
rubbed his eyes with one hand.

"Van," he said, his voice thick with fatigue. "S–sorry
about this. Shavri sent me out; they got two Healers that
can pain-block now—they finally caught the trick of it this
morning." He shifted around and grimaced as he tried to
move his head. "I couldn't make it back to m'room. Too
damned tired. Ordered some food for both of us and came
here. Didn't think you'd mind. Do you?"

Vanyel threw himself down in the other chair and reached
for a piece of cheese, suddenly ravenous. "Of course I don't
mind," he said. "But why in Havens didn't you take the
bed if you were so tired."

Stefen frowned at him. "I put you out of your bed once.
I'm not going to do it again. There's your mail." He pointed
to a slim pile of letters weighed down with a useless dress-
dagger. "Just came as I dozed off. Pass me some of that
cheese, would you?"

Vanyel passed the plate to him absently and used the
paperweight to slit the letters. He worked his way down
through the pile, and then froze as he saw the seal on the
last one.

"Oh, no," he moaned. "Oh, *no*. I do not need this."

"What?" Stef asked, alarmed. "What's the—"

Vanyel held up the letter, wordlessly.

"That's the Forst Reach seal," Stefan said, puzzled. Then
comprehension dawned and his expression changed to a
mixture of amusement and sympathy. "Oh. That. One of

your father's famous missives. What is it now—sheep, your brother, or your choice of comrades?"

"Probably all three," Vanyel said sourly, and opened it. "Might as well get this over with."

He skimmed through the first paragraph, and found nothing out of the ordinary. "Well, Mekeal's doing all right with his warhorse project, which means that Father's grousing about it, but can't find anything to complain about. Looks like the Famous Stud has a few good traits—well hidden, I may add." The second paragraph was more of the same. "Good gods, Meke's first just got handfasted. What's he trying to do, start his own tribe? Did I—"

"Send something? What about that really awful silver and garnet loving-cup I've seen around?" Stefen had curled up in the chair with his head resting on the arm and his eyes closed. "Savil told me you kept things like that for presents, and the worse they are, the better your family likes them."

"Except for Savil, my sister, and Medren, the concept of 'good taste' seems to have eluded my family," Vanyel replied wearily. "Thank you. Hmm. The last of the sheep has succumbed to black fly, and Father is gloating. Melenna and—good *gods!*"

"What?" Both of Stefan's eyes flew open, and he raised his head, staring blindly.

"Melenna and Jervis are *married!*" Van sat there with his mouth hanging open; the very idea of Jervis marrying *anyone*—

"Oh," Stef said indifferently. "There's a lot of that going around. Maybe it's catching" He put his head back down on the armrest, as Vanyel shook his head and proceeded to the third and final paragraph.

"Here's the usual invitation to visit home, which is invariably the prelude to something that kicks me in the—" Van stopped, and reread the final sentences. And read them a third time. They didn't make any more sense than they had before.

I suppose you know we've heard a lot about you from Medren. He's told us you have a very special friend, a Bard. 'Stefen' was the name he gave us. We'd really like to meet him, son. Why don't you bring him with you when you visit?

"Van?" Stefen waved a hand at him, and broke him out of his daze. "Van? What is it? You look like somebody hit you in the back of the head with a board."

"I feel like that," Van told him, putting the letter down and rubbing the back of his neck. "I feel just like that. There has to be a trick to it—"

"Trick to what?"

"Well—they want me to bring you with me. They want to meet you. And knowing my father, he's already assumed the worst about our friendship." Vanyel picked up the letter again, but the last paragraph hadn't changed.

Stefen yawned and closed his eyes. "Let him assume. He asked for it—let's give it to him."

"You mean you'd be willing to go with me?" Vanyel was astounded. "Stefen, you must be crazed! *Nobody* wants to visit my family, they're all insane!"

"So? You need somebody they can be horrified by so they'll leave you alone." Stefen was drifting off to sleep, and his words started to slur. "Soun's like—me—t'me. . . ."

I couldn't, Vanyel thought. *But—he's worn away to nothing. They do have two Healers to replace him, and those two can train more. Randi is as much recovered as he's going to get, and the Karse situation is stable. So—why not?*

"Why not?" Savil said, and chuckled. "He's certainly asked for it."

Vanyel had finally prevailed on her to have her favorite chair recovered in a warm gray; she looked like the Winter Queen, with her silver hair and her immaculate Whites. Taking her out of the Web had done her a world of good; there was a great deal more energy in her voice, though she still moved as stiffly as ever.

"But Savil," Vanyel protested weakly, "He thinks Stef is my lover! He *has* to!"

Savil leveled the kind of look at him that used to wither her apprentices. "So what if he does? *He* is the one who issued the invitation, entirely unprompted. Call his bluff. Then confound him. Tell you what. I'll come with you."

"Kernos' Horns, Savil, what are you trying to do, get me killed?" Vanyel laughed. "Every time you come home with me, I wind up ears-deep in trouble! I might as well go parade up and down the Karsite Boroder in full panoply— it'd be safer."

"Nonsense," Savil scoffed. "It was only the once. Seriously, I daren't travel by myself anymore. And I could cer-

tainly use the break. They can't afford to let Herald-Mages
retire anymore, there aren't enough of us."

"True," Van acknowledged. "You know, this really isn't
a bad idea."

:Stef is a sack of bones and hair,: 'Fandes chimed in. *:The
Healers are threatening mayhem if someone doesn't take him
away for a rest. Savil needs one, too, and so do you, and
neither of you will get one unless you're out of reach.:*

"Fandes thinks it's a good idea," he mused. "And to tell
you the truth, Mother and Father have been fairly civilized
to me the last couple of visits. Maybe this *will* work."

"Give me two days," Savil said, looking eager.

"Don't take more than that," Vanyel told her, as he got
up and headed for the door.

"Why?" she asked. "You don't take *that* long to pack!"

"Because if you take longer than that," he called back
over his shoulder, "my courage will quite melt away, and
you'll have to tie me to Yfandes' back to make me go
through with this."

Two days later, they were on the road out of Haven, with
Stefen riding between them on a sleek little chestnut palfrey, a filly out of Star's line. Vanyel's beloved Star had
lived out her life at Haven, a pampered favorite whose good
sense and sweet nature bred true in all the foals she'd
thrown. Star had, in fact, been Jisa's first mount. And
although once he'd been Chosen Van had no more need
of a riding horse, there had been trusted friends (and the
occasional lover) who did—so Star, and Star's offspring, had
definitely earned their keep. One of Star's daughters, this
palfrey's dam, was now Jisa's mount.

Vanyel had made a present of this particular filly, Star's
granddaughter Melody, to Stefen. Stef had reacted with
dubious pleasure—pleasure, because it meant he'd be able
to accompany Van on his daily exercise rides with 'Fandes.
Dubious, because he didn't know how to ride.

Van had been surprised until he thought about it, then
felt like a fool for *not* thinking. Stef had seldom had anything to do with a horse as a child; he was born into pov-
erty, and in the city, so there was no reason for him ever
to have learned how to ride. While Van, who had been
tossed onto a pony's back as soon as he could walk, was a

member of a privileged minority; the landed—which meant *mounted*—nobility.

He didn't often think of himself that way, but Stefen's lack of such a basic—to Van—skill made the Herald rethink a number of things in that light.

And then he'd seen to it that Stef learned to ride, among other things.

He was actually glad that Stefen was still such a tyro; it gave him a good excuse to stop fairly early each day. Savil wasn't up to long rides either, but she would never admit it. But with poor, saddle-sore Stefen along, she could be persuaded to make an early halt long before she ran into trouble herself.

By the third day of their easy trip, Stef was looking much more comfortable astride. In fact, he looked as though he was beginning to enjoy himself, taking pleasure in his mount and her paces. The chestnut filly was a good match for his dark red hair, and the two of them made a very showy pair.

:I imagine they'd attract quite a bit of notice if we weren't around,: Yfandes commented, echoing his thoughts.

:Don't look now, beloved, but they attract quite a bit when we are around.: With the late summer sun making a scarlet glory of the chestnut's coat and Stef's hair, and the two White-clad Heralds on their snowy Companions on either side of him, Stefen looked like a young hero flanked by savants.

:It's a good thing he isn't the clothes-horse I was at his age,: Van continued. *:Otherwise he'd outshine all of us.:*

:He is rather striking, isn't he?: There was a note of fondness in Yfandes' thoughts that pleased Vanyel. She didn't always like his friends; it was a relief when she did. One thing that helped was that Stef shared a habit with Jervis, the former armsmaster of Forst Reach. He talked directly to Yfandes, never talked *about* her in her presence, and included her in on conversations as if she could understand them—which, of course, she could.

Stef's filly snorted at a butterfly and pranced sideways, tossing her mane and tail playfully. Stefen laughed at her, and reined her in gently. A few weeks ago he would have clutched at the reins, probably frightening her and himself in the bargain. There was a patience and a confidence in the way he handled her that spoke to Vanyel of more than riding experience.

He's matured, Vanyel thought, with some surprise. *He's really grown up a lot in the last few weeks. He looks it, too, which is probably just as well. It's bad enough that my father is assuming he's my lover—if they knew how young he really is, my tail would truly be in the fire!*

He squinted ahead, trying to make out a distance post or a landmark through the bright sun. *Another week at most, even at this easy pace, and we'll be there. I wish I knew how much of a strain this was really going to be. It could be worse, I suppose. At least they're making an effort to be polite.*

The filly fidgeted, but Stef held her down to a fast walk, talking to her with amusement in his voice. Savil caught Vanyel's eye and grinned, nodding her head toward the young Bard.

:*A month ago she'd have put him on his rump in the dust. Boy's doing all right, Van. I like him.*: Her grin got a little wider. :*Beats the blazes out of some "friends" you've had.*:

He made a face at her. :*Now don't you start! I've told you; we're* just *friends and that's the way I intend to keep it.*:

She just gave him a look out of the corner of her eye that implied she knew better.

He ignored the look. By his reckoning, even if his parents were willing to admit that he was shaych that didn't imply they were minded to aid and abet him.

They're willing to meet my friends but they won't want to know they're *more than friends. I'll bet they keep half the hold between my room and Stef's,* he thought wryly. *Little do they know how much I'm going to appreciate that. It's been hard enough keeping things cool between us, and if they're going to help, that's just fine with me.*

Stefen slowed his filly and brought her alongside Yfandes. "If this is the way traveling always is, I'm sorry they jumped me out of Journeyman so quickly," he said, as Vanyel smiled. "I could get to like this awfully fast."

"You should have talked more with Medren," Van told him. "You're lucky. This is a good trip; the roads are fine, it hasn't rained once, and it's late summer. I'd say that on the whole, the bad days outnumber the good two to one. That's what it feels like when you're stuck out on the road, anyway."

Yfandes snorted and bobbed her head in agreement. Stef looked down at her.

"That bad, is it, milady?"

She whickered, and snorted again.

"I'll take your word for it. Both of you, that is. But this trip has been—entirely wonderful. I feel like a human being for the first time in weeks." He tilted his head sideways, and gave Vanyel a long, appraising look. "You look a lot better yourself, Van."

"I feel better," he admitted. "I just hope Joshel can hold things together for a few weeks."

"Huh," Savil said, entering the conversation. "If he can't, he's not worth his Whites."

"That's not fair, Savil," Vanyel objected. "Just because Joshe isn't a Herald-Mage—"

"That's not it," she replied. "At least, that's not all of it. You left him a clean slate, if he can't deal with it—"

"Then I'm sure we'll hear from someone," Stefen interrupted firmly. "I don't think it matters. They know where we are; if they really need you, they can contact you, Van. Why not relax?"

Stef was right, he thought reluctantly. He really *should* relax. This was another in a string of absolutely perfect summer days; the air was warm and still, without being sultry. They encountered a number of travelers, and all were completely friendly and ordinary, farmers, traders, children on errands—not a one had aroused his suspicions or Savil's. Birds chirped sleepily as they passed, and when the sun grew too oppressive, there always seemed to be a pleasant grove of trees or a tiny village inn to rest in for a little.

Maybe that's what's bothering me. It's too perfect. I mistrust perfection. I keep waiting for something to go wrong.

This afternoon was identical to the rest; at the moment they were passing through an area completely under cultivation. Open fields left fallow alternated with land under the plow. There were usually sheep or cattle grazing in the former, and farmfolk hard at work in the latter. The sheep would either ignore their presence or spook skittishly away from the road—the cattle gathered curiously at the hedgerows to watch them pass. Insects buzzed on all sides, in the fields and the hedges.

This is the way it should be, Van thought a little sadly,

thinking of the burned-over fields, and ravaged villages of the South. *This is how Valdemar should be, from Border to Border. Will I ever see it that way in my lifetime? Somehow I doubt it. Dear gods, I would give anything if I could ensure that day would come. . . .*

Stefen gave the filly her head, and she danced away ahead of them, her hooves kicking up little puffs of dust.

Vanyel shook his head. *No use in brooding. I'll just do what I can, when I can. And keep Stef at arm's length until he comes to his senses.*

The Bard let his filly stretch into a canter, outdistancing both the Heralds. Van chuckled; the filly was headstrong, but hadn't learned her own limits yet. He and Savil would catch up to the two of them eventually, probably resting in the shade of a tree.

With any luck, this whole trip may end up with Stef doing just that—learning his *limits. Especially after he meets Mother and Father. Chasing me is one thing, but trying to do so around them—and having to play little politeness games with them—* He chuckled to himself, and Yfandes cocked an ear back at him. *Oh, Stef, I think you may have met your match.* "Many's the marriage that's been canceled on account of relatives." *This might be exactly what's needed to make him realize that he's been throwing himself at a legend, not a flesh-and-blood human. And when he sees that this human comes with a package of crazed relations, I won't seem anywhere near as attractive!*

They rode into Forst Reach in the late afternoon of the one day that hadn't been completely perfect. Clouds had begun gathering in late morning, and by mid-afternoon the sky was completely gray and thunder rolled faintly in the far south. Farmers were working with one eye on the sky, and Stefen's filly fidgeted skittishly, her ears flicking back and forth every time a peal of thunder made the air shudder.

Nevertheless, there was the usual child out watching the road for them, and by the time they came within sight of the buildings of Forst Reach the multitude had assembled. Withen Ashkevron had given in to fate, and begun adding to the building some ten years ago; now two new wings spread out from the gray granite hulk, sprawling untidily to the east and north. And scaffolding on the southern side told Van that yet another building spree was about to begin. The additions had totally altered the appearance of the place; when Vanyel was first a Herald it had looked foreboding, and martial, not much altered from the defensive keep it had originally been. Now it looked rather like an old warhorse retired to pasture; surrounded by cattle, clambered upon by children, and entirely puzzled by the change in its status.

And it appeared, as they drew nearer, that the entire population of the manor had assembled to meet them in the open space in front of the main building. Much to Van's amusement, Stefen looked seriously alarmed at the size of the gathering.

"Van, that can't be your family, can it?" he asked just before they got in earshot. "I mean, there's hundreds of them. . . ."

Vanyel laughed. "Not quite hundreds; counting all the cousins and fosterlings, probably eighty or ninety by now. More servants, of course. Farewells can take all day, if you aren't careful."

"Oh," Stefen replied weakly, and then the waiting throng broke ranks and poured toward them.

The filly shied away from the unfamiliar scents and sounds, but the people pressed closely around her were all well acquainted with the habits of the horses. The children all scampered neatly out of the way of her dancing hooves, and before she could bolt, Vanyel's brother Mekeal took her reins just under the bit in a surprisingly gentle fist.

"This one of Star's get?" he asked, running a knowing hand over her flank. "She's lovely, Van. Would you consider lending me her to put to one of the palfrey studs one of these days? We're still keeping up the palfrey and hunter lines, y'know."

"Ask Bard Stefen; she's his," Vanyel replied, and dismounted, taking care to avoid stepping on any children. Not any easy task, they were as careless around adults as they were careful around horses. He moved quickly to help Savil down before she could admit to needing a hand, a service that earned him a quick smile of conspiratorial gratitude.

Stefen dismounted awkwardly in a crowd of chattering children and gawky and admiring adolescents, who immediately surrounded him demanding to know if he was a real

Bard, if he knew their cousin Medren, if he knew any songs about their cousin Vanyel, and a thousand other questions. He looked a little overwhelmed. There weren't a great many children at Court, and those that were there were usually kept out of sight except when being employed as pages and the like. Vanyel debated rescuing him, but a moment later found himself otherwise occupied.

Withen bore down on him with Treesa in tow, plowing his way through the crowd as effortlessly as a draft horse through a herd of ponies. He stopped, just within arm's reach. "Van—" he said, awkwardly. "—son—"

And there he froze, unable to force himself to go any further, and unwilling to pull away. Vanyel took pity on him and broke the uncomfortable moment. "Hello, Father," he said, clasping Withen's arms for just long enough to make Withen relax without making him flinch. "Gods, it is good to see you. You're looking indecently well. I swear, some day I'm going to open a closet door somewhere, and finally find the little wizard you've been keeping to make your elixir of youth!"

Withen laughed, reddening a little under the flattery; in fact, he *was* looking well, less like Mekeal's father than his older brother. They both were square and sturdily built, much taller than Vanyel, brown-eyed, brown-haired, brown-completed. Withen's hair and beard were about half silvered, and he'd developed a bit of a paunch; those were his only concessions to increasing age.

Withen relaxed further, and finally returned the embrace. "And as usual, you look like hell, son. Randale's been over-using you again, no doubt of it. Your sister warned us. Kernos' Horns, can't we ever see you when you *haven't* been overworking?"

"It's not as bad this time, Father," Van protested with a smile. "My reserves are in fairly good shape; it's mostly sleep and peace I lack."

"But don't they ever feed you, boy?" Withen grumbled. "Ah, never mind. We'll get some meat back on those bones, won't we, Treesa?"

Vanyel held out his hands to his mother, who took both of them. Treesa had finally accepted the onset of age, though not without a struggle. She had permitted her hair to resume its natural coloring of silver-gilt, and had given up trying to hide her age-lines under a layer of cosmetics.

Yet it seemed to Van that there might have been a little less discontent in her face than there had been the last time he was here. He hoped so. It surely helped that Roshya, Mekeal's wife, was accepting her years gracefully, and with evident enjoyment. Whatever stupid things Mekeal had done in his time—and he'd done quite a few, including the purchase of a purported *"Shin'a'in* warsteed" that was no more *Shin'a'in* than Vanyel—he'd more than made up for them by wedding Roshya. At least, that was Van's opinion. Roshya stood right behind Treesa, a young child clinging to her skirt with grubby hands, giving Treesa an encouraging wink.

"Run along dear," Roshya said to the child, with an affectionate push. The child giggled and released her.

Treesa smiled tentatively, then with more feeling. "Your father's right, dear," she said, holding him at arm's length and scrutinizing him. "You do look very tired. But you look a great deal better than the last time you were here."

"That's mostly because I am," he replied. "Mother, you look wonderful. Well, you can see that I brought Aunt Savil—and—" he hesitated a moment. "And the friend you wanted to meet. My friend, and Medren's. Stef—"

He turned and gestured to Stefen, who extracted himself from the crowd of admiring children and adolescents.

Van steeled himself, kept his face set in a carefully controlled and pleasant mask of neutrality, then cleared his throat self-consciously. "Father, Mother," he said, gesturing toward Stefan, "This is Bard Stefen. Stef, my Father and Mother; Lord Withen, Lady Treesa."

Stef bowed slightly to Withen, then took Treesa's hand and kissed it. "Mother? Surely I heard incorrectly. You are Herald Vanyel's younger sister, I am certain," he said, with a sweet smile, at which Treesa colored and and took her hand away with great reluctance, shaking her head. "His mother? No, impossible!"

Withen looked a little strained and embarrassed, but Treesa responded to Stef's gentle, courtly flattery as a flower to the sun. "Are you really a full Bard?" she asked, breathless with excitement. "Truly a Master?"

"Unworthy though I am, my lady," Stef replied, "that is the rank the Bardic Circle has given me. I pray you will permit me to test your hospitality and task your ears by performing for you."

"Oh, *would* you?" Treesa said, enthralled. Evidently she had completely forgotten what else Stef was supposed to be besides Van's friend and a Bard. Withen still looked a little strained, but Van began to believe that the visit would be less of a disaster than he had feared.

Thunder rumbled near at hand, startling all of them. "Gods, it's about to pour. Meke, Radevel, you see to the horses," Withen ordered. "The rest of you, give it a rest. You'll all get your chances at Van and his f–friend later. Let's all get inside before the storm breaks for true."

Treesa had already taken possession of Stefen and was carrying him off, chattering brightly. Van turned protectively toward Yfandes, remembering that his father never *could* bring himself to believe she was anything other than a horse.

But to his immense relief, Meke was leading Stef's filly to the stables, but his cousin Radevel had looped the two Companions' reins up over their necks and was standing beside them.

"Don't worry, Van," Radevel said with a wink. "Jervis taught me, remember?" And then, to the two Companions, "If you'll follow me, ladies, one of the new additions to the stables are *proper* accommodations for Companions. Saw to 'em m'self."

Vanyel relaxed, and allowed his father to steer him toward the door to the main part of the manor, as lightning flashed directly overhead and the first fat drops of rain began to fall. *Good old Rad. Finally, after all these years, I get* one *of my family convinced that 'Fandes isn't a horse!*

Eight

" ... SO, that's the situation," Withen continued, staring out the bubbly, thick glass of the crudely-glazed window at the storm outside. "I don't think it's going to change any time soon. Tashir is turning out to be a fine young man, and a good ruler. His second eldest is fostered here, did I mention that?"

Thunder vibrated in the rock walls, and Vanyel shook his head. "No, Father, you didn't. What about farther north though, up beyond Baires?"

Withen sighed. "Don't know, son. That's still Pelagir country. Full of uncanny creatures, and odd folks, and without much leadership that I've been able to see. It's a problem, and likely to stay one. . . ."

Vanyel held his peace; the *Tayledras* weren't "leaders" as his father understood the term, anyway, although they ruled and protected their lands as effectively as any warlord or landed baron.

Rain lashed the outside of the keep and hissed down the chimney. He and his father were ensconced in Withen's "study," a room devoted to masculine comforts and entirely off-limits to the females of the household. Withen turned away from the window and eased himself down into a chair that was old and battered and banished to here where it wouldn't offend Treesa's sensibilities; but like Withen, it was still serviceable despite being past its prime. Van was already sitting, or rather, sprawling, across a scratched and battered padded bench, one with legs that had been used as teething aids for countless generations of Ashkevron hounds.

"So tell me the truth, son," Withen said after a long pause. "I'm an old man, and I can afford to be blunt. How much longer does Randale have?"

Vanyel sighed, and rubbed the back of his neck uneasily.

"I don't know, Father. Not even the Healers seem to have any idea." He hesitated a moment, then continued. "The truth is, though, I don't think it's going to be more than five years or so. Not unless we find out what it is he's got and find a way to cure it, or at least keep it from getting worse. Right now—right now the Council's best hope is to be able to keep him going until Treven's trained and in Whites. We think he can hang on that long."

"Is it true the boy's wedded that young Jisa?" Withen looked as if he approved, so Vanyel nodded. "Good. The sooner the boy breeds potential heirs, the better off we'll be. Shows the lad has more sense than his elders." Withen snorted his disgust at those "elders." "It was shilly-shallying about Randale's marriages that got us in this pickle in the first place. Should have told the boy to marry Healer Shavri in the first damn place, and we'd have had half a dozen legitimate heirs instead of one girl out of the succession."

Withen went on in the same vein for some time, and Vanyel did not think it prudent to enlighten him to the realities of the situation.

"About the Pelagir lands, Father," he said instead, "The last few times I've visited home, I've heard stories—and seen the evidence—of things coming over and into Valdemar. Are they still doing that?"

When Withen hesitated, he began to suspect that something was seriously wrong. "Father, are these—visitations—getting worse? What is it that you aren't telling me?"

"Son," Withen began.

"No, Father, don't think of me as your son. I'm Herald Vanyel, and I need to know the whole truth." He sat up from his sprawled position, looked his father straight in the eyes. Withen was the first to look away.

"Well—yes. For a while they were getting worse." Withen looked at the fire, out the window—anywhere but at Van.

"And?"

"And we asked Haven for some help. For a Herald-Mage." Withen coughed.

"And?"

"And they said there weren't any to spare, and they sent us just a plain Herald." Withen's mouth worked as if he were tasting something bitter. "I won't say she was of no use, but—but we decided if Haven wasn't going to help us, we'd best learn how to help ourselves, and we sent her back. Let her think she'd taken care of the problem after a hunt or two. Had a talk with Tashir's people—after all, they've been doing without mages for one damned long time. Found out the ways to take out some of these things without magic. Worked out some more. Finally the things stopped coming across altogether. I guess they got some way of talking to each other, and let it be known that we don't like havin' things try and set up housekeeping over here."

"There's been no more sign of anything?" Van was amazed—not that there were no signs of further incursions, but that the people here had taken on the problem and dealt with it on their own.

"No, though we've been keepin' the patrols up. Tashir's people, too. But—"

"But what, Father?" Vanyel asked gently. "You can say what you like. I won't be offended by the truth."

"It's just—all our lives we've been told how we can depend on the Herald-Mages, how they'll help us when we need them—then when we need them, we get told there aren't any to spare, they're all down on the Karsite Border or off somewhere else—and here one of our *own* is a Herald-Mage—it just goes hard." Withen was obviously distressed, and Vanyel didn't blame him.

"But Father—you were sent help. You said so yourself. They sent you a Herald," he pointed out.

"A *Herald?*" Within scoffed. "What good's a plain Herald? We needed a Herald-Mage!"

"Did you give her a chance?" Vanyel asked, quietly. "Or did you just assume she couldn't be of any help and lead her around like a child until she was convinced there wasn't any real need for her?"

"But—she was just a Herald—"

"Father, nobody is 'just' a Herald," Vanyel said. "We're taught to make the best of every ability we have—Heralds and Herald-Mages. The only difference in us is the kinds of abilities we have. She would have done *exactly* as you did. She probably would have been able to help you, if you'd given her the chance. She wouldn't have been able to invoke a spell and destroy the creatures for you, but it's quite probable a Herald-Mage wouldn't have been able to either. I have no doubt she could have found the ones in hiding, perhaps, or uncovered their weaknesses. But you didn't give her a chance to find out what she could do."

"I suppose not," Withen said, after a moment. "I—don't suppose that was very fair to her, either."

Vanyel nodded. "It's true, Father. There aren't enough Herald-Mages. I'm afraid to tell you how few of us there are. I wish there were more of us, but there aren't, and I hope when you are sent help next time, you won't think of that help as 'just' a Herald."

"Because that's the best help Haven can give us," Withen concluded for him.

But he didn't look happy. And in a way, Van understood. But there was that stigma again—"just" a Herald—when there were Heralds who had twice the abilities of some of the Herald-Mages he'd known.

It was a disturbing trend—and unfortunately, one he had no idea how to reverse.

"Father, which would you rather have in a pinch—a Herald with a very strong Gift, a Gift that's exactly the kind of thing you need, or a Herald-Mage who may be able to do no more than *you* could on your own?" He paused for effect. "There have been no few Herald-Mages *killed* down on the Karsite Border precisely because they were mages, and because of that they tried to handle more than they were capable of. If I were spying on the enemy, I'd rather have a strongly Mindspeaking Herald doing it for me than a Herald-Mage who has to send up a flare of mage-fire when he needs to talk! If I were hunting up magical creatures, I'd rather have a Herald with powerful FarSight than a weak Herald-Mage who'd light up like a tasty beacon to those creatures every time he uses his magic."

"I never thought about it that way," Withen mumbled. "But still—"

"Please do think about it, Father," Van urged. "And please talk to others about it. Valdemar is short of friends and resources these days. We have to use everything we can, however we can. You have a powerful influence on the way people think in this area—"

"I wish your brother thought that," Withen mumbled, but he looked pleased.

"If you decide that I'm right, you can make an enormous difference in the way things are handled the next time. And that just may save you a great deal, including lives."

Withen sighed, and finally met his eyes. "Well, I'll think about it, son. That's all I'll promise."

Which is about as much of a concession as I'm ever likely to get out of him. "Thank you, Father," he said, hoping it would be enough. "That's all I can ask."

Dinner proved to be entertaining and amazingly relaxing. Only the immediate family and important household members assembled in the Great Hall anymore—there wasn't *room* for anyone else.

Vanyel was partnered with the priest who had replaced the late, unlamented Father Leren; a young and aggressive cleric with a thousand ideas whose fervor was fortunately tempered with wit and a wry good sense of humor. The young man was regrettably charismatic—before the meal was over, Van found he'd been lulled into agreeing to broach a half dozen of those ideas to his Father.

Treesa had kidnapped Stef and ensconced him at her side, with herself and Withen between the Bard and Vanyel. Since that was pretty much as Van had *expected* things would go, he ignored Stef's mute pleas for help throughout the meal. Given how much effort he'd been going to in order to avoid the less platonic of Stef's continued attentions, he found it rather amusing to see the Bard in the position of "pursued."

Immediately following dinner, Withen claimed his son for another conference. This time it included Withen, Radevel, Mekeal, and two cousins Vanyel just barely knew. That conference left him with a profound admiration for how well the folk in this so-called "Border backwater" were keeping up with important news. They knew pretty well how much impact Treven's marriage was going to have on situations outKingdom, had good guesses about what concessions Randale was likely to have to make with Rethwellan in order to gain their Queen's aid, and had a fair notion of the amount of help Tashir was likely to be able to offer Valdemar.

What they wantd to know was the real state of the situation with Karse. "We heard they'd outlawed magery," Radevel said, putting his feet up on the low table they all shared, "and there was rumors about fightin' inside Karse. All well an' good, if it's true, an' what's bad for Karse is likely to be good for us 'twould look like, but what's that really gonna do to us? That gonna end up spillin' across the Border, you reckon?"

Vanyel put his drink down on the table, and dipped his finger into a puddle of spilled ale. "Here's the Karsite Border," he said, drawing it for them. "Here's Rethwellan, and here's us. Now this is what we know so far—"

In a few sentences he was able to sum up his own and Randale's analysis of the situation, and the reasons why the alliance with Rethwellan was all the more necessary.

"So we end up takin' hind teat if there's trouble out here, hmm?" one of the cousins said cynically, around a mouthful of bread and cheese.

"To be brutally frank," Vanyel felt forced to say, "unless it's a major incursion, yes. I wish I could tell you differently."

Radevel shrugged philosophically. "Somebody's gotta take second place," he pointed out. "No way around that. Seems to me we've been doin' pretty well for ourselves; we got some Guard, we got our own patrols, we got Tashir an' his people. So long as nobody brings up an army, we should be all right." Withen nodded, and refilled all their mugs, letting the foam run over the tops with casual disregard for the state of the furniture.

"I can do this much for you," Vanyel told them after a moment's thought. Five sets of eyes fastened on him. "You know I have limited Crown authority. I can authorize a general reduction in taxes for landholders who keep their own armed forces. And I can get you weapons—and I think some trainers. We've got some Guards that are minus legs or arms that would still make good trainers, even if they can't fight."

All of them brightened at that. Mekeal looked as if he was counting something up in his head.

:Probably would-be young heroes,: Yfandes said cynically. *:And he's reckoning how much he can get taken off the tax-roles by encouraging young hotheads to take their energy off to the Guard.:*

:Probably,: Van replied, thinking a little sadly of all the aspiring heroes who had found only early graves on the Karsite Border. And how many more he'd send there, if indirectly. . . .

But the fighters had to come from somewhere. Better that they came as volunteers, and well-trained. "I can probably even authorize tax credit if you send trained fighters for the Guard instead of cash or kind at tax time," he continued. "Randale's pretty loath to hire mercenaries, but he wants to avoid conscription, and right now the ranks down South are getting thinner than we'd like."

"I got another thought," Mekeal put in. "Give that credit across Valdemar, an' send the green 'uns to us for training an' seasoning. We'll get 'em blooded without the kind of loss you get in combat."

That made him feel less guilty. "Good gods," Vanyel replied, "I'm surrounded by geniuses! Why didn't *we* think of that?"

Meke shrugged, pleased. "Just tryin' to help all of us."

:It's an excellent solution to getting youngsters used to real combat at relatively low risk,: 'Fandes observed, with approval. *:I like the way your brother thinks.:*

:So do I, dearling.: He nodded at Meke. "That will help immensely, I truly think."

They discussed other matters for a while, but it was fairly evident that they'd touched on all the topics the others considered of the most import. Vanyel got to his feet and excused himself when the conversation devolved to small talk about hunting.

"I'll make an effort to get in touch with Herald Joshel and get confirmation on everything we covered," he told them, and grinned, seeing a chance to bring a point home. "That's the advantage of having a strong Mindspeaking Herald around when you need answers in a hurry. Joshe is actually a stronger Mindspeaker than I am, and he's taking my place with Randale while I'm gone. I know when he'll be free tomorrow, and I'll contact him then."

He was surprised at how late it was when he left them. The halls were quiet; the servants had long since gone to bed, leaving every other lamp out, and the ones still burning turned down low. His room would be the guest room he'd used every visit he'd made home, and he knew exactly where it was, despite the additions to the manor and the darkness of the halls.

He found himself yawning as he neared his door. *I didn't realize how tired I was,* he thought sleepily. *It's a good thing I didn't drink that second mug of ale Father poured. I wonder what room they put Stef in? I hope it wasn't the one overlooking the gardens; ye gods, he'll be up all night with*

*mocker-birds screaming at his window. I'll take the old room
any time, even if it isn't as cool in the summer. Havens, that
bed is going to feel good. . . .*

He reached for the door handle and pulled it open just
enough to slip inside. Some kind soul had left two candles
burning, one above the hearth, one beside the bed. The
gentle candlelight was actually quite bright compared to the
darkened hallway; shadows danced as the candleflames
flickered in the draft he had created by opening the door.
As he stepped away from the door, he glanced automatically toward the right side of the hearth, beside the bed—
the servants always left his luggage there, and he wanted to
make sure his gittern was all right before he went to bed.

And he froze, for there were two sets of packs, and two
gitterns. His—and Stefen's. And—he looked beyond the
luggage to see if the furnishings had been changed; but they
hadn't—only one bed.

Behind him, someone shot the bolt on the door.

He whirled; Stefen turned away from the door and faced
him, the warm gold of candlelight softening his features so
that he looked very young indeed. His loose shirt was
unlaced to the navel, and his feet were bare beneath his
leather riding breeches.

"Before you ask," he said, in a soft, low voice, "this
wasn't my idea. This seems to have happened on your
father's orders. But Van—I'm glad he did it—"

Vanyel backed up a step, his mind swimming in little
circles. "Oh. Ah, Stefen, I'll just get my things and—"

Stef shook his head, and brushed his long hair back
behind his ears with one hand. "No. Not until I get a chance
to say what I have to. You've been avoiding this for weeks,
and I'm not letting the one chance I've had to really talk
to you get away from me."

Vanyel forced himself to relax, forced his mind to stop
whirling as best he could, and walked over to one of the
chairs next to the hearth. He stood beside it, with his hands
resting on the back so that Stefen could not see them
trembling. He glanced down at them; they seemed very cold
and white, and he wondered if Stefen had noticed. "Ah . . .
what is it you need to talk about that you couldn't have
said on the road?" he asked, as casually as he could.

"Dammit, Van!" Stefen exploded. "You know very well
what I want to talk about! You—and me."

"Stefen," Vanyel said, controlling his voice with an effort that hurt, "you are one of the best friends I've ever had. I mean that. And I appreciate that friendship."

Stef's eyes were full of pleading, and Vanyel forced himself to turn away from him and stare at a carved wooden horse on the mantelpiece. "Stef, you're very young; I'm nearly twice your age. I've seen all this before. You admire me a great deal, and you think—"

There were no footsteps to warn him; suddenly he found Stef's hands on his shoulders, wrenching him around, forcing him to look into the young Bard's face. Stef's hands felt like hot irons on his shoulders, and there was strength in them that was not apparent from the Bard's slight build. "Vanyel Ashkevron," Stef said, hoarsely, "I am shaych, just like you. I've known what I am for years now. I'm not an infatuated child. What's more—" Now the Bard flushed and looked away, off to Vanyel's right. "I've had more lovers in one year than you've had in the last ten. And— and I've never felt about *any* of them the way I feel about you. I—I think I love you, Van. I don't think I could ever love anyone but you."

He looked back up at Vanyel. The Herald could only gaze back into the darkened emerald of Stefen's eyes, eyes that seemed in the dim light to be mostly pupil. Vanyel was utterly stunned. This—this was considerably beyond infatuation. . . .

"Bards are supposed to be so cursed good with words," Stefen said unhappily, looking into Vanyel's eyes as if he was looking for answers. "Well, all my eloquence seems to have deserted *me*. All—all I can tell you is that I think I'd love you if you were a *hundred* years older than me, or a deformed monster, or—or even a woman."

The Bard's voice had lost any hint of training; it was tight and rough with tension and unhappiness. For his part, Vanyel couldn't seem to speak at all. His throat was paralyzed and his chest hurt when he tried to breathe. He felt alternately hot and cold, and his heart pounded in his ears. Stefen didn't notice his unresponsiveness, evidently, for he continued on without looking away from Van.

"Since you aren't any of those things," he said, his voice unsteady with emotion, "since you're w-wonderful, and w-wise, and beautiful enough to make my heart ache, and dammit, *not* old, I—I can't take this much longer." A single tear slid down one cheek, shining silver in the candlelight; Stefen either didn't notice it, or didn't care. "I—I'm only glib when it comes to making rhymes, Van. I love you, and I'm *not* a Herald. I can't *show* you how I feel—except physically. I want to be your lover. I don't want anyone else, not ever again."

When Vanyel didn't respond, a second tear joined the first, slipping silently from the corner of Stefen's eye; he swallowed, and broke eye contact to look down at his feet. He relaxed his hold on Vanyel's shoulders, but didn't release him.

"I suppose—I guess I must revolt you," he said, bitterly. "All my . . . other lovers . . . I don't blame you, I guess. I—"

That broke Vanyel's paralysis. That, and the ache his Gift of Empathy let him feel all too clearly, an ache that was matched by the one in his own heart. "No," he whispered. "No—Stef, I—just never knew you felt that strongly."

His hands hurt from clenching the back of the chair. He let go, and flexed them, then raised his right hand, slowly, and brushed the tear from Stefen's face with gentle, wondering fingers. "I never guessed," he repeated, no longer trying to hide the strength of his own feelings from himself.

Stefen let go of Vanyel's shoulders, caught Van's hand and looked back up into Vanyel's eyes, quickly. Whatever he read there made him smile, like the sun coming from behind a cloud; a smile so bright it left Vanyel dazzled. He kept Vanyel's right hand in his, and backed up a step. Then another. Vanyel resisted for a fraction of a second, then followed, drawn along like an obedient child. His knees were weak, and the room seemed too hot—no, too cold—

He's too young! part of him kept clamoring. *He can't possibly know what he's doing, what this means. He's hardly older than Jisa—*

His conscience nagged as Stefen blew out the candles; as the young Bard ran strong, callused hands under Vanyel's shirt, and drew him down onto the bed—

And then the voice was silenced as Stef gently proved beyond a shadow of a doubt that he was *just* as experienced as he had claimed. If there was someone being seduced, it wasn't Stefen. . . .

The last of Vanyel's misgivings dissolved as not-so-young Stefen showed him things he hadn't even imagined, and

then proved that the sweet giving and receiving the Bard
had just taught him was only the beginning. . . .

*Overhead, sky a dead and lightless black. To either side,
walls of ice—*

He turned to the one standing at his side. 'Lendel—

*But it was Stefen; wrapped in wool and fur, and so fright-
ened his face was as icy-pale as the cliffs to either side of
them.*

"You have to go get help," he told the Herald—no, the
Bard—

"I won't leave you," Stef said, stubbornly. *"You have to
come with me. I won't leave without you."*

*He shook his head, and threw back the sides of his cloak
to free his arms. "Yfandes can't carry two,"* he said. *"And
I can hold them off for however long it takes you to bring
help."*

"You can't possibly—"

"I can," he interrupted. *"Look, there's only enough room
at this point for one person to pass. As long as I stand here,
they'll never get by—"*

Blink—

*Suddenly he was alone, and exhausted; chilled to the bone.
An army filled the pass before him, and at the forefront of
that army, a single man who could have been Vanyel's twin,
save only that his eyes and hair were deepest black—a dark
mirror to Vanyel's silver eyes and silvered hair, and as if to
carry the parody to its extreme, he wore clothing cut identi-
cally to Heraldic Whites, only of ebony black.*

"I know you," he heard himself say.

The man smiled. "Indeed."

"You—you are—"

"Leareth." The word was Tayledras *for "darkness." The
man smiled. "A quaint conceit, don't you think?"*

And Vanyel knew—

He woke, shaking like a leaf in a gale; his chest heaved
as he gasped for breath, clutching the blanket.

He was cold, bone-cold, yet drenched with sweat. *It was
the old dream, the ice-dream, the dream where I die—I
haven't had that dream for years—*

Stefen lay beside him, sprawled over the edge of the bed,
oblivious to Van's panting for air. Though the candles were
out, Van could see him by moonlight streaming in the win-

dow. The storm had blown itself out, leaving the sky clear and clean; the moonlight was bright enough to read by, and Vanyel saw the bright points of stars glittering against the sky through the windowpane.

Vanyel controlled his breathing, and lay back, forcing his heart to slow. He blinked up into the dark canopy of the bed, still caught in the cold claws of the nightmare.

I haven't had that dream for years—except this time it was different. This time, it wasn't 'Lendel that was with me. Except—except it felt like 'Lendel. I thought it was 'Lendel until I turned around, and it was Stef. . . .

The young Bard sighed, and turned over, bringing his face into the moonlight. Lying beside Stef, for a moment—for a moment it had been, it had *felt* like being beside Tylendel, his love and lifebonded.

Lifebonded.

Only then did he realize why Stefen "felt" like Tylendel. The tie was the same; Vanyel was not only in love with the Bard, he had lifebonded to him. There was no mistaking that tie, especially not for an Empath.

No—

But there was no denying it, either. Vanyel suppressed a groan; if being attracted to Stefen had been a betrayal of 'Lendel's memory, then what was this? He couldn't think; he felt his stomach knot and a lump in his throat. He had loved 'Lendel; he still did.

He thought that he would lie awake until dawn, but somehow exhaustion got the better of confused thoughts and tangled emotions, and sleep stole over him. . . .

:It's about time you got here,: Yfandes said, with a knowing look. *:Honestly, Van, you make things so complicated for yourself sometimes. Well, come on.:*

She turned adroitly, and flicked her tail at him, looking back at him over her shoulder. *:Well? Aren't you coming?:*

"Where am I?" he asked, looking about himself. There wasn't anything to be seen in any direction; wherever he looked, there was nothing but featureless gray fog. He and Yfandes were all alone in it, so far as he could see.

:Where are you?: she repeated, her mind-voice warm and amused. *:You're dreaming, of course. Or rather, in Dream-time. There* is *a difference. Now are you coming, or not?:*

He followed her, having nothing better to do; the peculiar

fog thickened until he could hardly see her. He tried to catch up with her, but she always managed to stay the same distance ahead of him. Finally, all he could make out of her was a vague, glowing-white shape in the swirling fog.

A tendril of fog wrapped around his head, blinding him completely. He faltered, tried to bat it away—

And stumbled into an exact duplicate of the grove in Companion's Field where he and 'Lendel had spent so many hours. The same grove that 'Lendel had destroyed. . . .

"Well, *ashke*," said a heartbreakingly familiar voice behind him. "You certainly took your time getting here."

He turned, slowly, afraid of what he might see, especially after what he and Stef had done.

"Don't be an idiot," Tylendel said, shaking back hair as gold as the summer sun filtering through the pine boughs above him. "Why should I mind?"

Tylendel lounged against the rough trunk of a tree with his arms crossed over his chest, looking little older than when he'd died, but dressed in the Whites he hadn't yet earned in life. He raised one golden eyebrow quizzically at Van, then grinned. "Why, Van—that's twice in one day you've been moonstruck. Is this getting to be a habit?" Then, softer, "What's wrong Vanyel-*ashke?*"

As Vanyel stood, rooted to the spot, Tylendel pushed himself away from the tree, crossed the few feet between them and took him in his strong, warm arms. Sharp scents rose from the crushed pine needles beneath their feet. Vanyel returned the embrace; hesitantly at first, then, with a sob that was half relief and half grief, held his beloved so tightly his arms hurt.

"Here, now," 'Lendel said, holding him gently. "What's the matter? Why should I be angry with you because you found someone to love who loves you?"

"Because—because I love you—" It seemed a foolish fear, now—

"Van-*ashke*, what's the point in suffering all your life for one mistake?" 'Lendel let go of him and stepped back a little, so that he could look down into Vanyel's eyes. "You don't give up a chance at happiness just because you've already been happy once in your life! Havens, that's like saying you'll never eat again because you've been a guest at one grand feast!"

'Lendel chuckled warmly; as his smile reached and

warmed his brown eyes, Van found himself smiling back. "I guess that is kind of stupid," he replied with a touch of chagrin. "But I never did think too clearly when my emotions were involved."

'Lendel's smile faded a little. "Neither of us did," he said, soberly. "Me especially. Van—you know, I didn't love you enough, and I'm sorry."

Vanyel started to protest; 'Lendel put one finger on his lips to quiet him. "This is honesty; I didn't love you enough. If I had, I would have cared more about what was good for you than what *I* wanted. I'm sorry, *ashke*, and I think perhaps I've learned better. I hope so. Because—oh, Van—I want to make it up to you more than anything. If you can believe in anything, please, believe that. And believe that I love you."

He bent down and touched his lips to Vanyel's.

Vanyel woke with a start, wrapped in Stefen's arms. For a moment, he thought he could still smell the scent of crushed pine needles, and feel the breeze on his cheek.

"—love you," Stefen whispered in his ear, then subsided into deep breathing that told Van he was still really asleep.

-'Lendel. That was 'Lendel. What in hell did all that mean? Van wondered, still slightly disoriented. *What in* hell *did all that mean?* He stared, wide-eyed, into the darkness. He would have liked to talk to Yfandes, but a gentle Mindtouch showed her to be deep in slumber.

The next time Stef turned over, releasing him, he eased out of bed, far too awake now to fall back asleep. The room was chilly; the storm had cooled things off in its passing. He slipped into a robe and began slowly pacing the floor, trying to unravel his dreams and nightmares, and making heavy work of it.

That second thing didn't feel like a dream, he thought, staring at the floor while he paced. *That felt real; as real as the Shadow-Lover, and I* know *He was real. It was 'Lendel, it couldn't have been anything I conjured up for myself out of guilt. Could it? I've never done anything like that before this. . . .*

And the old ice-dream has changed. I thought I'd gotten rid of it—thought I'd purged it away after I faced down Krebain. Why has it come back?

The square of moonlight crept across the floor and up the

all, then vanished as the moon set. And still Vanyel was
wide awake, and too intent on his own thoughts to feel
chilled. He kept pacing the floor, pausing now and again to
look down on Stefen. The Bard slept on, his lips curved in
a slight smile, sprawled over the entire bed.

After a while, as the impact of the two dreams—if they
were dreams—began to wear off, that posture of Stef's
began to amuse him. *I never would have believed that someone that slight could take up that much room all by himself,*
he thought with a silent chuckle. *He's like a cat; takes up
far more space than is even remotely possible under the laws
of nature.*

It was nearly dawn; the pearly light of earliest morning
filled the room, making everything soft-edged and shadowy.
Vanyel continued to stare down at Stef; not thinking, really,
just waiting for some of his thoughts to sort themselves out
and present themselves to him in an orderly fashion.

Stefen stirred a little, and opened his eyes. He blinked
confusedly at Van for a moment, then seemed to recollect
where he was. "Van?" he asked, sleep bluring his voice.
"Is something wrong, Vanyel-*ashke*?"

Vanyel froze. The words, the very tone, brought back the
second dream with the impact of a blow above the heart.

*Tylendel leaning up against the shaggy tree trunk, a slight
smile on his lips, his arms crossed over his chest. "What's
wrong, Vanyel-ashke?"*

Ashke—it was the *Tayledras* word for "beloved," and
Tylendel's special name for him, a play on Vanyel's family
name of "Ashkevron."

But 'Lendel had been fluent in *Tayledras;* Savil had
insisted that 'Lendel and Vanyel both learn the tongue, as
she had always intended to take them to the Pelagir Hills
territory claimed by her Hawkbrother friends as soon as
Tylendel was ready for fieldwork. She didn't even offer the
lessoning to Donni and Mardic, her other two pupils.

Stefen, on the other hand, knew only one word of pidgin-
Tayledras; shaych, the shortened form of *shay'a'chern,*
which had become common usage for those whose preferences lay with their own sex. He couldn't ever have heard
the word he'd just used, must less know what it meant.

Wild thoughts of hauntings and possessions ran through
Vanyel's mind. He'd seen so many stranger things as a Her-

ald— "Stef," Vanyel said, slowly and carefully. "What did you just call me?"

"Vanyel-*ashke*," Stefen repeated, bewildered, and plainly disturbed by Van's careful mask of control. "Why? Did I say something wrong?"

"Is there a reason why you called me that just now?" Vanyel didn't move, though the hair was rising on the back of his neck. First the dreams, and now this . . . he extended a careful probe, ready at any moment to react if he found anything out of the ordinary.

"Sure," Stef replied, blinking at him, and rising up onto one elbow. "I've—" he blushed a little "—I've been calling you that to myself for a while. Comes from your name, Ashkevron. It—it seems to suit you. You know how a Bard likes to play with words. It has a nice *sound*, you know?"

The probe met with nothing. No resistance, no aura of another presence. Vanyel relaxed, and smiled. It was nothing, after all. Just an incredible coincidence. He wasn't being haunted by the spirit of a long-dead lover, nor was this love in any danger of being possessed or controlled by the last.

Not that 'Lendel would ever have done that, he reminded himself. *No, I'm just short on sleep and no longer thinking clearly, that's all. And so used to jumping at shadows that I'm overreacting to even a perfectly innocent pet-name.*

"Did I say something wrong?" Stefen asked again, more urgently this time, starting to sit up as he pulled tangled hair out of his eyes with both hands. "If you don't like it—if it bothers you—"

"No, it's all right," Vanyel answered him. "I was just a little startled, that's all. *Ashke* is the *Tayledras* word for 'beloved,' and I wasn't expecting to hear that from you."

"If you'd rather I didn't—" Stef hastened to say, when Vanyel interrupted him.

"I do like it—just, I had some odd dreams, and coming on top of them, it startled me. That's all." Vanyel touched Stefen's shoulder, and the Bard flinched.

"Havens, you're *freezing*," Stef exclaimed. "How long have you been up? Never mind, it's probably too long. Get *in* here before you catch something horrible, and let me warm you up. After all," he added slyly, as Van shrugged off his robe and slid into bed beside him. "Whatever you catch, *I'll* probably get, and you wouldn't want to have the guilt of ruining a Bard's voice on your conscience, would you?"

"Anything but that," Van replied vaguely, then gasped as Stef curled his warm body around Van's chilled one.

"Oh?" the Bard said archly. *"Anything?"*

Nine

After Stefen had warmed him and relaxed him—among other things—they both fell asleep for a second time as the first light of the sun sent strokes of pink and gold across the sky. This time Vanyel slept deeply and dreamlessly, and Stefen actually woke before him. Van awakened to find Stef lounging indolently next to him, watching him with a proprietary little smile on his face.

"Well, what are you looking at?" Van asked, amused by the Bard's expression. "And a copper for your thoughts."

Stefen laughed. " 'Acres and acres, and it's *all mine*,' " he said, quoting a tag-line of a current joke. "If you had any idea of the number of times I've daydreamed of being right where I am now, you'd laugh."

"You think so?" Van smiled, and shook his head. "Oh, no, I promise, I wouldn't laugh."

"Well, maybe you wouldn't." Stefen searched his face for a moment, looking as if he wanted to say something, but couldn't make up his mind how to say it. Vanyel waited patiently for him to find the words. "Van," he said, finally, "I have to know. Are you sorry? I mean, I'm just a Bard, I haven't got Mindspeech; I can't, you know, mesh with you when we—" He flushed. "I mean, does that bother you? Do you miss it? I—"

"Stef," Vanyel interrupted him gently. "You're laboring under a misapprehension. I've never had a lover who shared his mind with me, so I wouldn't know what it was like."

"You haven't?" Stefen was flabbergasted. "But—but what about Tylendel?"

"My Gifts were all dormant while he was alive," Van replied, finding it amazingly easy—for the first time in years—to talk about his old love. "The only bond we had that I could share was the lifebond."

141

"Do you miss *that,* then?" Stef asked, shyly, as if he was afraid to hear the answer, but had to ask the question.

"Do you miss *that,* then?" Stef asked, shyly, as if he was afraid to hear the answer, but had to ask the question.

"No," Vanyel said, and smiled broadly. "And if you look inside yourself for a moment, you'll know why."

"If I—"

"Stef, you're a trained Bard; Bardic Gift is enough like Empathy for you to see what I mean." Van sent a brief pulse of wordless love along the bond, and watched Stef's face change. First surprise—then something akin to shock— then a delight that resonated back down through the bond they shared.

"I never dreamed—" Stef's voice was hushed. "I never— How? Why?"

"I don't know, *ke'chara,* and I don't care." Vanyel shook his head. "All I know is that it's happened, it's real. *And* I know that if we don't get out of bed and put in an appearance, we're never going to do so before noon—I'm afraid they might break the door down and find us in a very embarrassing position."

Stefen laughed. "You know, you're right. We should spare them that, at least. It's only fair."

Vanyel grinned wickedly. "Besides, if I know my mother, she's dying to carry you off to perform for her and her ladies. So come on, Bard. Your audience awaits."

Stefen struck a pose, and held it until Vanyel slid out of bed and flung his clothing at him.

"I warn you, you'd better hurry," the Herald advised him, "or I'll send her in to fetch you."

"I'm hurrying," Stefen replied, pulling on his breeches. "Trust me, I'm hurrying—" Then he stopped, with his shirt half on. "Van, about your mother—is she—ah, *serious?*"

Vanyel knew exactly what Stef was trying to ask, and laughed. "No, she's not really chasing you. She would probably be horrified if you took her seriously; in her way, she really loves Father, I think. She's just playing The Game."

Stefen heaved an enormous sigh of relief. "I couldn't tell, she's a little heavier-handed at it than the ladies at the Court."

"Not surprising," Van replied, checking his appearance in the mirror. "She's playing by rules that are thirty years out of date." He straightened his hair a little, then turned back to Stef, who was struggling into his tunic. "Under all the posing, she really has a good heart, you know. *She* was the one that saw that Medren had talent, even if she couldn't recognize the Gift, and saw to it that he got whatever training was available out here. Not much, but it was enough to give him a start." He crossed the room, to tug Stef's tunic down over his head. "She could have ignored him; he was nothing more than the bastard son of one of her maids, even if his father *is* my brother Meke. She *could* have dismissed Melenna; she didn't. Granted, she *was* holding Melenna as a last effort to 'cure' me, but still—she did her best for both of them, and that's a great deal more than many would have done."

Stef solved the problem of his tousled hair by shaking his head vigorously, then running his fingers through his mane a couple of times. "Then I'll get along fine with her. Anyone who's done anything for Medren gets my nod."

Vanyel chuckled. "Don't misunderstand me; Treesa's far from perfect. She can be selfish, inconsiderate, and completely featherheaded. She didn't dismiss Melenna, but that was at least partly because she'd have had to train a new maid *and* take care of all the things Melenna had until the new one was trained. And the gods know she's a shrewd one when it comes to her own comforts; she knew Melenna would be so grateful that she'd have devoted service out of the girl for years. But for all of that, she's good at heart, and I love her dearly."

Stef unlocked the door, with a sly smile over his shoulder for Van. "You know, this business of having a family takes an awful lot of getting used to. I have to confess it kind of baffles me."

Vanyel laughed, and followed Stefen out into the hall. "Stef, I hate to tell you this, but for all the privileges I grew up with, there have been any number of times I'd have traded places with any orphaned beggar-child on the street. My life would have been a great deal simpler."

Stefen grimaced. "I'll keep that in mind."

True to Vanyel's prediction, Treesa descended upon them once they reached the Great Hall, and appropriated Stefen to perform for her and her ladies as soon as they'd finished a sketchy breakfast.

That left Vanyel alone, which was exactly what he wanted

right now. He strolled out the side door, heading ultimately toward the stables, taking care *not* to take a route that would put him along halls used by anyone except children and servants, or, once outside, under anyone's window. He wanted some time to think things through, and he'd had enough of family conferences for a while.

But there *was* someone who deserved his attention, first. :*'Fandes*,: he Mindsent, :*Good morning, love.*:

:*Good morning, sleepy*,: she Sent back, her mind-voice so full of pleased satisfaction that he chuckled. :*I trust you enjoyed yourself last night.*:

:*You trust correctly*,: he replied, just a tiny bit embarrassed.

:*Good*,: she said. :*It's about time. I want you to know that I heartily approve of this and I commend the lad's patience. The only question is, now what are you going to do?*:

He paused for a moment beside the mews, noting absently the chirrs and soft calls of the hooded raptors inside. :*That's something I need to work out, lover. Would you be terribly hurt if I borrowed one of the hunters and rode off without you for a little bit? I want to be alone to think this through properly.*:

He caught a moment of surprise from her, and half-smiled. It wasn't often that he was able to catch her off-guard anymore. :*I suppose that makes sense*,: she said after a long pause. :*This really affects you a great deal more than me. No, I won't be hurt. Just don't make any stupid decisions like trying to get rid of the lad, will you? You need him, and he needs you, and you are very, very good for each other.*:

He laughed aloud, one of his worries taken care of—he was afraid that while she approved of Stef as a friend, she might not be as approving of the new relationship. :*I doubt I could remove him now with a pry-bar, love. And—thank you for understanding.*:

She Sent him a reply, not in words, but in emotion; love, trust, and shared happiness. Then she released the link.

He managed to reach the stables without being intercepted by anyone, though there were a couple of close calls avoided only because he saw Meke and his father before they saw him. Fortunately the stables weren't far; the double doors were standing wide open to catch every breeze and he walked inside.

Mekeal's famous Stud still had the best loose-box in the place, and the years had not improved the beast's looks or temper. It laid its ears back and snapped at him as he passed, then cow-kicked the side of its stall in frustration when it couldn't reach him. The only ones who had ever succeeded in riding the beast were Radevel and Jervis, and it was a fight every step of the way even for them.

"Watch it, horse," he muttered under his breath, "or I'll turn 'Fandes and Kellan loose on you again."

The horse snorted as if it could understand him, and backed off into a corner of its box.

Make's warhorse mares were in this stable, along with the foals too young to sell. They watched him calmly as he passed them, some whickering as they caught his scent and recognized him for a stranger. That brought him the attention of one of the stablehands, a scruffy young man who came out of a loose-box at the sound of the first mare's call, grinning when he saw that it was Vanyel.

"Milord Herald," he said. "Can I serve ye?"

"I just want to borrow a hunter," he said. " 'Fandes is tired and all I want to do is take a ride through Wyrfen Woods. Has Father got anything that needs exercise?"

"Oh, aye, a-plenty." The stablehand scratched his sandy head for a moment, thinking. "Habout Blackfoot yonder?" He pointed about three stalls down at a sturdy bay hunter-mare with a fine, intelligent eye. "Not too many can handle her, so she don't ever get all th' workin' she could use. She got a touchy mouth an' goes best neck-reined, an' she's a spooker. Needs some'un with light hands an' no nonsense. Reckon ye can still ride abaht anything, eh?"

"Pretty well," Vanyel replied. "I gentle all of the foals out of Star's line, if I have the time. I like your watchdogs, by the way—" He waved at the warhorse-mares, who were still keeping an eye on him. "—they're very effective."

"They are, that," the stablehand agreed, grinning, and showing that he, like Vanyel's old friend Tam, had lost a few teeth to the hooves of his charges. "Better at night. Anybody they dunno in here, an' they be raisin' a fuss. Leave one or two loose, and *they* be out o' their boxes— heyla!" He illustrated with his hands and the handle of his rake for a wall. "Got us one thief an' three o' them uncanny things that way. That old Stud breeds better'n he shows."

"I should *hope!*" Vanyel laughed, and went to fetch saddle and harness for his assigned mount.

Blackfoot was exactly as predicted: very touchy in the outh, and working well under pressure of neck-rein and knee. Vanyel took her back to the stable long enough to switch her bridle for a bitless halter; as far as he was concerned, with a beast that touchy, it was better not to have a bit at all. If he *had* to rein her in, he was strong enough to wrestle her head down, and no horse out of Withen's hunter-line would ever run when she couldn't see.

He took one of the back ways into the Wood rather than the road through the village. Right now he didn't feel sociable, and the villagers would want him to be "Herald Vanyel Demonsbane," which was particularly trying. So he followed the bridle path out through the orchards, which were currently in fruit, but nowhere near ripe, so there was no one working in them. The apple trees were first, then nut trees, then the hedge that divided the orchards from the wild woods.

Riding a horse was entirely different from riding Yfandes; the mare required his skill *and* his attention. She tested him to see what she could get away with most of the way to the Wood, and subsided only when they had passed through a break in the hedge and the bridle path turned into a game trail. The silence of the Wood seemed to subdue her, and she settled down to a walk, leaving Vanyel free to turn most of his concentration inward.

Wyrfen Wood was still avoided by everyone except hunters and woodcutters, and those who had to pass it traveled the road running right through the middle of it. The place had frightened Van half to death the first time he'd ridden through it; even dormant, he'd had enough Mage-Gift to sense the old magics that had once permeated the place. Those energies were mostly drained now, but there was still enough lingering to make anyone marginally sensitive uneasy. Animals felt it certainly, birds were few, and seldom sang, and Blackfoot's ears flickered back and forth constantly, betraying her nervousness.

Vanyel had made a fair number of exploratory trips into the Wood over the years, and he was used to it—or at least as used to residual magics as anyone ever got. He was aware of the dormant magic, but only as a kind of background to everything else, and a possible source of energy in an emergency. For all that Wyrfen Wood was an eerie place, it was relatively harmless.

Except that it attracted things from outside that were *not* harmless, and gave them an excellent place to hide. . . .

Which brought him right around to one of the very things he needed to think out.

The mare had slowed to a careful walk, picking her way along a game trail that was a bare thread running through the dense undergrowth. Vanyel let her have her head, settled back in the saddle, and spoke his thoughts aloud to the silent trees.

"There aren't enough Herald-Mages. There won't *be* enough Herald-Mages for years, even if Karse stops being a major threat tomorrow. That means the Heralds are going to have to start taking the place of Herald-Mages. Right?"

Blackfoot's ears flicked back, and she snorted.

"Exactly. Most people, including the Heralds themselves, don't think they can. But that's because they're looking at Heralds as if they were—were—what? Replacements? No . . . substitutes. And when you substitute something, you're usually replacing something superior with something inferior, but—you substitute something *like* the original. And Heralds aren't necessarily like Herald-Mages at all."

He thought about that, while Blackfoot picked her way across a dry creek-bed.

"The point is that they *aren't* Herald-Mages. The point is to get Heralds to use *their* Gifts the best they possibly can, rather than trying to do something they can't. I'm a tactician. Where's the tactical advantage in that?"

The game trail widened a little, and they broke into a clearing, a place where lightning had set fire to a stand of pines last year to create a sizable area of burnoff. Now the secondary growth had taken over; grass stood belly-high to the mare, lush and tangled with morning-trumpet vines and bright golden sun-faces. A pair of deer that had been grazing at the farther end looked up at the noise they made, and bounded off into the deeper woods.

"The tactical advantage," Vanyel told their fleeing backs, "is that most mages *don't* have strong Gifts in anything other than sensing and manipulating magical energy. Which means—that they won't think of things like that. They won't be protected against a FarSeer spying on their work—or a ThoughtSenser reading their minds. Or a Fetcher moving something they need for a spell at a critical moment. That's it—that's it! I've got to do something to get the Heralds to stop thinking of themselves as second-rate mages and start thinking of themselves as first-rate in the areas of their Gifts. And we *have* to start matching the need *exactly* to the Gift, and not just throw the first Herald who happens to be free at the need."

It wasn't the entire answer, but it was a start. It was more than they had now.

Blackfoot had reacted to the lush meadow before her precisely as any horse would have; she put her head down and began grazing greedily. Vanyel was so used to Yfandes that the move took him completely by surprise. He started to pull her up, then thought better of the idea. The grass would keep her occupied while he contacted Joshe, and the residual magics made a good pool of energy to draw on so he wouldn't have to use his own strength. Right now Joshe should be with Randale, going over what the Herald would need to cover at the Council meeting. This would be an ideal time to contact him.

He let her graze while he closed his eyes, getting used to the sounds around him so that he would be alerted by anything out of the ordinary. There weren't many; a light breeze in the branches high overhead, an air current that did not reach the ground, a few crickets and a locust singing, and the noise of Blackfoot tearing at the juicy grass and chewing it. Once everything was identified, he extended his Mage-Gift and made careful contact with the trickle of magic directly underneath him.

:??:

A curious touch, and one he did not expect. But not hostile; he identified that much immediately.

:??:

The touch came again; he caught it—and began laughing at himself. "Caught by my own trap!" he said aloud, and opened his eyes. Nothing to be seen—until he invoked Mage-Sight. There, right in front of him, hovered a little cloud, glowing a happy blue. A cloud with eyes: a *vrondi*.

"Hello," he said to it. It blinked, and touched him a second time. This time he sent back the proper reassurance.

:!!: it replied, and—well, *giggled* was the closest he could come to it. Then it vanished, leaving him free to tap the magic current again.

So far as Van knew, the Herald-Mages of Valdemar were the only ones to have ever discovered the *vrondi*. Their touch was not something that outKingdom mages would recognize, and even their appearance only showed that they were air elementals, and nothing more. Air elementals were the ones most commonly used as spies or scouts, which would only reinforce the impression he was trying to give. And even he, who had set the spell in the first place, had found that unexpected contact alarming. So a strange mage would feel something watching him as soon as he invoked any aspect of Mage-Gift or set any spell in motion. He wouldn't be able to identify it, he wouldn't know *why* it was watching him, and Vanyel heartily doubted he'd ever be able to catch it—*vrondi* were just too quick, and they were incredibly sensitive to hostility. Van decided he could almost feel sorry for that hypothetical future mage. The *vrondi* would drive him crazy. Yes, he could almost feel pity for someone faced with that situation.

Almost.

He settled back again; Blackfoot chewed on, happily oblivious to the magics going on around her, intent only on stuffing herself with the sweet grass. Oblivious—or ignoring them; with an ordinary horse, it was often hard to tell which. *First she gets spooky because she feels magic, then she totally ignores it going on above her ears. Stupid beast.* But 'Fandes would have been laughing at him by now for forgetting his own protection-spell, so Van wasn't entirely unhappy that she wasn't with him at the moment.

He Reached carefully for Joshe, drawing on the little stream of magic he'd tapped to boost him all the way to Haven.

:Vanyel?: came the reply. He caught at the proffered contact and pulled Joshe in, strengthening Joshe's faltering touch with his own augmented energies. The line between them firmed and stabilized.

Concern, overlaid with the beginnings of foreboding. *:Vanyel—is there anything wrong?:*

:No,: he said quickly, *:No, just some things came up out here and I need limited Crown authority to guarantee the things I promised. Is Randi up to that?:*

Relief, and assent. *:He's been better, but he's been worse. We've got Treven in full training, poor lad. I don't think he sees Jisa until bedtime, and he's up at dawn with the rest of*

*us. A little more seasoning, and he'll be sitting in for Randale
on the Council. What is it you need?:*

Vanyel explained as succinctly as he could. He sensed
Joshe's excitement over the notion of taking more recruits
in lieu of taxes, and then sending them to the Western Border for toughening instead of throwing them straight into
combat after training.

:It's good, Van, all of it. Hold up a moment.: Van sensed
Joshe's attention going elsewhere for a moment, then the
contact strengthened as it came back. *:King Randale gives
you full permission; the official documents will get drafted
today or tomorrow, and go out by regular courier. He also
said to tell you he thinks your family is slipping. They're
not only degenerating into becoming normal, they're getting
sensible. He says he's not sure how to take that—it sounds
to him like the end of the world can't be far away.:*

So Randi was feeling good enough to make a joke. That
was an improvement over the state he'd been in following
Jisa's revolt. *:Tell him it isn't the end of the world, it's merely
the result of my own patient application of a board to their
heads for the last several years. Even* they *get the hint
eventually.:*

Joshe's Sending was a simple laugh.

*:I've also got some thoughts for you and the rest of the
Heraldic Circle. I'd like you to call a meeting and put this
before them, if you would. I really think it's important, especially now.:*

He explained his own thoughts on the dichotomy, per-
ceived and actual, between the Heralds and Herald-Mages,
the problems he could see it causing, and his own tentative
ideas for a solution to the problems. Joshe was silent all
through his explanation, and for a short time afterward.
Finally he answered.

:I'm surprised you noticed,: he replied slowly, with
thoughts just under the surface that Vanyel couldn't quite
read. *:Most of the other Herald-Mages either don't see it—
or agree with the common perception that Heralds are some
kind of lesser version of a Herald-Mage.:*

The bitter taste to his reply told Vanyel that this was
something Joshe himself had encountered, and it hadn't
gone down well. Joshe was immensely competent, and a
match for Van in any number of spheres, and Vanyel didn't
blame him for feeling resentment.

:It's a problem, Joshe,: he said, as carefully as he could. *:It's part of my peculiar mind-set to see problems. I think it needs to be dealt with now, before it causes serious damage. We can't do much about the perceptions of the general populace until we start to fix things in our own house.:*

Something followed that comment that was like a mental sigh of relief that follows after a far-too-heavy burden has been removed. Van nodded to himself, and pursued his advantage.

:You'll never have a better time than now. The King is a Herald, the Heir is a Herald, the Herald-Mage in charge of the Karsite Border is much *more Gifted in Fetching than magery and knows it, and you're sitting in for me. Savil will be sensible about this. You can keep this on the table as long as you need to in order to get the others to see that it is a problem, and you can call on the Heralds in the Circle to submit examples.:*

Now Joshe's resolution wavered. *:Do you think it's that important? It seems so trivial with everything else in front of us. The Karse situation, Randi's health. . . .:*

:It's important,: he replied grimly. *:And it's only going to get more so. I think you can make the rest of the Circle see that. Point out the attrition among the Herald-Mages, and then quote what happened out here. People are supposed to trust* us, *and how can they if they think of some of us as being better than others?:*

:Good point. Consider it on the boards.: Vanyel knew that once Joshe made up his mind about doing something, he pursued it to its end. He felt a breath of relief of his own. The problem wasn't solved, but it would be. At least a start was being made.

:Then I leave it in your capable and efficient hands. Wind to thy wings, brother.:

:And to yours.: Vanyel felt Joshe break the contact, and dropped his end of it with a sigh.

Blackfoot was still stuffing herself, and showed no signs of stopping any time within the decade. He hauled her head up; she fought him every thumblength of the way, and returned to the game trail sullenly, and with ill grace.

I wish I had as clean an answer to what I should do about Stef, he thought uncomfortably. *Gods, there's no denying what I feel about him—or the lifebond. But if I accept all that, and do so publicly, it flaunts the fact that I'm shay'a'ch-*

ern *in the faces of people I have to handle very carefully.
Can I afford that? Can Valdemar? Or will knowing I have
my weaknesses actually put me at an advantage? It might
. . . I know that an awful lot of people come to me with the
idea that I'm some kind of supernally wise and powerful
savant, and that I can't possibly be interested in their problems. Knowing I have problems and weaknesses of my own
might make me more accessible.*

*But it also puts Stef right where I don't want him—in a
position as an easy target for anyone who can't come directly
at me. And he doesn't have any way to protect himself from
that.*

*Maybe I ought to give him up. I don't know that I can
afford a liability like that. Just make this a wonderful little
idyll out here where it's safe to do so, then send him on his
way when we get back to Haven. I'll make him understand,
somehow. Maybe we could pretend to quarrel. . . .*

*No—I can't give him up. I can't. There has to be another
way.*

He was so intent on his own thoughts that he barely
noticed when Blackfoot left the game trail for the road, and
turned herself back toward Forst Reach.

*Why is it I can solve the problems of the Kingdom, but
can't keep my own life straight? Gods, I can't even control
a stupid horse.* He let her go for a moment, then reined her
in to turn her back onto one of the game trails. He was still
in no mood to face his fellows, and intended to return home
the way he'd left.

He got her turned, though not without a fight. She had
gotten her fill of picking her way through the brush, and
let him know about it in no uncertain terms. She balked
when they reached the break in the blackberry hedges that
lined both sides of the road, and he finally had to dismount
and lead her through.

That was when the spell of paralysis struck him, pinning
him and Blackfoot where they stood.

One moment everything was fine; the next, with no warning at all, he was completely unable to move. Every muscle
had locked, rigid as wood, and beside him Blackfoot shivered as the same thing happened to her. Magic tingled on
the surface of his skin, and Mage-Sight showed him the
cocoon of energy-lines that held him captive. It took him
completely by surprise.

But only for half a breath; he hadn't spent all those years on the Karsite Border without learning to react quickly, even after being surprised.

His body was trapped, but his mind was still free—and he used it.

He tested the barrier even as he searched for the flare of mage-energy that would betray the location of his enemy as the other mage held the spell against him.

There—

And it was someone who was reacting exactly as he'd postulated ordinary mages would when faced with a Herald; armored to the teeth with shieldings to magic, but completely open to any of the Heraldic Gifts.

Van *could* use his own magic, and not the Mind-magic, of course. The stranger was nowhere near Vanyel's ability, and Van knew he could break the spell with a simple flexing of his own power, if he chose. But if he did that, the man might get away, and Van had no intention of letting him do that. Too many enemies had come back, better equipped, for second tries at him. Mages were particularly prone to doing just that, even one who was as outranked as this one.

Perhaps—*especially* this one. Because this was one whose power was stolen; siphoned from others with neither knowledge nor consent. Van saw *that* the instant before he struck. That may have been the other's motivation; to catch Vanyel off-guard and steal his power. There was no way of knowing until Van had him helpless and could question him at length.

Which—Vanyel thought angrily, as he readied his mental energies for a mind-to-mind blast—would be very shortly now. . . .

No mage of ill-intent should have been able to concentrate long enough to set a trap, he thought, looking down at the trussed-up body of his would-be captor, lying on his side in a bed of dead leaves. *Especially not in my home territory. The* vrondi *should have had him so confused and paranoid that he should have been firing off blasts at nothing. At the* least *he should have been leaking mage-energy sufficiently enough for me to detect him. I can't understand why he wasn't. Or why the* vrondi *didn't reveal him.*

The man stirred and moaned; he was going to have a dreadful headache for the next several days. The bolt Van

leveled him with had been at full-power, just under killing
strength. Van *could* kill with his mind—in fact, he *had*,
once. It was something he never, ever wanted to do again.
It had left him too sick to stand for a month, and feeling
tainted for a year afterward. Even though the mage he'd
destroyed had been a self-centered, power-hungry bastard,
without a drop of compassion in his body, and with no
interests outside his own aggrandizement, experiencing his
death directly, mind-to-mind, had been one of the worst
things Vanyel had ever endured. No, unless there was no
other way, he didn't ever want to do *that* again.

*Maybe he's unusually good at concentrating. Or maybe
he's already so paranoid that having the* vrondi *watching him
didn't make things any worse for him.*

The mage at Van's feet was ordinary enough. He looked
no different, in fact, from any number of petty nobles Van
had encountered over the years; sandy hair and beard,
medium build, a little soft and certainly not much accustomed to exercise or physical labor. His nondescript, blue-
gray woolen clothing was that of "minor noble" quality,
though cut a little differently from what was currently popular in Valdemar, and of heavier materials.

*He must have come in over the Western Border; he cer-
tainly isn't from around here.* Van waited impatiently for
the mage to regain consciousness. He wanted to scan his
mind, and wouldn't be able to do that effectively unless the
mage was at least partially awake. The best information
came when people reacted to questions, especially when
they had something to hide.

The mage opened brown eyes that reflected his confusion
when he felt he was tied up, and realized that he was lying
in a pile of last year's leaves. Van moved closer, stirring the
branches, and the mage focused on him immediately.

With no outward sign whatsoever of recognition.

But inside—the man's mind was screaming with fear.

Thoughts battered themselves to death against the inside
of the mage's skull, none coherent, none lasting more than
a breath. The only thing they had in common was fear.
After a few moments of attempting to make sense of what
was going on in there, Vanyel gave up and withdrew.

The mage was completely insane. There *was* no reason
for his action, because he wasn't rational. He had trapped
Vanyel because he had detected Van's use of magic the way

the *vrondi* had, and thought that Van was after him. But then, he thought *everyone* was after him. His life for at least the past month had been spent in constant flight.

He didn't leak energy, because he *couldn't,* he had himself so wrapped up in mage-shields that nothing would leak past them. And the *vrondi's* constant surveillance was only confirmation of what he already knew, that everybody was after him. And they were probably so confused by his insanity that they hadn't been able to make up their tiny minds about revealing him.

Vanyel sighed—then felt a twinge of guilt, and a sudden suspicion that sent him back to the mage's mind, probing the chaotic memories for confirmation he hoped he wouldn't find.

But he did. And this time he retreated from the chaos still troubled. The man had never been more than a hedge-wizard, but had convinced himself that "someone" was thwarting him from advancing beyond that status. To that end he began stealing power from others, specifically those whose Gift was even weaker than his. But since he really *wasn't* terribly adept or adroit, he failed to clean that power of little bits of personality that came with it. . . .

For at least the past four years, he'd been going progressively closer to the edge of insanity. He'd have gone over eventually, of that Vanyel had no doubt. But he had still been clinging to the last shreds of rational thought, when he crossed the Border into Valdemar and used his powers to search for another victim.

That had triggered Vanyel's Guardian spell, and the *vrondi* swarmed on him. It was at that point that he lost his grip on reality.

"In other words," he told the man, who stared at him blankly, "I might well be the one who sent you mad, in a roundabout fashion. Damn."

He crossed his arms, leaned back against the trunk of a tree, and thought over what he was going to have to do. Blackfoot snorted her disgust at being tied to a bush for so long with nothing she wanted to eat within reach. When Van didn't respond, she stamped her hooves impatiently. He continued to ignore her, and she heaved an enormous sigh and turned as much as her reins would allow to watch a moth fly past.

"I guess I'm going to have to take you back to Forst

Reach," Vanyel said, reluctantly. "If I leave you with
Father Tyler, he can find a MindHealer to set you straight—
and power-theft is really more in the provenance of the
clergy than it is mine, since you didn't actually do any of
that *inside* Valdemar. I really hate to have to take you
there, but there's no place else."

With that, he hauled the mage to his feet, ignoring the
man's struggles. He'd learned a thing or two on the Border,
and one of those things was the best way to immobilize a
prisoner. Blackfoot snorted with alarm when they
approached her, but Van ignored her alarm as well as he
ignored the man's attempts to struggle free.

At that point, Vanyel gave the man a taste of his own
medicine; a touch of the paralysis spell he'd set on Van.
With the man completely helpless, Vanyel was able to haul
him bodily to lie facedown over Blackfoot's saddle, like an
enormous bag of grain. He felt the curious touch of the
vrondi, attracted by his use of the spell, but ignored the
creature; when he didn't invoke magic again, it got bored
and vanished.

He was sweating and annoyed when he finally got the
man in place; he considered using the spell to keep him
quiescent during the walk back—but decided against it. It
would be a waste of energy, since the ropes tying feet to
hands under Blackfoot's belly would hold him perfectly
well.

With a glance of annoyance at him, and a swat for Blackfoot, who decided to rebel against this unexpected burden,
Vanyel took the reins and began leading the hunter along
the game path, heading back to the manor.

And he couldn't help wondering if every half-mage in the
Kingdom was going to take it into their heads to go mad.

The prospect was not an appetizing one.

Ten

"Lamentable," said Father Tyler, regarding the trussed-up mage, who was propped against a corner of the low wall surrounding the father's stone cottage. From the look of things, the mage was neither happy nor comfortable, not that Van was inclined to wish him either of those states.

Father Tyler shook his head again, his tightly-curled blond hair scarcely moved. "Most regrettable."

"I wouldn't feel too sorry for him, Father," Vanyel said sourly, rubbing a pulled shoulder. The man had somehow gotten heavier when the time came to get him off Blackfoot's back, and Van had wrenched his back getting the mage to the ground. "He brought at least two thirds of this on himself. Maybe more; mages aren't supposed to cross into Valdemar without registering themselves, but I doubt you'll find a record of this one. Be that as it may, his problem stems from power-theft. He's certainly guilty of that, and he's managed to do as much harm to himself as he ever did to his victims."

"Just how serious is power-theft?" the priest asked, rubbing his chin, a look of intense concentration on his long face. "I admit the seminary never covered that."

"Somewhere between rape and larceny," Vanyel replied, absently, wondering if he could get Blackfoot back to the stables without running into his relatives. "Power becomes part of a mage; it has to, if he's going to be able to use it effectively. Because of that, having your power stolen is a little like rape; there's a loss of 'self' that's very disturbing on a purely mental level. But that's why this fool ran into trouble. He wasn't good enough to cleanse the power he stole of all the personality overtones, and they became part of him. Pretty soon he never knew if what he was thinking stemmed from his own personality, or what was from out-

side, and he couldn't control what was going on in his
dreams and random thought processes anymore. He put on
tighter and tighter shields to stop the problem, which only
made it worse. The pressure in there must have been intol-
erable. Then the *vrondi* started spying on him, and he
snapped completely. But if he hadn't stolen the power in
the first place, this never would have happened."

"Well, it is your job to judge, Vanyel," the priest said,
with a smile that made it clear he intended no insult. "But
it is part of mine to forgive, and mend. I'll see what can be
done for this poor fellow."

That only succeeded in making Van feel guiltier, but he
smiled back and thanked the priest. He thought about warning him that the mage was strong and far from harmless—

But Father Tyler was younger than Vanyel himself, quite
as strong as any of the stablehands; besides, he was the
successor to Father Leren. He had been part of the united
Temples' effort at cleansing their own ranks and was probably quite well acquainted with all the faces of treachery.

He'll be all right, Vanyel told himself as he made his
farewell and took Blackfoot's reins. She was quite willing
to go; in fact she tried her best to drag him to the stable. He
would have been amused if he hadn't been so preoccupied.

He held Blackfoot to a walk by brute force, and turned
again to his personal dilemma. The problem of Stef was no
closer to a solution. Van still couldn't see how he would be
able to reconcile all the warring factors in his life.

"What would *you* do?" he asked the mare, who only
strained at the reins on her halter and tried to get him to
quicken his pace. "Oh, I know what you'd do," he told her.
"You'd eat."

She ignored him, and tugged impatiently as they crossed
the threshold of the stable. Several of the stalls that had
been occupied were empty when Blackfoot hauled him back
to her loose-box. So luck was with him—it looked like the
masculine contingent of Forst Reach had taken themselves
off somewhere, en masse. And since Treesa had Stef as
a semi-captive provider of entertainment, she wouldn't be
looking for her son.

Vanyel unsaddled the mare and groomed her; evidently
she was one of those animals that liked being groomed, as
she leaned into his brushstrokes and sighed happily, behaving as charmingly as if she *hadn't* spent most of the ride

fighting him. While he curried her, Van tried to think of
somewhere about the keep he could go to think. What he
needed was someplace where he could be found if someone
really went looking for him, but a place no one would go
unless they really *were* looking all over for him.

Then it occurred to him: the one side of the manor that
hadn't yet been built on was the side with that relatively
inaccessible porch. It was tree-shaded and quite pleasant,
but since the only entry was through a pantry, hardly anyone ever used it. It was too open for trysting, and too awkward for anything else. Which meant it should be perfect
for his purposes.

Blackfoot whickered entreatingly at him and rattled her
grain bucket with her nose.

"You greedy pig—I'm surprised you aren't as fat as a
pony!" he exclaimed, laughing. "Well, you don't fool me.
I *know* the rules around here, girl, and you don't get fed
until after evening milking."

She looked at him sourly, and turned her back on him.

"And you don't get to lounge around in your stall,
either," he told her, as he swung the door to the paddock
open. "It's a beautiful day, now get out there and move
that plump little rear of yours."

He swatted her rump; she squealed in surprise and bolted
out the open door. She dug all four feet in and stopped a
few lengths into the paddock, snorting with indignation, but
it was too late. He'd already shut the door.

He laughed at the glare she gave him before she lifted
head and tail and flounced out into the paddock.

Then he turned tail himself, and headed back to the keep,
and a great deal of thinking.

Once he'd fetched his instrument from their room, Stefen
expected Treesa to lead him straight to the solar. That room
was normally the ladies' sanctum—or at least it was for all
the ladies *he* knew. But she didn't head in that direction;
in fact, she led him outside and down a path through the
gardens. The path was very well-used, and led through the
last of the garden hedges and out into a stand of trees that
continued for as far as he could see.

"Lady Treesa?" he said politely. "Where in Havens are
we going?"

"Didn't Van tell you?" she asked, stopping for a moment to look back over her shoulder at him.

He shook his head and shrugged. "I am quite entirely in the dark, my lady. I expected you to take me to your solar."

"Oh—I'm sorry," she laughed, or rather, giggled. "During the summer we don't work in the solar unless there happens to be a lot of weaving to do—we come out here, to the pear orchard. No one is working in it at this time of year, and it's quite lovely, and cool even on the hottest summer days. The keep, I fear, is a bit musty and more than a bit damp—who would want to be indoors in fine weather like this?"

"No one, I suppose," Stef replied. At about that moment, the rest of the ladies came into view between the tree trunks. They had arranged themselves in a broken circle in the shade, and were already at work. Sure enough, they had their embroidery frames, their cushions, and their plain-sewing, just as if they were working in the heart of the keep. Spread out as they were on the grass beneath the trees, they made a very pretty picture.

They came up to the group to a chorus of greetings, and Lady Treesa took her seat—she was the only one with a chair, an ingenious folding apparatus—which, when Stef thought about it, really wasn't unreasonable given her age.

Now Stefen was the center of attention; Treesa let her ladies stew for a bit, though they surely must have known who he was *likely* to be. After an appropriate span of suspense, Treesa introduced him as "Bard Stefen, Vanyel's friend," and there were knowing looks and one or two pouts of disappointment.

Evidently Van's predilections were now an open secret, open enough that there were assumptions being made about what being Vanyel's "friend" entailed. Stefen ignored both the looks and the pouts; smiled with all the charm he could produce, and took the cushion offered him at Treesa's feet, and began tuning his gittern, thankful that he'd put it in full tune last night and it only required adjusting now. The twelve-stringed gittern was a lovely instrument, but tuning it after travel was a true test of patience.

"Now, what is your pleasure, my lady?" he asked, when he was satisfied with the sound of his instrument. "For giving you pleasure is all my joy at this moment."

Treesa smiled and waved her hands gracefully at him.

"Something fitting the day," she said, "Something of love, perhaps."

For one moment Stef was startled. *She can't possibly have meant that the way it sounded. She can't possibly be alluding to Van and me, can she?*

Then a second glance at her face told him that she was just "playing The Game" of courtly love. She'd meant nothing more than to give him the expected opening to flatter her.

Well, then—flatter her he would.

"Would 'My Lady's Eyes' suit you?" he asked, knowing from Vanyel that it was Treesa's favorite.

She glowed and tossed her head coyly, and he congratulated himself on reading her correctly. "It would do very nicely," she replied, settling back into the embrace of her chair, not even pretending an interest in her needlework.

Stefen smiled at her—only at her, as The Game demanded—and launched into the song.

By the third song he had grown to like Treesa quite a bit, and not just because she was so breathlessly flattering to his ego, nor because she was Vanyel's mother. As Van himself had said, she had a very good heart. When he paused to rest his fingers, she asked him for news of Medren; and not just out of politeness' sake. Ignoring the sidelong glances of her ladies, she asked him several questions about her wood's-colt grandson after Stef's initial answer of "he's fine."

"Has he gotten advanced from his Journeyman status?" she asked, after several close inquiries to the state of Medren's health and progress—a question voiced wistfully, or so it seemed to Stef.

He paused for a moment to think, as the breeze ruffled his hair and sent a breath of cool down the back of his neck. "Not when we'd left, my lady," he replied, "But I honestly don't think it's going to be much longer. He's very good, my lady, and I'm not saying that just because he's my friend. The Council of the Bardic Circle is really waiting for the fuss to die down about my getting jumped to Master so quickly before they promote anyone else. And if you want to know the truth, I think they might have been waiting for me to leave so that no one could accuse me of using *my* influence to get him his full Scarlets."

"Bard Stefen," she said, and hesitated, looking at him

oddly. This time he was certain that expression was of hope, "Do you think when he gets it, he would be willing to come *here* for a permanent post?" She smiled, and blushed a little. "I'm perfectly willing to trade shamelessly on his family ties if you think he'd be willing. Forst Reach would *never* rate a Master Bard, else."

Stefen pondered his answer for a moment before replying. Treesa was entirely right; Forst Reach *was* too small a place to demand the attentions of a Master Bard. Certainly there would be no chance for advancement here, under normal circumstances. But Forst Reach was also on the Border, and within reach of the newly-combined "kingdoms" of Baires and Lineas which were now ruled by Herald Tashir. Remarkable things had happened here—in fact, the solving of the mystery of who slaughtered Tashir's family was the subject of Medren's own planned Masterwork—and it was entirely possible that more remarkable things might occur. These were the sort of events that the Bardic Circle really preferred to have a full Bard on hand to record.

Furthermore, Medren had never shown the kind of ambition Stef harbored—he'd never talked about advancing in Court circles or gaining an important patron. It might well be that he'd be happy here.

"I think it might be worth asking him, my lady," Stefen replied with perfect truth. "And I know that if he wants it, the Circle would grant him leave to be here. Especially if you'd agree to share him with Tashir."

"I'd share him with *anyone* if it meant we'd have a Bard here," Treesa exclaimed. "And Tashir is such a dear boy, I'm certain he'd work out schedules with me so that we wouldn't both need Medren at the same time. It shouldn't be that hard even for seasonal celebrations—if I scheduled *ours* a bit early, and he scheduled *his* a bit late. . . ." Her voice trailed off, and she tapped her lips with one finger, obviously deep in thought. Stefen held his peace until she spoke again.

"Then I'll request it formally," she said aloud, and turned to Stef with both hands out in entreaty. "Would you—"

"I'll speak to him, my lady," Stefen assured her.

The dazzling smile she bestowed on him showed him something of the beauty she must have had in her prime. He bowed slightly to her, reinvoking The Game before she could get him to promise more than he could deliver. He had the distinct feeling that if she exerted herself, she could do just that.

He heard the sound of hooves on dry ground behind him at that moment, the steps slow and unhurried. He was about to turn to see who was riding out here, when Lady Treesa looked over his shoulder and smiled a second dazzling smile.

"And here is the *other* reason we meet out-of-doors in fine weather when Vanyel is at home," she said happily. "Especially if we can get Van to perform for us, or we have some other musician available. Welcome, Lady Yfandes! It would certainly present some difficulties attempting to get you up to the solar, would it not?"

Stefen turned; sure enough, it was Yfandes, who bowed— there was no doubt of it—to Lady Treesa, and whickered with what sounded like amusement. The Companion made her stately way to a spot that had evidently been left empty just for her, and folded herself down to it. That was the only way Stefen could think of the movement—it was a great deal more graceful than the way a horse would lie down, and was strongly reminiscent of a lady slowly taking a seat on the ground while minding all her voluminous skirts.

"Lady Yfandes is as fond of music as I am," Treesa told Stefen seriously. "When Vanyel finally *told* me that, the thoughtless boy, I couldn't see any reason why she shouldn't be able to join us when she wished."

Stefen realized then, with a bit of shock, that Treesa was speaking of Yfandes as if she were a lady-guest, and doing so completely naturally. It seemed *she* had no problem with accepting Yfandes as a "person" and not a horse.

Which is a little better than I can manage at the moment, he thought ruefully. *I have to keep reminding myself that she's not what she seems. And I'm a Bard, so I should know better!*

"Well, in that case, my ladies all," he said, with a slight bow to Yfandes and another special smile for Treesa, "allow me to take up my gittern, and resume amusing you."

In fact, he was greatly enjoying himself. The entire little group seemed to be enthralled with having the talents of a full Bard at their disposal. Some of Treesa's ladies were quite pretty, and although Stef had no intention of following up on his flirtations, when they fluttered coyly at him, he preened right back. That was an accepted part of The

Game, too. Best of all, none of this was work—he used only the barest touch of his Gift to enhance his performance, hardly enough for him to notice, unlike the deep-trance, draining effort he'd been putting out for the King.

It was a pity that Van had decided to vanish somewhere, but Stef was getting used to that. *Van broods,* he thought wryly. *And I must admit, he's had a lot to brood about lately. If I know him, no matter what we managed to build between us last night, he's going to have to agonize over it before he can accept it. Thank the gods he can't repudiate a lifebond, or I'd probably spend every night we're here reconvincing him he's not going to be rid of me. Of course, that could be quite enjoyable—but it could also be exhausting.*

He wondered what the Companion was making of all this. It would certainly help if Yfandes was on his side. He cast a brief glance at her; glowing white against the green of the orchard grass, and obviously watching him, her head nodding in time to his music. There was no doubt that there was a formidable intelligence behind those soft blue eyes.

Maybe the fact that she came out here is a sign that she likes me, he thought, when he couldn't detect any sign of hostility in her posture or her conduct. *I hope so. It would make my life so much easier. . . .*

Shortly after his second rest, Yfandes got up—doing so with a quiet that was positively unnerving; *nothing* that big had a right to move that silently!—and meandered off by herself. Stefen took that as a basically good sign. If Van was having trouble thinking things through, 'Fandes was probably going to him. And no matter what was wrong, Stefen was certain that 'Fandes would help her Chosen get his head and emotions straightened out.

Just as he was about to begin again, Stefen spotted someone coming toward the little group on a wagon-road that bisected the grove of trees. He was moving slowly, and as he neared, Stef could see why; he was carrying two heavy baskets on a pole over his shoulders. A farmworker, then, not someone coming to look for himself or Treesa, and nothing to concern them.

He continued to exchange news of the Court with Treesa, while the other ladies leaned closer to listen, but there was something about the man that vaguely bothered him, though he couldn't put his finger on what it was. He watched the stranger draw closer out of the corner of his eye and could not figure out what it was about the man that gave him uneasy feelings.

Certainly none of the others seemed to think there was anything out of the ordinary about him. They ignored him as completely as if he didn't exist.

Then—*I thought Treesa said that no one works out here at this time of year. So what's he doing out here?*

He took a second, longer look at the stranger, and realized something else. Something *far* more alarming.

The man's clothing was of high quality—actually better than Stef's own Bard uniform.

What is that peasant *doing dressed like that?*

The feeling of *wrongness* suddenly peaked, and Stefen reacted instinctively, flinging himself at Treesa and her chair and knocking both to the ground.

Just in time, for something small, and with a deadly *feel* to it whizzed over both their heads, cutting the air precisely where Treesa had been sitting—

Vanyel leaned out over the edge of the balustrade. The granite was warm and rough under his hands; solid, and oddly comforting. *I want solid things around me,* he thought slowly. *So much of my life is in flux—so much depends on luck and the things others do. I'd really like to have one point of stability; something I could always depend on.*

Or someone. . . .

The balustrade overlooked nothing; bushes were planted right up against it with trees beyond them, and had been allowed to grow until they blocked whatever view there might have been. With trees on all three open sides and the wall of the keep behind him, the porch wasn't good for much except the occasional lounger.

Sun beat down on Vanyel's head, warming him even though his Whites were reflecting most of the heat away. He stood so quietly that the little yellow-and-black birds that nested year-round in the branches of the bushes resumed the chatter he'd disturbed when he came out onto the porch, and actually began flitting to sit on the balustrade beside him.

:Brooding again, are we?:

He blinked, and came out of his nebulous thoughts. Yfandes was below him, barely visible through the thick branches of the bushes, a kind of white shape amid the green.

:*I suppose you could call it brooding,*: he admitted. :*It's about—*:

:*Stefen, of course,*: she interrupted. :*I thought you'd probably had enough time to stew over it and make your insides knot up.*:

:*Huh.*: He raised an eyebrow. :*Dead in the black. Am I that predictable?*:

:*On some topics, yes. And I expect by now you've laid to rest the fact that you're lifebonded, and that he really does love you on top of that. And that you love him. So what is it that's turning you inside out?*:

He sighed, and looked up at the clouds crossing the cerulean sky. :*Danger, love. To him, and to me. To me, because he can be used as a hostage against me. To him, because he's going to be in harm's way as soon as it's obvious we're a pairing. I don't know that I can afford that kind of liability, and I don't know that it's right to put him at that kind of risk.*:

Yfandes withdrew for a moment. :*Well, as to the first—he's assigned to Haven, and a very valuable commodity, even with the Healers learning how to duplicate what he does. They still have to be in physical touch, and their subject responds best if both parties are in a trance. Try conducting negotiations that way, and see how far it gets you!*:

He chuckled at the mental image that called to mind.

:*So far, Stef's the only answer to keeping Randi on his feet and functioning when he's in pain,*: she continued. :*And as such, he'll have the best guards in Haven. And as for your second question—Stefen's a grown man. Why don't you ask him if he's willing to take the risks that come with being your lover? My bet is that he's already thought about them, and accepted them as the price he pays for having you.*:

He pushed away from the balustrade and folded his arms across his chest. :*Do you really think so?*: he asked, doubtfully.

He heard her snort in exasperation below him. :*Of course I think so, I wouldn't have said it otherwise! You know I can't lie mind-to-mind!*:

He felt comforted by her matter-of-fact attitude, and by her solid *presence*. No matter what happened, no matter what went wrong in his life, 'Fandes was always there for him. It made all of this a little easier—

In a single moment, the feeling of comfort vanished, to be replaced by one of immediate danger. All his internal alarms shrilled, and without a second thought, he leaped the balustrade and crashed through the intertwined bushes to land in a crouch at Yfandes' side.

She felt it, too—they were so closely linked she couldn't have ignored it. In the next second he had vaulted onto her back—

She evidently had signals of her own, for she plunged forward through the undergrowth, aimed toward the orchards, as soon as he was securely on her back. That gave him a direction: he clamped his legs around her barrel and twined his fingers in her mane, and invoked FarSight and Mage-Sight together.

Magic—

Strong, controlled, and near at hand.

Dear gods— his mind screamed. *The pear orchard!*

'Fandes leaped the hedge surrounding the gardens—they hurtled through, her hooves tearing great gouts of turf from the lawns—she leaped the second hedge on the other side and flew into the orchard.

Women were screaming at the tops of their lungs, and scattering in all directions—not with any great success, at least not the highborn. Their heavy skirts encumbered them, and they fell as much as they ran. The serving maids had already hiked their dresses above their knees and taken to the dubious shelter of tree trunks. Cushions were tumbled every which way, and the air was full of feathers where one or two of them had burst.

It was obvious whom they were fleeing, as a brown-clad stranger with his back to Vanyel and Yfandes raised his hands above his head.

A mage—and his target was equally obvious. Treesa and Stef lay sprawled helplessly just before him, and Van felt the gathering forces of energy as the mage prepared to strike them there where they lay.

But—that's the man I caught—

Yfandes screamed a battle-challenge just before the man let loose a bolt of mage-fire. He half-turned in startlement at the noise, and the bolt seared the turf just beyond Bard Stefen and Vanyel's mother.

He was quicker than any mage Van had ever encountered in his life, at least in combat; before Vanyel could ready a blast of his own, he'd let fly with a second—just as Van realized that he and 'Fandes were completely unshielded.

Vanyel expanded the core of his own energies with a rush outward in a shield to cover the two of them, but just a fraction too late. Yfandes writhed sideways as she tried to evade the bolt, but was only partially successful. The edge of it hit them both.

He was protected; the shielding had covered that much— but Yfandes squealed as the bolt clipped her. She collapsed, going down in mid-leap, falling over onto her side. A sudden blank spot in Van's mind told him that she'd been knocked unconscious.

'Fandes!

He wanted, *needed* to help her. But there was no time— no time.

He managed to shove himself clear of her as she fell; hit the ground and rolled, and came up with mage-bolts of his own exploding from both hands. His hands felt as if he'd stuck both of them in a fire, but he ignored the pain.

The stranger dodged the one, and his shields absorbed the other. He struck back; a firebolt.

Vanyel sidestepped his return volley and let fly with a crackle of lightning at the stranger's feet. As he'd hoped, the mage's combat-shields did not extend that far down, and Vanyel's lightning found a target. The stranger shrieked and danced madly, but would not budge from his position, which was far too close to Stef and Van's mother for safety—

Vanyel sent a *sandaar,* a fire-elemental, raging straight for the enemy's face. He flinched, but stood his ground, and blew the elemental away with a shattering blast of power. That gave Van enough respite to take the offensive. Before the other mage had a chance to ready a counterblast, Van let fly three levinbolts in succession, and succeeded in driving him back, one step for each bolt.

When Van saw that the ploy was working, that the mage *was* being driven away from the Bard and Treesa, he Reached for energy in a frenzy, and sent bolt after bolt crashing against the enemy's shields. Though nothing penetrated, the force of impact was enough to continue to drive him backward, deeper into the orchard.

Van continued to fire off levinbolts as his own body shook with the strain of producing them out of raw magic, and his Mage-senses burned with the backlash of power. His whole world narrowed to the flow of energy, the target, and a vague awareness of where Treesa and Stefen lay.

Finally the enemy mage came exactly opposite the two lying on the ground. He didn't seem aware of them; certainly Van was keeping him occupied in defending himself. A few more steps, and Van would be able to include them in his own shielding—

Treesa chose that moment to struggle erect, though Stefen was trying to keep her down and protected with his own body. Her movement caught the mage's attention—

He looked directly into Vanyel's eyes, and smiled.

And reaching down into a pocket at the side of his boot, cast, not a weapon of magic or force, but one of material steel, following that with a levinbolt of his own. But not at Vanyel. At his mother.

"NO!" Vanyel screamed, and threw himself between Treesa and the oncoming blade—

And felt the impact in his shoulder as he crashed into his mother, sending them both to the ground—

And then a shock that twisted the world out of all recognition in a heartbeat, picked him up by the scruff of the neck, shook him like a dog shakes a rag, and flung him into the darkness.

Stef was trying to get Treesa down on the ground again, when another of those blinding flashes of light went off practically in the Bard's face. He cried out in pain as it burned his eyes; cried out again as two bodies crashed into his.

Can't see—can't breathe. Got to get out—

He struggled to get out from underneath them, his eyes streaming tears, with everything around him blurred.

He tried to make his eyes work. The only person still standing was the brown blot that was the mage that had attacked them. It raised two indistinct arms, and Stef struggled harder still to get free, knowing that there was nothing to stop him this time—that somehow he'd gotten rid of Van—

"Hey!"

A hoarse yell. The mage started, and turned just as Stef's

eyes refocused. The mage's mouth opened in shock, and he tried to redirect the power he had been about to cast at his three victims.

Too late.

Radevel was already on him; he swung his weighted practice blade down on the mage's head as he tried to fend off the blow—or possibly hit Radevel with the mage-bolt meant for the others. It didn't matter. The blunt-edged metal sword snapped both his arms like dry sticks, and continued with momentum unchecked. When the blade connected, it hit with a sound unlike anything Stef had ever heard before; the dull *thud* of impact, with a peculiar undertone of something wet breaking—like Rad had just smashed a piece of unfired pottery.

The mage collapsed, and Stef swallowed hard as his gorge rose and he fought down the urge to vomit. He'd seen any number of people dead before this—of cold, hunger, disease, or self-indulgence—but he'd never seen anyone *killed* before. It wasn't anything like that in songs.

He was having trouble thinking; vaguely he knew he should be looking for Vanyel, but he couldn't seem to get started. Finally he noticed that Van was one of the two people collapsed on top of him.

Van—he's not moving—

Yfandes struggled to her feet and shook her head violently, then looked around for Vanyel. She spotted him and the downed mage; pounded over and shouldered Radevel out of the way with a shriek of rage, and began trampling the body with all four hooves.

If he wasn't dead when he hit the ground, he is now.

Radevel stuck the blunt sword into his belt and turned. Half a dozen white-faced young men and boys walked slowly toward him from behind the trees—the sound of retching told Stef that there were probably more of them out there who weren't in any shape to walk yet.

"I hope you were paying attention," Radevel said matter-of-factly. "If you get the value of surprise on a mage about to spellcast, that's the best way to take him. Get his attention and interrupt his magic, then rush him before he has a chance to redirect it. Go for his arms *first*—most of 'em seem to have to wave their arms around to get a spell off. If you can, you want to keep 'em alive for questioning."

He glanced back over his shoulder at Yfandes, who was

still squealing with rage and doing her best to pound what was left of the mage into the dirt.

"Of course," he continued, "when family or Heralds are involved, that usually isn't practical."

His expression didn't change, nor did the tone of his voice, but Stef noticed (with an odd corner of his mind that seemed to be taking notes on everything) that Radevel's eyes widened when he'd looked back at Yfandes, and he was retreating from her a slow, casual step at a time.

Servants had materialized as soon as the mage was down, and pulled Stef out from under the Herald and his mother. They ignored Stef, concentrating on trying to revive Lady Treesa and Vanyel. Radevel gathered his group of students and plowed his way through them to get to his aunt and cousin's side.

"What happened?" One of the ladies grabbed Radevel's arm as he passed. "Where did this man come from?"

"Van brought him in," Radevel said shortly, prying her hand off his arm. "Bastard jumped him, and Van thought he was crazy. Left 'im with Father Tyler. Must not've been as crazy as Van thought; first chance he got, once Tyler left him alone, he cut himself loose and stabbed the priest. Me, I was on the way to practice with this lot, and I found him— good thing, too, he'd've bled to death if I hadn't found him when I did. Anyway, just about then I saw Van pelting off this way, and I followed."

Radevel shook the lady off before she could ask him anything more, and knelt down beside Stef.

Stefen didn't know what to do; Van was as white as snow and about as cold, and Treesa wasn't much better off. He watched the servants trying to bring them around, and felt as helpless and useless as a day-old chick. Radevel looked at the haft of the tiny knife in Van's shoulder, but didn't touch it; laid his hand to the side of Treesa's face.

"Something's wrong here," he said to Stef. "This isn't natural. We need an expert. You—" he reached out and grabbed one of the older servant-women. "You keep anybody from muckin' with 'em. And don't nobody touch that knife. I'll get the Healer."

"I'll get Savil—" Stef offered, glad to find *something* he could do, getting unsteadily to his feet. He set off at a dead run before anyone could stop him, ignoring the way his eyes kept blurring and clearing, and the dizziness that made him stumble.

His breath burned in his throat, and his sides ached by the time he was halfway across the garden.

There seemed to be something wrong—he shouldn't have been that winded. It felt like something was draining him. . . .

Savil was already on the way—he was practically bowled over by Kellan in the entrance to the gardens. Her Companion stopped short of trampling him, and he scrambled out of the way, just barely avoiding her hooves.

"What happened?" Savil asked, reaching down to grab his arm, missing, and seizing his collar instead.

"A mage," Stef panted, holding his side. "He attacked me and Treesa—no, that's not right, he attacked Treesa, and I was just in the way. Van took him out, but he got Van—gods, Van is hurt and—and we can't get him or Treesa to wake up—"

"Enough, that's all I need to know for now." She turned away, dismissing him, and Kellan launched herself across the garden, leaving him to make his own way back.

He arrived winded and unable to speak; Savil was kneeling beside the Healer, and examining Vanyel's shoulder.

"I've been treating them for poison," the Healer said in a flat voice, "I thought Lady Treesa might have gotten nicked by one of those knives. But they aren't responding, and I don't know why."

"It's because you're not fighting poison, lad, you're fighting magic," Savil muttered, as Stef limped up and collapsed on the ground beside her with a sob. "It's a good thing you didn't try to pull that knife, you'd have killed him."

She looked up—in Stef's direction, but more *through* him than *at* him. "We can't do anything for them here," she said, after a moment. "Let's get them back to their beds. I hate to admit this to you, but I'm out of my depth. Van could probably handle this, but—well, that's rather out of the question at the moment."

Stef clutched his side and stifled a moan of panic, and she glanced sharply at him. "Don't give up yet, lad," she said quietly. "I'm out of my depth, but I'm not ready to call it finished."

Stef clenched his jaw and nodded, trying to look as if he

believed her, while Van lay as pale as a corpse on the ground beside her.

Savil completed a more thorough examination than she was able to give in the orchard, and sat back in her chair, watching Van and thinking.

He wasn't prepared for a magic weapon, so he wasn't shielded against it. But something's got the thing slowed down considerably. Damned if I know what. Huh. A leech-blade. That's something I've only read about. I didn't know there was anyone that was enough of a mage-smith to make one anymore.

She glanced over at Stefen, who was recovering from magic-induced shock adequately on his own. Savil hadn't done anything to help him mostly because she reckoned that the lad could do with a little toughening. But he hadn't recovered as quickly, nor as completely as she'd expected, and Savil didn't know why that was happening either.

He sat on the other side of the bed, holding Vanyel's hand, in a pose that reminded her poignantly of the way Van had held 'Lendel's when her trainee was coming out of the trauma his twin's death had induced.

There was something else there that was poignantly like Van and her protege.

When it finally occurred to her, it was such an astonishing thought that she double-checked with her Companion to make sure she wasn't imagining things.

:Kell! Would you check with Yfandes and ask her if that boy's gone and lifebonded to Van?:

:If he's—: A moment of surprise. *:She says he has.:*

:Damn. Would that be why the leech-blade isn't draining Van as fast as I thought it would?:

:It's a good guess.: A pause. *:She says probably; something as deep as a lifebond is hard to monitor. She says Van is being fed from somewhere besides her, anyway.:*

:Sunsinger's Glory.: She invoked Mage-sight and stared at the evil thing. *It's working its way deeper, but slowly enough that I can take my time. He's got a couple of days before it'll do any lasting harm. Stef said it was thrown at Treesa; I wonder what it was supposed to do to her? Take her over, maybe; we'll never know now. So. I may be out of my depth, and Van may be out of reach, but I haven't exhausted the quiver yet. The only problem is that all the others that can*

handle this kind of weaponry are Tayledras. *And I certainly can't take Van through a Gate in his condition; it would kill him.*

Well, that just means they're going to have to come to him, if I have to truss them up and drag them.

She heaved herself out of her chair, and saw Stef's eyes flick briefly to her before returning to Vanyel.

"Stefen," she said. "I want you to stay with him. Don't let anyone move him, and especially don't let anyone touch that blade. I'll be back shortly."

"Where are *you* going?" he asked, his head jerking up, his expression panicked.

"To get help," she replied. "Just remember what I told you, and do it."

And before he could get himself organized enough to stop her, she limped out of the room, and ducked down a side stair only an Ashkevron would know about.

I'll bring them, all right, she thought grimly, as she made her way down the twisting little staircase entirely by feel. *Whether they like it or not.*

Eleven

Savil emerged from a linen closet on the ground floor, a legacy of her father's legendary building spree. At the far end of this hallway was the old family chapel, whose door Savil intended to use as a Gate-terminus. It had been used that way a number of times in the past, and the border-stones "remembered" those configurations. It was easier, and took far less energy, to build a Gate where one had been built before. And it was safer to anchor one end of a Gate on holy ground; there was less likelihood that something would come along and take control of it away from you.

We've shielded this chapel to a fair-thee-well, Savil thought, surveying the door for a moment. *It was well-shielded before, but it's a magical fortress now. That's good; less chance that the Gate-energy is going to get out and turn poor Van inside out. It's been twenty years, and his channels are still sensitive to Gate-energy. I'd rather not take a chance on making his condition any worse right now.*

A few months ago, she wouldn't have been able to do this, because she wouldn't have had the strength to spare. But when Van had changed the Web-Spell, he'd freed her and the other Guardians from the constant drain on their resources required by the Web. Now she had energy for just about any contingency, for the first time in years.

That freedom couldn't have come at a better time.

She braced herself, and invoked the four sides of the Gate; right side and left, threshold and lintel. When she had the "frame" built on the actual doorjambs, and the sides, bottom and top of the door were all glowing a luminous white, she invoked the second half of the spell. She fought a wave of weakness back for a moment, then sent the energy of the Gate out in little seeking threads, "looking" for the place she showed them, where they would build the second terminus.

It was easier this time than the last Gate she'd built to the Pelagirs, because she knew now where the k'Treva had relocated their Vale the last time they'd moved, and knew also where they built their own Gates inside the Vale.

Easier in terms of time; it was never "easy" to build a Gate, and the energy all had to be drawn from the mage himself; no outside sources could be used. As always, it felt as if bits of herself were spinning off and leaving her; as if she was trying to Fetch something that was just barely beyond her strength. It was hard to think; as if someone was actively preventing her mind from working. But there were no more than a few heartbeats between the moment she began the search and the moment she made contact with the other terminus.

There was a flare of light—and the chapel door no longer opened on a prosaic little family shrine, but on a riot of green leaves and twisted rock, with a hot spring bubbling off to the right.

K'Treva Vale.

She stumbled across the threshold, and into a circle of unblinking and hostile guards.

A half-dozen golden-skinned, blue-eyed warriors stared at her over the crystalline points of spear- or arrow-heads. Though not mages themselves, these guards knew the tiniest signs of the Gate being activated, and were prepared to handle anything or anyone coming through. This was the first time Savil had actually seen the Gate-guards at their posts, though she had met several of them during her visits to Moondance and Starwind—whenever one of the k'Treva mages needed to use the Gate, the guards generally cleared discreetly out of the way.

They stared at Savil for a very long moment, and she was altogether glad that she hadn't come with the intention of trying to cause trouble, because they looked more than capable of handling it.

Their no-nonsense attitude extended to their appearance. Most wore their hair shorter than was usual for *Tayledras*, barely past shoulder-length; and since it was summer, the normal silver-white had been dyed in mottled browns and dull yellow-greens. Their elaborate clothing was also dyed that way. In a tree or hiding in underbrush, they would be very hard to see.

Some few of them had the Mage-Gift, but none were primarily mages. These were members of the *Tayledras* Clan who, whether or not they had the Mage-Gift, preferred not to use what Gift they had. They served the Clan in other ways; as Healers and craftsmen, as scouts and border-guards, and as guards of the few places within the k'Treva shield that needed both tangible and intangible guards. After all, they didn't have to be sensitive to know when the Gate had been activated—the effect was fairly obvious.

Most of them were young; the life-expectancy of a *Tayledras* scout was about that of a Field-Herald, and for many of the same reasons.

"Savil!" exclaimed one of them, as Savil fought off her weakness and looked up. The circle of suspicious and hostile expressions changed in an instant. Someone knew her and recognized her. The weapons were lowered or set aside entirely, and two came to her aid as she swayed with fatigue and dropped to her knees on the bare stone in front of the Gate itself.

"Wingsister!" exclaimed the same one, a lean, sharp-faced young woman Savil knew as Firesong, whose spear clattered onto the smooth, bare stone as she tossed it aside. She helped Savil to her feet, and before the Herald-Mage could even voice her need, snapped out a series of commands.

"Windblade, get tea and honey. Hawkflight, find Brightstar; he should be with his weapons-teachers. Dreamseeker, find Starwind and Moondance. Suncloud, get me three more guards. Move on it!"

The four so designated handed their weapons to comrades, and sprinted off. Firesong helped Savil over to a seat on a magically smoothed boulder, supporting the Herald-Mage with one arm around her shoulders.

"How long can you hold the Gate?" Firesong asked as soon as Savil was settled.

"As long as I have to," Savil replied dryly. "Don't worry, the other terminus is secure. I wouldn't put k'Treva into any danger I could avoid."

"Good." Firesong looked as if she might have said more, but the youngster sent off for tea returned, as did the boy sent to fetch replacements. The guardswoman then had her attention fully claimed by the newcomers.

Like every set Gate-terminus Savil had ever seen constructed by *Tayledras,* this one was built around a cave-mouth. Unlike the last one, which she had helped shape, it was a very shallow cave this time; it went into the solid rock of the cliff-face scarcely more than two horse-lengths. The entrance had been cleared of dirt down to the bare rock, and ringed with boulders. It wasn't wise to allow anything to grow too near a place used often as a Gate-terminus; strange things happened to the plants. . . .

In spite of her claim to be able to hold the Gate, Savil was coming to the end of her strength. She huddled with her hands cupped around the hot cup of tea, and shivered. *They'd better come soon,* she thought, *or I'm going to lose this thing. We could call it up again, but that would take time, a good day before I'd be fit to try. We have time, but I don't think we have that much.*

But as if they heard her thoughts, Starwind and Moondance finally made their entrance, dramatically as always, bondbirds on their shoulders. Savil looked up from her tea, sensing them, more than hearing them—and there they were.

They *were* mages—Adepts, in fact—so their hair was its normal silver-white, elaborately braided and beaded, and flowing down past their waists. And being Adepts, they tended to a sense of the flamboyant that showed in their fantastically designed green tunics.

Savil smiled weakly at them; they wasted no time in formal greetings on seeing the depleted state she was in. They moved as one to augment her own failing energy.

She sighed as they each caught up one of her hands and she felt their energy flowing into her, strong and pure. With one sitting on either side of her, feeding her power to replace what she had lost, she felt able to talk to them.

It had been a while since she was last at k'Treva, but the years hadn't made much change in either of her friends. It was impossible to tell that Starwind was Savil's age, and Moondance only a little older than Vanyel. Adepts were long-lived, normally; node-magic tended to preserve them. *Tayledras* Adepts were even more long-lived, for they lived amid a constant flow of node-derived magic, magic that touched even the non-Gifted, whether born or raised among

them, bleaching their hair and eyes to silver and blue in a
matter of two years.

That bleaching effect was even more pronounced and
took less time for the mages, a sign that working with node-
magic changed them in deeper ways. The drawback was that
when they *did* near the end of their allotted span—and not
even an Adept could know when that would be—they would
fail and die within a matter of weeks, as the magic burned
them up from within.

Savil knew all that, but growled, "You two have little
simulacrums locked away somewhere, don't you, that age
for you."

"Now, Wingsister," Starwind chuckled, "You know that
isn't true. You could enjoy the benefits we do, if you would
accept our invitation to live here."

"Can't," she said shortly. "I have duties, and we've been
through all that. Listen, I need your help—"

Briefly, she outlined everything that had happened, and
waited for their response.

The initial reaction was pretty much as she'd expected.

"We do not leave k'Treva," Moondance began, uneasily,
when she had finished. "You know that. Our place is here,
as it has been for centuries—"

"That, *ash'ke'vriden,* is no excuse," said a light tenor
voice from just beyond the trees planted at the edge of the
"safe" boundary. A huge, white owl winged silently into
the clearing to perch on a boulder, and following it was a
younger version of the two *Tayledras* Adepts.

Except that instead of blue eyes, this striking young man
had luminous silver, and there was something about the
timbre of his strong, vibrant voice that would remind anyone who heard it of Vanyel.

Hardly surprising, since Vanyel was Brightstar's father—
and apparently Brightstar was going to be Savil's unexpected ally.

"You yourselves have taught me that *Tayledras* have left
their territories at need before," Brightstar said, taking a
stand beside his owl, "and the world being what it is, likely
will again." He lifted his chin in a way that reminded Savil
irresistibly of Van in one of his aggressive moods. "If the
need is great enough, what harm in answering it?"

Savil explained again, and Brightstar stiffened his back in
outrage. "But you *must* go! I owe Wingbrother Vanyel my

very existence. *I* would go, if I knew how to deal with these 'leech-blades'—" He spread his hands in a gesture of helplessness. "But I cannot."

"What, humility from the falcon who refused to admit there was any height he could not soar to?" Starwind raised a sardonic eyebrow.

They were taking this a little too lightly for her comfort, and evidently their adoptive son felt the same. Brightstar glowered. "I do not think that we have time to waste while Vanyel lies in danger from this thing," he said. "And you are quite right that there are some things I am not suited for."

"So at last you recognize that yours is the Gift of changing the living and Healing the earth, and not things made by the hand of man." Moondance looked up, theatrically. "Has the sun turned green? Are fish learning to fly?"

"Is my honored father going to return to the point?" Brightstar retorted. "The question is—Vanyel is in need of us and cannot come to us. How do we answer that need? *I* say you must go to him before he comes to harm!"

Starwind nodded reluctantly. "Vanyel needs us, and indeed, we owe him much—but is our Clan served by our leaving the Vale? Or would this bring harm that outweighs any good we could do? My son, there are good reasons for keeping our presence as secret as we may."

A polite cough interrupted them. Savil turned slightly, and saw that Firesong was standing there, obviously waiting to be heard.

Starwind nodded at her, and she coughed again, self-consciously. "If you will excuse my intrusion," she said, standing at rigid attention with her hands clasped behind her, "It seems to me that the better question would be if the Vale and Clan are *harmed* by your leaving. And I cannot see that this would be the case. The debt of k'Treva to Wingbrother Vanyel is a high one, and our honor would be in doubt if we did not proffer help when it was asked of us. In my opinion, and speaking as the head of the scouts, I think that this overrides even our tradition of secrecy."

"So, I am twice rebuked," Moondance said with a slight smile. "And by the infants. I do believe that I hear a turtle singing."

"Lest the ground itself rise up to rebuke us a third time, *shay'kreth'ashke*," Starwind said, rising and holding out his hand to Savil, "or our son strike us down and drag us across the threshold, let us go."

"I'm very glad to hear you say that, *ke'chara*," Savil said, as they walked toward the Gate, and steeled themselves for the shock of crossing.

"Whyfor?" Starwind asked, pausing on the threshold of the Gate itself.

"Because," she said, "I'm getting too old to hit attractive men over the head and carry them off. And the sad part is, I'm so old that's the only way I can get them!"

And with that, she took his elbow and stepped across the threshold, taking him with her.

Though she was so exhausted that it felt like days since she'd left, it was hardly more than a candlemark. Either weariness had made it seem longer, or time did odd things when you passed through a Gate.

Or both, she thought, turning to face her creation. *No one really knows how the damn things work, anyway. Someday maybe an artificer will discover how to make us fly, and we can do without them altogether. If I had the choice between a nice journey in a comfortable seat, and one of these gut-wrenching Gates, I'd take the journey every time.*

She held up her hands and began unweaving her Gate, strand by careful strand, taking the energies back into herself. Tedious work, and dangerous; going too fast could send the power back into her at a rate she couldn't handle. And at her age, a shock like that could all too easily kill her.

Then again, that journey would probably mean entrusting myself to the competence of strangers. There's plenty of folk I wouldn't trust my baggage to, let alone my safety. Ah, well, it's a nice dream, anyway.

Building a Gate took most, if not all, of a mage's energies, but taking it down put a sizable amount of that energy back. Savil was feeling very much her cantankerous self when she turned back to Starwind.

"Well," she said, dusting her hands off on her tunic, "what kind of an entrance do you want to make?"

"Your pardon?" Starwind replied, puzzled by her turn of phrase.

"Do you want things to stay as quiet as possible?" she asked. "Would you prefer we kept your presence at Forst

Reach a secret? It'd be hard, and frankly, we'd waste a lot of magic doing it, but we could, if that's what you want."

Starwind exchanged glances—and probably thoughts—with Moondance. He bit his lower lip, and looked at her measuringly before replying.

"I am of two minds," he said. "And the first thought is that it would be worth any effort to keep our presence unknown. Yet if we were to do that, we would be unable to accomplish many things that *I* would like. Moondance wishes to have speech of Vanyel's father, for one. If we are to do such a thing, we must be here openly."

Savil did her best to keep her surprise from showing. "I can't imagine why you'd want to talk to Withen, but—all right. So what's your choice?"

"Open," Moondance said promptly. "With as much drama as we may. If we are to break *Tayledras* silence, then I say we should leave your folk with a memory that will follow them all their days."

"You'll do more than that, my lad," Savil muttered, but nodded anyway. "However you want," she said a little louder. "I'd like you to look at Treesa first, if you would. Van can wait a little, and I'd rather get her on her feet before Withen comes home and has hysterics."

Starwind nodded. "Lead the way, Wingsister. We will follow your lead."

I doubt that, she thought, but didn't say it.

It was worth every odd look she'd ever collected from the members of her family to see their faces as she sailed into Treesa's sickroom, followed by the two *Tayledras*. They certainly knew how to time things for a particularly dramatic entrance, she gave them that. She shoved open the doors first, then made a half-turn to see if they were still coming—then, just before the doors swung completely shut, they flowed through, side by side, and paused to look around.

There were roughly half a dozen people in the room, all told. The only two Savil recognized were the Healer and Father Tyler, both of whom stared at the exotic Adepts with their mouths slowly falling open.

The rest drew back as far as they could get; years of being told as children to "be good, or the Hawkbrothers will get you" were bound to have an effect. And no one could doubt for a moment that these two were a pair of the fabled outlanders—for their birds were still perched calmly on their shoulders, as if they passed through Gates and were carried around strange keeps every day of the month.

Both birds were stark white now, though when Savil had last seen him, Starwind's bondbird, the younger of the pair, was still marked with gray where the darker colorations hadn't yet bleached out. She found herself marveling anew at the birds' calm; no falcon in the Ashkevron mews would sit unjessed and unhooded on a human's shoulder, nor tolerate being taken all over the keep. But then, these birds were to ordinary raptors what *Shin'a'in* warsteeds were to horses. Bred for centuries to be the partners of those they bonded with, their intelligence was a little unnerving. Just now Starwind's bird was watching Savil with a quiet, knowing look in its eyes, and Moondance's was watching the priest with what had to be an expression of wicked amusement.

Moondance himself strode toward the bed where Treesa had been placed. Those at her bedside melted out of his way without a single word. He held his hand briefly above her forehead, frowned for a moment, and then announced without turning around, "You were correct, Wingsister. It is simple mage-shock from being too near a blast. I can bring her out, if you'd like. It makes no difference to her recovery if she is awakened now or later."

"Do it now," Savil advised, "before Withen comes crashing in here like a bull with its tail on fire."

Moondance took both of Treesa's hands in his, and held them for a moment with his eyes closed. Treesa began to stir, muttering unintelligibly under her breath. Moondance waited for a moment, then opened his eyes and called her name, once.

"Treesa," he breathed. Only that, but somehow the name took on the flavoring of everything she was, and things Savil hadn't guessed she could be.

Treesa's eyes fluttered open, and the first thing she focused on was Moondance.

"Oh—" she said, weakly. "My." She gulped, and blinked at the *Tayledras* as if she could not look away from him, though he dazzled her. "Am—am I dead? Are—are you an angel?"

Starwind was too polite to burst out laughing, but Savil could tell by his too-calm expression and the creases around his twinkling eyes that he was doing his very best not to laugh at the notion of Moondance as an angel.

Moondance is never going to hear the last of this, Savil thought, holding back a smile that twitched the corners of her mouth despite the seriousness of the overall situation.

"No, my lady," Moondance said haltingly in the tongue of Valdemar. "I am only a friend of your son. We came here to help him, and you as well."

"To help—" All the color drained from Treesa's face. "Van—how badly is he hurt? Dear gods—"

She struggled to sit up, but the Healer prevented her from moving by holding her down with one hand on her shoulder. Moondance put his hand atop the Healer's, eliciting a gasp from both the Healer and Treesa.

"We go to him now, my lady," Moondance said, and smiled sweetly. "Be at ease; all will be well."

And with that, he turned and swept out of the room, Starwind joining him so that they left as they had entered, together. Savil smiled at Treesa, as reassuringly as she could, and followed them.

"Where is young Vanyel?" asked Starwind as soon as they were all in the stone-walled corridor.

"Up a flight and over a bit," Savil told him, taking the lead again, and moving as quickly as her aching hip would permit. "I should warn you about something. Seems he's lifebonded again, this time to a young Bard about half his age—"

Starwind exchanged a wry glance with Moondance. "Indeed? And where have I heard *that* tale before?"

"I would have no idea," Savil replied, her tone heavy with irony. "Just because you were near thirty and Moondance was all of sixteen. . . . At any rate, the boy's with him. Don't frighten him; he's had a bad few hours, and he's part of the reason why I haven't been frantic to get you here."

Moondance looked puzzled, but Starwind nodded knowingly. "Ah. The blade feeds on both of them. I had wondered why you were so calm about all this."

"So long as you didn't take a week to make up your minds, I reckoned we had time." She paused outside Vanyel's door. "Here. And remember what I told you."

This time Starwind held the door open for her, and followed her inside with no dramatics at all. Stefen, white-faced, was absorbed in Van—so completely that he didn't even notice they were there until Starwind laid a gentle hand on his shoulder.

Stefen jumped; he looked up at the *Tayledras* Adept, and his eyes grew very large, and very round. His mouth opened, but he couldn't seem to make a sound.

"We are here to help young Vanyel, little one," Starwind said kindly. "But for us to do so, you must move away from him."

Stefen lurched to his feet, knocking over the chair he'd been sitting on, and backed away, tripping over it in the process. Moondance caught him before he fell, and Savil wondered for a moment if the poor boy was going to faint on the spot. He recovered, and edged over to Savil, standing slightly behind her, his eyes never once leaving the *Tayledras*.

Starwind held one finger near to the leech-blade, but did not touch it. "A nasty piece of work, that," he said in his own tongue to Savil. "More than ordinary malice went into its making."

"But can you get rid of it?" Savil asked anxiously.

"Oh, aye. Not easily, but it is by no means the hardest task I have ever undertaken. *Ashke*—"

Moondance nodded, and moved to stand immediately behind him, with one hand resting lightly on his shoulder. Starwind ripped part of the ornamental silk from his sleeve; the cloth parted with a sound like the snarl of a hunting cat. He wrapped the bit of silk around his hand, and only then grasped the hilt of the leech-blade.

"Now we give it something else to seek after," he murmured, and held his other hand a few thumblengths away from the wicked little knife. Invoking Mage-Sight, Savil Saw that his hand glowed with life-force; far more than Vanyel possessed, even at the core of him. And she Saw how the blade loosened its hold on the Herald-Mage; how it turned in Starwind's hand, and lurched out of the wound like a hunger-maddened weasel.

"*Not* this time, I think," Starwind said aloud, pulling his unprotected hand away before the writhing blade could strike it. "Now, *ashke*—"

Moondance made an arc of pure power between his two hands, and Starwind brought the blade down into it.

The thing *shrieked*.

Stefen screamed, and clasped his hands over his ears. Savil very nearly did the same. The only reason she didn't try to block her ears was because she knew it wouldn't do any good. That hideous screaming was purely mental.

The scream of the blade continued for four or five breaths, then, as suddenly as it had begun, the thing fell silent. Moondance damped the power-arc, and when Savil's eyes and Mage-Sight recovered from the dazzle, she saw that Starwind held only a hilt. The blade itself was gone, and the air reeked of charred silk.

"And that," the *Tayledras* said with satisfaction, turning the blackened hilt over in his hand, and examining it carefully, "is that." He looked up at Savil. "And now, dearest Wingsister, we four can all join to bring our brother back to us."

She was placing her hands over Moondance's when she realized what he'd said.

Four? Huh. Well, why not?

"Come here, lad," she said over her shoulder to Stefen, who was hovering worriedly in the background. "They won't bite you."

"Much," Moondance said, in her tongue, with a sly grin for Stefen. Oddly enough, that seemed to relax him.

"What can I do?" he asked, taking his place at Savil's side.

"I have no idea," she admitted. "But *he* knows. So let's both find out."

Starwind smiled, and placed his hands atop theirs.

Savil took a long, deep breath and looked quickly down at Vanyel. He was breathing normally, deeply asleep, and his color was back. *He'll probably wake up in a candlemark or so. 'Fandes will be out about as long.*

"What happened?" Stef asked, dazedly. "What did we do?"

"Sit, Singer," Moondance said, pushing him down onto the bed. "We gave young Vanyel a path back to himself, and the strength to return upon it. But that strength came from us, you most particularly, and you should now rest." He nodded at the bed. "There is plenty of room there, and Vanyel would feel comforted by your presence."

"He would?" The youngster looked on his last legs, but

was stubbornly refusing to admit his weariness. "Well—if
you think so—"

"I think so." Moondance threw a light blanket over the
Bard's shoulders. "Rest. You do not hasten his recovery by
fretting."

"If you—" he stifled a yawn "—say so."

Moondance shook his head at Starwind. "Children. Was
I that stubborn-minded?" he asked in *Tayledras.*

"Oh, you were worse." Starwind grinned, and took Savil
by the elbow. "Kindly show us where we will be staying,
Wingsister. I think we will have to remain here some few
days more, else Vanyel will foolishly exert himself and it
will be all to do again."

:And just what do you have up your sleeve?: she asked
him. *:You're right, of course, but there's more that you aren't
telling the boy.:*

:Perceptive as always,: he replied. *:I wish you to hear this
from Moondance, however.:*

She nodded at Moondance, who joined them at the door.
"Sleep, Stefen," he ordered as he closed it. An indistinct
mumble came from the general direction of the bed. It
sounded like agreement.

"In the absence of anyone else I guess I'll make the decision of where to put you two," Savil said. "And because I
don't know where else, I guess you might as well take the
room next to Van's."

She opened the door to the next guest room, which
looked about the same as Vanyel's in the dim light; with
Forst Reach entertaining as many as a hundred visitors during the course of a year, no room ever sat long enough to
take on an air of disuse. The only real sign that it was not
occupied was the fact that the shutters were closed, and
what light there was leaked in through the cracks.

"So, now, what was it you wanted to tell me about?"
Savil asked Starwind, closing the door behind him. The
older *Tayledras* went directly to the window and threw the
shutters open.

"Not I," he said, "but Moondance." He sat on the window ledge and leaned out, looking with interest—though
real or feigned, Savil couldn't tell which—at the grounds
below.

"Well?" she asked impatiently of Moondance. The Heal-
ing-Adept looked very uncomfortable.

"I do not know how much you give credence to our beliefs," he said doubtfully.

"Depends on which one," she replied, sitting on the edge of the bed. "If it's the one about how people should live in trees, I still think you're out of your mind."

He ignored the sally. "We think—and have proved, insofar as such a thing is possible to prove—that souls are reborn, sometimes even crossing species' boundaries. Rebirth into something of like intelligence, a *hertasi* perhaps being reborn as a *kyree,* or a *kyree* as a human—"

"Must make things interesting at dinnertime," Savil jibed.

He glared at 'her. She gave him a sardonic stare right back.

"This is all very fascinating philosophy, but I don't see what it has to do with Van," she pointed out, tilting her head a little.

Moondance shook his head. "Not with Vanyel—with the Singer."

"Stef?" she exclaimed incredulously. "Why on earth Stefen? And why is it important?"

"Because my *shay'kreth'ashke* believes—as do I—that your Stefen is, or was, the young one called Tylendel," Starwind called from the window.

Savil's first reaction was surprise, then skepticism. "What, just because they lifebonded? Really, isn't that a little too neat, too pat? It makes a very nice tale, but—" She shrugged.

"No," Moondance said, walking to the window to stand beside Starwind. "No, it is not because of the lifebond, or not primarily. There are other things—memory traces of Vanyel many years ago, ties other than the lifebond." He paused, and looked up at the ceiling as if gathering his thoughts. "And there are reasons, pressing reasons, for this to have happened. The bond between Tylendel and Vanyel was strong, stronger even than most lifebonds I have seen. There is a debt owed to Vanyel because of what happened. There is unfinished business because Tylendel failed as a Herald." He looked at her expectantly for a moment, then shrugged. "I could go on at length, but that would only bore you."

"I doubt it," Savil replied, fascinated in spite of her skepticism. "But I can't see what relevance it has to the current situation, either."

Starwind left the window. "Only that the past has bearing on the present, and will color what happens in the present."

"So, should I tell them about this speculation of yours?" she asked curiously.

"Ah." Starwind clasped his hands behind his back, and gave his lifebonded a wry smile. "That is where we differ. I think perhaps yes, but I do not feel at all as strongly as Moondance, and am willing to be overruled."

"And I think that on no account should you tell them," Moondance said adamantly, leaning his back against the windowframe. "But our reasons for our feelings are much the same."

"We feel," Starwind took up the thread of conversation, "that this relationship should be permitted to develop without the baggage of the previous one. It is not the same set of circumstances at all, their meeting and bonding; nor are their relative status or ages the same. Therefore I think they should be told so that they may avoid misunderstandings that echoes of the past may bring."

"And I think that being told will only bring problems; that Vanyel will cease to react to Stefen as he has become, and that he will begin behaving in ways that will warp the relationship out of all recognition and health." Moondance crossed his arms over his chest, and looked very stubbornly at Savil.

"I can think of one problem right off," she said slowly. "If Van thinks Stef's his old love, he's likely to do one of two things—pay *more* attention to Stef's opinions and advice, or *less*. Neither is healthy. Stef's got a good head on those shoulders, but he also has a lot of growing up to do yet. Right now Van's giving him about the same amount of slack he'd give any lad his age, and listening to him when he makes sense—"

"Which is the way it should remain," Moondance concluded.

She shook her head at Starwind. "Sorry, old friend, but my vote goes with Moondance."

He shrugged. "I had already told you I did not feel that strongly; I am content to be overruled."

"To change the topic, how long do you want to stay?" she asked. "I'll have to tell Withen something when he gets back."

"Three days, perhaps five. No more, certainly." Starwind

shook his hair back. "Two days to keep Vanyel from over-exerting, then however long it takes to unravel *who* did this thing, and *why*."

"If we can," Moondance said with resignation. "It is by no means certain. But with four Adepts at work, the odds are that what can be uncovered, will be."

"Which brings me to a request, dearest Wingsister," Star-wind grinned. "Do you think this place is capable of producing garments of a suitable size for us? It seems that we forgot to pack. . . ."

"Oh, probably nothing good enough for you, you preen-ing snow-birds," Savil grinned wryly, "but we may be able to rummage up *something*."

Twelve

Yet another of Treesa's ladies had Savil and the elder *Tayledras* trapped in a conversation, this time just outside the keep as Starwind sent his falcon up for some exercise. There was no reason for this one-sided discourse; she'd done it purely for an excuse to gawk at the exotic. Savil closed her eyes for a moment, and wished that the chattering child-woman would come to the point. "This," said Starwind under his breath, in his own language, "is not a family, it is a small army. And half of them are mad." He nodded to the young woman, smiled, and tried to interject a single word. "It—"

She ran right over the top of him without pausing for breath, and without taking her eyes from Starwind's face. "But my mother's cousin twice removed, you know, the Kyliera Grove Brendewhins not the Anderlin's Freehold lot, the ones who—"

:*Does she never cease speaking?*: Starwind asked. :*Even in sleep?*:

:*Not to my knowledge,*: Savil replied the same way.

:*Then I shall have to do something rude to free us from the chains of her words,*: he told her.

:*You're forgiven in advance,*: Savil assured him.

Suddenly, with no forewarning whatsoever, Starwind's white gyrfalcon swooped down out of the sky above them, and dove at the girl, missing her by a goodly distance, but frightening her into silence. The bird hovered just over Starwind's head, screaming at her, threatening to dive again.

"Your pardon," Starwind said, with a completely disarming smile, "but I think my bird must have taken a dislike to your apparel. I have never seen him act in this way before. He must believe that you are a threat to me."

The bird dove again, and this time the girl shrieked and fled. Starwind held up his arm, and the falcon settled on it immediately, then hopped to his shoulder and began preening itself with every sign of being completely calm.

Kellan wandered up, and put her nose up to the bird. It reached out with its wicked beak and gently nibbled at her upper lip before resuming its preening.

:*A bird with sense,:* Kellan told her Chosen, a wicked twinkle in her eye. :*I was considering charging you three just before Starwind asked Asheena to threat-dive.:*

:*The only problem with that is Lytherill would never have believed threat out of you,:* Savil said. :*She believes in the unquestionable goodness and purity of Companions.:*

Kellan hung her head and moaned. :*Does this mean I can expect her to garland me with roses, try to hug my neck, and speak to me in babytalk?:*

Savil laughed. :*No love, she's not quite* that *young, though a couple of years ago, before she discovered boys, you'd have been in danger.:*

:*How close are you to finding out what that mage was up to?:* Kellan asked, with the kind of abrupt change of subject Savil had come to expect from her over the years.

:*Close. We'll probably be able to run the spells tomorrow.:*

:*Indeed, Wingsister.:* A new mind-voice entered the conversation and both Savil and her Companion suppressed startlement. Adepts—or very powerful Mindspeakers—were so few that Savil seldom remembered that the *Tayledras* shared with Vanyel the ability to "overhear" any conversation that was not shielded against them. :*Pardon,:* he said apologetically. :*Yes, we should be prepared enough and Vanyel recovered enough to make the attempt tomorrow. Would the one who struck him were still in condition to be questioned.:*

Starwind sent his falcon up once more, this time in response to a pigeon taking wing from the keep eaves. Wild raptors, Savil knew, missed more often than they struck, but *Tayledras* bondbirds seldom stooped without a kill at the end. Starwind had his eyes closed, and his entire body stiffened with tension as his bird dove. A scream of triumph rang out as the bird pulled up for the kill and Starwind shivered a little, a tiny smile of satisfaction on his lips, as the falcon's talons struck home.

The gyrfalcon carried its prey to the roof to feed, and Starwind opened his eyes and smiled a little more broadly at Savil's knowing grin.

"Fantasizing someone other than a pigeon at the end of that stoop, hmm?" Savil asked.

"I?" Starwind was all innocence. And Savil didn't believe it for a moment.

"You. If I had that bastard in my reach right now—never mind. Come on, let's finish this walk." Savil headed out into the paddocks, and Starwind fell in beside her, Kellan following noiselessly behind.

"As for being waylaid by half-grown girls, half the problems you and Moondance are having you brought on yourself," she told him frankly. "You two insisted on being spectacular, well, now you see what happens to a spectacle. I'm sorry, but I can't feel terribly sorry for you."

"I would not have insisted, had I known the sheer number of inhabitants in this place," he replied ruefully. "Gods of my fathers—*five* families, with no less than seven children in each, hundreds of men-at-arms, and then there are the servants, the fosterlings—" He shook his head in disbelief. "K'Treva is little larger, and it is an entire clan! It staggers the imagination."

"And every one of those people is dying for a close-up look at you," Savil sighed. "I tried to warn you."

"The warning came too late." He shrugged. "Though— I am glad to have met Withen's falconer, for all that he salivates every time he looks upon our winged brothers. And I am doubly glad to have met Vanyel's father and mother."

Savil strolled over to a fence surrounding the field that held the yearling fillies, and leaned on it, putting one foot on the lowest rung. "Withen's gotten better the last five years or so. I must say, I'm rather proud of him. Most men go more hidebound with age, but the old bastard seems to have relaxed some of his attitudes. Hellfires, he hardly ever bellows at me anymore."

"You think so?" Starwind replied, looking out over the field. "That is good. That is *very* good."

But why it was good, he refused to say.

Every night after dinner, Withen and Treesa had taken to inviting the *Tayledras*, Savil and Vanyel up to their private suite or (more often, since the weather was excellent) out to the secluded side porch Vanyel had favored before the orchard incident. In part, it was out of pity—to get them away from the Forst Reach hordes. And after the first

evening, they included Stefen in on the invitation, although
the Bard begged off, saying he had promised to entertain
the younger set.

Tonight was no exception, but this time Vanyel, too, had
gracefully asked pardon to decline. He didn't give a reason,
but Savil told Withen as she joined the group out on the
porch that he was missing an unusual experience.

"What is it?" Withen said curiously, handing Starwind a
cup of wine. He'd had servants line the porch with festival-
lanterns so that the place was well, but not brightly, lit.

"Someone managed to goad your son and his friend into
challenging each other, musically speaking," she replied.
"That's what they're up to right now, in front of most of
the younglings of the keep—no, Treesa, trust me, it isn't
anything you want to subject yourself to."

Treesa had begun to rise, but sank back down to her seat.
"I do trust you, but why? I trust Van not to do anything
that would upset the children's parents, so it can't be a
bawdy-song contest, can it?"

"No, it's not," Savil said, grinning. "It's a *bad* song contest. They've challenged each other to come up with the
worst songs they know. Trite, badly-rhymed, badly-
scanned—you name it. Right now Van's going through
some piece of drivel about being trapped in a magic circle
for seventeen years, and it sounds like it may take seventeen
years to sing it."

Treesa laughed. "It may, at that," she said, and filled a
cup for the younger *Tayledras*.

Moondance took it, but his face was sober. "Lady Treesa,
Lord Withen, I have a great wish to speak of something
with you, and as it concerns your son, I think this moment
of his absence gives me the opportunity. If you will permit."
He paused, and looked first into Treesa's eyes, then into
Withen's. "It is not comfortable."

Treesa dropped her gaze, but nodded. Withen cleared his
throat. "Nothing about my son is particularly comfortable.
I'm not sure he was ever created to inspire comfort. I think
I would like to hear what you have to say. No, I would not
like it, but I think I should hear it."

Moondance sighed, and sat down on the stone railing.

"Then, let me tell you something about a very young
man, a boy, named Tallo."

Savil was considerably more than a little surprised; Moon-

dance found the story of his own past so painful that he
had rarely divulged it to anyone. She knew it, of course;
she had found the boy . . . she had brought him to Starwind, nearly dead.

Moondance told his story in as few words as possible, his
voice flat and without emotion.

"Some thirty years ago, in a village far from here, there
lived a boy named Tallo. He was a recluse, a lone runner,
an odd boy, given more to thought than deed. His parents
hoped he would become a votary, and sent him to the priest
to learn—but in the priest's books he found what he was
truly Gifted with. Magic. His parents did not understand
this, nor did they sympathize, for their lives had little to do
with magic and mages. This made him further alone, more
different, and his parents began to try to force him back to
their own simple ways. It was too late for that—there were
arguments. There were more when they attempted to bring
him to wed, and he refused. He could not tell them what
he felt, for what he yearned for were those of his own sex,
and such a thing was forbidden."

Moondance's soft voice did not betray the pain the *Tayledras* Adept felt. Savil knew; no one better—but certainly
Withen could never have guessed.

"One summer, after a winter of arguments and anger,
there came a troupe of gleemen to the village—one among
them was very handsome, and quite different from his fellows. Thus it was that Tallo learned he was not the only
boy to feel yearnings of that kind. They became lovers—
then they were discovered. Both were beaten and cast out
of the village. In anger Tallo's lover repudiated him—and
in pain and anger, Tallo called lightnings down upon him."

Moondance sighed, and shook his head. "He did not
mean even to hurt, only to frighten—but he did not know
enough to control what he called, and the young gleeman
died in agony, crying out Tallo's name. And in remorse for
what he had done, Tallo tried to take his own life. It was
Herald Savil who found him, who brought him to her new
friend, Starwind of the k'Treva. Who was also *shay'a'chern*,
and Healed the young boy in body and spirit—but still,
there was such grief, such remorse, that Tallo felt something
must be given in sacrifice to the harm he had done. So did
Tallo die, and in his place came Moondance."

Withen started. Moondance glanced sideways at him, and

only now did the *Tayledras* show any emotion. "Tallo is no more," he said, his voice subdued. "And no one in Tallo's village would know Moondance. The *Tayledras* are stories to frighten children with, and they would not dare to recognize him. Those that were his family would only be afraid of what he has become. Never can the one who became Moondance reconcile with his family; he did not when he was Tallo, and now it is impossible to do so. And that, Lord Withen, Lady Treesa, is a desperate sadness."

He sipped his wine, as the insects sang in the darkness around them, and the lights in the lanterns flickered.

"It seems to me, Lord Withen," Starwind said, finally, just before the long silence became too much to bear, "that a man's life must be judged by what he has done with it. Your son is a hero, not only to your people, but to ours, to the peoples of Baires and Lineas, even to some outside the Borders of your realm. Look at the good he has done—and yet always with him is a deep and abiding hurt, because he feels that *you* have seen nothing of the good he has done, that you feel he is something evil and unclean."

Withen swallowed his cup of wine in a single gulp. He stared up at the stars for a long time, then lowered his eyes to meet Starwind's for just a moment. He dropped them, then toyed with his cup, until the silence grew too much even for him to bear.

He cleared his throat, and furrowed his brow, looking very unhappy. "Thank you. You've given me a lot to think about," he said, awkwardly, and turned to lock gazes with Moondance. "Both of you have. And I promise you that I *will* think about it." He looked down at his cup, as if he was surprised to find it empty. "I think at the moment that I have had quite enough wine for one night." He smiled suddenly, stood up, and held out his hand to Treesa, who took it with a surprised expression. "By now that little contest should be over, and I do believe I'd like to find out who—and what—won."

And with that, he set his cup down, aided Treesa to her feet, and exited with a certain ponderous grace.

Savil blinked, and took a sip of her own wine. "What was that supposed to accomplish?" she asked. "And why on earth did you broach that subject now?"

Moondance put down his cup of wine untasted. "It was

something that needed Healing," he replied. "I have done my poor best, and we may only see what time will bring."

Starwind nodded without speaking.

Savil looked up at the velvet of the night sky; no moon tonight, which made the stars seem all the brighter. "It felt right, if my opinion means anything to you," she said at last. "Right words, right time. If anything is going to happen—"

"It is in Withen's hands," Starwind sighed, then stretched. "Gods of my fathers—if there is anything more difficult than dealing with the heart, I do not know what it may be. I am to my rest."

"And I to mine," Savil said, putting her cup down. "Tomorrow is another day."

"Yes. And tomorrow we shall have finished the preliminaries over that evil hilt. Tomorrow we shall look into its past, and that of its wielder." Moondance shook his head. "This will not be pleasant."

"No," Savil agreed, moving toward the door with the other two. "And I don't think the answers we're going to get will be pleasant either. So let's enjoy our peace while we have it, hmm?"

"Indeed." Starwind said, pausing to let her precede him. "For it is all too fleeting and fragile a thing, peace."

Vanyel knew that Savil would have been happier in a fortified Work Room, but the current situation wouldn't allow it. There really was no place suitable in all of the keep. The *Tayledras* felt more comfortable out-of-doors, and the orchard was the place where the strange mage had died, so to the orchard they had all come. Savil had brought a cushion with her; the ground was too much for her bones. The *Tayledras* sank down in their places with no sign of discomfort at all. Vanyel wished belatedly that *he* had thought to bring something to sit on, but it was too late now.

They sat in a circle, but with their backs to each other, rather than face-to-face. All four of them would Hear this reenactment of the recent past; all four of them would Hear the thoughts that had been strong enough to have left an imprint there. They were looking outward, not inward, and hence, the seating arrangement.

They were all in place now, as Vanyel eased himself down between Savil and Starwind.

The little circle did not include Stefen, who was keeping

Treesa and her ladies occupied and out of the mages' way, but it was Starwind's opinion that he was better employed in that capacity than in watching them work magic he could not participate in.

Vanyel unwrapped the blackened hilt and laid it on the bare earth. He looked up at Savil, whose expression made him think that her insides were probably in knots. "You don't have to do this, you know," he reminded her. "You don't have to help."

"I know that," she replied, "but I'd worry myself to bits until you three finished this little exercise. I'd rather be in on it."

Vanyel nodded. "All right, then. Let's link."

He linked to Savil, while Starwind gathered Moondance in; familiar bonds to familiar. Then the two halves joined, forming a meld that was as close to seamless as anything Van had ever seen. It helped that the four of them had wielded magics as a group before; it also helped that their friendship was as close as it was. But what made this work was that all four of them had actually trained together. They would take turns as leader and supporters in this, and there was no room for temperament or pride.

Savil took the lead for the first part; invoking from the hilt and from the blood-soaked ground the mage's last moments.

The peaceful orchard and his companions vanished from Vanyel's sight. Now he approached a ring of Treesa's ladies, listening to Stefen's music, as if he rode upon the mage's shoulder, and Vanyel knew that the others were Seeing what he Saw. All of the stranger's surface thoughts were open to them for that time period. Savil froze the scene at the moment the mage had attacked Treesa and Stefen, and they read then what was uppermost in his mind.

Vanyel was so startled he nearly fell out of the link. The man he had captured in the Wood and this mage might just as well have been two entirely different people! Not only was *this* mage not crazed, but his attitudes were drastically different, as well as what could be read of his past history and training.

The mage had not known that Vanyel was home; he had deduced who Vanyel was quickly enough, but had entrapped him by pure accident. He had been assuming that he would trap Withen's house-mage; most nobles outside Valdemar had one, to weave protections for themselves and their interests. Since he hadn't detected any of the arcane protections that would have shown him Withen's house-mage had a Work Room, he had supposed that his enemy must be some kind of woods' witch, or hedge-wizard, to do all of his spellcasting out-of-doors. The Wood, with all of its residual magics, would have been perfect for that. So the stranger had waited, snare at the ready, for the first sign of spellcasting. He had expected to catch another hedge-wizard.

He had gotten Vanyel. This was rather akin to setting a trap for a sparrow and catching a firebird. The mental blow that knocked him unconscious had caught him completely by surprise.

So when he came to, he had done so behind a screen prepared for just such an occasion. He had retreated behind a disguise that had been created for him by another mage—just in case he had discovered that the one he intended to neutralize had been more powerful than he. This was the false persona whose thoughts Vanyel had skimmed, the madman who interpreted everything as an attack or a threat to himself.

At this point the stranger had still not known that he'd caught Vanyel; he had only thought that Withen's house-mage was far more skilled than he had guessed. It wasn't until Vanyel actually came into his line-of-sight that he had realized who and what had caught him.

That had been the spark of recognition Vanyel had seen. After that, the man buried himself even deeper beneath the false persona, deciding to fall back on his secondary plan.

That involved getting inside Forst Reach itself—and Vanyel played right into his hands by taking him to Father Tyler.

He'd waited for Vanyel to probe him more carefully, and had been relieved when Van was too preoccupied to see if there was anything behind the persona-screen. That made his job all the easier.

He had disposed of Father Tyler, and had gone looking for Treesa or Withen. He'd found out where they were by the simple expedient of asking a servant. Then he'd gone hunting.

The final thought Vanyel read as the mage prepared to launch the leech-blade at Treesa was that his master would be very pleased.

That was, maddeningly, all.

Savil tried to Read farther into the past than the moment of the attack, but once he was off Forst Reach lands, the mage had been screened and shielded, and there was nothing there to be Read. There was no image in the mage's mind connected with this "master"; he'd never seen the unknown mage in person. The "master" had only given him his orders, then given him the means to carry them out—*he* had set up the disguise-persona, had screened his servant against detection and back-Reading while off the Forst Reach lands, and had constructed the twin leech-blades for him.

The mage had only been a tool in the hands of someone bigger.

Vanyel shook off his disappointment, and began gently disengaging himself from the spell. Gradually the frozen scene faded from Mage-Sight and ordinary sight; then, with an abrupt, gut-wrenching shudder, it vanished completely, and Vanyel was back in the present, with a numb behind, and far too many unanswered questions.

He got up, breaking the circle, and stretched. He stood staring at the tree just in front of him for a while, trying to get everything he'd learned and everything he *hadn't* learned sorted out. When he turned around, Starwind was staring at him, a slight frown on his lips.

"You do realize what this attack means, do you not?" he said to Vanyel. "That you were vulnerable to the leech-blade was the purest accident; if you had been warded against magic the thing would have had no purchase upon you. Nevertheless, *you* were the target; the mage recognized you and knew that. He was to destroy you by indirect means, by destroying those you love. The one who sent him does not want to confront you—but does want you eliminated. This time the targets were to be Lady Treesa, Lord Withen, or both—hence the two blades."

"The protections I put on them won't hold against direct attacks," Savil admitted unhappily. "I can't stop an assassin. I don't think this is going to end with one attack, either, not with what I picked up. Van, I don't know what to say."

Vanyel sighed, and ran his fingers through his hair. "It's nothing I haven't anticipated, Savil. That's always been my worst fear, you know that. But if there is somebody, some powerful enemy of mine out there—where has he been all this time? What does he really want? And is he just *my* enemy, or is he Valdemar's enemy as well?"

Moondance stretched as Starwind clasped his shoulders and rubbed them absently. "This comes as quite a surprise to us as well, Wingbrother. We are reclusive, yes, but there are still signs of such a mage as this "master" seems to be which we should have detected long before this."

Vanyel offered Savil his hands to pull her to her feet. "Except that you have a peculiar blind spot, my friends," Savil, said, accepting the aid. "You never look outside your own territory. Even the *Shin'a'in* Clans work together, but you don't; each of your Clans operates on its own. That's your strength, but that's also your weakness."

"Strength or weakness, it matters not," Starwind said shortly. "The question is, how is Vanyel to ensure the continued safety of his parents? As you have pointed out, Wingsister, this is not going stop at one attack."

"There's only one thing I can do," Vanyel said. "Since I can't be where they are—"

"Get them to move to where you are." Savil shook her head. "I don't know, Van. That may be harder than getting yourself transferred to Forst Reach."

"That may be," Vanyel said grimly, "But it has to be done."

Dinner was a cold lump in Vanyel's stomach, and his weariness made the lamplight seem harsher than it really was.

". . . . I have no choice but to insist on this, Father," Vanyel concluded, clasping his hands around his ale mug, and staring at the surface of the table. "I know you never want to leave Forst Reach—and the gods know you never asked to have a Herald-Mage for a son. I'm asking this because I have to. I can't protect you, Savil can't protect you, Randale can't afford to keep a Herald here full-time to keep you safe; there aren't enough of them, and nothing less would do it. You could hire all the guards you wanted to; none of them would do any good against a mage. Hire a mage, and whoever this is will send a better one. This enemy of mine knows me very well, Father. If you or Mother died because of what I am—I—I'd never get over it." He looked up; at Withen's troubled face, and at Treesa's frightened one. "There's no help for it, Father. You'll have to take up the Council seat for this district and move to Haven. Everyone would be glad to see you in it, and

Lord Enderby never wanted it in the first place. You'd do a good job, and the Council could use your experience."

Treesa sighed happily and lost her fear instantly; *she* had wanted to move to Haven for years, ever since the last of her children wedded. "Oh, Withen," she said, her eyes sparkling, "You must! I've hoped for this for so long—"

Withen winced. "I think you mean you've hoped for a reason to make me go to the capital, and not that the reason would be that we're in danger otherwise!"

Treesa pouted. She'd recovered very quickly, showing a resilience that Moondance called "remarkable." "Of course that's what I meant! Withen, for all that you like to pretend that you're a plain and simple man, you've been running not only Forst Reach, but most of the county as well. And you very well know it. When something goes wrong, where's the first keep they go to? Here, of course. And it *isn't* to ask advice of Medren! I think Van is right; I think you'd make a fine Councillor."

Withen shook his head, and took a long drink of ale. "Ah, Treesa, I hate politics, you *know* that—and now you want me to go fling myself into them right up to the neck—"

Vanyel put his mug down. *I'm going to have to shock him into taking the seat, or he'll go, and pine away with boredom.* "Father, it's either that, or move to Haven *without* anything to do but sit around the Court all day and trade stories with the other spavined old war-horses," he said bluntly. "I was offering you an option that would give you something useful to do. You *are* going to Haven, whether or not you like it. I cannot afford to leave you here."

Withen bristled. "So I'm a spavined old war-horse, am I?"

Vanyel didn't rise to the bait. Withen expected him to try and back down, and he couldn't, not with so much riding on his persuading Withen that he was right. "In a sense, yes; you're too old to rejoin the Guard, even as a trainer. There's nothing else there for you. But that Council seat is crying for someone competent to fill it, and you *are* competent, you're qualified, and you won't play politics with Valdemar's safety at stake—and that puts you ahead of half the other Councillors, so far as I can see. And you, Father, are trying to change the subject."

Abruptly, Withen put his mug down and held up both hands in surrender. "All right, all right. I'll take the damned seat. But they'll get me as I am. No Court garb, no jewels and furbelows. Treesa can dress up all she likes, but I'm a plain man; I always have been, and I always will be."

Vanyel's shoulders sagged with relief. "Father, you can be anything you like; you'll be a refreshing change from some of the butterfly-brains we have on the Grand Council. Trust me, you won't be alone. There are two or three other old war-horses—no more 'spavined' than you, I might add—former Bordermen like you, who have pretty much the same attitudes. And I say, thank the gods for all of you."

Withen glowered. "I'm only going because you've got work for me," he said, grumbling. "Meke may think he runs Forst Reach, but Treesa's right: when there's trouble, it's me they all come to."

All the better for Meke, Vanyel thought. *Let him make his own mistakes and learn from them*.

But what he said was, "Then it's time to expand your stewardship, Father. More than time. I think you will serve Valdemar as well or better than you served Forst Reach."

He started to get up, when Withen's hand on his wrist stopped him. "Son," his father said, earnestly. "Did you really mean that about how you'd be hurt if something happened to your mother or me?"

"Father—" Vanyel closed his eyes, and sank back into his seat, swallowing an enormous lump in his throat. "Father, I would be devastated. I would be absolutely worthless. And somehow this mage knows that, which is why it's so important for you to be somewhere safe. Valdemar needs me, and needs me undamaged. And I need you. You're my parents, and I love you." He took a deep breath; what he was going to say was very hard, and it had cost him a lot of soul-searching. "I can't change the past, Father, but I can manage things better in the future. You've been very—good—about my relationship with Stef. If it would make you feel better, though, I'll see to it that he and I—don't see much of each other. That way you won't have—what I am—rubbed in your nose at Haven."

Withen flushed, and looked down at the table. "That's . . . that's very good of you, son. But I don't I want you to do that."

Vanyel bit his lip with surprise. "You don't? But—"

"You're my son. I tried to see to it that you learned everything I thought was important. Honor. Honesty. That there are things more important than yourself. It seems to

me you've been living up to those things." Withen traced
the grain of the table with a thick forefinger. "There's only
one way you ever disappointed me and—I don't know, Van,
but—it just doesn't seem that important when you stack it
up against everything else you've ever done. I don't see
where I'd have been any happier if you'd been like Meke.
I *might* have been worse off. Two blockheads in one family
is enough, I'd say."

Withen looked up for a moment, then back down at his
cup. "Anyway, what I'm trying to say is—is that I love you,
son. I'm proud of you. That youngster Stefen is a good-
hearted lad, and I'd like to think of him as one of the
family. If he'll put up with us, that is. I can understand why
you like him." Withen looked up again, met Vanyel's eyes,
and managed a weak grin. "Of course, I'll admit that
I'd have been a deal happier if he was a girl, but—he's
not, and you're attached to him, and any fool can see
he's the same about you. You've never been one to
flaunt yourself—" Withen blushed, and looked away again.
"I don't see you starting now. So—you and Stef stay the
way you are. After all these years, I guess I'm finally getting
used to the idea."

Vanyel's eyes stung; he wiped them with the back of his
hand. "Father—I—I don't know what to say—"

"If you'll forgive me, son, for how I've hurt you, I'll
forgive you," Withen replied. He shoved his seat away from
the table and held out his arms. "I haven't hugged you since
you were five. I'd like to catch up now."

"Father—"

Vanyel knocked over the bench, and stumbled blindly to
Withen's side of the table. "Father—" he whispered, and
met Withen's awkward embrace. "Oh, Father," he said into
Withen's muscular shoulder. "If you only knew how much
this means to me—I love you so much. I never wanted to
hurt you."

Withen's arms tightened around him. "I love you, too,
son," he said hesitantly. "You can't change what you are,
any more than I can help what I am. But we don't have to
let that get in the way any more, do we?"

"No, Father," Vanyel replied, something deep and raw
inside him healing at last. "No, we don't."

Thirteen

Ordinarily Stef would have been fascinated by the activities in the fields—he was city-born and bred, and the farmers at their harvest-work were as alien to him as the *Tayledras,* and as interesting. But Vanyel had been brooding, again, and finally Stef decided to ferret out the cause.

The road was relatively clear of travelers; with the harvest just begun, no one was bringing anything in to market. That, Savil had told Stef, would happen in about a week, when the roads would be thick with carts. This was really the ideal time to travel, if you didn't mind the late-summer dust and heat.

Stef didn't mind. But he *did* mind the way Van kept worrying at some secret trouble until he made both their heads ache.

And it seemed that the only way to end the deadlock would be if he said or did something to break it.

"Something's bothering you," Stefen said, when they were barely a candlemark from Haven. "It's *been* bothering you for the past two days."

He urged Melody up beside Yfandes, who obligingly lagged a little. Vanyel's lips tightened, and he looked away. "You won't like it," he said, finally.

Stef swatted at an obnoxious horsefly. "I don't like the way you've been getting all knotted up, either," he pointed out. "Whatever it is, I wish you'd just spit it out and get it over with. You're giving *me* a headache."

He eyed Savil, who was riding on Vanyel's right, hoping she'd get the hint. She raised one eyebrow at him, then held Kellan back, letting herself fall farther and farther behind until she was just out of earshot.

Though how much that means when she can read minds— Stef thought, then chided himself. *Oh, she wouldn't probe unless she had to. Heralds just don't do that to people, not*

205

*even Van comes into my mind unless I ask him. I've got to
get used to this, that they have powers but don't always use
them.* . . .

"It's you," Van said quietly, once Savil had withdrawn
her discreet twenty paces. "I'm afraid for you, Stef. The
way I was afraid for my parents, and for the same reason."
He shaded his eyes from the brilliant sun overhead, and
looked out over fields full of people scything down hay, but
Stef sensed he wasn't paying any attention to them. "I have
an enemy who doesn't want a direct confrontation, so he'll
strike at me through others. Once it's known that you and
I are lovers, he won't hesitate to strike at you."

*Gods. I was afraid I'd shocked or offended him. He's so—
virginal. And Kernos knows I'm not.* "Ah," Stefen said,
relieved. "I was hoping it was just something like that, and
not that—that I'd upset you or anything."

Vanyel turned to face him with an expression of complete
surprise. "Stef, you've just *had* a taste of what it's like to
be a target! How can you brush it off so lightly?"

"I'm not treating this lightly, but why are you bringing
your parents to Haven if it isn't safe there?" Stefen pointed
out with remorseless logic. "I thought that was the whole
idea behind making them move there."

Vanyel looked away from him, up the road ahead of
them.

It won't work, lover. You're never getting rid of me. Stefen
had already made up his mind to counter any argument Van
gave him, so he used Van's silence as an excuse to admire
his profile, the way his long, fine-boned hands rested on his
saddle-pommel, his perfect balance in the saddle. . . .

"It's safer," Vanyel said, after a strained silence. "That
doesn't mean it's safe. I don't want you hurt."

"I don't want to *be* hurt," Stefen said vehemently, then
laughed. "You keep thinking I'm like a Herald, that I'll go
throwing myself into danger the way you do. Look, Van, I
am *not* a hero! I promise you, I have a very high regard for
my skin! Bards are supposed to sing about heroes, not imitate them—there's no glory for a Bard in dying young, I
promise you. I'll tell you what; at the first sign—the *very*
first sign of trouble, I will most assuredly run for cover. I'll
hide myself either behind the nearest Guard or the nearest
Herald. Does *that* content you?"

"No," Vanyel said unhappily, "But I can't make you

leave me, and that's the only thing that would keep you safe."

"Damned right you can't," Stefen snorted. "There's *nothing* that would make me leave you, no matter what happened."

"I only hope," Vanyel said soberly, peering up the road at the gate in the city walls, "that nothing makes you eat those words."

"I only hope nothing makes you eat those words." Was it only a few months ago I said that? I knew it could come to this, but will he understand?

"I'm sorry, Stef."

Vanyel spoke with his back to the Bard, looking out the window of his room as he leaned against the windowframe; he couldn't bear to look at Stefen's face. He didn't know how Stef felt, though he expected the worst; he was so tightly shielded against leaking emotions that he couldn't have told if Stef was angry, unhappy, or indifferent. But he didn't expect Stef to understand; the Bard couldn't possibly understand how a Herald's duty could come ahead of anything else.

Maybe nothing would make you leave me, ashke, *but nobody said anything about me leaving you. And I don't have a choice.*

"I can understand why you have to go—you're the only real authority who can speak for the King. But why can't I go with you?" Stefen spoke softly, with none of the anger in his voice that Van had expected—but Stef was a Bard, and used to controlling his inflections.

"Because I'm going to Rethwellan. They don't like shaych there. Actually, that's an understatement. If you came with me, they'd probably drive us both across the Border and declare war on Valdemar for the insult, if—when—they found out about the two of us." Vanyel gripped the side of the window tightly. The beautiful late-autumn day and the garden beyond the open window were nothing more than a blur to him. "We need that treaty, and we need it now—and the Rethwellan ambassador specifically requested me as Randi's proxy. I want you with me, but my duty to Valdemar comes first. I'm sorry, Stef."

Arms around his shoulders made him stiffen with surprise. "So am I," Stefen murmured in his ear. "But you said it yourself; Valdemar comes first. How long will you be gone?"

Vanyel shook his head, not quite believing what he'd just heard. "You mean you don't mind?"

"Of *course* I mind!" Stef replied, some of the anger Van had expected before this in his voice. "How can I not mind? But if there's one thing a Bard knows, it's how Heralds think. I've known all along that if you had to make a choice between me and your duty, I'd lose. It's just the way you are." His arms tightened around Vanyel's chest. "I don't *like* it," he continued quietly, "but I also don't like it that you can speak directly to my mind and I can't do the same to yours, and I'm learning to live with that, too. And you didn't answer me about how long you think you'll be gone."

"About three months. It'll be winter when I get back." The silence lasted a bit too long for Van's comfort. He tried to force himself to relax.

Stefen slid his hands up onto Van's shoulders, and began gently massaging the tense muscles of his neck.

"I'll miss you," the Bard said, eventually. "You know I will."

"Stef—promise me you'll stay safe—" Van hung his head and closed his eyes, beginning to relax in spite of himself.

"I'm the safest person in the Kingdom, next to Randale," Stefen chuckled. "Frankly, I'm much more concerned with knowing that you'll keep *yourself* safe. And one other thing concerns me very deeply—"

"What's that?"

"How I'm going to make sure tonight is so memorable you come *running* back here when you've got the treaty," Stefen breathed into his ear.

If 'Fandes wasn't so bone-deep tired, Van thought through a fog of weariness and cold, *I'd ask her to run. Ah, well.*

Dull gray clouds were so low they made him claustrophobic; the few travelers on the road seemed as dispirited and exhausted as he was. Sleet drooled down as it had all day; the road was a slushy mire, and even the most waterproof of cloaks were soaked and near-useless after a day of it. Dirty gray snow piled up on either side of the road and made walking on the verge impossible. Van had stopped at an inn at nooning to dry off and warm up, and half a candle-mark after they started out again he might as well not have

bothered. Both he and Yfandes were so filthy they were a
disgrace to the Circle.

  :No one would be able to stay clean in this,: 'Fandes grumbled. *:How far are we? I've lost all track of distance. Gods,
I'm freezing.:*

  *:I think we're about two candlemarks out of Haven at this
pace,:* Vanyel told her.

  She raised her head, a spark of rebellion in her eye. *:To
the lowest hells with this pace,:* she said, shortly. *:I'm taking
a new way home.:*

  And with that, she pivoted on her hindquarters and
leaped over the mounds of half-thawed snow that fenced
the sides of the road. Vanyel tightened his legs around her
barrel and his grip on the pommel with a yelp of surprise.
He tried to Mindspeak her, but she wasn't listening. After
three tries, he gave up; there was no reasoning with her in
this mood.

  She ranged out about twenty paces from the road, then
threw her head up, her nostrils flaring. *:I thought so. This
is where the road makes that long loop to the south. I can
cut straight across and have us at the Palace gates in half a
candlemark.:*

  "But—" he began.

  Too late. She stretched her weary legs into a canter, then
a lope. She was too tired for an all-out run, but her lope
was as good as most horses' full gallop.

  "Look out!" Vanyel shouted. "—you're going through—"

  She leaped a hedge, and cut through a flock of sheep,
who were too startled by her sudden presence to scatter.
Something dark and solid-looking loomed up ahead of them
in the gusting sheets of thick sleet. She leaped again, clearing the hedge on the opposite side of the field; then lurched
and slipped on a steep slope. Vanyel clung to her back as
she scrambled down a cut, splashed through the ice-cold
creek at the bottom, and clambered up the other bank.

  Van gave up on trying to stop her, or even reason with
her, and hung on for dear life.

  The sleet thickened and became real snow; by now
Vanyel was so cold he couldn't even feel his toes, and his
fingers were entirely numb. Snow was everywhere; blown
in all directions, including up, by the erratic gusts of wind.
He couldn't see where Yfandes was going because of the
snow being blow n into his face; only the tensing of her

muscles told him when she was going to make another of
those bone-jarring jumps, into or out of someone's field,
across a stream, or even through a barnyard.

Finally she made another leap that ended with her hooves
chiming on something hard. Presumably pavement; she
halted abruptly, ending in a short skid, and he was thrown
against the pommel of his saddle before he could regain his
balance. When he looked up, the walls of the city towered
over them both, and here in the lee of the walls the wind
was tamed to a faint breath. Already snow had started to
lodge in the tiny crevices between the blocks of stone, creating thin white lines around each of them.

She moved up to the gate at a sedate walk, bridle bells
chiming cheerfully as a kind of ironic counterpoint to her
tired pacing.

The Guard at the gate started to wave them through,
then took a second look and halted them just inside the
tunnel beneath the walls, with a restraining hand on Yfandes' bridle. This tunnel, sheltered from the wind and snow,
felt warm after the punishing weather outside.

Vanyel raised his head tiredly. "What—" he began.

"You're not goin' past me in *that* state, Herald," growled
the guard, a tough-looking woman who reminded Van of his
own sister, Lissa. "Old man like you should know better than
to—"

Old man? He shook his head so that his hood fell back,
and she stopped in midsentence, her mouth falling open.

"If there were any flies to catch," he said, with tired good
humor, "you'd be making a frog envious."

She shut her mouth with an audible snap.

"Beg your pardon, milord Vanyel," she said stiffly. "Just
saw the white in your hair, and—"

"You did quite right to stop me, my lady," he replied
gently. "I'm obviously not thinking, and it's from cold and
exhaustion. We're far from infallible—*someone* had better
watch out for us. Now what were you planning on doing
with me—aside from telling me what a fool I was to be out
in this muck?"

"I was goin' to give you a blanket to wrap up in," she
said hesitantly. "Make you take off that soggy cloak. Gods,
milord, it looks like you're carryin' half the road-muck
'twixt here and the Border on you."

"I think we are, but the Palace isn't far, and that's where

we're heading," he said. "I think we can make it that far."
He managed a real smile, and she smiled back uncertainly.

"If you say so, milord." She took her hand off Yfandes'
rein, and stepped aside; he rode back out into the cold and
snow.

But at least within the city walls they were sheltered from
the wind. And it wasn't that far to the Palace. . . .

He must have blanked out for a while; a common enough
habit of his, when he knew he was in relatively safe, but
uncomfortable surroundings—riding on a patrolled road in
the dead of winter, or waiting out an ambush in the pouring
rain, for instance. The next thing he knew, he was in the
dry and heated warming shed beside the stable; one of the
grooms was at his stirrup, urging him to dismount.

:'Fandes?: he queried.

She turned her head slowly to stare at him, blinking. *:Oh.
We're home. I must have—:*

*:You did the same thing I did; the minute we crossed inside
the city we went numb. Get some rest, love. I'm going to do
the same as soon as I make my report.:*

"Get her closer to the heat," he told the groom, dismounting with care for his bruises. The warming shed was
heated by a series of iron stoves, and on very cold nights,
the door into the stable would be left open so that the heat
would carry out into the attached building. "Get her dry,
give her a thorough grooming, then a hot mash for her
supper."

:Bless you.:

"Put two blankets on her, and take that tack away. It
needs a complete overhaul." He took the saddlebags from
the cantle and threw them over his shoulder, mud and all.

"Anything else, milord?" the groom asked, eyes wide
with surprise at his state.

"No," Vanyel said, and dredged up another smile.
"Thank you. I'm a little short on manners. I think they
froze somewhere back about a candlemark ago."

:Where are you going?: Yfandes asked, as she was being
led away.

:To my room long enough to change, then to report,: he
told her. *:Check with the others and tell me if Randi's holding Audience today, would you?:*

:He is,: she replied immediately. *:Stef's with him.:*

:Good. Thank you. Go get some rest, you deserve it.: He

found a little more energy somewhere, and quickened his steps toward the door.

:*So do you, but you won't take it,*: she replied with resignation. Van sent her a tired but warm mental hug.

He strode out into the snow, which was coming down so thickly now that it completely hid the Palace from where he stood. :*I'll take it, love. Later. Randi's good hours are too rare to waste, and I have too much to report.*:

He was afraid; afraid of what he'd find when he saw Randale, afraid that Treven was not going to be able to cope with so many duties thrust on him so young, afraid that Shavri was going to fall apart at any moment—

Yes, and admit it. Afraid Stef's lost interest. That's what is really eating at you. He shivered, and forced himself to walk a little faster, as the snow coated him with a purer white than his uniform cloak was capable of showing just now.

The stable-side door opened just before he reached it, and someone pulled him inside, into warmth and golden light from the oil lamp mounted in the doorframe.

It took Vanyel a moment to recognize him; not because Tantras had changed, but because his numb memory couldn't put name and face together.

"Tran—" he croaked. *Ye gods, I doubt I'd recognize my own mother in this state.*

"Give me that cloak," Tantras said briskly, unfastening the throat-latch himself. "Delian has been watching for you two for days; as soon as he saw how mind-numb you were, he called me. There." The cloak fell from Van's shoulders, landing in a sodden heap on the floor. "Good. There isn't a lot of time to spare; Randi's Audiences rarely last more than a candlemark or two even with Stef to help. Come in here—"

He pulled Vanyel into a storage-chamber. There was a small lantern here on a shelf, and a set of Whites beside it. "Strip, and put these on," Tantras ordered. "What do you need out of your saddlebags?"

"Just the dispatch cases," Vanyel said, pulling at the lacings of his tunic, with hands that felt twice their normal size.

"I take it that you did all right?" Tantras pulled out the pair of sealed cases and laid them on the shelf where the uniform had been.

"It wasn't easy, but yes, I got the treaty Randi wanted." He had to peel his breeches off, they were so soaked. Tran handed him a towel, and he dried himself off, then wrapped it around his dripping hair before he began pulling on the new set of breeches. "Queen Lythiaren—gods, that's a mouthful!—has only heard rumors of what we are and what we can do. Heralds, I mean. She isn't familiar with Mind-magic; the very idea that someone could pick up their thoughts and feelings frightens most of the people of Reth-wellan. I spent about as much time undoing rumor as I did at the bargaining table. But it's over, and I must say, it's a good thing Randi sent *me,* because I'll tell you the truth, I don't think anyone else has the peculiar combination of Gifts that would have let them pull it off."

"Your reputation doesn't hurt, either," Tran observed wryly.

Vanyel pulled the tunic over his head—one of Tran's and much too loose, but that wouldn't matter. He began towel-ing his hair, still talking. "That's true, though it almost did more harm than good. That's why I got out of there before the passes snowed up. I make them all very uneasy, and they were very happy to see my back."

"Here're your dispatches," Tran said, handing the cases to him as he ran his fingers through his hair to achieve a little order. "I'll take the rest of your stuff back to your room. And Randi looks like hell, so be prepared."

Vanyel took the twin blue-leather cases from his friend, and hesitated a moment. He wanted to say something, but wasn't certain what.

"Go," Tran said, holding open the door with one hand while he grabbed the lantern with the other. "You haven't got any time to waste."

Just how much worse can Randi have gotten in three months? he wondered, forcing tired legs into a brisk walk. The corridors were deserted; in fact, the entire Palace had an air of disuse about it. It was disquieting in the extreme, especially for someone who remembered these same corri-dors full of courtiers and servants, the way they had been in Elspeth's time. It was as if an evil spirit had made off with all the people, leaving the Palace empty, populated by memories.

The Throne Room was mostly empty; no sycophants, no curious idlers, only those who had business with Randale.

Hardly more than twenty people, all told, and all of them
so quiet that Van clearly heard Stef playing up at the front
of the room. At first Van couldn't see Randale at all; then
someone moved to one side, and Van got his first look at
the King in three months.

With a supreme effort of will he prevented himself from
crying out and running to Randale's side. Randale *had*
changed drastically since summer.

It wasn't so much a physical change as something less
tangible. Randale looked frail, as fragile as a spun-glass
ornament. There was a quality of transparency about him;
he could easily have been a *Tayledras* ice-sculpture, the kind
they made for their winter-festivals, but one of a creature
other than a man. One of the Ethereal Plane *Varrir*,
perhaps.

That was, perhaps, the most frightening thing of all. Randale no longer looked quite human. Everything that was
nonessential had been burned away or discarded in the past
three months; he held to life by nothing less than sheer will.
There was something magnificent about him; Vanyel would
never have believed that poor, vacillating Randi, Randale
who had never wanted to be King, could have metamor-
phosed into this creature of iron spirit and diamond
determination.

He's holding on until Treven is ready, Van thought,
watching as Randale listened carefully to the messenger
from the Karsite Border. *He won't let go until Trev can
handle the job. But that's all that's keeping him. I wonder if
he realizes that?*

Shavri bent over him and touched his shoulder. He raised
a colorless hand to cover hers, without taking his eyes or
his attention away from the messenger. Vanyel Felt the
strength flowing from her to him, and realized something
else. Shavri was as doomed as Randi. She had, out of love,
done the one thing no Healer ever did—she'd opened an
unrestricted channel between them. She was giving him
everything she had—they would burn out together, because
she no longer had any way to stop that from happening.

She knew what she'd done; she *had* to. Which meant that
was what she wanted.

*Neither of them knows what the other is hiding. Randi
doesn't know the channel Shavri opened is unrestricted; Shavri doesn't know how little Randi has left. I should tell*

them—but I can't. I can't. Let them keep their secrets. They have so little else except love.

Joshel beckoned to Van as the messenger bowed in response to something Randale said. Vanyel forced himself to walk briskly to the foot of the throne, as if he'd just come in from a pleasure ride. Randale was focused entirely on what came immediately before him; too focused to read past any outward seeming of well-being, if Van chose to enforce that kind of illusion. Which was precisely what Vanyel intended to do.

"Majesty," he said quietly, "your business with Rethwellan is successfully concluded." He handed the dispatch tubes to Joshel, who opened them and handed them to the Seneschal. "Here is your treaty, my King; exactly what you requested I negotiate for. Mutual defense pact against Karse, extradition of criminals, provision for aid in the event of an attack, it's all there."

Plus a few more things the Queen and I worked out. He watched as the Seneschal scanned each page and handed it on to Randale; noted with tired satisfaction the surprised smiles as they came to the clauses he had gotten inserted into the document. It was a *good* treaty, fair to both sides. The rulers of Karse would have a rude awakening when they found out about this particular agreement.

He was proudest of the fact that he had negotiated the agreement despite having no formal training as a diplomat. Everything he knew, he'd picked up from Joshel or the Seneschal.

Randale knew that, and his smile showed that he realized the value of Van's accomplishment. "Well done, old friend," he said, in a breathless voice that told Van how much each word cost him in effort. "I couldn't have asked for more. I wouldn't have thought to ask for some of the things you got for us. I'm tempted to ask you to give up mage-craft in favor of politics."

"Oh, I think not, my liege," Vanyel said lightly. "I am far too honest. This is one situation where honesty was an asset, but that's usually not the case in politics."

Randale laughed, a pale little ghost of a chuckle, and leaned back into the padded embrace of his throne. "Thank you, Vanyel. I'm sure the Council will want to go over this with you in detail shortly, and I'd appreciate it if you'd brief Trev on how to handle the Queen."

This was clearly a dismissal, and Vanyel bowed himself out. He left the Throne Room entirely; he couldn't bear to see anything more of what Randale had become. Joshel followed him out into the corridor.

"I know you're exhausted, Van, but we need to convene the Privy Council on this and the Karse situation right away—" The haggard young Herald paused, concern for Vanyel warring with the needs of the moment, and the conflict evident in his expression.

"It's all right, Joshe," Van told him. "The Council room is warm, and that's what I need most right now. I'm cold right down to my marrow."

"Can you go there now? I can get pages to bring everyone there in next to no time." Joshe's relief was so plain that Van wondered what else had gone wrong in his absence.

"Certainly," he replied. "Provided that no one minds that I look like a drowned cat."

"I doubt they'll mind," Joshel said, "We've got other things to worry about these days. They'd take you looking like a stablehand covered with muck, you're that important."

Frustration and anguish inside Vanyel exploded into words. "Important? Dammit, Joshe, what's the use of all this? I can level a building with the power I control, but I can't do anything for a friend who's dying in front of my eyes!"

Joshel sighed. "I know. I have to keep telling myself that it isn't Randi that we're working to preserve, it's Valdemar. Most of the time, it doesn't help."

"What good is having power if you can't use it the way it needs to be used?" Vanyel asked, his hand clenched into a fist in front of him. "I'm Vanyel Demonsbane, and I can't even keep my parents safe in their own home, much less keep Randi alive."

Joshe just shook his head; Vanyel could Feel the same anguish inside him, and unclenched his fist. "I'm sorry, Van. I wish I knew some answers for you. I should tell you one thing more before the Council meeting. The Heraldic Circle met today, and we're promoting Trev to full Whites."

Vanyel felt the news like a blow to the stomach. To promote Treven so young could only mean one thing—the King had to be a full Herald, and the ForeSeers did not see

Randale living through the next two years it would ordinarily take Treven to make his Whites.

Joshe nodded at Vanyel's expression. "You know what that means as well as I do," he said, and turned back to the door to the Throne Room.

Van walked the few steps down the corridor to the Council Chamber. Unlike the rest of the Palace, this room looked, and felt, as if it were in use. Heavy use, from the look of all the papers and maps stacked neatly about, and the remains of a meal on a tray beside the door. Here, then, was where the business of the Crown was being transacted, and not the Throne Room. Evidently Audiences were just for those things Randale had to handle personally, or for edicts that needed to come from the lips of the Sovereign in order to have the required impact.

This treaty, obviously, was one of those things, which was why Tran had hustled him into the Throne Room. Randale was probably signing it now, with what there was of the Court as witness, which made it binding from this moment on.

Van took his usual seat, then slouched down in it and put his feet up on the one beside it. *If Stef hasn't had a change of heart while I was gone, I could certainly use a massage,* he thought wistfully. The fire in the fireplace beside him burned steadily, and the generous supply of wood beside it argued that it had become normal practice to keep the Council Chamber ready for use at a moment's notice. That was in keeping with the rest of Van's observations, so it meant that the business of the Kingdom was being conducted at any and all hours.

After being told of Treven's promotion, he wasn't surprised when the door behind him creaked open, and Treven eased into the room, wearing a brand-new set of Whites.

The youngster sat down in the chair beside Vanyel with an air of uncertainty, as if he didn't know what his welcome would be. Van watched him through half-closed eyes for a moment, then smiled.

"Ease up, Trev. We're still friends. I've come to the conclusion that you and Jisa did the right thing."

The young man relaxed. "We've managed to convince Randale and Shavri, too," he said. "Though Jisa and her mother came awfully close to a real fight over it. I'm still not sure how I kept them from each other's throats. Early training for diplomatic maneuvering, I guess." He adjusted the fit of his white belt self-consciously.

"Feeling uncomfortable about that?" Van asked, gesturing at the white tunic.

Treven nodded. "I hadn't expected it quite so suddenly. I don't feel exactly like I've earned it. It feels like a cheat. And—and I don't like getting it because—because—"

The young Herald hung his head.

"I understand," Vanyel said. "I'd think less of you if you didn't have doubts, Trev. I'll give you my honest opinion, if you want it."

Treven grimaced. "Lady bless, that sounds like a bitter pill! Still—yes, I think so. At least I'd know what to measure myself against."

Vanyel took his feet off the chair, and straightened his aching back before facing Treven. The young man's honest blue eyes met his fearlessly, and Vanyel felt a moment of satisfaction. There weren't many people who could meet his gaze.

"I think you were rushed into this, Trev, and we both know why. No, I don't think you're ready—quite. I think you will be when you have to be, if you don't let that uniform fool you into thinking the Whites make the Herald."

Treven looked disappointed, and Vanyel knew he'd been hoping to be told—despite Van's warning that this would be an honest opinion—that he really was ready to be called a full Herald.

In some ways Treven was a boy still, and that had something to do with what Van had told him. He had a boy's optimism and a boy's belief in the essential fairness of the universe. This wouldn't have been a problem in an ordinary Herald—but neither belief had any place in the thinking of a Monarch. A King never assumed anything was fair; a ruler must always expect the worst and plan for it.

Treven would learn, as Randale had learned. As Jisa had learned.

As if his thought had summoned her, Vanyel felt Jisa's presence before she entered, the little mind-to-mind brush that was the Mindspeaker's equivalent of a knock.

:Hello, love,: he replied. *:Holding on?:*

:As well as I can,: she replied. *:You saw.:*

So, she hadn't missed what her mother had done, binding herself to her lifebonded's fate. And she wasn't blinded to

Randale's condition by her love of him. There was resignation in her mind-voice, and a sadness as profound as if her parents were already gone.

:They've closed me out,: she said, in answer to the questions he couldn't bring himself to ask. *:They've closed everyone out except each other. Most of the time I could be a thousand miles away, for all they notice I'm there.:*

:Well, I notice you're here. Come on in.:

The door behind him creaked again, and Treven looked up and smiled. Vanyel started to get up, but Jisa pushed him back down into his chair with her hands on his shoulders.

"No you don't, Uncle Van. There's enough Healer in me to know how tired you are." She kissed him on the top of his head, and Sent *:Treven doesn't know, Father. I don't see any reason why he has to.:*

:Thank you, dearheart.: "I won't deny you're right. Are you part of the Council now, too?"

She sat down beside Treven. "Both of us; I'm here as Mother's proxy. I have been ever since late fall."

"And doing very well at it, too." Jisa had left the door open, and the rest of the Council filed in, taking their usual seats. The Seneschal had said that last, and he stopped on the way to his seat at the head of the table, pausing with his hands on the back of Jisa's chair. His inflection told Vanyel he meant the compliment; there was nothing paternalistic or condescending in his voice. "I frankly don't know what we would have done without her earlier this fall; We had a situation with someone who claimed to be a high-ranking Karsite refugee. We suspected his motives, but he was shielded against casual Thought-sensing, and we didn't want to tip our hands by probing him. We badly needed someone whose Gift was Empathy—"

"But Mother was exhausted and in any case, wouldn't leave Father," Jisa said matter-of-factly. "So I went. He was a spy for the Prophet, sent to see if we were giving aid to their mages. It's hard to mistake fanatic devotion for anything else."

"That was when we put her on the Council," the Seneschal said, taking his seat. "And that brings us around to the Karsite situation."

The situation, so Seneschal Arved told them, was stalemate. The followers of the Prophet had won, and were consolidating their victory. As yet they had shown no signs of resuming the war the previous regime had begun—but they had also been probing to see if Valdemar had been aiding mages, or were offering aid to those who continued to evade the "witchfinders."

"They're just looking for an excuse to start things up again when they're ready," said the representative for the South, Lord Taving, with a sour grimace.

"I'm inclined to agree," Vanyel's father replied. "You know what they say: 'Nothing comes out of Karse but brigands and bad weather.' Whether they say their cause is for their god or for their greed, the Karsites always have been robbers and always will be."

Lord Taving looked gratified to find someone who shared his basic feelings toward Karse. "The only problem is, we're still in no shape to fight a war," he said, "or at least that's my understanding."

"You are correct, my lord," the Lord Marshal said. "Thanks to Vanyel's suggestions, we haven't had to resort to conscription, but our new Guards are still green as new leaves, and if faced with troops of seasoned fanatics they wouldn't stand a chance."

"And why aren't they ready?" asked Guildmaster Jumay. "Zado knows we pay enough in taxes!"

"Largely because we've already lost more men to this war with Karse than in the whole of Elspeth's reign!" the Lord Marshal shot back heatedly.

"Which is why the treaty Vanyel brought back from Rethwellan is vital," the Seneschal said, pouncing on the opportunity to introduce the subject.

The rest of the Councillors—who had not been at the Audiences—reacted according to their natures. Lord Taving was not inclined to trust anything South of Valdemar's Border. Withen wanted to know where the catch was. The Lord Marshal heaved an audible sigh of relief, until he realized the thing included a mutual assistance pact.

Vanyel explained the details of the treaty at length until his head ached, pointing out the ones Randale had requested and the ones he had gotten inserted. They finally agreed that it was an excellent treaty as it stood—which was just as well, since Randale had already signed it.

When they finally let him go, it was clear that they were already preparing for Randale's death and a period in which

Treven would be just one of the Council when it came to decision-making. Which was a good idea—but it brought home the fact that Randi's days were numbered, and probably less than a year.

He returned to his room very depressed, and paused outside the door for a moment to think where Stefen might be.

Then the door opened under his hand—

"I'm glad you're back," Stef said simply, and took his hand to pull him inside.

Fourteen

Stefen had been waiting for Van ever since the Audience session ended. He'd come straight to Vanyel's room once Randale had been put to bed. He'd had a page bring food and wine, and had gotten everything set up exactly like the supper he'd had with Vanyel the first night the Herald had brought him to this room. Except tonight he expected the end of the evening to be somewhat different.

He'd known Van was expected back at any time, but no one had been able to tell him exactly when the Herald would arrive, so he'd been as nervous and excited as a kid waiting for Festival for the past week.

When Van had made his presentation at the Audiences, even though he'd been in trance, Stef had known he was there. He had thought his heart was going to pound itself to pieces with joy. To stay in trance until Randale had no further need of him had been the hardest thing Stefen had ever done.

"I'm glad you're back," Stefen said simply, letting his voice tell Vanyel exactly how glad he really was. "I've missed you." He reached behind Vanyel and closed the door.

"I've missed you," Vanyel said, then unexpectedly pulled the Bard into his arms for an embrace with more of desperation in it than passion. Stef just held him, not entirely sure what had prompted the action, but ready to give Vanyel whatever he needed. Behind him, the fire crackled and popped, punctuating the silence.

Finally Van let him go. "I was afraid once I was gone you'd find someone who suited you better," he said hoarsely.

"We've lifebonded," Stef reminded him, pulling the Herald into the room and getting him to sit in the chair nearest the fireplace. "How could I find anybody who suited me better than that? That's not something that goes away just because there's some distance between us."

Vanyel laughed weakly. "I know, I was being stupid. It's just that in the middle of the night, when you're leagues and leagues away from me, it's hard to see why you'd choose to stay with me." Stefen reached for the food since Van was ignoring it, and poured some wine for him.

"You're still being stupid," Stef said, and put bread and cheese in one hand, and a mug of hot mulled wine in the other. "Eat. Relax. I love you. There, see? Everything's all right." He sat in the chair opposite Vanyel, and glared at him until he took a bite.

"I wish it could be that simple," Vanyel sighed, but he smiled a little when he said it. He ate what Stef gave him, then sipped at his wine, watching Stefen, his strange silver eyes gone dark and thoughtful.

"I have a surprise for you," Stef said, unable to bear the silence anymore. He got up, went to the desk, and took out the box he'd put there earlier. "I left it here in case you came back to your room before I got done. Here—"

He thrust it into Vanyel's hands and waited, hardly breathing, for the Herald to open it.

Vanyel turned the catch on the simple wooden box, saying as he did so, "You didn't have to do this—you don't have to give me things, Stef—" The lid came open, and he saw what nestled in the velvet and his mouth opened in a soundless "oh."

He took it out, his hands trembling a little. He'd told Stef once or twice that he was hampered in his mage-craft by not having a good focus-stone. The mineral he worked best with was amber, which wasn't particularly rare, but he had a problem similar to his aunt Savil's. For mage-work, the clearer and less flawed the stone, the better it focused power. And amber rarely appeared totally clear and without inclusions. When it did—it was expensive. Since the loss of his first focus-stone a few years ago, Van had never again found a piece even in the raw state that was flawless and large enough to be of use. Flaws in a stone could make it disintegrate or even explode when stressed by magic energies.

So, like Savil, Vanyel had to do most of the work that required a focus through his secondary stone, an egg-shaped piece of tiger-eye.

Stefen's present was a faceted half-globe of completely flawless, water-clear, dark gold-red amber, set in a thin silver band with a loop at the top so that it could be worn as a pendant. He'd begged a silver chain of Jisa just so that Van could wear it immediately. Jisa had given one to him without asking why, but when he'd told her, she'd been as pleased as if the gift had been for her.

"Stefen," Van said in a strange, strained voice. "You have to tell me. Where—and more importantly, *how*—did you get this?"

"I didn't steal it!" Stef exclaimed, stung.

"I didn't think you did, love—but there's no ordinary way *you* could afford something like this, and we both know it." Vanyel put the pendant back in the box and closed it. "I can't in good conscience wear this until I know."

He thinks I sold my bed-time for it, Stef thought suddenly. *Oh, gods—I have to put him right.*

"I met this gem-merchant," he said quickly. "He was giving some of the ladies I was playing for a private showing; amber, pearls, and coral, really unusual things, but he says he's been all over the world at one time or another. Anyway, he had this and I saw it, and he saw me looking at it. He told me it would be useless to me, that it was made to be a mage-focus . . . well, we got to talking, and I told him I wanted it for you, even though I knew I couldn't afford it."

He remembered what the merchant had told him, too: "What, a Bard like you? Gods, my friend, in my country you'd have been showered with baubles like this a thousand times over. A Gift such as yours is rarer than all my collection put together."

Then the merchant's face had grown thoughtful. "On the other hand, perhaps we could do each other a service. . . ."

"So anyway, he offered to give me the stone if I'd do him a favor. He had some more private showings planned, at the house he'd rented, for fellow gem-merchants. He said they were a lot harder to convince than pretty ladies and he wanted me to play for them—"

He faltered, for Vanyel was looking at him in a way that made him feel as if he *had* sold himself. "—he didn't ask me to do anything like make them buy things. Just to put them in a pleasant mood; make them feel good, and allow him to drop the fact that I was the King's Bard to impress them. That was all! I didn't do anything wrong!"

Vanyel was still looking at him doubtfully.

"Did I?" he asked, in a very small voice.

The Herald weighed the box in his hand. Stefen felt worse with every passing moment. He'd intended this to be a love-offering, and instead the thing had turned into a viper and bitten them both.

Finally Van opened the box, and took the amber out. Stef heaved a sigh of relief. Vanyel stared at the beautiful thing, and shook his head. "You didn't do anything wrong—but only by accident and the fact that I don't think your friend wanted you to get into trouble," he said, in a low voice. "You came so close to misuse of your powers that I shudder to think about it. You must *never* use your Gift to manipulate people except at the orders of the Crown, Stef. You can be stripped of it, if you do. And it's wrong, Stef, it's just plain wrong. What if this man had been unscrupulous, and had been trying to sell trash—and what if he'd actually asked you to influence people to buy? What if he'd drastically overpriced his wares and asked you to make them think he was giving them a bargain? What if he'd brought in those who couldn't afford his merchandise and told you to make them want it enough to buy it no matter what?"

"Stop!" Stef cried, horribly ashamed of himself. Now he almost wished he *had* sold himself; it seemed more honest.

"Stef—"Vanyel caught his hand and drew him down beside his chair. "Stef, I didn't want to make you feel bad. You *didn't* do any of those things; you didn't misuse your powers. But it was a very near thing. You can thank that merchant for being an honest fellow, and *not* leading you into temptation."

Stefen vowed silently to *think* about what he was being asked to do before he did it. And he marveled a little at this change in himself. A year ago he would have done any of those things, and never considered them wrong.

"Van," he said quietly, "Being with you . . . you've shown me that it's as wrong to play with peoples' minds and emotions as it is to steal—" He hesitated a moment, then added, "In a way, it *is* stealing from them. It's stealing their right to think and feel at their own will. I wouldn't have understood that before I met you, but I do now."

Vanyel relaxed completely, and closed his hand around the amber half-globe. "Then I can wear this, Stef, and I will, gladly, and I'll use it knowing it was a gift of love *and* honor." He bowed his head and chuckled. "I suppose that sounds rather pretentious and pompous, like something out of a ballad—but it's how I really feel, Stef."

"If you thought any differently, you wouldn't be Vanyel," Stef replied, flushing happily as Van pulled the chain over his head and laid his right hand on Stef's shoulder.

"You give me too much credit, lover," Vanyel said quietly. "I'm as prone to being a fool as anyone else. And just now, I'm a very sore fool. Could I possibly get you to use those talented hands of yours to unknot my shoulders?"

"And give me a chance to have my hands on you?" Stef grinned. "Of course you could, and I will. Gladly."

Vanyel finished off his wine in a single gulp, peeled off his tunic, kicked off his boots, and sagged back into his chair. Stefen got up and moved around behind him, and began kneading his shoulders with steady, firm pressure.

"What's wrong, Van?" he asked. "You just got back with everything the King asked you for and more."

"Sometimes I feel like everything I've done is useless," Vanyel said dispiritedly. "Randi is going to be dead before the year's out, every enemy Valdemar has will take that as a signal to strike while Treven is so young, and a good half the treaties we made will fall apart, because they were made with Randale and not Trev. Karse is likely to declare holy war on us any day. The West is full of half-mad mage-born, any one of whom might be another Krebain, but with wider plans. I have a personal enemy out there somewhere; I don't know who or why, only that he, she, or it is a mage."

Stefen dug his thumbs into Vanyel's shoulders a little harder and tried to think of things to say that would make a difference. "Randale is the mind behind the Crown, but about half of the work is being done by Trev and the Council," he offered. "Trev's bright, especially on short-term planning, and Randale's doing long-range planning that ought to hold good for the next five years. Trev's a little too idealistic, maybe, but he'll get that knocked out of him soon enough—and Jisa is practical enough for two. They'll be all right."

"How do *you* know so much about this?" Vanyel asked suddenly, after a long silence.

"I'm right there whenever Randale is working, and I'm beginning to be able to listen to what's going on while I'm in trance." Stefen was rather proud of that. It wasn't much compared with the kinds of things Vanyel could do, but it was more than he'd been able to manage before Van's trip.

"That's pretty impressive," Vanyel told him, without even a trace of patronization. "Bards usually don't have a Gift that requires being in trance, and I'm surprised you learned how to manage that on your own. What about Jisa and Trev?"

"I spent a lot of time with them after you'd gone," Stef replied, working on Van's neck, flexing and stroking as though he were playing an instrument. The muscles were very stiff, so tight they were like rope under tension, and Stef had no doubt they were giving Van a headache of monumental proportions. "With Jisa especially. The Seneschal is the only one who doesn't underestimate her, and he likes it that way."

"A very wise lady," Vanyel said, his voice a little muffled. "Did you know she's my daughter, and not Randi's?"

It should have been a shock. Somehow it wasn't. "No. But it makes sense. She's very like you, you know." He thought about the situation for a moment. "Obviously Randale must know; I mean, a Healer like Shavri can prevent any pregnancy she cares to, so it wasn't an accident, which means she *wanted* Jisa. . . ."

"Shavri was desperate for a child, and the two of them asked me to help. I've never told anyone but you, not even my parents," Van replied. "I have three other children. but the only one I ever see is Brightstar, the boy Starwind and Moondance are raising. The others are a mage-Gifted girl one of the other *Tayledras* has, named Featherfire, and a girl two of Lissa's retired shaych Guards are raising, who has no Gifts at all so far as I can tell."

Stefen wasn't sure how he should be feeling about these revelations. "Why?" he asked finally. "I mean, why did you do it? I can see why Shavri would have asked *you*, rather than somebody else, but why the others?"

Vanyel sighed, and flexed his shoulders. "For pretty much the same reasons as Shavri had. People I knew and cared for wanted a child, but for one reason or another couldn't produce one without outside help. Featherfire's mother isn't shaych, but there wasn't a single *Tayledras*

male she felt the right way about to have a child with. She
had twins; Brightstar is Feather's brother."

Stef recalled all the fantasies he'd had about his parent-
age, how he'd never known who even his mother was. "Do
you ever wish you'd—I don't know, had more of a hand in
their raising?" He worked his thumbs into the nape of
Vanyel's neck, with the silky hair covering both hands. "I
know they've got parents who really want them, but—"

"That's just it; they have parents who really *want* them,"
Van replied. "Ah, that's it, that's the worst of the aches,
right there. I see what 'Fandes means about musicians having talented hands. Really, love, the only reason Brightstar
and Jisa know I'm their father is that it's necessary for them
to know. Brightstar evidently has all my Gifts; Jisa could
get backwash from a magical attack on me, because she has
Mage-Gift in potential. They have to be prepared. Featherfire is so like her mother they could be twins, and Arven
doesn't even carry potential as far as I was able to check.
They all know who their *real* parents are—the ones who
love them."

. He chuckled then. "What's funny?" Stef asked.

"Oh, just that whatever it is that makes someone *shaych*,
it probably isn't learned *or* inherited. Brightstar has a half
dozen young ladies of the *Tayledras* with whom he trades
feathers on a regular basis, and he'd probably have more if
he had the stamina."

"Trades feathers?" Stef said with puzzlement.

"*Tayledras* custom. When you want to make love to
someone you offer them a feather. If you want a more permanent relationship, it's a feather from your bondbird."

"Oh." That gave his fertile imagination something to
work on. And feathers were easier come by in the dead of
winter than, say, flowers. . . .

Van was finally relaxing under his hands. In fact, from
the way his head kept nodding, the Herald was barely
awake. Which meant Stef could probably coax him into bed
without too much trouble.

Of course, he may not get much sleep. Stefen sighed con-
tentedly, and slowly ran his fingers through Vanyel's hair,
grateful just for his lover's presence.

Van relaxed for the first time in three months, and gave
himself over completely to the gentle strength of Stef's cal-

lused hands. Stef felt the cold more than most—he was so thin it went straight to his bones—so he'd built the fire up to the point where *he* was comfortable. That meant that even without his tunic, Van basked in drowsy warmth.

The mage-focus glowed just above his heart, touching him with a different sort of warmth. That piece of amber was truly extraordinary. It might have been made for him, fitting into his cupped hand perfectly, meshing with his power-patterns and channeling them with next to no effort on his part. Given how things had worked out, perhaps it had been; in the same way that the rose-quartz crystal he'd given Savil years ago had seemingly been made for her, though it had been given to him.

He'd told Stef the truth, though; if the Bard had bought the thing with the dishonorable coin, he couldn't have worn it. If Stef had failed to realize *why* that kind of perversion of his Gift was wrong, Vanyel would have had misgivings every time he put it on.

Stef had changed, though Van had never tried to change him. He'd become a partner, someone Van could rely on, despite his youth. *And because he's my partner, he had to know about Jisa and the others. Partners shouldn't have secrets from one another. That information could be important some day. It's good to be able to tell someone—especially him. . . .*

It was so easy to relax, letting all his responsibilities slide away for a moment. He felt himself drifting off into a half-doze, and didn't even try to stop himself.

PAIN!

He didn't realize that he'd jumped to his feet until he found himself staring at Stef from halfway across the room. He blinked, and in that instant between one breath and the next, knew—

Kilchas! That pain was Herald-Mage Kilchas, and he was dying. Or being killed. Suddenly. Violently.

An unexpected side effect of the new Web. Unless someone was magically cut out of the Web, every Herald would know when another Herald died, as the Companions already knew.

And as Vanyel knew that something was wrong.

The Death Bell began tolling, and he grabbed his tunic from the back of the chair beside the one he'd been sitting in, pulling it on hastily over his head. Something was wrong, something to do with Kilchas, and he was the only one who might be able to see what it was. But he had to get there.

Stef fell back a step, startled. "Van, what did I—"

The Death Bell tolled, drowning out the rest of his words.

Stef had been at Haven long enough to know what *that* meant. But he'd never seen a Herald react to it the way Vanyel had—and he'd never heard of a Herald who had reacted *before* the tolling of the Bell.

"Van?" he said, and the Herald stared at him as if he'd never seen him before.

"Van?" he said again, which seemed to break Vanyel out of whatever trance he'd gotten stuck in. Vanyel grabbed his uniform tunic and began pulling it on over his head.

"Van," Stef protested, "It's the Death Bell. There's nothing you can *do,* and even if there were, you just got back! You're tired, and you've earned a rest! Let somebody else take care of it."

Van shook his head stubbornly, and bent down to reach for his boots. "I have to go—I don't know why, but I have to."

Stefen sighed, and got both their cloaks; his, that had been draped on a hook behind the door, and Vanyel's spare from the wardrobe. As soon as the Herald straightened up from pulling his boots on, Stef handed him the white cloak and swung his own scarlet over his shoulders. Vanyel paused, hands on the throat-latch of his garment.

"Where are *you* going?" he asked, in a startled voice.

Stefen shrugged. "With you. If you're going to run off the first night you're home, at least I can be with you."

"But Stef—" Vanyel protested. "You don't have to—"

"I know," he interrupted. "That's one reason why I'm doing it anyway, lover." He held the door open for the Herald, and waved him through it. "Come on. Let's get going."

Someone had already beaten Vanyel to the scene; there were lights and moving shadows at the base of one of the two flat-topped towers at the end of Herald's Wing. The storm had blown off some time after Vanyel got in; the sky was perfectly clear, and the night windless and much colder than when he'd arrived. The slush had hardened into icy ridges that he and Stef slipped and stumbled over to get to the death-scene.

Kilchas lay facedown on the hardened snow, one arm twisted beneath him, head at an unnatural angle. He was dressed in a shabby old tunic and soft breeches, with felt house-shoes. Treven, cloak wrapped tightly around him, knelt beside the body. A very young, blond Guardsman stood next to him, holding a lantern that shook as the hand that held it trembled. "—there was this kind of cry," he was saying, as Van stumbled within hearing distance. "I looked up at the tower, and he was falling, limplike; like somebody'd thrown a rag doll over. I ran to—to catch him, to try to help, but he was—" The young man shuddered and gulped. "So I came to get help, my lord."

"Which was when you bowled me over in the corridor," Treven said coolly, touching the body's shoulder with care. "You can go get me a Healer, but I think he'll just confirm that the poor old man died of a broken neck and smashed skull." Though the young Heir spoke with every sign of complete composure, Van Felt him shaking inside. This was Trev's first close-up look at the violent death of a fellow human, and all his calm was pretense.

Not that it ever got easier emotionally with time and repetition; it was just easier to be calm about taking care of it.

"Trev." Vanyel touched the young man's shoulder at the same time as he spoke; Trev and the Guardsman both jumped. The lantern swung wildly in the Guardsman's hand, making the shadows jerk and dance, and making the body appear to move for an instant.

"Trev, I'll take it from here if you want, but I think you've got things well in hand." His first impulse had been to take over; this, after all, was not the first time he'd seen death near at hand—it was not even the first time he'd seen the death of someone he knew and cared for. No, that had happened so often he'd given up counting the times. . . . But taking over from Trev would have meant shoving the young Heir into the position of hanger-on, when what he *needed* to do was start assuming his authority. The sooner he started doing so, the more readily others would accept that authority when Randi died.

So even if the young Heir didn't have any experience in handling situations like this, Trev should be the one in charge.

Treven took a deep breath, and looked very much as if he wanted to hand that authority right back to Van. But instead, he said only, "This really isn't my area of expertise, Herald Vanyel. Would you mind having a look here?"

Van nodded. Beside him, Stef shivered, and pulled his cloak a little tighter. Vanyel knelt down beside the white-faced Heir, and examined the body without visible sign of emotion, though he wanted to weep for the poor old man. "The neck is broken, and the front of the skull as well," he said quietly. He looked up, though all he could see of the top of the tower was the dark shape of it against the sky. "Kilchas has an observatory up on the top of this tower," he told Treven. "Did he say anything about going up there tonight?"

Another pair of heralds had joined them; Tantras and Lissandra; Lissandra huddled in on herself, as though she was too cold for her cloak to warm her. "Oh, gods," the woman said brokenly. "Yes, he told me that he was going up there if it cleared at all tonight. Phryny was conjuncting Aberdene's Eye, or some such thing. Only happens once in a hundred years, an he wanted to see it. He was so excited when it cleared up at sunset—" She sobbed, and turned away, hiding her face on Tran's shoulder. He folded his cloak around her, and looked down at the three kneeling in the snow.

"Poor old man," Tantras said hoarsely. "He must have gotten so wrapped up in what he was doing that he forgot to watch his step."

"There're probably ice patches all over the top of that tower," Trev replied, "And the parapet is only knee-high. It's only enough to warn you that you're at the edge, not save you from falling." He stood up, folding dignity around himself like a new cloak that was overlarge, stiff, and a trifle awkward. "Guard, would you please see that Kilchas' body is taken to the Chapel? I'll inform Joshel, and have him see to what's needed from there." The Guardsman stood up, saluted, and trudged toward the Guard quarters, leaving the lantern behind. Before too long his dark blue uniform had been absorbed into the night.

Treven turned to Vanyel. "Thank you, Herald Vanyel. If Tantras and Lissandra don't mind, I'll have them stay with me to get things taken care of. You've just come in from a long journey, and you should get some rest." He coughed uncomfortably, as if he wasn't sure what to say or do next.

Vanyel started to object, but realized that he didn't have any grounds for objection. It *looked* like an accident. Everyone else accepted it as an accident.

But Van didn't—couldn't—believe that it was.

Nevertheless, all he had to go on were vague and ill-defined feelings. Nothing even concrete enough for a Herald to accept.

So he thanked Treven—to Stefen's quite open relief—and returned across the crusted snow to the warmth and light of the Herald's Wing.

He was at the door, when Yfandes Mindtouched him. *:Van,:* she said, sounding troubled. *:We've found Kilchas' Companion, Rohan. He's dead. He was off in the far Western corner of the Field.:*

:And?: he prompted her.

:And I don't like it. There's no sign of anything wrong, but I don't like it. We just don't—fall over like that. Unless we die in battle or by accident, we're Called, and we generally have time to say good-bye to our friends before we go.:

:Could the shock of his Chosen dying like that have killed Rohan?: Van asked.

:Maybe,: she replied reluctantly. *:Most of the others think that's what did it.:*

:But you're not convinced.: It was kind of comforting that she shared his doubts.

:I'm not convinced. It doesn't feel right. I can't pinpoint why, but it doesn't.:

"Van, are you going to stand there all night?" Stef asked, holding the door open and shivering visibly.

"Sorry, *ashke,*" Vanyel said giving himself a little mental kick. "I was talking to 'Fandes. The others found Kilchas' Companion. Dead. She says it doesn't feel right to her."

The heat of the corridor hit him and made him want to lie down right then and there. He fought the urge and the attendant weakness. Stefen looked at him with puzzlement. "I thought that Companions never outlived their Chosen," he said. "And vice versa. So what's wrong?"

" 'Fandes just doesn't like the way it seems to have happened—Rohan was off by himself in the farthest corner of the Field, and none of the others knew he was gone until they found him."

Stefen looked disturbed. "That's not the way things are supposed to happen," he replied slowly. "At least not the way I understand them. I think you're both right. There's at least something odd about this."

Van reached the door of his room first, and held it open for the Bard. "It may just be the new Web-spell," he said as he closed the door behind them, took off his cloak, and flung it into a chair. "It's supposed to bind us all together; some of that may be spilling over in unexpected ways, like onto our Companions."

Stefen draped his own cloak on top of Vanyel's. "Here," he offered. "Let me help you out of that tunic and go lie down; we can talk about this while I give you a better massage than the one that was interrupted. I'll play opposition, and try to find logical explanations for everything you find wrong."

"Stef, I'm absolutely exhausted," Vanyel warned, unlacing his tunic and allowing Stef to pull it off. "If you really get me relaxed, I'll probably fall asleep in the middle of it. And once I do, you wouldn't be able to wake me with an earthquake."

"If that's what you need, then that's what you should do," the Bard replied, pushing him a little so that he sat down—or rather, collapsed—onto the bed. "Meanwhile, let me get the knots out of you while we talk about this. Why don't you pull 'Fandes into this, too? If she's worried, you probably should, anyway, and she may find holes in *my* arguments."

:*'Fandes?*: Van called

:*Here*—:

:*Want to listen in on this? We're going to try and see if I'm just overreacting to Kilchas' death because of exhaustion.*:

:*Neatly put, and that could be my problem, too. Go ahead. I'll be listening.*: She sounded relieved.

Vanyel yielded to Stef's wishes, and sprawled facedown on the bed. Stefen straddled him and reached into the top drawer of the little bedside table.

"What—" Vanyel began, turning his head to look; then when Stefen pulled out a little bottle of what was obviously scented oil, asked in surprise, "How did that get in there?"

"I put it there," Stef said shortly. "Get your head back down and relax." In a few moments, his warm hands were slowly working their way upward along Van's spine, starting from the small of his back. Vanyel sighed, and gave himself up to it.

"Now, what doesn't fit in the way Kilchas died?" Stef asked. "And don't you start tensing up on me. You can think *and* stay relaxed."

"Kilchas has a little enclosure up there," Van said, thinking things through, slowly. "The roof is glass. If he doesn't want to, he doesn't *have* to go out in the cold. I can't see why he would have been outside, and he certainly wasn't dressed for the cold."

"What if the glass was covered with snow or ice?" Stef countered. "It probably was, you know."

:I agree,: Yfandes said reluctantly. *:Everything else was.:*

"Good point. But why was he wearing slippers, rather than boots?"

Stefen rolled his knuckles along either side of Vanyel's spine while he thought. "Because he didn't know the glass was going to be iced over until he'd already climbed the stairs to the roof, and it was too far for him to climb down and back up again just for his boots. He was an old man, after all, and his quarters are down here on the ground floor."

Van gasped as Stef hit a particularly sore spot. "All right, I can accept that, too. But he's had that observatory for years. He always knows—knew—exactly where he is up there. Why should he suddenly misstep now?"

"Because he didn't," Stef answered immediately. "He was doing something he'd never had to do before. He was cleaning the glass on the roof of his little shelter, trying to chip the ice off. He lost his balance, or he slipped."

:That sounds just like Kilchas. Stubborn old goat.:

Vanyel tried not to tense as Stef hit another bad knot and began working it out. "Why not get a servant to do it?" he asked.

"No time?" Stef hazarded, as the fire in the fireplace cracked and popped. "This thing he was going to be watching—it would have been about to happen, and he figured if he had to find a servant, then wait for him to do the job, he'd miss part of what he wanted to see. Either that, or he was sure a servant wouldn't do it right. Or both."

:That sounds like Kilchas, too,:

The air filled with the gentle scent of sendlewood. Vanyel felt sleep trying to overcome him and fought it off. "If he just fell—" he said, slowly, "Why, when I felt him die, did I only feel pain? Why didn't I feel him fall?"

"I don't know," Stef said, pausing with his hand just over Van's shoulderblades. "I don't know how these Gifts of yours are supposed to work. But Kilchas was an old man, Van. What if he was already dead when he fell? What if his heart gave out on him? That's pretty painful, I guess. And if *his* heart suddenly gave out, couldn't that cause his Companion's to do the same? Maybe that's why *he* was found the way he was."

Vanyel closed his eyes, suddenly too tired to try to find something wrong with what appeared to be a perfectly ordinary situation.

"You're probably right," he said, :*'Fandes, do you agree?*:

:*Quite reasonable,*: she said, wearily. :*That's very typical of heart-failure; the shock goes straight to us, too. And Kilchas' Rohan was as old as he was. That's a much more logical explanation than foul play—it's just that so few of you live long enough these days for your hearts to fail that I forgot that. I think we may be overreacting because we're tired and we're so used to treachery and ambush that we ignore other answers, love.*:

" 'Fandes agrees with you—" he began; the Stef started something that had nothing to do with a therapeutic massage, and he murmured a little exclamation of surprise.

"Have we disposed of the topic, *ashke?*" Stef asked, breathing the words into his ear, his chest pressed against Vanyel's back.

:*I think,*: Yfandes said tactfully, :*that it's time for me to get some sleep. Good night, dearheart,*:

:*Good night, love,*: he replied—then his attention was taken elsewhere.

And it was quite a while before either he or Stefen actually slept.

Fifteen

Vanyel forgot all about his misgivings in the weeks that
followed. His time was devoured by Council meetings,
Audience sessions where he and Treven stood as proxies
for Randale, and long-distance spellcasting. Desperation at
being unable to be two places at once had led him to discover that he could work magic *through* a Herald without
the Mage-Gift, provided that the Herald in question was
both a Thoughtsenser and carried Mage-Gift in potential.
He immersed himself in the nodes so often he began to feel
very much akin to the *Tayledras*.

He often returned to his room at night long past the hour
when sane folk retired. When he did so, he found Stef
invariably curled up sleepily next to the fire, light from the
flames making a red glow in his hair, for he refused to take
his own rest until Van returned. The Bard's patient care
was the one constant in his life besides Yfandes, and as fall
deepened into winter, he came to rely more and more on
both of them, just to keep a hold on sanity and optimism
in a world increasingly devoid of both.

Karse *had* declared holy war on the "evil mages of Valdemar," though as yet they had done nothing about it. The
agents both the Lord Marshal and the Seneschal had in
place reported that the Prophet-King (as he styled himself)
had his hands full with rooting out "heresy" in his own land.
But no one was under any delusions; the consensus was that
as soon as the followers of the Sun Lord needed an outside
enemy to unify what was left of the populace, there would
be an army of fanatics hammering the Southern Border.

That would only add to the bandits who had taken over
the buffer zone between the two countries, motley bands of
brigands who had escaped or been turned loose during the
revolution, those who had been accused of magery and fled

237

their homes but had declined to cross the Border, and
opportunists who preyed on both sides.

"At least there won't be any mages in the Prophet's pay,"
the Seneschal said, as they all leaned over the maps and
tried to find weak points in their defenses.

"Maybe," the Archpriest replied dubiously. His tour of
the south had garnered mixed results. On the whole he was
happy with the outcome, for his presence had kept any
overt activities to a minimum. The net result, however, was
that there were no enclaves of the Sun Lord in Valdemar
any more. Roughly half of the devotees had been so
revolted by the Father-House's actions that they had con-
verted to some other way. The rest had decamped across
the Border to Karse, to join their fellows. The holdings
themselves had gone to those who had remained behind,
thus staying in the hands of those who had remained loyal
to Valdemar.

Supposedly loyal, at any rate. Both the Seneschal and the
Archpriest were keeping a wary eye on them in case some
of these "conversions" were intended as a ruse, to cover
later subversion. That there were spies planted in the midst
of these enclaves was a given.

"What do you mean, 'maybe'?" asked the Seneschal,
hand poised above a marker representing a Guard
detachment.

"What's the difference between a miracle and a magic
spell?" the Archpriest asked, looking from Arved to Van
and back again.

"A miracle comes from the gods; magic comes from a
mage," the Seneschal replied impatiently.

"That's purely subjective," the Archpriest pointed out.
"To the layman, there is no discernible difference. The
Prophet can easily have mages *within* his own ranks, claim
their powers are from the Sun Lord, and be completely
within strict doctrinal boundaries."

"Damn. You're right," the Lord Marshal said softly. "I
wonder how many he *does* have?"

"There's no way of knowing," Vanyel replied, as they all
turned to look at him. "I *don't* think he has anyone a Herald couldn't counter, though. My operatives aren't reporting
any 'miracles' other than Healing and the odd illusion, not
even when the Prophet's Children are trying to capture
mages. The powerful mages in the pay and employ of the

Karsite Crown were all known as such, and have either been killed or fled the country. That's not to say that the Mage-Gifted won't end up in the Sun Lord's priesthood in the future; I'd virtually guarantee that. but they won't get effective training, because there won't be anyone experienced enough to train them thoroughly, and they probably won't be permitted to use their Gift combatively."

"Why not?" the Archpriest asked.

Van smiled thinly, and fingered a marker representing an agent. "Because if they learn what they can do, what's to stop them from declaring *themselves* the chosen of the God and doing exactly what the Prophet did?"

"Only with more success, because they have 'miracles' to prove their power," the Archpriest mused, his eyes half-closed. "Interesting speculation. It's fortunate that you are on our side, Vanyel."

Van bowed with intended irony. "A Herald tends to be altogether too well acquainted with the ways of treachery for anyone's comfort, including his own, my lord," he said. "One could say that it is part of the job."

"To know, and not use?" The Archpriest's smile was genuine and his eyes warmed with it. "I am aware of that, my son. I think that most of you would have been comfortable within the ranks of the clergy had there been no Companions to Choose you."

"Most?" Vanyel chuckled, knowing the Archpriest was blissfully unaware of his relationship with Stefan. "Some, maybe, but I assure you, my lord, not all. By no means all. We are far too worldly for most orders to ever accept us!"

He would have said more, but suddenly—

His eyes burned. A giant hand closed itself around his chest, as his lungs caught fire. He tried to breathe, and only increased the pain. His heart spasmed; once, twice—then exploded.

He found himself sprawled facedown over the table, the rest of the Councillors, his father among them, frantically trying to revive him. He stared at the lines of the map just under his nose, unable to remember what they were.

"Vanyel!"

He was very cold, and his chest hurt.

"Turn him over you fools, he can't breathe!"

He blinked as the shadows danced around him, trying to recall exactly where—and who—he was.

:Van?: Yfandes said weakly, making a confusion of voices inside his head and out. *:Are you all right?:*

"What's wrong? What happened? Has he ever had a spell like this before?"

He stirred, dazed, the map-paper under him crackling.

The Council meeting. I was in the Council meeting.

:Van?: A little more urgent.

:'Fandes.: Give me a moment. . . . :

"What—" he gasped. He tried to push himself away from the table, but his arms were too weak and trembling, and he was too dazed to even think of what to do. Someone—two someones—grabbed his arms, one on either side, and pulled him up. Trev and Joshel; they lowered him into a chair—

Just as the Death Bell began tolling.

Lissandra— He knew it, even as the other two looked at each other over his head and spoke the name simultaneously.

"You go," Treven told Joshel. "Find out what happened." He shook Vanyel's shoulder gently. "Is that what you Felt? Is that what happened to you just now?"

Vanyel nodded, and schooled himself to reply. "I—yes. Something very painful, very sudden. Like what happened with Kilchas, only worse." He shuddered. "I don't understand—why am I Feeling them die? Why is this happening to me, and no one else?"

"Maybe because you set the spell," Treven hazarded. "The rest of us know what happens after the fact, but you feel it at the time. Or maybe it's happening just because the two of them were in the original Web with you. Or because they're close by physically. We haven't had any Herald deaths at Haven but Kilchas and Lissandra."

"I suppose. . . ." He put his head down on his knees, still dizzy. "A lot of good I'm going to be if I black out every time a Herald dies." He was still in too much quasi-physical pain and too much in shock to feel the emotional impact of the other Herald-Mage's death.

:'Fandes? What about her Companion?:

:We're looking,: Yfandes said shortly. *:Shonsea dropped out of our minds just as you Felt Lissandra die. Are you going to be all right?*

:I think so—I—:

:We found her,: Yfandes interrupted. *:The northern end*

*of the Field. It looks as though she was running, and fell
and broke her neck.:*

Vanyel sighed and closed his eyes. *:If she felt what I did,
I'm not surprised it came as enough of a shock to make her
fall. Something horrendous happened, whatever it was.:*

His head throbbed with aftershock, and it was increasingly hard to think. He raised his head with an effort when
Joshel came back into the Council Chamber, coughing.

"It looks like she had an accident with her alchemical
apparatus," Joshe said. "When we got to her chamber, it
was full of fumes of some kind. We had to open a window
to clear them out. Look—"

He held up a glass jar; it was frosted on the outside.

"That's what those fumes did closest to the spill; ate into
things. We found a container of some kind over a small
firepot had broken. That was where the fumes were coming
from. All we can guess is that it cracked and spilled the
stuff into the fire, and Lissandra breathed in a fatal dose
before she could get the window open."

"It *Felt* like my lungs were on fire," Vanyel said. "I
couldn't breathe, and my eyes were burning."

"She might not even have been able to see to get the
window open," Joshe continued. "As corrosive as those
fumes were, she must have been nearly blind. We found
her halfway between her workbench and the door."

*Lissandra should have known better than to work with
something that dangerous in her chamber,* Vanyel thought
vaguely. *What on earth possessed her to do such a thing?
The still-room at Healer's Collegium has adequate ventilation
against accidents, and she hasn't got any secrets from the
Healers. . . .*

But his head was pounding, and he couldn't seem to get
any further than that.

"I need to get something for my head," he said thickly,
getting to his feet. Treven looked at him in concern.

"This hit you awfully hard," he said. "I know you've been
overworking. Do you want to take this session up later?"

He shook his head. "No," he replied. "We haven't the
time to spare. You have Audiences right after this, then
Randi has a private Audience session with the Rethwellan
ambassador. I'll be all right."

Treven smiled weakly. "You always are," he said with
gratitude. "I don't know what we'd do without you."

"Some day you'll *have* to do without me," Van reminded him grimly. "I'm not immortal. Well, let's get on with this. My operatives say the next move will be for Karse to declare holy war on Rethwellan, too, trusting that the mountains will keep the Queen from coming at them."

"The more fools, they," the Lord Marshal replied. "Here's what she's pledged us if they make a move like that. . . ."

The fire in Savil's room hissed and popped at them, and the late-afternoon sun shone weakly down on the gardens outside the window. Van sat back in his chair and tried not to look as if he were tired of hearing his aunt's plaints.

"I don't like it," Savil said fretfully. "First Kilchas, then Lissandra. Both of them Herald-Mages. It's no accident."

"What else could it be?" Vanyel asked reasonably, rubbing one of his shoulders. He was still stiff and sore from his fit this afternoon. "We've been all over that. No one found anything out of the ordinary. No signs of tampering, magical or otherwise. Just the result of miscalculation."

A coal fell down to the grate, and a shower of sparks followed it.

'I still don't like it," she replied, stubbornly shaking her head. "What if the tampering wasn't with their equipment, but with *them*—their minds or their bodies? A Healer could easily have stopped Kilchas' heart. A MindHealer could have made Lissandra think she was putting something harmless on the fire. You'd never detect that kind of tampering."

She's getting old, he thought sadly. *She's getting old, and frightened of everything.* In her oversized, overstuffed chair she looked thinner, and terribly frail. There were lines in her face that had never been there until this winter. It seemed that, like the *Tayledras,* she was failing all at once. *She's aged more in the last six months than in the last six years.* "Savil, love, why would a Healer do something like that?" he asked. "It just isn't logical."

"You don't have to be a Healer to have Healing Gifts," she countered. "You have them; so do I. Moondance *is* a Healing Adept. It could be a rogue mage with the Gift. A kind of anti-Healer."

Great good gods. Now she's inventing enemies. Whoever heard of anything like that? "All right, then," he replied patiently. "*Who*? We've no indication that anyone is using mages against Valdemar right now."

She frowned. "What about the one that nearly killed you?"

"There's no sign of that kind of magical attack in either Kilchas' death or Lissandra's," he reminded her. "And the attempt on me was not directed at Valdemar. I think that must have been a purely personal vendetta and nothing more. I've made a lot of enemies in the last few years, and it's all too likely to have been one of them."

"Van," she said unhappily, "I'm worried. I think it's stretching coincidence—first the incident with you, then Kilchas is killed, then Lissandra. Please listen to me—"

Vanyel sighed. "I'll tell you what, Aunt Savil. If it'll make you feel more confident, I'll strengthen your wards. But I don't think they need it. You're an eminently capable mage, as you very well know—you're *my* superior at ritual magics. Kilchas was very old and inclined to try and do things he shouldn't because he was stubborn. Lissandra worked with very dangerous substances all the time. The odds just caught up with both of them."

Savil scowled at him, and the fire hissed as if it felt her anger. "Vanyel Ashkevron, you're being more than usually dense. If I were ten years younger—"

Abruptly she deflated, and shrank back down into her chair. "But I'm not," she said sadly. "I'm older than Kilchas, and just as vulnerable. I'm holding you to your promise, Van. Strengthen my wards. I'll take any help I can get, because I believe I will be the next target and I can't get anyone else to agree with me, not even you."

Vanyel stood up, feeling guilty. "Savil, I don't blame you for overreacting. You knew both of the others better than I did. I'll be happy to strengthen your wards as soon as I get a moment free, and I'm absolutely certain that in a few more weeks we'll be laughing about this."

"I hope so," Savil said unhappily as he moved toward the door. "I truly hope so."

He stifled a surge of annoyance, and bade her good night as affectionately as he could manage. It wouldn't cost him more than a candlemark and a little energy to strengthen her wards, and if it made her less paranoid, it was worth it.

He closed the door behind himself, and literally ran into Stefen in the hall outside.

"I hope you're through for the day," the Bard said in a weary voice as he caught Vanyel's arm. "Because I certainly am. It's my turn to need a backrub. The Rethwellan ambassador wouldn't talk unless I was out of the room and Randale couldn't sit up unless I was *in* the room, so they compromised by sticking me in a closet."

Vanyel chuckled tiredly, and put his arm around Stefen's shoulders. "Nobody has me scheduled for anything more, and I'm not inclined to let them know I'm free. Let's go; I'll give you that backrub."

"More than a backrub, I hope," Stef said, shyly.

"I think I might be able to manage that," Vanyel said into the Bard's ear.

"Good," Stef said. "I'll hold you to that. . . ."

Later, much later, as Vanyel drifted off to sleep, he remembered what he had promised Savil.

Oh, well, he thought drowsily. *I can take care of it tomorrow. It's not that urgent. And I didn't promise exactly when I'd do it, just that I would when I got some free time.*

The fire had burned down to coals, with a few flames flickering now and again above them, and Stef was already asleep, his head resting on Vanyel's shoulder. It was the first moment of peace together they'd had since returning from Forst Reach—the first entire evening they'd been able to spend together without either of them being utterly exhausted or worried about something.

And it was the first evening Van hadn't had to spend in the nodes, drawing energy for later use, or channeling it elsewhere.

He stroked Stef's silky, fine hair, and the Bard murmured a little in his sleep. *I'm not going to spoil it now. It can wait until morning.*

He watched the fire through half-closed eyes, listening to Stef breathe, and waited for sleep to take him.

Then the peace of the evening shattered.

:VANYEL!:

He was out of bed and grabbing his clothes before Stef woke.

:VAN—:

Savil's cry was cut off, abruptly, and Vanyel doubled up and fell to the floor—

Pain—

—knives of fire slicing him from neck to crotch—

—lungs aching for air—

—teeth fastening in his throat—

Then, nothing—

He found himself gasping for breath, curled in a fetal position on the floor, Stefen staring at him from the bed with his eyes wide with fear. It had felt like an eternity, yet it had taken only a few heartbeats from the moment Savil called him until now.

Savil!

He grabbed his robe from the floor beside him where he had dropped it and struggled to his feet, pulling it on. He burst out the door and ran down the corridor—joined by every other Herald in the wing just as the Death Bell tolled. *This* time he hadn't been the only one to feel the death-struggle.

And this time there was no doubt. This was no accident.

Savil's door was locked; Vanyel kicked it open. His aunt lay in the center of a circle of destruction; furniture overturned, lamps knocked over, papers scattered. Blood everywhere. Some of the others, Herald-trainees who had probably never seen violent death before, gasped and turned green—or blanched and fled.

Claw and teethmarks on Savil's throat and torso showed that she'd put up a fight. A trail of greenish ichor and a broken-bladed knife told that her enemy had not escaped unscathed.

But there was no sign of it, and the trail ended at the locked door.

Not that it mattered to him. The damage was already done, and this time Vanyel's hard-won detachment failed entirely. While the others checked the locks, and looked for clues or any sign of what had attacked her, he sank down to his knees beside the body, and took one limp hand in his—and wept.

Oh, gods—Savil, you were right, and I didn't listen to you. Now you're gone, and it's all my fault. . . .

Some of the others stopped what they were doing, and looked at him with pity and concern. Very few of them had ever seen Vanyel emerge from behind the cool mask of the

first-ranked Herald-Mage of Valdemar. Fewer still had seen
him break down like this, especially in public. He had heard
that he had a reputation for such coolness and self-isolation
that even fellow Heralds seemed to think nothing could
crack his icy calm.

They were finding out differently now. "She—thought
someone was—targeting the Herald-Mages," he said brokenly, to no one in particularly. "She was afraid she was
going to be next; she asked me to help her, and I just
thought she was being hysterical. I promised to strengthen
her wards, and I didn't; I forgot. This is all my fault—"

*She's never going to sit there in her chair and expound at
me again. I can't ever ask her for advice. She'll never take
on Father for me—she was my mother in everything but flesh,
and I failed her, I failed her, when I'd promised to help her.*

He hung his head, and closed his eyes, choking down the
sob that rose and cut off his breathing.

*Savil, Savil, I'm so sorry—and sorry isn't enough. Sorry
won't bring you back.*

Tears escaped from under his closed eyelids, and etched
their way down his cheeks. He couldn't swallow; he could
hardly breathe.

A hand touched his shoulder. He looked up, slowly,
through eyes that burned and vision that wavered with
tears.

"Van?" Tantras said quietly. "I know you're in no shape
to do anything, but you're the only Herald-Mage left, and
we can't check all the magical locks she had to see if they
were violated."

He blinked, then reckoned up in his head all the deaths
over the last couple of years.

*Oh, gods—I'm not just the only Herald-Mage they have
left here, I'm the very last Herald-Mage. There aren't any
more but me.*

He wiped the back of his hand across his eyes and rose
slowly to his feet. "Clear everyone out," he said in a low,
and deadly calm voice, as a coldness settled in his heart and
icy anger steadied his thoughts. "I'll need some room to
work."

The wards weren't violated. Van stood in the middle of
the room and scanned every inch of it with Mage-Sight. The
wards were fading now that Savil was dead, but they were

still strong enough to read. She had warded all four directions, above and below, weaving protection atop protection, and all glowed with the bright blue that meant no strand and no connection had been broken, and the only hole was the one he himself had made when he broke down the door.

The wards weren't violated. The locks and locking-spells are all intact. Whatever it was came in before she set the wards.

What was the damned thing, anyway?

There was still a trace of the greenish ichor left; more than enough to identify the creature if it was something Vanyel had encountered before this. But it wasn't; it wasn't even close to anything he knew, and the magical signature it had left behind when it broke the spell that gave it its disguise was entirely new.

It's intelligent, he decided. *It has to be. And it's not Abyssal, or I'd at least recognize that much of its signature, which only leaves one possibility. It's created, or it's from the Pelagirs. Or both—*

His only option now was to try alone what he and Savil and the two *Tayledras* had done together; try to See into the immediate past. He wouldn't have tried it if he hadn't seen it done by an expert; and if the time he wanted to See hadn't been so recent, he wouldn't have been able to do it alone.

The longer he waited, the fainter the traces would be. His best chance at discovering anything would be to cast the spell now, this instant.

You son of a bitch, whoever, whatever you are, you're not getting away! I'm going to hunt you down if it takes me the rest of my life—

He sat down on the cold, bare floor, next to where Savil had been found, and tapped recklessly into the node far below Haven. His need, anger, and sorrow drove him deeper into it than he had ever been or dared to go before; he grasped the raw power with unflinching "hands," manipulating it like soft, half-molten iron. He forged it into the spell on the anvil of his will and tuned it to himself through the medium of his mage-focus. Then he cast it loose.

When he opened his eyes, the room was as he had left it when he'd last seen Savil alive. He was sitting just beside Savil's big chair; it was early evening by the thin light coming in the windows, and she didn't seem to be in the room.

This must be just after I met Stef, he thought, and guilt ate at him, acid in his wounds of loss. The wards were *not* up. And there was nothing in the room that did not belong there.

Vanyel froze the moment and searched everywhere, even behind and underneath the furniture. Nothing. Everything was entirely as it should be.

He gritted his teeth and let time proceed again, waiting as the twilight deepened and became true night; as one of the servants came in, lighting the lamps and leaving fresh candles in the sconces. Another brought in a heavy load of wood, and fueled the fire. Nothing at *all* out of the ordinary—

Wait a moment!

He froze the time-stream again, and examined the candles, minutely, with Mage-Sight.

Nothing at all odd about the candles—but when he turned his Sight on the wood, the entire pile glowed an evil green, and when he dug deeper at it, the wood gave him the same signature as the ichor.

But it wasn't enough; not quite. He needed to see how the thing had looked when it dropped its disguise, and where it had gone afterward.

He forced himself to let the time-stream start up again; his heart lurched when he saw Savil enter the room. *No, not now,* he told himself, forcing himself to be cold and unemotional. *I'ts not the time for that—not while I'm tapping a node. I can't afford to give up concentration for emotion.*

He regained control over himself, just as his aunt turned away from him and put up her wards.

Even though he was watching the woodpile, he didn't see it actually change; the creature was that fast. He froze time again; catching it in mid-leap and Savil in mid-turn.

Well, at least I'm not slipping, he thought, still locked in that icy detachment. *That creature isn't anything I've ever encountered before.* It was mostly like a raven, but with toothed beak, evil red eyes, and powerful legs that ended in feet bearing knife-sharp, hand-sized talons.

Not even the *Tayledras* knew all of the creatures that roamed the Pelagirs, but somehow this bird-thing didn't have the feeling of anything natural—if that word could ever be applied to a beast from that magic-haunted area. Still, the bird looked wrong; the teeth were too long for it to be able to actually eat with them, and those claws were no good for anything except rending. Certainly it couldn't perch on anything like a tree limb with those talons. And how would it feed young?

Vanyel could not leave his own position, but he could let the beast continue its leap, little by little, until he could see all of it. He did so, steadfastly ignoring the look of fear on his aunt's face, the panic as she realized she could not ready a blast of mage-energy before it reached her. It was thumb-lengths away from her when he stopped the thing again, and close examination of the rear proved what he had suspected. It had no genital slit; in fact, it had nothing at all, not even a vent. It was as featureless behind as a feather-covered egg.

It was a construct, a one-of-a-kind, probably created specifically for this task out of a real raven. The only way it could obtain nourishment would be magically; it was utterly dependent on the mage that created it, and there would be no young that might escape the mage's control. That meant that the mage who had targeted Savil was at the least more ruthless than Vanyel, and very likely more powerful as well.

Power doesn't count for everything, Vanyel thought, clenching his jaw on a rising tide of anger. *There's skill, and there's how much you're willing to pay for what you want. I want this bastard, and I don't intend to lose him.*

He sped up the time-stream, skipping ahead to the moment when Savil was already dead and he had started to kick in the doorway. He watched dispassionately as the bird-thing, wounded and bleeding, again assumed its guise of a pile of wood, this time beside the door. He watched as he allowed himself to be overcome with grief, and the creature took that moment of distraction to slip out the door.

He tracked it as it fled from the Palace by the first exit. It paused just long enough to attack one lone Companion, down and in shock with the loss of her Chosen—the others came to Kellan's aid, but too late. The thing rose up in triumph and fled, its talons and beak red with the mingled blood of Herald and Companion, while the rest of the herd shrieked their impotent anger after it.

And still he tracked it. North. North for several days' ride, on wings sped by more magic, until it dropped back down to earth, exhausted and weakened by its injury. He sensed from its primitive thoughts that it was going to stay there for at least a week, healing. It knew it was safe enough. No one knew it was there . . . and no one could follow it that quickly.

That was all he could bear to see. He let loose his control of the spell, and it dissolved away, leaving him sitting alone in the middle of the empty, ruined room, with dawn just beginning to color the sky outside the windows, and Stefen huddled in a cloak just inside the door.

"They t-told me not to disturb you," the Bard stuttered, looking pale and wan in the thin, gray light. "But nobody said I couldn't wait here until you w-were done. Van, I'm sorry, I w-wish I could do something—"

"You can," Vanyel replied shortly. "You can guard the door and keep everyone else out." There was hurt in Stef's eyes at his coldness, but he ignored it.

:'Fandes?: he called.

The rage in her mind-voice colored everything a bloody red. *:Gods damn them to the lowest hells! That thing got Kellan on its way out, Van—:*

:I know that,: he interrupted. *:And I'm about to extract a little revenge right now. Will you link and cover my back while I go hunting?:*

:Hunt away,: she snarled, *:I'm right behind you.:*

That was all the assurance he needed. Once again he dove into the node, pulled in all the raw power he could hold through the buffering effect of his amber focus, and launched himself out again with all his channels scorched and tender but still perfectly functional.

He knew the general area where the thing had gone to earth, and he still had that trace of ichor to use to find its exact location. While he had that bit of the beast's life-fluid, it could never escape him, no matter how many disguises it assumed, or how much magic it called up to cloak its presence.

With Yfandes guarding his back, he knew he needn't waste half his energy watching for ambush; he tracked the thing into its hiding place with infinite patience. He still had his tap into the node, he could afford whatever expense of power it took to find the construct.

When he found it, he also found something else; it had shielding far more powerful than he had expected. The creature's master wanted it back, evidently, which made it all

the more valuable to Vanyel. His resources were already
stretched thin by distance; he couldn't smash through those
shields at this range.

But he didn't need to. . . .

It was protected against "real" magic, not Mind-magic.
And one of his Gifts was Fetching—with all of the power
of the node to back him. Because he had both real and
Mind-magic, he could fuel his mind-powers with mage-ener-
gies as no other Herald could. Which was where his enemy
had made a fundamental misjudgment.

He seized the thing, shields and all; belatedly it tried to
escape, but it hadn't a chance at that point and its master
hadn't given it the ability to call for help. It had been too
late for the creature to escape the moment he knew its
physical location. As it struggled, he could Feel its rising
panic, and he smiled—

And *Pulled.*

:Yes—: Yfandes hissed eagerly in his mind—by no means
enough to distract him; he was used to her commentaries
and encouragements in the back of his thoughts after all
these years. *:Yes! Bring it* here *and we'll show them we're
not to be slaughtered at anyone's whim—:*

The thing grabbed on to where it was and resisted his
pull; he simply tapped deeper into the node, ignored the
pain, the rivers of fire that ran along his channels, and
pulled harder. He ripped it loose as it shrieked in desperation; Yfandes supported him as he hauled it in. She cush-
ioned him from the effects of a reaction-headache,
something she'd never done before, enabling him to fling
the creature down right on the spot where it had killed
Savil, and pin it to the floor with raw node-power.

Stefen gave a strangled croak when it appeared, but
wisely remained where he was. Wise—or perhaps frozen
with fear; Van Felt the panic coming from him in waves,
but had no time to worry about the Bard just now. While
the beast squirmed and screamed both mentally and vocally,
he stripped the protections from its crude thoughts and
ripped away every detail he could concerning its master.

North, the direction it had fled in the first place; the
direction no one expected for an enemy. North, and an
impression of the vast wilderness that could only be the
Forest of Wendwinter and the Ice Wall mountains beyond.
But of the master himself, nothing; only darkness. After

ruthless probing that left the bird's mind a broken, bleeding rag, Vanyel decided that this was all the construct had ever seen of its master.

He contemplated the writhing creature at his feet with his mouth set in a grim line. He had left it a ruin, with nothing remaining to tell it how to get home, or even how to defend itself. It could no longer work the borrowed magics it had been given, and it might not even remember how to fly. If he let it go, it would slowly starve itself to death, and its master would never know what had become of it, or even whether or not it had been successful in its task.

Even Yfandes' lust for revenge seemed satisfied now; at any rate, she was silent, and her anger no longer seethed at the back of his mind.

But *his* need for vengeance was not filled.

He gathered all the node-power he could handle, poured in channels that burned as hotly as his own need for revenge. He made certain that there was still a line open between the bird and its creator. It was too bad that the line was such a thin one—one that he could not follow to its source. He was going to have to find the perpetrator the hard way.

But the line was enough to punish the master through. . . .

And he smashed the thing with one hammer-blow of pure, wild power.

The construct screamed its agony, and as it died in the cold flames of magic, the energy backlashed up the line Van had left open to its creator.

The scream ended; the thing glowed with the power Van poured into it—then incandesced until it was too bright to look at. And still he fed the fire, until the last of it was eaten away, and there was nothing left but a few wisps of white, feathery ash.

He turned toward Stefen, knowing that at any moment he would feel the effects of what he had just done. Yfandes couldn't protect him from the reaction-headache of overexertion of Mind-magic much longer; it was incredible enough that she'd done it in the first place. And his channels were pure agony that would take several hours of self-Healing to repair.

The Bard stared at him, his eyes wide and frightened, his face pale as skimmed milk. "W-what did y-you do th-that for?" he whispered, looking at Vanyel as if he expected the Herald to lash out at him next.

"I sent a message," Vanyel said quietly. "One that can't be mistaken for anything but what it is. A challenge, and a warning. Whoever did this, whoever murdered Savil, is going to pay for it with his own life. Because this wasn't a personal vendetta; this bastard is the same one that's responsible for Kilchas' death, and Lissandra's and probably made the attempt on me as well. So it's a threat to Valdemar, and as such, I am going to eliminate the source of the threat."

The reaction-headache hit then; he brought one hand slowly to his head and swayed a little. Stef was instantly at his side, supporting him.

He recalled the hurt in Stefen's eyes when he'd cut him off earlier, and grimaced. "Stef," he said, awkwardly, "I'm sorry. I loved Savil, she was—she was—" He couldn't continue; tears interrupted him.

"She was the most remarkable and sweetest old bitch the gods ever created," Stef replied angrily, with tears in his own eyes. "There's never going to be anyone to match her. Whoever did this to her—I want his hide, too. Not as much as you do, but I want it too, and I'll do anything I can to help you get it." He held Vanyel, half supporting him, half embracing him. "It's all right, I understand."

Vanyel shook his aching head. "I just hope you can keep understanding, Stef," he said through the pain, "because this isn't finished yet. It isn't even close."

Sixteen

Vanyel had convened the entire Council as soon as he was able to speak coherently. The *entire* Council, including Randale, which meant that they met in his bedroom with Shavri in attendance.

Four stone walls surrounded them; like the Work Room, the Royal Bedchamber was an interior room, entirely windowless. Hard on Randi, who seldom got to see the sun anymore—but mandated by security. Assassins can't climb in the window if there aren't any windows.

The room was warm, but not stifling. For the sake of appearances, Randi had been moved from his bed to a couch, one as soft and comfortable as his bed, but with a padded back so that he could sit up with full support. The rest of the Councillors brought in chairs from the outer rooms of the suite, and arranged them around the couch with no regard for rank.

Most of them took in Vanyel's pronouncement—framed as a request—with a stunned silence.

All but the King.

"Absolutely not," Randale said, actually sitting up in alarm. His voice sounded stronger than it had in months. Shavri paled a little and clutched the side of the couch. "We can't possibly spare you."

"You can't afford not to let me go, Randale," Vanyel replied tightly, keeping a rein on his temper. "Whoever this is, whatever his motive, he's been targeting Heralds, and that makes him an enemy of Valdemar. And if he can pick Herald-Mages off from *outside* the Border, he can pick off anyone, including you, any time he chooses."

He'd hoped that personal threat would give the King pause, but Randale didn't hesitate a second. "That's not a factor. What is a factor is that you are the *last* Herald-Mage. Who's going to train the youngsters with the Mage-Gift?

Who would even know what the Mage-Gift *looks* like? And
who is going to counter attacks by mage-craft on the Border
if you aren't here?"

"To answer the last question first," Van replied, "Heralds. 'Ordinary' Heralds. They're not only capable of it,
I've managed to convince them that they *can*, which was no
mean feat."

"He has trained several Heralds in just that already,"
Joshel said reluctantly. "And we've learned from our operatives that there aren't any mages on the Karsite side any
more; at least, none with any power. After declaring magic
anathema, *they* won't have anyone to train mages either—"

"As for the youngsters—" Van continued, grimly, "In
case you hadn't noticed, no one has had any trainees with
Mage-Gift for the past two years. It was never that common
to begin with, and it seems to be appearing entirely in
potential now."

"Only in potential?" Shavri said, looking shocked, her
glance going from Vanyel to Joshel and back again. "But—
why? What's happened?"

Van shrugged, and rubbed his thumb nervously along the
arm of his chair. "I don't know—but consider this—so far
as I can tell, this enemy has picked Herald-*Mages* as his
targets. What if he's been making his job easier by killing
the children with the Mage-Gift before they can be Chosen?
It wouldn't be that hard. All you'd have to do is wait for
the Gift to manifest and send something to cause an 'accident.' No one would ever guess that the deaths were connected in any way."

"That makes it all the more imperative that you stay—"
Shavri began, her face settling into a stubborn scowl.

"That makes it all the more imperative that I *go*," Vanyel
countered, pounding the arm of his chair with his fist.
"What am I supposed to do, tap into the nodes and sit
around scanning the entire countryside, waiting for some
spell or creature to target an unknown child somewhere? I
don't even know if that's what's happening—and if it is,
how do I stop it?" His throat tightened with grief and guilt,
but he forced himself to continue. "The thing that got Savil
spirited itself *into* the Palace, in *Haven*, and killed an experienced Herald-Mage under our very noses! Dear gods, she
called to me for help, and I'm just down the hall from her
and I was *still* too late to save her! How in the seven hells

am I supposed to catch this enemy again when I not only
don't know where and when he'll strike, but who? I *have*
to carry the fight to him; it's the only way to neutralize him.
And if we don't—he has to have a larger plan, he can't be
doing this for the fun of it. Do we wait for him to be ready
to make his move, or do we take him *before* he's ready?
Which is better tactics?"

"I can't argue tactics with you, Vanyel," Shavri said
resentfully, as Randale collapsed back against his cushions,
"But I can't see what good it's going to do you, us, *or*
Valdemar to go haring off into the unknown after some
nebulous enemy who may just be—"

Vanyel was about to interrupt her, when Yfandes stopped
him. *:Hold your temper, Van,:* she said firmly. *:We're
behind you. And we're going to take care of this.:*

We? he thought in surprise. But before he could ask her
what she meant, the face of every Herald in the room went
blank, and Shavri stopped in midsentence.

There was a long moment of silence, broken only by the
sounds of non-Heralds stirring restlessly in their seats. The
candles placed in sconces all around the room flickered only
when someone moved, creating a momentary current in the
air. Someone coughed uncomfortably.

:'Fandes?: Vanyel Sent. *:What's going on?:*

:You have to go, Van,: she replied firmly. *:This mage is
too much of a threat. We—the Companions, I mean—have
been talking it over since you decided to go after him, and
we think you're right. So we're backing you. And if the others won't listen to their own Companions, they'll hear from
all of us.:* The overtones to her mind-voice sounded both
smug and a little ominous. *:We'll just see how long any of
them can hold out against that.:*

Joshel shook his head at that point. "All right," he said
aloud, breaking the silence so suddenly that the non-Heralds started. He gave Vanyel a long-suffering look. "I don't
know how you managed this," he told the dumbfounded
Herald-Mage, mixed admiration and annoyance in his
expression, "I've never heard of all the Companions uniting
to back a Herald against King and Council before. I hope
you're right, Vanyel Ashkevron—and I hope this isn't going
to be too much for even you to handle."

One by one the others gave in, Shavri the last, possibly

because Shavri's bond with her Companion was the weakest.

But finally even she acquiesced, though not happily. "I hope you're satisfied, Herald Vanyel," she said, on the verge of tears. "I thought you were our friend—"

The others of the Council looked uneasy, embarrassed, or both, at this display of "womanly vapors." Vanyel, who knew it was more than that, dared not waver from his resolve. He knew why she was trying emotional blackmail; she was afraid for Randale and Jisa, but there was too much riding on this for him to allow her to manipulate his feelings for her, Randi, and their daughter.

"I am, Shavri. But Valdemar comes first, you know that as well as I do," he replied coolly, bringing home to her the same lesson he'd given Randale years ago.

"Then how *dare* you ride off and leave Valdemar unprotected?" she cried passionately, making her hands into fists.

"Because I *am* protecting Valdemar," he said, just as passionately. "This mage, whoever he is, doesn't dare leave me alive, not after the way I destroyed his creature. While he concentrates on me, he'll be ignoring Valdemar and anyone in Valdemar. You should all be perfectly safe while he brings all his resources to bear on me."

"And what if he k-k-kills you?" Shavri said miserably. "What will protect us then?"

"Shavri," he said, leaning toward her and catching and holding her gaze, "If I die, I'll either take him with me, or leave him so crippled he'll be no threat. So help me, I will protect Valdemar with my last breath, and if there is a way to protect her after my death, I'll find it!"

He stared into her eyes for a long moment, during which no one seemed to breathe. Then he sat back, breaking the spell himself. "But I don't intend to die," he said, with a grim smile. "I intend to find this bastard, and make him pay for what he did to Savil and the others. And if I have your permission to do so—?"

Randale nodded wearily. "There doesn't seem to be much choice in the matter," the King said. "For what it's worth, you have the permission of Crown and Council."

Vanyel stood, an bowed with deliberate grace to all of them. "I'm sorry if you feel that your decision has been forced," he said, "But I can't feel sorry that you came to it. Valdemar is more important than any one man, however powerful he seems to be. Thank you; I'll be leaving in the morning. Treven is ready to take full responsibilities as Randale's proxy and the Heir, Joshel knows how to contact my operatives in Karse, and Tantras can take over everything else I've been doing, just as he's done in the past." He looked around at the various faces of the Councillors, his father included. "I'm not indispensable, you know," he finished quietly. "No one is. You're all the most capable people I know, and if there's safety for anyone in this realm, it's in your hands, not mine, ultimately. *Zhai'helleva*, my friends."

And with that, he turned and left the room before anyone else could break down—including himself.

Stefen slipped inside Vanyel's door and shut it behind him, quietly. Van was beside the bed, neatly folding clothing and stowing it away in his travel-packs. While he did not look up from his packing, Stefen knew that Vanyel was well aware he'd come in.

Stef bit his lip, unable to think of how to start, what to say. Vanyel continued to ignore his presence, perhaps hoping that Stef would become discouraged and leave. The silence lengthened, as Stefen's palms grew sweaty and his throat tighter and tighter. Finally he blurted out the first words that came into his head.

"You're not leaving without me." He tried to make it sound defiant, but it came out plaintive. He pressed his back against the wood of the door as if he could physically bar Vanyel's way and waited for Van's response.

"Stef," Van said without turning around, "I can't take you with me, you know that." He sounded as distant and cold as if he were on the moon.

"Why not?" Stefen asked, around the lump in his throat. He was well aware that his words were very similar to what might be coming out of a petulant adolescent, and too anxious to care. "You're not going into Rethwellan this time. There's no one to care if we're lovers! What's the difference if I'm with you or not?"

Finally Vanyel turned around; his face was set in a stony mask, and his eyes were inward-focused, as if he was trying not to see Stef, only his shadow. "The difference is that you're not a Herald, you're not combat-trained, you can't even defend yourself from one man with a sword. You're a liability, Stef. I told you when we first—"

"How am I any safer here?" he interrupted, desperately, playing shamelessly on the guilt he knew Vanyel felt over Savil's death. "Savil wasn't safe! If someone wants to use me against you, all they have to do is wait until you're gone, and *take* me. Anybody who can do what's been done so far could make one of those Gate-things, grab me while everybody's asleep, and be gone before I could yell for help! You said yourself I couldn't protect myself from one man with a sword—how am I going to protect myself against something like *that?*"

He balled his hands into fists, to keep from gouging the wood of the door with his nails. The room was much too hot, and it was very hard to breathe. Vanyel seemed to waver for a moment, the mask cracking—then his lips tightened. The fire flared up, making his face look even harsher and more masklike.

"I don't have time for this, Stef. I have a job to do, and you're only going to get in the way." The words were deliberately hurtful, and if Stef hadn't felt a trace of contrary emotions through the bond that tied them together, he might have fled at that moment.

He's so driven—but I can crack that shell. I have to. Just enough so that he'll let me come with him . . . but it's a mistake to bring up Savil again. That's what's driving him.

"I'm coming with you," he said stubbornly, moving away from the door and toward Vanyel. "If you won't take me with you, I'll follow you. If you set somebody to watch me, I'll get away somehow. If you won't let me stay with you, I'll ride an hour behind you." He stopped for a moment, then made the last two steps in a rush, taking Vanyel in his arms before the Herald could evade the embrace. Vanyel held himself away, as stiffly as the night they'd first met, but Stef hid his face in Vanyel's jerkin anyway. "I don't care what you do," he said into Vanyel's shoulder, his cheek pressed tightly against the smooth leather. "I love you, and I'm following you. I don't care what happens to me, as long as I can be with you."

"What about Randale?" Vanyel asked in a strange, hollow voice.

"I'm not in love with Randale," Stef replied, a little defensively. "I'm not a Herald, you said that yourself, and

I don't see that I owe him anything. There're a dozen Healers that can pain-block now; three of them can do it while Randale's awake and talking. I'm just a convenience; he doesn't *need* me any more, and with Treven taking over full Heir's duties, he won't even have to do anything he doesn't feel up to."

"Shavri would probably dispute that," Vanyel said dryly, but his rigid posture was softening.

"She did," Stefen told him, encouraged by that tiny sign. "And I told her she could force me to stay, but she couldn't force me to play. She looked like she wanted to throw something at me, but she didn't. She just told me what she thought of me. It started with 'traitor' and went downhill from there."

"I imagine it did," Vanyel replied with a little cough.

"She told me she'd have me demoted, that she'd have me banned from the Bardic Circle," Stef continued, feeling that Vanyel was relaxing further. "I told her I didn't care. And I don't." He released Vanyel a little, and looked up into the Herald's face, lifting his chin defiantly. "It doesn't matter to me. If I wantd a high position and all the rest of that, I could have gone with that gem-merchant. I *used* to want that kind of thing, but I don't anymore."

"What do you want, Stef?" Vanyel asked softly, his strange silver eyes full of pain, and haunted by thoughts Stef could only guess at.

"Besides you? I don't know," Stefen said truthfully. He'd *intended* to say "just you," but something about the way Van had asked the question compelled him to the exact truth. "I only know that without you, no rank or fame would be worth having."

"And what would you have done if Randale had still needed you?" Vanyel continued, holding Stef's eyes with his.

Stefen swallowed. His throat tightened again, and a cold lump formed in the pit of his stomach. "I d–d–don't know," he replied miserably. "It's too hard a choice, and I didn't have to make it, so does it matter? He *doesn't* need me, and he told Shavri so."

"He did?" For the first time since Savil's death, Vanyel smiled—a very faint smile, but a genuine one. "You didn't tell me that part."

"You didn't let me get to it," Stef reminded him, with

an uncertain grin. "Randale told Shavri that *he* didn't need me, and that I'd only pine myself away to nothing if I had to stay. He said I should follow my heart, and that I shouldn't let you stop me. And that we needed each other."

Vanyel's arms came up and slowly closed around Stefen. "I guess we do, at that," he said in a whisper, and held Stef so tightly the Bard could hardly breathe.

"Will you let me come with you now?" he asked, when he was certain Van wasn't going to let go of him any time soon.

"Don't you ever give up?" Vanyel asked, amusement warring with exasperation, and amusement winning.

"No," the Bard replied, sure now that he'd won. "I already told you that." He felt Van's hand stroking his hair, and sighed, relaxing himself, the cold lump in his stomach vanishing.

"All right—but only because I think you're right." Vanyel pushed him away enough so that the Herald could look into his eyes. "You're probably a lot safer with me than here. I can put better protections on you than I've ever put on anyone else, including myself, you'll be invisible to Mage-Sight because I'll make them all passive defenses that don't manifest unless you're attacked, and it's harder to find a moving target. But Stef—please, *please* promise me that if it comes to a physical battle, you'll run. You *don't* know anything but street-fighting, and I don't have the time to teach you enough of anything to do you any good. I've lost Savil—if I lost you—"

The look in Vanyel's eyes was not altogether sane, and reminded Stef uneasily of the expression he'd seen once in the eyes of a broken-winged bird. Stefen shuddered, and pulled the Herald back into an embrace. "I promise," he said. "I told you, I value my skin. I won't risk it doing something stupid."

"Good," Vanyel sighed. "Well—I guess I should let you go pack. . . ."

He let go of Stef, reluctantly. Stefen backed a step away, and grinned up at the Herald. He returned to the door, opened it, and pulled his packs in from the hallway.

"I already have," he said simply.

Vanyel was awake at dawn, and Stef somehow managed to shake himself into a facsimile of alertness, even though his body protested being up at such an unholy hour, and his mind refused to admit that he was actually moving about.

Van had gone completely over his packs the night before; fortunately Medren had helped Stef put his kit together, and there was nothing Vanyel insisted upon that he did not already have, and very little he insisted Stef discard. Stef had already been in bed and asleep by the time Van finished his own packing, but he could be a very light sleeper if he chose, so the night had not been entirely wasted.

Although as he yawned his way through a sketchy breakfast, he wondered if the night might not have been better spent in sleeping, after all.

It was so dark that the stablehands were working by lantern light. Vanyel saddled Yfandes with his own hands, but suggested absently to Stefen that he stand back and let the experienced grooms deal with his little filly.

They placed a different sort of saddle on her than Stef was used to; one identical to Vanyel's, with the rear and front a little higher than his riding saddle, and rings and snaffles all over the skirting. He couldn't imagine what all those fastenings could be for, especially when there weren't any straps in evidence to be attached to them.

But then he didn't know much about horses, anyway. If that was the kind of thing Vanyel wanted him to use, he and Melody would cooperate. At least, he hoped Melody would cooperate; she looked rather affronted by the rump-band.

Then the grooms brought out two of the oddest animals Stefen had ever seen. Horse-tall, spotted brown and white, as hairy as the shaggiest of dogs, they had long necks and rabbit like faces with big, round, deep-brown eyes. One of them craned its long neck in Stefen's direction, its nostrils widening and its split upper lip lifting.

Stef tried to back out of its reach, but Melody was in the way and he was hemmed in by stalls on either side. The grooms were so busy loading the beasts with packs that they didn't notice what the one nearest Stef was trying to do.

He braced himself, waiting for the thing to try and bite him, hoping he could dodge out of the way before it connected.

But the creature only snuffled at him, stirring his hair with its warm, sweet breath. Melody twitched the skin of her neck and turned her head to see what was disturbing her.

Stefan fully expected her to have a fit when confronted

by the odd beast, but she didn't even widen her eyes. She just snorted in equine greeting, and the beast stretched its neck still further to touch noses with her before going back to snuffling Stefen's hair as if in fascination.

Finally the groom looked up from strapping the last pack down, and saw what the creature was doing. "Here now," he said, slapping its shoulder lightly. The beast pulled its head back, and turned a gaze full of disappointment on its handler.

"Don't you go a-lookin' at me like that, missy," he said. "Them's not roses you was a-smellin', 'twas the young lad's hair."

She sighed, as deep and heartfelt as any crestfallen maiden, and closed her eyes. The groom pulled the final strap tight, and turned toward Stef. "Chirras," he said, shaking his head. "Curious as cats, they are. You watch this 'un; she likes flowers, an' anything that's bright-colored she'll go sniffin' at just in case it might be some posy she ain't never seen afore." He grinned. "Some fool Herald name of Vanyel gave 'er a snow-rose once, an' ever since she's been lookin' fer flowers where there can't be none."

"She'd just carried my packs through a blizzard, Berd," Vanyel replied without turning around. "I thought she deserved a reward, and I didn't have any sweets with me. Listen, we plan to leave these two at the Border, at the last Guard post. Is that all right?"

"What're you gonna do for supplies?" the groom asked skeptically.

"What I generally do; live off the land." Now Vanyel turned to face them. "I wouldn't have asked you for them now except that Stef isn't used to this kind of trip, and I don't want to make it too hard on him at the beginning."

"Whatever you say," the groom replied. "The Guard post is fine. Next replacement to come back down can bring 'em with."

"That's pretty much what I thought." Vanyel took the lead-rope of the other chirra from a young boy and fastened it to the cantle of his saddle, while Berd did the same with the flower-loving chirra and Melody's saddle. Van mounted once his chirra was secure, and Stef followed his example.

"You take care, m'lord Van—" Berd called after them, as they rode out into the dark and cold. Vanyel half-turned in his saddle to wave, but he neither replied nor smiled.

Outside the walls of the city, there was nothing to be seen except snow-covered hills and a farmhouse or two. By the time they were a candlemark from Haven, the sky was as light as it was likely to get for the rest of the day. The clouds hung low, heavy, and leaden; the air felt a little damp, and the only place Stef wasn't cold was where his legs were warmed by contact with his horse.

Vanyel lifted his head and sniffed the light breeze, a few strands of silvered hair escaping from the hood of his cloak. "Smells like snow," he said, the first words he'd spoken since leaving the Palace grounds. Stef sampled the air himself, but it didn't smell any differently to him. "How can you tell?" he asked, his voice sounding loud over the snow-muffled footfalls of the beasts on the road.

"It just does," Van replied. "Like rain, only fainter and colder." He looked back at Stef, and got Yfandes to slow so that they were riding side by side. "I won't stop for you, and I won't hold my pace back for you, Stef," he said warningly. "I don't dare. I'm holding back enough as it is, taking chirras for the first leg. The *only* reason I'm catering to your inexperience on this first stage is because my enemy is going to assume I'm coming straight for him at a Companion's pace, and I hope this will throw him off."

"I understand," Stef hastened to say. "I won't hold you back. I'll keep up."

"You might, but your filly isn't a Companion," Van began. Then he got that "listening" expression that meant his Companion was talking to him. " 'Fandes says she'll help," he replied, looking a little surprised. "I don't know what she plans to do; maybe do something so that Melody can keep up with her. I hope so; a Companion is good for a lot more in the way of speed and endurance than an ordinary horse. I bred both those qualities into Star's line, but there's still only so much a horse can do."

"I'll keep up," Stef repeated, vowing to himself that he'd die before he complained of soreness or fatigue.

He's so strange, he thought, *so cold. It's like there's nothing in the world that's important except getting this enemy of his. I've never seen him like this before. Is he always like this when he's working, I wonder?*

"I have to stop this mage," Vanyel said quietly, as if he'd heard Stefen's thoughts. "I have to, Stef, it's the most important thing I've ever had to do. Can you understand that? I'm sorry if it seems as though I'm being cold to you—"

Stefen shook his head. "No, it's all right," he said hastily, even thought it *didn't* feel all right. "I told you I wouldn't fall behind, and I won't. You'll have no reason to feel that bringing me along was a bad idea."

"I hope you're right," Van replied bleakly. "Although I must admit that it looks as though the weather is going to be a bigger factor in our progress than you are."

Even as he spoke, the first big, fluffy flakes began falling from the lowering clouds. Stef looked up in puzzlement. "It doesn't look that bad," he protested, shifting in his saddle to relieve strained muscles inside his thighs.

Vanyel's eyes were closed, and his brows knitted with concentration. "It's not bad now," he said slowly. "But it could get that way very quickly, very easily. This storm system goes all the way up to the Border, and the balances in it are quite delicate. Right now it looks as though it's going to snow steadily, but things can change that balance all too easily."

"Oh," Stef replied. "I didn't know you could predict weather like that."

Vanyel opened his eyes and raised an eyebrow at him. "I can't," he said. "I can only read weather, I can't predict what it's going to do. It's one of the first things I was taught after I got control of my Mage-powers. The kind of magic I can do often disrupts weather patterns, and I need to know if I'm going to kick up a storm if I build a Gate or something of that nature."

"Oh, like when 'Lendel died—" Stef replied absently, lost in his own worries.

But Vanyel stiffened, and turned completely in his saddle to face the Bard. "How did you know that?"

Stefen brushed snow away from his face, and felt an odd little chill down his spine at the tone of Vanyel's voice and the odd expression he wore. Van actually looked frightened. Mostly startled, but a little frightened.

"Savil must have told me, or maybe Jisa," he said, trying to make sense of his own muddled memories and Vanyel's reaction. "I remember *somebody* must have told me there was a big storm caused mostly by the Gate being made. It was probably Savil, since there was a lot of stuff about how magic works involved in the explanation. I know Savil talked to me about it after I asked her—"

"Why?" Van asked. "Why did you ask her?"

"Because it's a part of you that's important," Stefen replied in a quietly defensive tone. "I never asked you about it because it seemed like you avoided the subject—I didn't want to hurt you or anything. So I asked Savil if *she'd* mind talking about it, and she said no, it had been long enough ago that she didn't mind anymore. That was while you were getting back to yourself after that mage attacked us."

Vanyel relaxed, and lost his haunted look.

"I talked to your parents a lot, too," Stef said. "I hope you don't mind." He tried to muster up a hint of mischief. "Treesa and I have a lot in common; she says I'm more fun to have as company than any of her ladies. I helped her get herself settled in when they got here, you know."

"I didn't know," Vanyel replied with a kind of absent-minded chagrin. "I just saw Father taking to the job of Councillor like a hound to the chase, and I guess I just assumed Mother would be all right."

She wasn't all right; she got here and found out that she was in the same position Savil said you were in when you first came here—a provincial noble from the backwater, twenty years behind the fashions, with no knowledge of current gossip or protocol, Stef thought. *She saw less of you than before. She was terribly lonely, and if there had been a way to get home, she'd have taken it.*

"I thought she was fine. It just seemed like after the first couple of weeks, she was as happy as Father," Van continued, peering through the curtain of snow at the road ahead. "Every time I'd see her she was the center of attention, surrounded by others." He paused for a moment, then said, "Was that your doing?"

"Some of it," Stef admitted. "I coached her, and I introduced her to Countess Bryerly and Lady Gellwin. You probably hadn't noticed, but there isn't much 'court' at Court with Randi so sick and Shavri's time taken up with it. The real Court, the social part, has pretty much moved out of the Crown section of the Palace and into the nobles' suites. And those are the two that really run it. Countess Bryerly is distantly related to the Brendewhins, so that made everything fine. Lady Gellwin took Treesa under her wing as a kind of protege, put her in charge of a lot of the younger girls once she found out that your mother did a lot of fostering."

A month ago, Vanyel would have been deeply upset that he hadn't thought to make sure his mother was well settled in. Now he only said, "Thank you, Stef. I appreciate your helping her," and continued to peer up the road.

That's not like him, Stef thought, worriedly. *I've never seen him so obsessed before. If he thought we could make any better time by getting off 'Fandes and pushing her, he'd do it. I don't understand what's gotten into him.*

The snow was getting thicker; there was no doubt about that. It still wasn't enough to stop them, or to slow them by too much, but Vanyel was obviously concerned. He spoke in an absent tone of voice whenever Stef asked him a direct question, but otherwise he was absolutely silent and inward-centered. The morning lengthened into afternoon, and Stef was afraid to ask him to stop for something to eat and a chance to warm up, even though they passed through three villages with inns that Stef eyed longingly. He was hungry, but worse than the hunger was the cold. Snow kept getting in under his hood and melting, sending runnels of icy water down the back of his neck. He could hardly feel his hands or his nose. There wasn't any wind, but they were creating their own breeze just by moving, and it kept finding its way in through the arm-slits of his cloak. And Melody was suffering, too; she walked steadily in Yfandes' wake with her head down and her eyes half-closed; she was tired, and probably missed her warm stable as much as Stefen missed his room and fireplace.

Finally Yfandes planted all four hooves in the middle of the road and refused to go any farther. Melody actually ran right into her rump before the filly realized the Companion had stopped.

Van seemed to come out of a trance. "All right," he said crossly. "If that's the way you want it, I guess I don't have a choice."

"What?" Stef said, startled.

"Not you, *ashke,* Yfandes. She says she's cold and hungry and she's stopping whether I like it or not." He dismounted and led her and the chirra over to the side of the road, kicking his way through the soft snow. Stef had to make two tries at dismounting before he could get off; he'd never been so stiff and sore in his life, and he had the sinking feeling it was only going to get worse.

But when he got under the tree, he felt a little resistance in the air—and when he passed it, a breath of warmth melted the snow stuck to his hair. It was more than just a breath of warmth; the entire area beneath the branches was warm, about as warm as a summer day; what snow Van hadn't cleared away was melting, and Yfandes was looking very pleased with herself.

"Van—" Stef said hesitatingly. "Is this a good idea? I mean, I guess you used magic to do this, won't somebody spot it?"

Vanyel shook his head. "I used a *Tayledras* trick; it's how they shield their valleys. From the outside, even to Mage-Sight, this place looks absolutely the same as it did before we got here; snow-covered trees, and no humans. It'll stay that way until well after we've gone on." He brushed snow from his cloak and grimaced. "There will still be a trace of magic-use here, though, and if my enemy knows I trained with the *Tayledras* he'll be able to track us by that, about two days behind our real trail. I'd rather not have done this, but 'Fandes said her joints were getting stiff and she had to get warm, so I didn't have much choice."

Stef had a sneaking suspicion that 'Fandes had insisted as much for *his* sake as her own, and he gave her a look of gratitude he hoped she could read. To his astonishment, she turned to look right at him and gave him a slow, deliberate wink when Vanyel's back was turned, rummaging in the chirras' packs.

"Could we sort of change direction every once in a while to throw him off?" Stef said, hoping this meant Van was going to warm up their resting place every time they stopped.

"It won't do much good; he knows we're coming north after him, and there's only a limited number of ways we can travel." Vanyel sighed, and looked over Stef's shoulder as if he wished they could get back on the road immediately.

Stefen ate his meal in silence. Yfandes sidled up to him and he leaned on her, grateful for the support and for her warmth. *It looks like the best I can hope for is that he'll wait until I'm warm clear through before getting back on the road.*

"At any rate, this is how we'll camp at night," Vanyel continued, handing him cold meat, bread, and cheese, and two apples. "I don't want to stop at inns; there could be spies there, and I don't want this mage to know exactly where we are."

Stef split his second apple and fed half to Yfandes and half to Melody. "Whatever you say, Van," he replied, hoping he'd be able to get back *on* his horse when Vanyel wanted to leave. "As long as I can be with you."

Seventeen

Snow fell, as it had fallen for the past three weeks, as it seemed it would continue to fall for the next three weeks. Not a blizzard; the wind, when there was one, was gentle, and the temperature relatively warm. But the snow was wet and heavy; good snow for playing in, as dozens of children making snow-beasts in their yards attested—but it increased their travel time fourfold. Ironically, considering how much stress Vanyel had put on the fact that he would leave Stef behind if he had to, the chirras were forcing a path through the snow for the two riding, and their progress was set by the chirras' pace.

"How many days can a snowstorm last?" Stef asked, huddled on Melody's back, shivering despite woolen underdrawers, a sweater and a shirt under his tunic, and two sweaters and his cloak over that.

"It's not the same storm, *ashke,*" Vanyel replied, as he consulted a map, then looked for landmarks. They were supposed to reach the last Guard outpost today, at least according to Vanyel's calculations. That outpost marked the end of the lands Valdemar claimed, and the beginning of territory held by no one except wolves—two and four-legged. And other things—the Pelagirs reached into that territory, and where they ended was anyone's guess. Probably only the *Tayledras* knew. It also marked the point at which Vanyel and Stefen's "easy" travel ended. They'd be leaving the chirras behind, and what little was left of the supplies, and going on with what Yfandes and Melody could carry—and what Vanyel could conjure up.

By now, Stef was no longer so sore in the morning that he would far rather have died than get up and remount his horse—but the cold never varied, and once out of their little shelter of mage-born warmth in the morning, he was chilled and miserable within a candlemark.

"What do you mean, it isn't one storm?" Stef asked. "It hasn't stopped snowing since we left Haven."

"It's a series of storms, all coming out of the north," Van replied, folding the map and storing it carefully in a special pocket on his saddle. "They generally blow out during the night, and a new one moves in just before dawn. The post isn't more than a couple of furlongs away; we should make it there by dusk." He looked back critically at Stefen. "If they have it to spare, we should get you some warmer clothing. And a better cloak. If I had known you'd feel the cold this badly, I'd have gotten it for you before we left."

Stefen held his peace.

"You're going to need it," Vanyel continued, urging the chirra forward, with Yfandes following at its tail. "After this, when we leave the gear and the extra supplies, this trip is going to be much harder on you."

And not on you? What are you made of, Van? Stone and steel? "I don't see how it can," Stef replied, since for once, Van seemed to be waiting for an answer. "I'm already frozen most of the time."

"Because we may be frozen *and hungry* most of the time," Vanyel told him, looking back over his shoulder. "We'll eat what I can hunt. I refuse to use magic to bring helpless creatures to me unless I'm literally starving to death."

"I'm probably a lot more used to being hungry than you are, Lord Vanyel Ashkevron," Stefen snapped. "I spent most of my life being hungry! I may not be woods-wise, but I'm not as helpless as you keep trying to make me out to be!"

Vanyel recoiled a little; his mouth tightened, and he turned away. "I hope for your sake that's true, Stefen," was all he said as he presented his back to the Bard.

Stef bit his lip and tasted the salt-sweet of blood. *Bright move, Stef. Very bright move. What do you use for a mind, dried peas?* He brushed snow and hair out of his eyes with a movement that had become habit, and stared at the snow-blanketed woods to his right and left. *But dammit, I wish he'd give me credit for being something more than a useless piece of baggage. All right, I'm not a Herald, I don't know how to survive on my own in the woods—but I can help and I've been helping—when m'lord bothers to give me instructions.*

Unhappiness, colder and more bitter than the cold, welled up in his throat. *Maybe he was right. Maybe I shouldn't have come. Maybe this whole trip is just showing him how little he needs or wants me. Maybe I should stay behind at this Guard post—*

Suddenly Yfandes stopped; Melody kept moving past the Companion until Vanyel reached over and caught her reins out of Stefen's hands.

Then he caught Stefen's hands, themselves. "I'm sorry, Stef," he said, that same wounded-bird look back in his eyes. "I don't give you enough credit. 'Fandes just gave me an earful for some of the things I've been saying and doing to you."

Stefen tried to smile. "It's all right, really it is—"

"No it's not, but I can't help myself, Stef," the Herald said through clenched teeth. "I'll probably go right on doing this to you, making you hurt, making you feel like you wish you'd stayed behind. I just hope you can forgive me, because it isn't going to stop. Everything has to take second place to what I'm doing about this enemy of mine, can you understand that?"

"No," Stefen said truthfully. "But I'll try."

Vanyel dropped his eyes. "I'm glad you're with me, Stef," he said, in a whisper. "I'm glad you're sticking this out with me. It would be a lot harder without you. You remind me I'm still human just by being here. You remind me there's something else besides the task I've been set. Something worth more than revenge . . . but I say things I shouldn't because sometimes I don't want to be reminded of that."

Stefen couldn't think of anything profound to say, but the lump in his throat and stomach were gone, and he felt a great deal warmer than he had in weeks. He freed one hand from Vanyel's and touched his glove to Van's cheek. "I love you," he said simply, as Vanyel's silver eyes met his again. "That's all that matters, isn't it?"

Vanyel smiled, a flicker of his old self, and patted Stef's hand. "Let's go," he said, and let go of the Bard's other hand. "The sooner we get into shelter, the happier you'll be."

The listening look crossed his face again, and he coughed. " 'Fandes says, 'to the nine hells with you humans, you

have cloaks. The sooner we get to the shelter, the happier
I'll be.' "

Stefen smiled—and when Vanyel had turned his attention
back to the trail ahead, exchanged winks with the
Companion.

Lady, he thought at her, *We may not be able to Mind-*
speak at each other, but I have the feeling you and I are
communicating very well, lately.

The Guard post meant a real fire, a real bed, and hot
food. And, almost as important, human voices, voices that
weren't his and Vanyel's.

There was warmer clothing available, wool underclothes
from the Guards' winter stores, sweaters one of the Guards-
women knitted from mixed sheep and chirra wool, the
new, fur-lined cloak that had belonged (Stef tried not to
think of the ill omen) to a Guardsman that had died of
snow-fever before he could ever wear it.

And there was news of the North, news that was at odds
with their own mission.

They sat by the fire, hot cider brewing in a kettle. Vanyel
and the Post Commander slouched across a tiny table in the
corner, while Stef warmed his bones right on the hearth.

"Lady bless, not a thing but the occasional bandit and a
bout of snow-fever," said the Commander, a handsome
woman with iron-gray hair and a firm jaw. "Since last summer we haven't even seen the odd Pelagir critter coming
over."

"Not even rumors?" Vanyel asked, as Stef warmed his
feet at the fire and played someone's old lute that had been
found in the storeroom. The tone wasn't exactly pure, but
the Guardsfolk were certainly enjoying it, so he tried not
to wince at the occasional dull note. "No hint of activity up
there at all?"

"Not a thing," the Commander replied positively. "The
only odd thing's this snow. Never seen it snow so much as
it has in the past few weeks. Well, you can see for yourself;
we shouldn't have more than one or two thumblengths on
the ground right now, and we've got it up to our waists with
no end in sight."

"You mean this *isn't* normal winter weather?" Vanyel
asked, sitting up straight. "I thought—my nephew was up

here and carried on like the snow was above the rooftops
by midwinter!"

"Hellfires, no, this isn't normal," the woman laughed.
"If your nephew was that young Journeyman Bard we had
through here—poor lad, one snowfall and he thought the
end of the world was coming in ice! But that was *after* some
of my people scared him half to death with their tales. Normal winter gives us snow every couple of weeks, not day
after day. Can't say as I mind it, though. Weather like this
is harder on the bandits than it is on us. We got clearing
crews; they don't, and it's damn difficult to move through
woods this deep in soft snow."

Stef knew that look, the one Vanyel was wearing now.
He finished the song he was on, just about the same time
as Van made a polite end to his conversation and headed
back to their room.

He gave the lute back to its finder, claiming weariness,
and ignoring the knowing looks as he hurried after the
Herald.

The guest room did not have a fireplace, and it was in
the area of the barracks farthest from the chimneys. Given
his choice, this was not where Stef would have gone. The
corridor was lit by a couple of dim, smoking lanterns, and
Stef would have been willing to swear he saw the smoke
freeze as it rose into the air. Vanyel was a dim white shape
a little ahead of him; he managed to catch up with the
Herald before he reached their door.

"What was it?" he asked, seizing Van's elbow. "What
did she say?"

He was half afraid that Van would pull away from him,
but the Herald only shook his head and swore under his
breath.

"I can't believe how stupid I was," he said quietly, as he
opened the door to their room and motioned Stef to go
inside. The candle beside the door and the one next to the
bed sprang into life as they entered—the kind of casual use
of magic that impressed Stef more than the nightly creation
of their shelter, because the use of magic to light a candle
implied that Van considered it no more remarkable than
using a coal from the fire for the same purpose. *That* was
frightening—that Van could afford to "waste" power that
way. . . .

"How were you stupid?" Stef persisted. "What did she

tell you other than the fact that they're having odd weather this winter?"

"Odd weather?" Vanyel grimaced. "That's rather like saying Randi's a little ill. You heard her, they've had *weeks* of snow, not the couple of days' worth they should have had."

He took his cloak down from the hook next to the door and bundled himself up in it. "Do you still want to be useful?" he asked, sitting down on the edge of the bed and looking up at Stef with the candle flames reflecting in his eyes.

"Of course I want to be useful—" Stef said uncertainly.

"Good. Stand by the door and make sure nobody comes in." Vanyel put his back against the wall, and pulled the cloak in tightly around himself. He cocked an eyebrow at Stef as the Bard shuffled his feet, hesitantly. "That's *not* a light request. I'm going into trance. I made the basic mistake of assuming that since I didn't sense any magic in the weather *around* us that it wasn't wizard weather. Obviously I was wrong."

"Obviously," Stef murmured, seeing nothing at all obvious about it.

"So, I'm going to be doing some very difficult weather-working, but I'm going to have to do it at some distance, where these snowstorms are being generated. When I do that, I'll be vulnerable." He waited for Stefen to respond.

After a moment, light did dawn. "Oh—so if there're any agents here—"

"Right. This would be the time for them to act. And since my magical protections are pretty formidable, the easiest thing would be to come after me physically." Vanyel settled back and closed his eyes.

"Van, what do you want me to do if somebody forces their way in here?" Stef asked, feeling for the hilt of his knife.

Vanyel opened his eyes again. "I want you to stop them however you have to," he said, his eyes focusing elsewhere. "This is one place where your street-fighting skill is going to do us some good. Take them alive if you can, but don't let them touch me. One of those leech-blades just has to touch the skin to be effective."

"All right," Stefen replied, feeling both a little frightened, and better than he had since this trip started. At least *now* he was doing something. And Van had admitted to needing him to do it. "You can count on me."

"If I didn't think I could," Van told him, closing his eyes again, "I wouldn't have asked you, lover."

Stef started at another noise; the candle had long since burned down to nothing, but he hadn't dared light another. Several times he'd thought he'd heard something outside the locked shutters on the room's single window, but nothing had ever happened.

The sound came again, but this time he realized it was coming from the bed. He groped his way over and sat down; the shapeless bundle of Van moved, and the cloak parted, letting out a faint mist of golden light. Stef gaped in surprise; his present, the amber mage-focus around Van's neck, was glowing ever so slightly. The light it gave off was just enough to see by.

"Anything happen?" Van asked, shaking long, silver-streaked hair out of his eyes. He looked like the old Vanyel; his face had lost some of that hard remoteness. And he *sounded* like the old Van, as well, his voice held concern for Stef as well as need to know if anything had gone wrong.

"I thought I heard something a couple of times, but other than that, nothing," Stef told him, still staring at the pendant. "Does it always do that?"

"Does—oh, yes, at least it has for a while. That's the best gift anyone's ever given me, especially now," Van said, his eyes and voice both warming. He stretched, throwing his cloak back a little and reaching high over his head, ending with one hand lying lightly on Stef's knee. "Having the focus to feed raw power through has made a lot of this much easier on me. I don't always have *time* to use it, but when I do, it extends my reach and my strength. I'm glad you cared enough about me to find it for me, *ashke*." He smiled, and Stef warmed all through. "The snow should stop in about a candlemark, and it won't start again the way it has been."

The abrupt change of subject didn't confuse Stef as much a it might have this time. "So it *was* wizard weather, then. Did you find out where it was coming from?"

"Vaguely. On the other side of this forest; possibly up in the mountains." Van massaged his right hand with his left. "That's the strange part, Stef, I've never heard of a power-

ful mage coming out of that area before. A few tribal sha-
mans, certainly, but never an Adept-class mage."

"Who says he has to have come from there?" Stef
replied, taking Van's hand and massaging it for him. *He's
treating me like a partner now, and not like a liability.* "He
could have come from somewhere else, the Pelagirs or Iftel,
maybe, and moved in there *because* there's no one there.
That's what *I* would do if I were a mage and wanted to
build myself up before I took on the world. I'd go up where
there aren't any mages. No rivals, no competition."

"That's reasonable, I suppose," Van admitted. "Listen,
lover, how upset would you be at not staying the couple of
days we planned here—at leaving at first light?"

"I told you I wasn't going to hold you back," Stefan said,
with a purely internal sigh of regret. "I'm not going to start
now by breaking that promise. If you want to leave, we'll
leave."

"I was hoping you'd say that," Van replied, kicking off
his boots. Stef took his cloak from him, and started peeling
off his own clothing, expecting that, as usual, the use of
magery would have left Vanyel too tired to do anything but
sleep.

Until he felt Van's hands sliding under his shirt.

"Here," the Herald breathed in his ear. "Let me help you
with that. This may be our last real bed for a while. . . ."

In the morning, that brief glimpse of the old Vanyel was
gone. Van was back to his new patterns; remote, silent,
face unreadable, eyes wary. Stef sighed, but he hadn't really
expected anything different. *At least I know that down under
the obsession, he's still the same person,* he thought, dressing
quickly in a room so cold that his breath frosted. *So when
this is over, I'll have him back again the way he was. It was
beginning to look like I'd lost the Van I love. . . .*

They saddled up and rode out without more than a cursory farewell. Stef had learned now to take care of Melody
entirely on his own while they'd been on the road, now he
didn't even think twice about getting her brushed down and
saddled, he just did it without waiting for the groom's help.

Most of what they were carrying was food for Yfandes
and Melody. There was a certain amount of provender out
here, even in the depth of winter, and Vanyel could, if he
chose, force-grow more overnight in their shelters. He could

even Fetch a limited amount every night from the stores
here at the Guard post, which was probably what he was
going to do. But the fact was it was harder to feed the horse
and the Companion out here in the winter woods than it
was to feed the humans, so their needs took priority over
Van and Stef's.

Stef was very glad for his new clothing, motley though it
was, the moment they got out of the shelter of the palisade
around the Guard post. Though the sky was as clear as Van
had promised—in fact, for the first time in weeks, Stef saw
the Morning Stars, Lythan and Leander, on the eastern
horizon—it was colder than it had been while it was
snowing.

A lot colder. Already Stef's nose was numb, and he was
very glad of the wool scarf wrapped around his ears under
the hood of his cloak.

Vanyel looked to the east, where the sky was just beginning to turn pink, and frowned a little. But he said nothing,
only urged Yfandes on, into the marginally clearer place
between the trees that marked what passed for a road up
here.

The sun rose—and at the moment it got above the tree-
tops, Stef knew what had caused Van to frown. Though
weak by summer standards, the clear sunlight poured
through the barren branches and reflected off of every surface, doubling, even tripling its effect on the eyes. The
ground was a blinding, undulating expanse of white, bushes
and undergrowth were mounds of eye-watering whiteness—
in fact, Stef pulled his head completely inside the hood of
his cloak and rode with his eyes squinted partly shut after a
few moments. The only relief was when they passed through
sections of conifers that overshadowed the road and blocked
the sunlight. Once out of their shade, the reflected sunlight
seemed twice as painful as before.

Still Vanyel pressed on, even though Melody and even
Yfandes tripped and stumbled because they couldn't see
where they were going, and couldn't guess at obstacles
under the cover of snow. The farther they got from the
Border, the thinner the snow-cover became, but the snow
and the light reflected from it were still *there,* still a problem, even past midday—and they did not take their usual
break to eat and rest. Finally Stef pulled Melody to a halt.
She hung her head, breath steaming, sweating, obviously

grateful for a chance to stop. Yfandes went on for a few more lengths, then paused. It took Vanyel several moments to notice that Stef was no longer behind him.

He turned and peered back through the snow-glare; hooded, White-clad Herald on his white Companion, he was hard to make out against the snow, and he looked like an ice-statue.

His voice was as cold as the chill air. "Why did you stop?"

"Because Melody and Yfandes need the rest you didn't take," Stef told him bluntly. "Look at Yfandes, look at how heavily she's breathing, how she's sweating! They don't have the chirras in front of them to break a path, Van, they need their rest at noon more than ever—"

"We don't have the time," Vanyel snapped, interrupting him.

"We don't have a *choice,*" Stef countered. "Yfandes will carry you until she drops, but what good are you going to be able to do if you kill her?" He nudged Melody with his heels, and she covered the few steps between them stiffly and reluctantly. He gestured at Yfandes, who had taken the same posture as Melody; head down, eyes closed, sides heaving. "Van, look at her, look at what you're doing to her. Hellfires, look at what you're doing to yourself! You can't see, you haven't eaten or had anything to drink since before dawn, and for what? This enemy of yours isn't *going* anywhere—he's going to be right where he's been all along!"

"But he knows we're coming—" Vanyel began.

"So what difference does that make?" Stefen sniffed, fighting back that traitorous lump that kept getting in the way of what he wanted to say, and rubbed his nose with the back of his glove. "He hasn't done much except throw a little snow at us so far, and that snow might not even have been thrown at *us*. Van, you're forgetting everything that makes you someone special, that makes you a Herald, every time you start focusing in on this enemy of yours. I mean, that's really it, he isn't an enemy of Valdemar anymore, he's a personal enemy, someone *you* want to take on by yourself—and you're running over everything and everybody in your path to get at him! Me, Randale, even Yfandes; none of us matter, as long as you can personally *destroy* this mage! Don't you see that? Don't you see what you're becoming?"

"You—" Vanyel's expression hardened still more, and he drew himself up, stiffly. "You have no idea of what you're talking about. You aren't a Herald, Stefen—you wouldn't even stand by Randale. How can you presume to judge—"

That was as far as he got. Yfandes jerked her head up, and trumpeted an alarm, but it was too late.

Men—hundreds, it seemed—burst through the snow-covered bushes on either side of the road. Melody started awake at Yfandes' scream, then shied violently at the shouting creatures running toward her. Stef clung to her saddle, bewildered—

Ambush? he thought, trying to hold onto Melody as she bucked and shied again, while Vanyel did something with his hands and balls of fire appeared from nowhere to burst in their attackers faces. *But—*

The exploding fire was the last straw so far as Melody was concerned. She screamed and fled, stumbling, down their backtrail, and bucked Stef off before they had gone more than two lengths.

Stefen went flying headfirst into a snowdrift, and came up, scraping snow out of his eyes, just in time to see Vanyel cut an axe-wielding attacker in half with his sword, while Yfandes mashed in a second man's face with her hindfeet.

At that moment Stef forget everything he ever was, and everything he ever knew. He was no longer thinking, only feeling—and the only thing he felt was fear.

And the only thing of any importance in the entire world was getting *away* from there.

He turned and ran. Ran as hard as he'd ever run in his life, with fear driving him and nipping at his heels. Ran along the backtrail and then off into the bushes, with branches lashing at him and buried protrusions tripping him.

Ran until he simply *couldn't* run anymore, until the sounds of fighting were lost in the distance, until he ran out of breath and strength and collapsed into the snow, lungs on fire, mouth parched, sides an agony, legs too weak to hold him.

He lay where he fell, waiting for one of the ambushers to come after him and kill him, fear making him whimper and tremble, but too spent even to crawl.

But nothing happened.

He pulled in great shuddering breaths of air, sobbing with fright, while his body finally stopped shaking with exhaustion and began shivering with cold. And still nothing happened.

He levered himself up out of the snow, and there was nothing in sight; no enemies, not even a bird. Only the snow-covered bushes he had fallen into, blue sky, bare tree-branches making a pattern of interlace across it, and the churned-up mess of snow and dead leaves of his backtrail through the undergrowth.

He listened, while fear ebbed and sense returned, slowly. He heard nothing, nothing whatsoever.

And finally thought returned as well. *Van! Dear gods—I left him alone back there—*

He struggled to his feet, and fought his way back through the bushes, staring wildly about. Still there was neither sight nor sound of anything.

Dearest gods, how could I do that—

Once again he ran, this time driven by guilt, along the swath his flight had cut through the snow and the forest undergrowth. He burst through a cluster of bushes onto the road, and literally stumbled onto the site of the ambush.

There was blood everywhere; blood, and churned-up snow and dirt, and bits of things that made Stef sick when he saw them—bits of things that looked like they had belonged to people.

Then his eyes focused on the center of the mess, on something he had first taken for a heap of snow.

Yfandes. Down, lying in a crumpled heap, like a broken toy left by a careless child, blood oozing from the stump where her tail had been chopped off.

No sign of Vanyel.

No—

Stef stumbled to Yfandes' side, afraid of what he would find. But there was nothing, no body, nothing. Yfandes had been stripped of her harness and saddle, and a trail of footprints and bloody snow led away from where she lay.

No—

His legs wouldn't hold him. His mind could not comprehend what had happened. In all the endless things he had imagined, there had been nothing like this. Vanyel had never been defeated—he never *could* be defeated.

No, no, no—

His heart tried to deny what his eyes were telling him; his mind was caught between the two in complete paralysis. He touched Yfandes' flank with a trembling hand, but she did not move, and Vanyel did not reappear to tell him that it was all a ruse.

His heart cracked in a thousand pieces.

NO!

He flung back his head, and howled.

"Damen!"

The boy started, fear so much a part of him that he no longer noticed it, and looked up from the pot he was tending on the hearth across the smoke-filled hall to the doorway.

The Lord. He cringed into the ashes on the hearthstones, expecting Lord Rendan to stalk over and deliver a blow or a kick. The men had gone out every day for the past two weeks on the orders of Master Dark, and had always come back empty-handed. Tempers were short, and Damen was usually the one who bore the brunt of those tempers.

But nothing happened, and his fear ebbed a little; he coughed and took a second look, raking his hair out of his eyes with a greasy hand and peering through a thicker puff of smoke and soot that an errant breeze sent down the half-choked chimney. Lord Rendan stood blocking the open doorway, arms laden with something bulky, a scowl on his face. But it wasn't the scowl Damen had come to dread these past two weeks, the one that told of failure on Rendan's part and punishment to come for Damen—

The boy scrambled to his bare feet, slipping a little on a splash of old tallow, and scuttled through the rotting straw and garbage that littered the floor to the lord's side. "Here," Rendan growled, thrusting the bundle at him. Damen took it in both arms, the weight making him stagger, as Rendan grabbed his shoulder and turned him toward the hearth. "Put it over there, on the bench," the lord snapped, as his fingers dug into Damen's shoulder, leaving one more set of bruises among the rest. The boy stumbled obediently toward the bench and dropped his burden, only then seeing that it was a saddle and harness, blood-spattered, but of fine leather and silver-chased steel.

A saddle? But we don't have any horses—

The lord threw something else atop the pile; white and shining, a cascade of silver hair—

A horse's tail; a white horse's tail, the raw end still bloody.

Before Damen could stir his wits enough to wonder what that meant, the rest of the men crowded in through the keep door, cursing and shouting, bringing the cold and snow in with them. Damen rubbed his nose on his sleeve, then scuttled out of the way. He stood as close to the fire as he could, for in his fourth-hand breeches and tattered shirt he was always cold. He counted them coming in, as he always did, for the number varied as men were recruited or deserted and may the gods help him if he didn't see that all of them had food and drink.

One hand's-worth, two hands, three and four hands—and five limp bodies, carried by the rest. One cut nearly in half; Gerth the Axe—

An' no loss there, Damen thought, with a smirk he concealed behind a cough. *One less bastard t' beat me bloody when 'e's drunk, an' try an' get into me breeches when 'e's sober.*

The others dropped Gerth's hacked-up body beside the door. Two more bodies joined his, bodies blackened and burned; Heverd and Jess. Damen dismissed them with a shrug; they were no better and no worse than any of the others, quite forgettable by his standards.

A fourth with the face smashed in was laid beside the rest, and Damen had to take account of the other faces before he decided it must be Resley the Liar. A pity, that— the Liar could be counted on to share a bit of food when the pickings were thin and there wasn't enough to go around, provided a lad had something squirreled away to trade.

But there was a fifth body, white-clad and blood-smeared; certainly no one *Damen* recognized. And that one was thrown down beside the pile of harness, not next to the door. An old man, he thought, seeing the long, silver-threaded hair; but that was before they dumped him unceremoniously beside the bench. Then the face came into the flickering firelight, and Damen blinked in confusion, for the face was that of a young man, not an old one, and a very handsome young man at that, quite as pretty as a girl. He was apparently unconscious, and tied hand and foot, and it occurred to Damen that *this* might be what Master Dark had set them all a-hunting these past two weeks.

He didn't have any time to wonder about the prisoner, for a few of the men set to stripping the bodies of their fellows and quarreling over the spoils, while the rest shouted for food and drink.

Damen gathered up the various bowls and battered cups that served as drinking vessels, and balanced them in precarious stacks in his arms. He passed among the men while they grabbed whatever was uppermost on the pile in his arms and filled their choice from the barrel atop the slab table in the center of the hall. Drink always came first in Lord Rendan's hall; sour and musty as the beer always was, it was still beer and the men drank as much of it as they could hold. Damen returned to the hearth, wrapped the too-long sleeves of his cast-off shirt around his hands and grabbed the end of the spit nearest him, heaving the half-raw haunch of venison off the fire. It fell *in* the fire, but the men would never notice a little more ash on the burned crust of the meat. He staggered back to the table under his burden of flesh, and heaved it with a splatter of juices up onto the surface beside the barrel, on top of the remains of last night's meal. Those that weren't too preoccupied with gulping down their second or third bowl of beer staggered over to the table to hack chunks off with their knives.

Now the last trip; the boy picked up whatever remained of the containers that hadn't been claimed as drinking vessels, and filled them one at a time from the pot of pease-pottage he'd been tending. He brought them, dripping, to the table, and slopped them down beside the venison, saving only one for himself. *He* was not permitted meat until the last of the men had eaten their fill, and he was not permitted beer at all.

He sat on his heels next to the hearth, and watched the others warily, gobbling his food as fast as he could, cleaning the bowl with his fingers and then licking it and them bare of the last morsel. Too many times in the past, one or more of the men had thought it good sport to kick his single allotted bowl of porridge out of his hands before he'd eaten more than half of it. Now he tried always to finish before any of the rest of them did.

But tonight the men had other prey to occupy them. As Damen tossed his bowl to the side and wrapped his arms around his skinny legs, Lord Rendan got up, still chewing, and strolled over to the side of the prisoner. The man was showing some signs of life now; moaning a little, and twitching. The Lord kicked him solidly in the side, and Damen winced a little, grateful that he wasn't on the receiving end of the blow.

Then Rendan reached down and untied the man, who didn't seem to understand that he'd been freed. The man acted a great deal like Rendan's older brother had, after his skull had been broken. Lord Gelmar hadn't died, not right away, but he couldn't walk or speak, and he'd acted as if he was falling-down drunk for more than a week before Rendan got tired of it and had him "taken outside."

"Careful, Rendan, he's like t' do ye—" one of the men called out.

"Not with that spell on 'im," the Lord laughed. "That powder Master Dark sent down with his orders was magicked. This 'un can hear and see us, but he can't *do* nothing." He kicked the man again, and the prisoner cried out, scrabbling feebly in the dirt of the floor.

"Just what *is* this beggar, anyway?" Kef Hairlip asked. "What's so bleedin' important 'bout him that the Master wants 'im alive an' talkin'? 'Ow come 'e 'ad us an' ever' other bunch 'twixt 'ere an' the mountains lookin' fer 'im?"

Tan Twoknives answered before the Lord could, standing up with a leaky mug in one hand and one of his knives in the other. "Kernos' balls, boy, haven't you never seen a Herald before?" He hawked and spat a gobbet of phlegm that fell just short of the prisoner's leg. "Bloody bastards give us more trouble'n fifty Kingsmen 'cross the Border, an' stick their friggin' noses inta ever'body's business like they got nothin' else t'do."

He shoved his knife back into his belt and swigged the last of his beer, then slammed the mug down on the table and strode forward to prod the prisoner himself.

Some of the others muttered; they all looked avid, greedy. More than half the band had long-standing grudges against Heralds; Damen knew that from the stories they told—though few of them had ever actually seen one. Mostly they'd been on the receiving end of Herald-planned ambushes or counter-raids, or been kicked in the teeth by Herald magic, without ever seeing their foe face-to-face. Heralds, Damen had reckoned (at least until now) were like the Hawkmen of the deep woods. You heard plenty of stories about them, and maybe even saw some of what they did to others that crossed their path, but if you were lucky, you never encountered one yourself.

Well, now they *had* one, and he didn't seem quite so formidable. . . .

"So, what's the Master's orders about this bastard, Rendan?" Tan asked prodding the prisoner with his toe again. "He's gotta be alive and talkin', but what else?"

Rendan crossed his arms, and looked down at the man, who had gone very silent and stopped moving. "He hasta be alive," Rendan said after a moment. "But the Master didn't say no more than that. The reward's th' same whether or not he's feelin' chipper."

Tan smiled crookedly, his yellowed and broken teeth flashing as he tucked his thumbs into his belt. "Well, if *that's* all he said—what'dye say t' gettin' some of our own back, eh?"

Damen nodded to himself, and tucked himself back farther next to the fireplace in the damp corner that he called his own. He knew that smile, knew that tone of voice. He blanked what had followed the *last* time he heard it out of his mind. He did *not* want to remember.

"I think that's a very good idea, Tan," Lord Rendan replied with a matching smile. He hauled the prisoner up by the front of his tunic, and threw him to Tan, who held him up until he stood erect—

Then punched him in the stomach with all his considerable strength.

The man doubled over and staggered backward toward Rendan, who leaned back against the table and kicked him toward one of the other men.

This amused them for a while, but after everyone had a turn or two, the novelty of having a victim who couldn't fight back and couldn't really react properly to the pain he was in began to bore them—as Damen had known it would, eventually. The only thing that actually did fight back was the thing the man had around his neck—it had burned whoever tried to take it, and eventually they left it on him.

Tan was the last to give up; he kneed the man in the groin and let him drop to the ground, limbs twitching. He stared at the Herald for a long time, before another slow smile replaced the scowl he'd been wearing.

He picked up a piece of the fancy horse-harness, a blue-leather strap embellished with silver brightwork, and turned it around and around in his hands. The prisoner moaned, and tried to crawl away, but succeeded only in turning over onto his back. He opened blind-looking silver eyes and stared right at Damen, though there was no sign that he actually saw the boy. There was a bruise purpling one cheekbone, and his right eye was just beginning to swell—but those injuries were nothing at all. Most of the blows had been to the vulnerable parts of the body, and Damen knew of men who'd died from less than the Herald had taken.

The Herald closed his eyes again, and made a whimpering sound in the back of his throat. That seemed to make up Tan's mind for him.

He reached for the man's hair with one hand, still holding the harness-strap in the other.

"Ah . . . y'sweet little horsey! Hah!" Tan rose from his knees, breathing heavily, refastening his breeches. "Who's next?" he asked, laughing. "Which o' ye stallion's gon' mount our little white mare? Little pup's's good's a woman!"

Damen couldn't watch. *He'd* been in that position before, when they'd first lured him out here, and away from another band, with promises of gold and feasting. Exactly the same position, except that he'd been forced over the bench, not a saddle, and he'd been whipped and brutally tied with rope-ends instead of harness. That was what he had tried hard not to remember—

He curled up in his corner, and buried his head in his arms, trying to block it all out. He could hide his eyes, but there was nowhere to hide from the sounds; the weak cries of pain, the rhythmic grunts, the soft wet sounds and throaty howls of pleasure, the creak of leather and jingle of harness.

It ain't me this time, he said to himself, over and over. *It don't matter. It ain't me.* He rubbed his wrists and stared in frightened paralysis at the floor, remembering how the ropes had torn into *his* skin, and how the men had laughed at *his* cries of agony.

And finally, he managed to convince himself, though he waited with shivering apprehension for the ones who hadn't yet had a turn to remember that *he* was in the hearth-corner, and that the bench was still unoccupied.

Not everyone had a taste for Tan's sport, though—either they weren't drunk enough, or the man wasn't young enough to tempt them, or any other of a dozen possible reasons, including that they still secretly feared the Herald despite his present helplessness.

Or they weren't convinced that Master Dark would be pleased with the results of this little diversion.

They all forgot Damen was even there—those that joined Tan in the helpless man's rape and those that simply watched and laughed, then wandered off to drink themselves stuporous and fall into one of the piles of old clothing, straw, and rags that most of them used for beds. Finally even Tan had enough; the noises stopped, except for a dull sound that could have been the Herald's moaning, or the wind.

Damen dozed off then, only to feel the toe of a boot prodding the sore spot on his rib cage from the last kick he'd gotten. He leapt to his feet, cowering back against the wall, blinking and shivering.

It was Lord Rendan again. "Go clean that mess up, boy," he said, jerking his chin at the huddled, half-clothed shape just at the edge of the firelight. "Clean him up, then lock him in the storeroom."

Damen edged past the Lord, then fumbled his way across the drunk and snoring bodies to where the prisoner still lay.

He'd been trussed and gagged with the harness, knees strapped to either end of the saddle, and as a kind of cruel joke, the silvery-white horse-tail had been fastened onto *his* rump. He was very thin, even fragile-looking, and his pale skin was so mottled with purple bruises he looked like the victim of some kind of strange plague.

Damen struggled with the strange straps and buckles and finally got him free of the saddle, but even after the boy had gotten him completely loose, the prisoner wouldn't—or maybe couldn't—do anything but thrash feebly and moan deep in his chest. Damen tugged his clothing more-or-less back into place, but the Herald didn't even notice he was there.

Get 'im inta the storeroom, 'e says. 'Ow'm I s'pposed t' do that? Damen spat in disgust, squatted on his heels to study the situation, and finally seized the man by the collar and hauled him across the floor and through the storeroom door.

The Lord lit a torch at the fire and brought it over, examining the prisoner by its light. The Herald had curled upon his side in a fetal position, and even Damen could tell he was barely breathing.

They did 'im, fer sure, he thought. *'It 'im too hard one way or 'tother. 'E don' look like 'e's gonna last th' night.*

Evidently Lord Rendan came to the same conclusion. He cursed under his breath, then threw the torch to the ground, where it sputtered and went out. Damen waited for the accustomed kick or slap, but the Lord had more important matters to worry about.

When Lord Rendan wanted to make the effort, he could have even hardened animals like Tan jumping to his orders. Before Damen could blink, he had a half dozen men on their feet, shaking in their patched and out-at-heel boots. Before the boy had any idea what the Lord had in mind, those men were out the door and into the cold and dark of the night.

The Lord returned to the storeroom with another torch, and stuck it into the dirt of the floor. And to Damen's utter surprise, Lord Rendan wrapped the prisoner in his own cloak, and forced a drink of precious brandywine down his throat.

"Stay with him, boy," the Lord ordered, laying the man back down again. "Keep him breathing. Because if he don't last till the Healer gets here—Master Dark is goin' t' be real unhappy."

Damen began shivering, and squatted down beside the man, piling everything that could pass for a covering atop him. He remembered what had happened to Lord Rendan's younger brother, the last time Master Dark had been unhappy with the band.

Sometimes you could hear him screaming when the wind was right. Master Dark had decided to recreate a legend, about a demigod whose eyes were torn out, and whose flesh was food for the birds by day and regrew every night. . . .

Not even Tan ate crewlie-pie after that, though the carrion-birds grew sleek and fat and prospered as never before.

No, Damen did not want Master Dark to be unhappy. Not *ever*.

*   *   *

Old Man Brodie bent over and ran his hands along the roan colt's off foreleg. He let his Healing senses extend—carefully—into the area of the break, just below the knee.

And let the energy flow.

A few moments later, he checked his progress. *Bone callus; good. And under it . . . hmm . . . knitting nicely. No more running about creekbeds for you, my lad; I'll bet you learned* your *lesson this time.*

He withdrew—as carefully as his meager skills would allow him to. The horse shuddered and champed at the unexplainable twinge in its leg, sidled away from the old man, then calmed. *Ach . . . too rough on leaving.* He regretted his lack of polish every day of his life since he'd failed as a Healer, the way he'd barely get a job done, never completely or with anything approaching style.

And never without causing as much pain to his patient as he was trying to cure—pain which he shared, and pain which he could, after several years of it, bear no longer.

His teachers had told him that he was his own worst enemy, that his own fear of the pain was what made it worse and made him clumsy. He was willing to grant that, but knowing intellectually what the problem was and doing something about it proved to be two different matters.

And *that* hurt, too.

Finally he just gave up; turned in his Greens and walked north until the road ran out. Here, where no one knew of his failure and his shame, he set himself up as an animal Healer, making a great show of the use of poultices and drenches, purges and doses, to cover the fact that he was using his Gift. His greatest fear had been that someday, someone would discover his deception, and uncover what he had been.

He stood up, cursing his aching back; and the colt, with the ready forgiveness of animals, sidled up to him and nibbled his sleeve. Brodie's breath steamed, illuminated by the wan light from the cracked lantern suspended from the beam over his head. He was glad the farmer had brought the colt into the barn; it would have been hellish working on a break kneeling in the snow. "That'll do him, Geof," Brodie said, slinging the bag that held his payment—a fat, smoke-cured ham—over his shoulder. The farmer nodded brusquely, doing his best to mask his relief at not having to put down a valuable animal. "He won't be any good for races, and I'd keep him in the barn over winter if I was you, but he'll be pulling the plow like his dam come spring, and a bad foreleg isn't going to give him trouble at stud."

The colt sniffed at the straw at his feet.

"Thankee, Brodie," Geof Larimar said, abandoning his pretense at calm. "When I found 'im, allus I could think of was that 'is dam's over twenty, an' what was I gonna do come spring if she failed on me? I 'preciate your comin' out in th' middle of th' night an' all."

"I appreciate the ham—" Brodie replied, scratching the colt's ears, "and I'd rather you called me when the injuries are fresh, it's easier to treat 'em that way."

"I coulda swore that leg was broke, though," Geof went on inexorably, and Brodie went cold all over. "He couldn't put a hair worth o' weight on it—"

"Bad light and being hailed out of bed are enough to fool any man," Brodie interrupted. "Here—feel the swelling?" he guided the farmer's hand to the area he'd just treated, still swollen and hot to the touch from the increased blood flow he'd forced there. "Dislocation, and a hell of a lot easier to put back in when it's just happened than if he'd had it stiffen overnight."

"Ah," the farmer said, nodding sagely. "That'd be why 'e couldn't put weight on it."

"Exactly." Brodie relaxed; once again he'd managed to keep someone off the track. He yawned hugely. "Well, I'd best be on my way. Could stand a bit more sleep."

Geof showed him out and walked with him as far as the gate. From there Brodie took the lonely little path through the creek-bottom to his isolated hut.

Not isolated enough, he brooded. *That Dark bastard managed to find me. . . .*

For he hadn't been able to keep his secret from everyone. Three years ago, a handsome young man had come strolling up to his very door and proceeded to tell him, with an amused expression, everything he *didn't* want anyone to know. Then informed him that he would make all this public—unless Brodie agreed to "do him a favor now and again."

The "favors" turned out to be Healing an endless stream of ruffians and bandits who came to his door by night, each bearing "Master Dark's" token. Their injuries were always the kind gotten in combat—Brodie asked no questions, and they never said anything. But after the first two, when it became evident that these patients were never better than thieves and often worse, Brodie began taking a twisted sort of satisfaction in his *lack* of skill where they were concerned. It only seemed right that in order to be Healed these cutthroats suffered twice the pain they would have if they'd recovered naturally.

Brodie was altogether glad that it was the dead of winter. He seldom saw more than two or three of them during the coldest months. . . .

He squinted up at the sky; first quarter moon, and the sky as clear as crystal. It would be much colder, come dawn.

He heaved himself up the steep, slippery side of the cut, and onto the path that led to his hut.

And froze at the sound of a voice.

"About time, ye ol' bastid," growled a shadow that separated itself from a tree trunk and strode ruthlessly toward him. "Time t' pay yer rent agin. Th' Master needs ye."

Eighteen

"What in Kernos' name did you *do* to him?" Brodie spluttered, white and incoherent with rage. Having to patch up one of these bastards was bad enough—but being called on to save one of their half-dead victims, presumably so that they could deliver similar treatment to him again—it was more than Brodie was willing to take silently.

The man was catatonic and just barely alive. Raped, beaten to unconsciousness, a cursory examination told Brodie he was bleeding internally in a dozen places, and only a wiry toughness that gave the lie to his fragile appearance had saved him from death before Brodie ever got there.

The so-called "Lord" Rendan shrugged. "It's none of your concern, Healer," he growled. "Master Dark wants this man, and he wants him alive and able to talk. You Heal him; that's all you need to know. You'd better do a good job, too, or else. . . ."

Rendan smirked, showing a set of teeth as rotten as his soul, and his less-than-subtle threat chilled Brodie's heart. This was more than simple risk of exposure, then, this was his life that was in danger now.

But if he showed his fear . . . working with beasts had taught him that displaying fear only makes the aggressor more inclined to attack.

"Get out of here, and let me work in peace," he growled, hoping the flickering of the single candle Rendan had brought into the storeroom hid the shaking of his hands. "Animals, the lot of you. Worse than animals, not even a rabid pig would do something like this! Go on, get out, and I'll see if anything can be done. And leave the damned candle! You think I'm an owl? And send in the boy—I may need him. He's practically useless, but the rest of you are worse."

Rendan lost his smirk, confronted by defiance where he
didn't expect it, demands where he expected acquiescence,
and reluctantly sidled out, leaving Brodie alone with his
desperate work.

Gods of light—Brodie didn't have to touch the man to
know that it was a good thing he was unconscious. Every
nerve was afire with pain. Brodie removed the heap of rags
covering him carefully, all too aware of how the least little
movement would make what was agony into torture for
both of them.

The man was already a strange one; hair streaked with
silver as any old gaffer, yet plainly much younger, and
under the bruises was a face that would set maidens swoon-
ing. When Brodie got down to his clothing he frowned,
trying to remember where he'd heard of white garments like
this man wore.

*Something out of Valdemar wasn't it? Kingsmen of some
kind. Not Harpers—Heralds? What's a Kingsman of Valdemar doing outside his borders?*

Well, it didn't much matter; the man's labored breathing
told Brodie that if he didn't do something quickly, this particular Kingsman would be serving from under the sod.

All right, you poor lad, Brodie thought, nerving himself
for the plunge. *Let's see how bad you really are. . . .*

Stef's throat was raw, and his eyes swollen when he finally
got control of himself again. He scrubbed at his eyes with
the back of his hand, and carefully slowed his breathing.

*Oh, gods, control yourself. Look at the facts, Stef; Van's
gone. This isn't doing anybody any good. He's not dead, or
there'd be a body. Besides, I'd know if he was dead. That
means they took him away somewhere. They left a trail even
I can follow, which means wherever they took him, I can
find him. And if I can find him, maybe I can get him loose.*

He took steady, deep breaths of air so cold it made his
lungs ache, and looked up at the dark, star-strewn sky.
Night had fallen while he'd cried himself senseless; there
was a clear quarter-moon, so he should have no trouble
reading the trail the ambushers had left. The moon was
amazingly bright for the first quarter; so bright he had no
trouble making out little details, like the drops of blood
slowly oozing from the stump where poor Yfandes' tail had
been chopped off—

Suddenly his breath caught in his throat. *She's bleeding! Dead things don't bleed!*

But if she isn't dead, why does she look dead?

Magic—has to be. And magic's the only way they'd have taken Van down . . . like the magic that got Savil and the others. And since I didn't see anything that acted like a mage before I—

Well, that means it was probably a magic weapon, something any fool could use. Probably something still here.

Galvanized by the thought, he began searching Yfandes' body meticulously, thumblength by thumblength, searching for something—anything that might qualify as a weapon. He wasn't certain what it would be, except that he had a vague notion it might be something very like that leech-dagger—the ploy had worked once, and people tended to repeat themselves . . . another dagger, maybe, or an arrow.

Almost a candlemark later, he found what he thought might be what he was looking for; a tiny dart, hardly longer than the first joint of his index finger, buried in Yfandes' shoulder, hidden by her mane. It tingled when he touched it, in the way he'd come to associate with magic. Maybe it wasn't what he thought it was—

But he gripped it as carefully as he could, and pulled, praying he wasn't leaving anything behind.

Yfandes drew a great, shuddering breath. Then another.

And suddenly Stefen was bowled over backward into a heap of bloodstained snow as she surged to her feet, and pivoted on her hindquarters, teeth bared, eyes rolling, looking for a target.

Her eyes met his.

Brodie ignored the aches of his body, the noisy breathing of the child beside him. He found himself doing things he never thought he could, driven by a rage that increased with every new injury he uncovered.

The young man had some slight Gift of Healing, and a boundless store of energy, which was certainly what had kept him alive all this time.

The Feel of blue-green Healing power was unmistakable, and Brodie approached the man's injuries cautiously after he first passed the man's low-level shields and encountered it. It was well that he did so. . . .

Dear gods— Everywhere he looked there was Healing

magic; low-level, but comprehensive. There was a fine net of Healing holding each critical hurt stable, sealing off the worst of the bleeding, keeping the swelling down. Brodie had to insinuate himself delicately into that net, replacing its energies with his own. But once he did that, he found that he now had an awesome amount of power available to him—such a tremendous amount that it was frightening.

He isn't a Healer—and I can't See that he's a mage, much less an Adept-class— but where in the gods' names did he get this reservoir of power from? What is he? And why is it Dark wants him?

But there was something subtly interfering with Brodie's own powers, and keeping the man from doing anything effective about his hurts. Then Brodie identified what it was—when he finally had a breath to spare and could take a more leisurely look at the major repair work he had ahead of him.

For when he probed into the man's abilities, beneath a shell of *external* blockage was something that Brodie suspected had to be Mage-Gift, though the blockage had it so sealed off that until then the Healer had not seriously considered that the man might be a mage. But Mage-Gift tied in and integrated with all the others in quite a remarkable way, so that interference with it rendered the rest of the man's abilities ineffective or impaired.

Brodie smiled, withdrew a little, and contemplated the external matrix of the spellblock. From within it was perfectly smooth, perfectly created to leave no crack and no opening that a mage so entrapped could use to break it open.

But from the outside—that was a different story entirely. The outside of the thing was rutted, creviced and full of weak spots. Brodie had no doubt that even a simple Healer like himself could find some way to break it open. After all, if a Healer could get through another person's shields to treat him, he ought to be able to break into a blocking-spell providing he could find something *his* power could work on. Half the battle was being able to See what was wrong; or so his teachers had always told him. "If you can See it, you can act on it—" was the rule.

Brodie had never heard of a Healer breaking a spell, but after all the things he'd done so far, things he'd have sworn that *he,* at least, couldn't do, he was willing to try this one.

The spell probably accounted for the man's catatonia—and no one had ordered Brodie *not* to interfere with it. Rendan had, in fact, told him to do "whatever it takes." He actually had permission, if oblique, to do exactly what he wanted to do.

He smiled again, seeing the perfect revenge for everything Rendan and Master Dark had done to him within reach, for when this man came back to himself again and found he was no longer blocked. . . .

"I just can't Heal him without cracking this thing," he said aloud to the boy, just on the chance that the child might be a spy for his master. He savored the words as he spoke them. "My goodness, I can't imagine what it could be for, but it's certainly keeping me from doing *my* job."

The boy scratched his head, then caught and killed a flea crawling across his forehead. He looked at the wall beyond the Healer incuriously. Brodie smiled again. *The child's no more than he seems. No one is going to interfere.*

And with that, he set himself to examining the spell-net, energy-pulse by energy-pulse. And found, much sooner than he expected, the point of vulnerability.

The spell was also tied into the man's physical condition, rendering his sense of balance useless and confusing his other senses, so that sight and sound were commingled and impossible to sort out. The man would be *seeing* speech as well as hearing it, for instance, and hearing color as well as seeing it.

But where the spell touched on the physical, the Healer had a point where *his* power could affect it. And since the spell was an integrated unit, once a weakness was exploited, the rest could be dis-integrated and destroyed from within.

Brodie laughed out loud, formed his power into a bright green stiletto-point, and set to work, chiseling his way into the spell.

Stef froze. Yfandes' eyes were glowing, a deep, angry red that cast a faint red light on the white skin around them. He'd never seen or heard of anything like it; it was a reflection of rage he guessed, and he wasn't sure she even recognized him. He'd seen what those hooves could do—

:*Where is he?*: growled a female voice, seeming to come from everywhere and nowhere.

He couldn't help himself; he gasped and looked wildly

around, wondering how anyone had come up on him without him noticing.

:It's me, Bard.: Yfandes stalked stiffly up to him, and shoved his shoulder with her nose, knocking him over sideways. *:What happened to Van? Where is he? All I remember is being darted.:*

He stared at Yfandes, stunned. *She must be Mindspeaking me, but how? I don't have the Gift—* "I don't know," he said aloud. "I—I ran away—"

:I know that, boy,: she snorted, mentally and physically. *:Which was exactly what Van told you to do, if you'll exercise your damned memory and stop having a crisis of conscience. And I can Bespeak anyone I choose to, it's one of the abilities Companions try not to use if there's any way around it. Now how much time have you been wasting? Were the bastards still around, or were they gone when you came back here?:*

"I—uh—they were gone," he stammered, clambering to his feet. "But they didn't exactly try to hide their trail—"

He pointed at the trampled snow just beyond her. She swung her head around then turned back to him. *:How long?:* she demanded again.

"It isn't much past sunset now—" he gulped, and continued bravely, "It was late afternoon when I found you. I thought you were dead. I just sort of—"

:Tyreena's blessed ass, you went into shock, Bard, you've never seen combat, you've never lost a beloved, and you went into thrice-damned shock. You pulled yourself together, which is more than I would have given you credit for being able to do. Now, are you ready to come with me and save him?:

He nodded, unable to speak.

:Then tie off my tail-stump so I don't leave a track for the wolves to follow, and let's get on with it, shall we?: She raised her head, and her eyes continued to glow with that strange crimson light. *:I can't Sense him, which probably means they had more than just the dart and he's spellblocked from me. But he's not dead. They couldn't kill him without my knowing.:*

Stefen searched what little had been left behind, and found a thong tied to the handle of a broken axe. He approached her flank with trepidation, the thong held out stiffly in front of him.

She swung her head in his direction and snorted again. *:Pelias' tits, Bard, I'm not a horse, I'm not going to kick you! Get on with it!:*

He stumbled over the lumps of frozen snow in his haste, but managed not to fall too heavily against her. He could feel her muscles stiffening, bracing herself to keep him erect until he regained his balance. He tied the bleeding stump of her tail off as hard as he could; felt her wincing a little, but didn't quit binding it until the bleeding stopped.

She craned her neck and rump around to survey his handiwork, and nodded with approval. *:Good. Gods, that hurts, though. Now, have you ever ridden bareback?:*

"No—" he replied.

:Well, you're about to learn.:

Vanyel prowled the dark, sheltered corner of his mind that was the only place free of pain, the only place that was still *his* and his rage seethed with all the red-hot, pent fury of a volcano about to erupt. Periodically he tested his bonds, but they never yielded, and he was forced to retreat again. He wanted revenge; he wanted to feel *those others* die beneath the lash of his anger as the construct had died. He wanted to hear them shriek in pain and fear; he wanted to destroy them so utterly that there would not even be a puff of ash to blow away on the breeze when he was finished.

And there was nothing he could do. The spell confusing his senses was too strong to break out of; even when they'd freed his hands and feet, he'd been unable to act on that freedom. Whoever had sent that spell powder had known what Van was capable of, and had integrated magic-blocking with Mind-magic-blocking, until there was nothing he could use to lever himself out of his encapsulation.

Whoever? No—this could only be the work of his enemy. No one else knew him so well, knew his weaknesses as well as his strengths. And Vanyel had tipped his hand by using Fetching to retrieve the construct, telling his enemy, in effect, exactly what he was dealing with.

He cursed himself for having the stupidity to play right into his enemy's hands.

And his anger built until that was all there was—white rage and the hunger to kill.

Then, suddenly, one of the walls he had been flinging himself against vanished, giving him the opening he needed.

He burst his mage-born bonds and roared up out of himself, wild as a rabid beast, every deadly weapon in his arsenal sharp and ready, and looking only for a target.

Any target.

Stef found that riding bareback—at least on Yfandes—was not as hard as he'd thought it would be. Moon or no, in broad daylight Melody had stumbled and missed paces, and he had no idea how Yfandes was finding her way in the near-darkness. She flowed along the rough ground like a scent-hound, nose to the ground, relying on him to keep watch for enemies. What he was supposed to *do* about those enemies, he had no idea—

Snow had blown over the tracks they were following once they got up out of the sheltered hollow where they'd been ambushed. That didn't seem to bother Yfandes, much. Only once did she cast about herself for the trail, when they came up on a large meadow, silver and seamless under the moonlight, with a stiff breeze still scudding snow across it in sinuously snaking lines.

She looked out over the white expanse, and circled around the edge under the trees until she came to a place where she could pick the trail up again.

Stef felt entirely useless, just a piece of baggage on Yfandes' back.

:You won't be useless when we find them,: came the dry, unsolicited voice in his head. *:You may be more involved than you'd prefer. Now will you kindly think of snow, please?:*

"What?" he replied, startled.

:You're broadcasting distress to anyone able to pick up thoughts, and that distress is very much centered on Van. I don't think they have a real mage or Mind-Gifted with them, but we daren't take the chance. So will you please think about snow? Or concentrate on how cold you are. Those are ordinary enough thoughts that they shouldn't give us away.:

He huddled down a little farther into his cloak, and did as he was told, looking up at the thin clouds drifting over the moon, shivering every time the breeze found its way down the back of his neck or in the arm-slit of his cloak. He tried very hard to concentrate on how miserable he was

feeling, on how he wished he was sitting beside a roaring
fire, with wine mulling on the hearth, and Vanyel—

Dammit.

With wine mulling on the hearth and nowhere to go. Or
sinking into a warm featherbed—

He stopped that one before it started.

Or standing before a feasting-hall crowded with adoring
listeners, his stomach full of a fine dinner and better wine,
and his ears full of praise—

He managed to dwell on that image for quite some time,
until a particularly sharp gust of wind cut right through his
cloak and gave him more thoughts of cold and misery to
dwell on.

He managed to feel quite sorry for himself before too
very long, and dwelling on his own unhappiness made it a
lot easier to "forget" Van, and what their attackers might
be doing to him.

It seemed as if they'd been traveling for an awfully long
time, though.

:It's nearly dawn,: 'Fandes said. *:But that's not too surprising. I hardly expected them to ambush us too near their own
stronghold. The trail is getting very fresh, though, and—:*

She stopped, suddenly, and flung her head up to catch
the breeze, hitting *him* in the face with the back of her
skull, and nearly knocking his front teeth out.

*:Sorry. They're near. I smell woodsmoke, heated stone,
burned venison, and them. Get down, and we'll take this
quietly. There's bound to be a sentry, but whether it'll be on
the walls or outside them—:*

Let's hope it's outside, Stef thought, flexing his stiff hands,
then sliding off her back to land knee-deep in snow. *We
won't be able to get past him if there's a sentry on the wall,
and I don't know the first thing about taking one out.*

He let Yfandes lead the way, picking his feet up carefully
to keep from falling over anything. Finally she stopped,
right on the edge of a screening of bushes.

:Careless, lazy, or stupid,: she said, and for a moment he
wondered if she meant *him*—

*:They've let all this undergrowth spring up on the edge
of their clearing,:* she continued, her mind-voice thick with
contempt. *:We can come right up to the walls without anyone
ever seeing us. Ah, there he is. Stef, look up there, just above
the door. See him?:*

Stef picked his way up to the bushes and looked—sure
enough, there was *something* there, pacing back and forth
a little. A shadow among shadows, on the top of a wall
that even in the dim moonlight showed severe neglect. The
square-built keep would not have lasted a candlemark in a
siege.

   :That's the sentry and that's the only one they have.: She
paused a moment. *:Now what that means is that this is probably the only way into the building, which is not very good
for us.:*

   "I could just walk up there," he offered. "I'm a Bard, I
could just pretend I'm a traveling minstrel—"

   *:In the dead of winter, the middle of nowhere? Minstrels
don't travel in winter if they can help it. How the blazes did
you get out here, and why did you come? They may be
stupid, but they're probably suspicious bastards.:*

   "Uh—I could say I was turned out of my post—"

   She snorted. *:Have you seen any Great Houses since three
days before the Border?:*

   "My inn, then—the innkeeper's wife and I——"

   *:Why here? This isn't a very promising place. It's all but
falling to pieces.:*

   "I'm cold and hungry, and I wouldn't care if it was the
first place I saw with people and food and fire—"

   :Wait.: She raised her head to look over his. *:Some-
thing's happening.:*

   With no more warning than that, the center of the building went up with a ear-numbing roar in a sheet of red and
green flames.

   Stef squeaked, and hid his eyes with his forearm, then
peeked under the crook of his elbow. The entire front of
the building had burst outward in the time he'd hidden his
eyes; the door was splinters, and the right side of the keep
had already collapsed outward. There were screams, but no
sign of fire, and Stef realized then that what he'd just seen
was an explosion of mage-power.

   :Get on!: Yfandes ordered, and he scrambled onto her
back. She didn't even wait this time until he'd settled himself; she just leapt through the bushes with the Bard clinging
to her mane and trying desperately to get a grip on her with
his legs.

   She raced across the small expanse of clear ground
between the bushes and the keep, and crashed through what

was left of the door, coming to an abrupt halt just inside.
He blinked, his eyes burning from the foul smoke blowing
into them, and tried to make out what was going on. Here,
inside the building, there were fires, small ones. Furniture
burning. Piles of rags, smoldering—

Men.

With horror and nausea, Stefen realized that fully half of
what he had thought were burning piles of flotsam were
actually burning bodies, aflame with the same blood-red
fires Van had used to destroy the raven-thing. And some
of the piles were thrashing and screaming.

He tumbled from Yfandes' back as she pivoted, lashing
out with hooves and teeth at a man running by. He tried
to make some sense of the confusion, looking, without consciously realizing he was doing so, for Van.

And then the fires rose higher, reflecting off a single figure, the red glare concealing until this moment the fact that
the man wore shredded Whites. Scarlet mage-fires turned
his white-streaked hair into a cascade of ripping shadow
threaded with blood. Just beyond, a group of terrified men
crouched against the far wall, cowering away from him;
some pleading, some simply trying to melt into the stone of
the wall in numb fear.

"Vanyel!" Stef shouted. The Herald turned around for a
moment, but a movement by one of the men he had cor-
nered made him turn back to face them. It *was* Vanyel, but
not a Van that Stefen recognized. Like Yfandes, his eyes
and the mage-focus around his neck glowed an identical,
angry red, and beneath the glow the eyes were not sane.
His clothing was tattered and bloodstained, and his face
disfigured with bruises, but it was not that mistreatment that
made him impossible to identify. It was those furious, mad
eyes, eyes which held nothing in common with humanity at
all.

Vanyel gestured, and one of the men shivering against
the wall jerked upright, and stumbled toward him. As he
did so, the last of the screaming stopped, though the fires
continued to burn in eerie silence. In that silence, the man's
whimpering pleas for mercy were sickeningly clear.

Vanyel laughed. "What mercy did you grant *me,* scum?"
he replied in a soft, conversational voice. "It seems to me
that I remember you. It seems to me that you were the first
and the last to sate yourself. 'Little white mare,' I believe

you called me." He gestured again, and the bandit stooped, like a clumsily-controlled marionette, and picked something up from the floor.

It was the splintered end of a spear-shaft, ragged, but as sharp as anything of metal. The bandit's arms jerked again, and the jagged end of it was placed against his stomach.

The bandit's eyes widened; his mouth opened, but nothing emerged. There was a popping sound, and as the point of the wood penetrated the bandit's clothing, Stefen realized with horror that Vanyel was forcing the brigand to disembowel himself, controlling his body with Mind-magic.

"No!" he screamed. *"Van, no!"*

He flung himself between the two, and faced that frightening mask of insanity, his hands held out in pleading. "Van, you're a *Herald,* no matter what they did to you, you *can't* do that to him!"

The red glow died from Van's eyes for a moment; then his jaw hardened, and something like an invisible hand pushed Stefen out of the way. The Bard stumbled and fell to the filthy floor, but was up again in a breath, and right back between the Herald and his victim. The brigand fell onto his back, writhing, then stiffened as Vanyel stepped forward.

"Van—Van, don't! If you do this, *you'll be just as bad as he is.* Don't let *him* do that to you! Don't let *them* make you into something like they are!"

Vanyel froze, with his hand still outstretched.

Then the angry red glow faded, first from his eyes, then from the pendant at his breast. He blinked, and sanity returned to his face.

He looked around at the carnage he caused, and his face spasmed; his mouth twisted as if he was going to be sick, but his eyes went to two bodies beside a storeroom door, and stayed there. One of those bodies was that of an old man, with the kind of pouch an herb-Healer often carried spilled out on the floor beside him. The other body was too small to be an adult; it had to be a child.

Van's posture betrayed him—tense, and legs slightly bent.

He's going to bolt— Stef realized, wondering if he could tackle the Herald before he broke and ran.

:No, he's not,: Yfandes said firmly, and interposed herself between Vanyel and the door.

Something—broke open. And suddenly Stef felt what

Vanyel was feeling. Absolute revulsion at the deaths, the massacre *he* had caused. Despair at the knowledge that he had killed at least one innocent; two if the boy could be counted in that category. Contemptible. Worse than contemptible . . . *hateful. Insane.* . . .

Under the self-loathing, the fear that Yfandes and Stef would both repudiate him, would hate him for what he'd done, and cast him out of their lives and hearts.

"No—Van—" Stef walked carefully toward him, slowly, with Yfandes maneuvering to keep Van's escape blocked. "Listen to me, it's not your fault. You were in pain, your mind was confused, you weren't able to think of anything except hurting them back. That's part of you—*everybody* has that as a part of them. You're not a god, above mistakes! It's just a part of you that you lost control of for a little. If it had been *me*, I'd probably have done a lot worse things than you did—"

'Fandes herded the Herald in close enough that Stef could get Vanyel in his arms. He did so, before Van could evade his embrace. The Herald shuddered all over his body, like a terrified animal.

:We've a problem, Bard: Yfandes said grimly. *:There's a lot worse damage than we thought.:* And through her powers, she permitted him a glimpse of a little of what had been done to Van, a glimpse that suddenly made Van's speech about being "sated" and "little white mares" understandable. Stefen choked—and then had to make a conscious effort to start breathing again.

The bandits seemed to realize that Vanyel was no longer a threat, and began slipping past the three of them to vanish into the thin, gray light of dawn beyond the walls. Stef ignored them; they didn't matter. What mattered was Van.

He held Vanyel, but not in a way that would confine him—lightly—and tried to send back love along the link between them. The last of the brigands, the man who'd nearly impaled himself at Vanyel's command, crawled toward the shattered door, leaving a blood-smeared trail. He scrambled to his feet when he reached it, and tumbled out of sight beyond a pile of toppled stone blocks. *I don't think he'll live long out there,* Stefen thought. *I can't really admit to caring much if he does.*

Gray light filled the hollow of the wrecked hall, and the mage-fires died and went out, leaving smears of black ash

where the burning bodies had been. Vanyel stood shivering
and tense in Stefen's arms, while the sun rose over the walls
of the keep. Finally, as the sun touched his blood-soaked,
tangled hair, he collapsed into Stef's embrace.

Yes, Stefen thought. *We've won the first round—*

:*It won't be the last,:* Yfandes said, smoldering anger
beneath her words. :*They've broken him.:*

Then it's up to us to put him back together.

"Come on, Vanyel-*ashke*," he said softly. "Let's go. Let's
get you somewhere warm and safe."

Stef found the tack, and the configurations it had been
twisted into made him tight with anger. He managed to get
it all untangled, got Yfandes saddled and bridled, then she
knelt and Van practically fell into her saddle.

:*I'd ask you to put the supports on him,:* she said after
she stood up again, :*—but—:*

"I have a pretty good idea," Stef answered her, wishing
that the bandit Van had nearly impaled hadn't gotten away.
"I'm nowhere near as innocent as Van still thinks I am.
He'd just get thrown back to last night if he felt restraints."

Vanyel had fallen into a half-stupor; shock, Stef guessed.
And at this point, the last thing he wanted to do was rouse
him.

"I can walk beside, and steady him in the saddle, if you
don't go too fast," he told the Companion.

:*Good. Thank you.:* She moved off a few steps. :*How's
that?:*

"That will do." He kept one hand in the small of Vanyel's
back, holding his sword-belt, and one clutching the front of
Van's saddle. Now, if Stefen tripped, he wouldn't fall and
take Van with him. "Where are we going?" he asked, as
she led him through the wreckage of the doorway and into
the sunlight. Several trails of footprints led away from the
place, and she looked around for a moment.

:*Anywhere except where those lead,:* she replied, finally.
:*Other than that, I really don't know. . . .:*

:*Perhaps, white sister,:* said a strange, very dry voice, :*you
should determine a direction before setting out.:*

The bushes directly ahead of them rustled, and something
large—*very* large—stepped out from among them.

:*Perhaps I can help,:* the voice continued.

Stef groped after a knife, his eyes fixed on the creature,

his heart right in his throat. This beast—whatever it was—
looked something like a wolf, but was much bigger than any
wolf Stef had ever heard of or seen. Its shoulder was as tall
as his waist; it had a thin, rangy body with long legs, and
a head with a very broad, rounded forehead, forward-facing
eyes, and jaws—

*Dear gods, that thing could bite my arm in half and never
notice—*

:I could, singer, but I won't.: The thing lolled out its
tongue in a canine grin. *:I see you recognize my Folk, white
sister. Tell him:*

:That's a kyree, *Stef. A neuter, I think.:* Yfandes bowed
her head to the creature, and Stef relaxed marginally. *:One
with a very powerful Gift of Mindspeech, or you wouldn't
be able to hear him . . . er, it.:*

:Indeed, right on all counts.: The *kyree* padded elegantly
across the snow toward them. *:I am the FarRanger for the
Hot Springs Clan. I felt the magic, and I came. We are like
in power, white sister, and you know my kind. Can I give
you a direction?:*

:Do you know the Tayledras?: she asked. The *kyree* nodded. *:We have a treaty with them, all Clans of the Folk.:*

:This one is Wingbrother to k'Treva.: She tossed her head
at her rider.

He raised his head and, peered keenly at Vanyel. *:Then
we are honor-bound to give you more than direction, we
must give you aid and shelter. Though of my own will,:* he
added over his shoulder as he turned, *:I would have done
so anyway.:* His lip lifted as he sniffed audibly. *:The things
here were a foul, uncleanly folk, and the world is well rid of
them. In time, they might have been a danger to my Clan.:*

Yfandes followed the *kyree* beneath the trees, where it
turned northward. *:I am Yfandes, this is Stefen, and my
Chosen is Vanyel,:* she said formally.

The *kyree* looked back over its shoulder for a moment.
:I am Aroon,: he replied, just as formally. *:There is deep
mind-hurt with the one you call your Chosen.:*

Stef felt Yfandes' shoulder muscles relax a little. *:Yes.
Have you a MindHealer among your Clan?:*

:I fear not,: Aroon replied, regretfully. *:Yet the talents of
the singer and yourself, and the safety of our caves may
suffice. Do not count the prey escaped until it wings into the
sky.:*

I think you should know, sir," Stef said hesitantly, "That the men that were here served someone who is our enemy. He's killed a lot of people, and he's a very powerful mage."

:*Adept-class, easily:* Yfandes interjected.

"I doubt very much that he'll be pleased with the way things have turned out. And he won't hesitate to kill *you* if you give us shelter and protection." Stef took a deep breath, afraid this would mean the creature would change its mind, yet feeling better that he'd *told* the *kyree* about the dangers involved.

The dry voice warmed a great deal. :*We have often been called insular, and isolationist,:* Aroon replied. :*And there is some truth to that. But if the one you speak of would indeed kill those of whom he knows nothing to achieve his vengeance on you, then he is our enemy as well, and you are well deserving of our protection. And as the* Tayledras *and the white sister will tell you, that is not inconsiderable, particularly for a Clan with a Winged One.:*

Yfandes heaved a great sigh. :*You have a shaman, then?:*

:*Indeed,:* the *kyree* chuckled. :*Comparable to your Adept-class. And I doubt me that this enemy of yours has ever encountered the magic of the Folk. If he can even find you on this continent, I would be greatly surprised. So—tell me all that you know of him. Warned ahead is armed ahead.:*

Yfandes touched Van's leg with her nose before answering. :*They called him Master Dark—:*

Sunset saw them entering the mouth of the cave-complex that the *kyree* called home, in the foothills of the very mountains Vanyel had been aiming for. To Stefen's considerable amazement, the caves were not dark; they were lit by glowing balls of light of many colors—each one, so Aroon told them, representing the last life-energy of a *kyree* shaman, created before he, she, or it passed out of the world.

:*The blue are those that were mages,:* he told them, as he led them through a gathering crowd of curious *kyree* that had gotten word of their arrival. The *kyree* didn't press about them, or hinder them in any way, but Stef felt their eyes on him, alight with a lively curiosity. :*The green,:* Aroon continued, :*those that were Healers. The yellow, those that were god-touched, and the red, those that had mostly Mind-magic.:* The globes of softly glowing light showed Stef wonders he'd have been glad to stop and examine more closely, if he hadn't been so worried about Van. Stone icicles grew toward stone tree trunks; stone pillars flowed toward the ceiling on either hand. Stone curtains, as rippling and fluid as real fabric, cloaked off farther chambers—light from globes behind them showed that, and the light passing through them made Stef catch his breath in wonder at their beauty.

And it was warm down here, and getting warmer.

"What's making it so warm?" Stef asked, throwing his cloak back and taking off his scarf.

:The springs,: Aroon told him. *:We have both hot and cold springs here. I shall ask you while you stay here that you light no fires—the smoke will be trapped, you see, and cause us difficulties. But do not fear the winter's cold, or that you must eat your food raw. There is one spring fully hot enough that you may cook meat in it. And as for the white sister, I think we can provide—:*

:I'd worried about that,: she admitted.

:Tubers, grain that we shall Fetch from those humans greedy enough to deserve being robbed, and mushrooms that we grow ourselves.: He laughed silently. *:We are not wholly carnivores.:*

:I'm relieved to hear it,: Yfandes began, when they passed beneath a smooth, nearly circular arch and into an enormous cavern centered with a stone formation so incredible Stef could hardly take it in. The *kyree* apparently appreciated it as well, for it was surrounded by glowing lights, placed to display it best. The thing looked like some kind of incredible temple, but one that had grown rather than been built. . . .

At the foot of this enormous structure lay a snow-white *kyree*, one with eyes as blue as Yfandes', Stef saw when they approached her closely.

:Forgive me for not rising,: the *kyree* whispered into their thoughts, *:But I am fatigued from cloaking your arrival.:* She chuckled. *:Something I am sure you appreciate. I am Hyrryl, the shaman of the Hot Springs Clan. Be welcome.:*

Yfandes bowed as deeply as she could without dislodging Van.

"Our thanks, gracious Lady," Stef said for them both.

:My thanks for your honesty with Aroon. I think that first, to warm you from your journey and to cleanse you, the

springs would be the best place for all of you.: She looked
up at the semi-conscious Herald appraisingly. *:You have one
deeply hurt; the Healing will not be easy.:*

Stef finally blurted out what he'd been thinking since they
met Aroon. "Lady—I don't think I can! I'm just a Bard, I
don't know anything about—about Healing something like
this! I—"

:You are one who loves, and is beloved,: she replied
gravely. *:That is not the answer to everything, but it will give
you a beginning. You are a Bard, and you are practiced with
words. Use that. Words can Heal—words and love together
can more often achieve what magic cannot.:*

Aroon bowed and moved away then; Yfandes followed,
and Stef had no choice but to go along. As they left that
cavern for another, Stef noticed it was getting hotter—and
there was a great deal of moisture in the air. Shortly after
that, he knew why, as they emerged into a cave filled with
multileveled hot springs.

Yfandes stopped beside one that steamed invitingly, lit
from above by a globe as yellow as sunshine. *:Get him
down, Stef. Strip him, and get him into the water. And get
into there yourself. Then—do what seems best.:*

"Why?" he asked, doing as he was told.

*:I'm going with Aroon. Hyrryl is a Healer, and I need that
Gift right now. Don't worry, I'll be back—and if Van starts
having problems, I'll be there in a blink.:*

He stripped Vanyel of his boots, shirt, and tunic—hesitated over the underbreeches, and decided to leave them
on. Yfandes turned and headed wearily back toward the
cavern entrance, and Stef saw how she limped—the cuts he
hadn't noticed before in his anxiety for Van—how worn and
exhausted she looked, and decided not to ask her to stay,
even though he felt badly in need of her support.

"All right, *ashke,*" he said quietly, as he slipped Van
down into the hot water, and the Herald started to revive
from the stupor he'd been in. "Let's see if words and love
really *are* enough."

Life in the *kyree* caverns had a curious, dreamlike quality
to it. Stef ate when he was hungry, slept when he was
weary, and forced himself to put all thoughts of time and
urgency out of his mind. Any weakness in Vanyel would be
fatal once he left the caverns—Master Dark would surely

be eager to have them in his hands, and sooner or later, they *had* to leave the protection and hospitality the *kyree* Clan was providing them. Yfandes helped, helped a great deal, in fact—but it became very obvious that since most of Van's mental and emotional trauma stemmed from the brutal serial rape he'd suffered, it was his lover that would have to be the prime mover in helping him become whole again.

Stef discovered a patience in himself that he had never once suspected. He took things so slowly that it was frequently Yfandes who fretted at the pace he was setting. Sometimes Van needed to be alone more than he needed either of them—when that happened, Stef took himself off to some other cavern, and made Yfandes come with him. There he usually found himself surrounded by *kyree*, all as hungry for music as any group of humans he'd ever encountered. He didn't have an instrument, but they considered his voice instrument enough. They'd accompany him with surprisingly complex rhythms tapped out on skin drums made for the use of paws and tails, and a low crooning drone they sang deep in their chests. Their sound was so unique, it filled him with a compulsion he would never have expected: it made him want to *compose* something for them, something to use their distinct sound.

He soaked with Vanyel in the hot springs, Yfandes lying in the heat nearby. It was days before Van could bear to have Stef touch him. . . .

And far longer for anything more.

And sometimes Stef was so tied up inside with frustration, longing, and emotions so confused he couldn't sort them out himself that he'd go off to some dark corner and cry himself hoarse. Hyrryl would find him there, and when he was ready he would talk to her, for hours, as Van talked to him, never minding that his was the only voice, and she ran on four feet instead of two. She spoke to him in strong, affectionate terms, and gently encouraged him to continue his "song-carving" with the *kyree*. He was flattered, and admitted that it actually seemed to be helping him more than it was entertaining the Clan. Hyrryl closed her eyes and chuckled silently, assuring him wordlessly not to be too sure about that. Stefen found himself telling her everything about his life over the "days," many things he had never told Vanyel, and some things he'd never before thought of as significant. He often wondered if Van ever confided in her as well, but if he did, Stef never learned of it.

Then, one "night," Van sought his solitary bed. Not for loving—but for comfort, which was by far the harder for him to need again—the comfort of arms around him, and the trust to sleep in the same bed as someone else.

And from that moment, there was no turning back.

Nineteen

Vanyel had called a private meeting of the three of them as soon as he felt he was ready to face the world again. Aroon had directed them to a small side-chamber lit only by a single green globe.

"All right," Vanyel said quietly, sitting cross-legged against a stone pillar, sipping at a tin cup (rescued from his saddlebags) full of cold water. "Here's what we're up against."

He looked from Stef's troubled eyes to Yfandes' calm ones. *At least I had enough sense to clean out Rendan's mind before I killed him—even if I didn't do it in the approved manner.*

"I got all this from ransacking the bandit lord's thoughts. This mage, this 'Master Dark,' has been operating for a long, long time." Vanyel sat back, and grasped his crossed ankles, nervously. "Rendan's *father* served him, in fact. This past year he actually began recruiting bandit groups seriously, but before that, he had at least four or five along the Border at any one time."

"Why?" Stef asked, puzzled. "What's the point, if he's up past the mountains and we're down here?"

:Because he didn't plan to stay there,: Yfandes replied.

Van nodded, and ran his hand through his hair. "Exactly. As I said, he's been operating a *long* time. Long enough that he began all this before Elspeth was born. The northlands are harsh, cold, and populated mostly by nomadic hunters and caribou herders. He wanted power over somewhere more civilized."

:Valdemar.: Yfandes cocked her head sideways. *:Why us?:*

"Because—this is a guess, mind—the Pelagirs are protected by the *Tayledras*, and Iftel was too tough a nut to crack." He smiled, crookedly. "Iftel is very quiet unless you

313

rouse them, and that deity of theirs—*whatever* it is—takes a very proprietary and active interest in the well-being of its people. Not even a circle of Adept-class mages wants to tackle a god."

I could wish we could get it to act beyond its Borders. . . .

"So, he decided he wanted Valdemar." Stef sat in the far corner and mended Van's tunic with careful, tiny stitches. Some of the gear had been retrieved with Yfandes' saddle-bags, but most was lost, and Vanyel hadn't wanted to go back for it. "What's he been doing about it?"

"He's been killing Heralds," Van said bluntly. "But doing it so carefully that no one ever suspected. Rendan knew a fair amount, more than he ever told his men—Rendan's father was in a real position to know a great deal, since he had enough Mage-Gift to be useful to Master Dark."

Vanyel knew a great deal more than that; since he hadn't been exactly concerned with ethics at the time, he'd raped Rendan's mind away from him in a heartbeat. *He couldn't subvert us, he couldn't take us on openly, so he destroyed us singly. The Herald-Mages were the easiest for him to identify at a distance—and the ones he considered most threatening. And I was right; he's been killing children and trainees, making it look like accidents, for a very long time now. Getting the children the moment their Mage-Gift manifested, if he could. Like Tylendel. . . .*

Like me.

"He's been doing this for *years* without detection," Vanyel continued, "And the only reason he tipped his hand with me is because I was a different and more powerful mage than he expected. And because I'm the last; he didn't have to worry about detection by the others, and he really *wanted* me out of the way. And—"

"And?" Stef prompted.

Vanyel closed his eyes a moment. "And because he's ready. He's bringing his forces down here to invade. Rendan didn't know when, but probably this spring."

He was lying, and he knew it. So did Yfandes, but she didn't call him on it. *All those dreams—the ones of dying in the pass. They weren't allegories for something else, they were accurate. But I still don't know when he's coming through—if I go get help now, it could be too late to stop him. One mage can hold him and however many troops and minor mages he has with him if it's done in the pass. But an army couldn't stop him if he makes it to the other side, and the Forest.*

"So what are we going to do, get help?" Stef asked, looking relieved.

Vanyel shook his head. "No, not until I've got accurate information. We're going up through Crookback Pass, so I can see what he's got." *That's why I've been fighting myself, love. I knew just as well as you did that any weakness would give him an opening to destroy me. And that* includes *wanting vengeance.*

Van felt strangely calm—whatever came, he hoped he was ready. He had tried to deal with all his fears alone, and what he had left was resignation and purpose. He hoped it would be enough to carry him through what was to come.

Master Dark *had* to be stopped. If it would take a sacrifice of one to stop him, Vanyel would willingly be that sacrifice.

Yfandes understood; she, too, had fought for Valdemar and the people of Valdemar all her life. But Van didn't think Stef would. So Stef wouldn't learn the truth until it was too late.

This was something quite different from the need for revenge that had driven him up here. He didn't hate Master Dark with the all-consuming passion that had eaten him as well—he hated coldly; what the mage had done, and what he wanted to do. Valdemar was in peril—but more than that, if this mage was permitted to take Valdemar, he would move on to other realms. Yfandes and Hyrryl agreed—

I'll cherish the time I have left—and I'll stop him however it takes. And if my death is what it takes—I'll call Final Strike on him. Not even an Adept can survive that.

"All right," Stef agreed reluctantly. "If that's what you want, that's what we'll do."

Van smiled, a little sadly. "Thank you, *ashke.* I was hoping you'd say that."

Stef trudged alongside of Yfandes, with Vanyel walking on the other side, both of them holding to her saddle-girth so that she could help them over the worst obstacles. The path was knee-deep in snow, and wound through stony foothills covered in virgin forest. Fallen limbs and loose rocks provided plenty of things to stumble over.

Crookback Pass was so near the *kyree* caverns that Hyrryl

and Aroon were visibly agitated to learn of Master Dark's plans. The Pass was the southernmost terminus of the only certain way through the mountains that anyone knew—at least in Valdemar.

Stef looked over 'Fandes' back at the Herald, toiling along with his head down and the sun making a halo of the silver strands in his hair. Van caught him at it, and gave him one of those peculiar, sad smiles he'd been displaying whenever he looked at Stef lately. Van had been very strange since he'd recovered. Loving—dear gods, yes. But preoccupied, inward-focused, and a little melancholy—but quite adamantly determined on this expedition.

So far it had been fairly easy, except for the heavy snow and the odd boulder. The *kyree* kept this area of the forest free of snow-cats and wolves—and it was really quite beautiful, if you had leisure to *look* at it. Which they didn't; both Van and Yfandes seemed determined to get up to the Pass as quickly as possible. With only one riding beast (Melody had vanished completely, and Stef only hoped she'd found her way to some farm and not down a wolf's throat) the only way to make any time was to do what they were doing, both of them walking, but using 'Fandes' strength to get them over the worst parts.

The hills they'd been traversing got progressively steeper and rockier, and by midafternoon they were in the mountains just below the Pass itself.

That was when Vanyel called a halt. Stef was afraid that Van was going to insist on a cold camp—but he didn't. They searched until they found a little half-cave, then spent the rest of the time until dark searching out dead wood. With the provisions the *kyree* had given them—more dead rabbits than Stef had ever seen at one time in his life—and the fire Van started, they had a camp that was almost as comfortable as the *kyree* caves.

Stef would have preferred a real bed over the pine boughs and their own cloaks, but that was all they'd have.

Van smiled at him from across the fire, the damage to his clothing and person a bit less noticeable in the dim fire-light. "Sorry about the primitive conditions, *ashke*, but I'd rather not let him know we were coming. Any display of magic will do that. If he's still trying to guess where we are, I'll be a lot happier."

Stef tore another mouthful of meat off his rabbit-leg,

wiped the grease from the corners of his mouth, and nodded. "That's all right, I don't mind, I'm just glad you're not *after* him the way you were. And *I'd* rather he didn't know where we were, either! I'm just glad we're finally going to get this over with. Then we can go home and just be ourselves for a while."

Vanyel blinked, rapidly, then pulled off his glove and rubbed his eyes. "Smoke's bad on this side—" He coughed, then said softly, "Stef, you've been more to me than I can tell you. You've made me so happy—happier than I ever thought I'd be. I—never did as much for you as I'd have liked to. And if it hadn't been for you, back there, I—"

Stef scooted around to Van's side of their tiny fire. "Tell you what—" he said cheerfully. "I'll let you make it up to me. How's that for a bargain?"

Vanyel smiled, and blinked. "I might just do that. . . ."

By midafternoon of the third day, they were into real mountains; though sunlight still illuminated the tops of the white-covered peaks around them, down on the trail they were in chill gloom. Stef shivered, and hoped they'd be stopping soon—then they rounded a curve in the trail and Crookback Pass stretched out before them.

A long, narrow valley, it was as clean a cut between two ranks of mountains as if a giant had cut it with a knife.

Too clean. . . .

Stef took a closer look at the sides of the pass. The rock faces looked natural enough until about ten man-heights above the floor of the pass. From there down they were as sheer as if they *had* been sliced, and as regular.

"Magic," Van whispered. "He must have carved every difficult pass from here back north this way. Dear gods— think of the power—think of what it took to *mask* the power!"

He looked up, above the area that had been carved. "If we walk along the floor of the pass, we'll be walking right into the path of—of anything coming along—"

Stef looked where *he* was looking and saw what looked like a thin thread of path. "Is that the original pass up there, do you think?"

Van nodded. "Look—see where it joins the route we're on? This is the original trail right up until this point. Then the old trail climbs, and the new one stays level."

Stef studied the old trail, what he could see of it. "You couldn't bring an army along that—at least not quickly."

"But you can on this." Van studied the situation a moment longer. "Let's take the old way as far as we can. We might have to turn back, but I'd rather try the old route first. I'd feel too exposed, otherwise."

Stef sighed, seeing his hopes for an early halt vanish. "All right, but if I spend the night camped on a ledge, I won't be responsible for my temper in the morning."

Van turned suddenly and embraced him so fiercely that Stef thought he heard ribs crack. "It's not your temper I'm worried about, *ashke*," he whispered. "It's you. I don't want anything to happen to you. I need that, to know you're safe. If I know that, I can do anything I have to."

Then, just as suddenly as he had turned, he released the Bard. "Let's get going while there's still light," he said, and began picking his way over the rocks to the old trail. Yfandes nudged Stef with her nose, and he took his place behind Van, with the Companion bringing up the rear.

From then on, he was too busy watching where he put his feet to worry about anything else. The trail was uneven, icy, and treacherous; strewn with spills of boulders that marked previous rockslides. After they came across one pile that had what was clearly a skeletal hand protruding from beneath it, Stef started looking up nervously at every suspicious noise.

And to add to the pleasure of the climb, the right side of the trail very frequently dropped straight down to the new cut.

It was not an experience Stef ever wanted to repeat—although for the first time in days—or the daylight, at least—he wasn't cold; the opposite, in fact. There was *something* to be said for the exertion of the climb, after all.

Night fell, but the full moon was already high in the sky, and Vanyel elected to push on by its light. They were about halfway across the Pass, and according to the *kyree*, there was a wide, flat meadow on the other side, and a good-sized stand of trees. That meant firewood, and a place to camp safe from avalanche.

Stef was very much looking forward to anything wide and flat. His back and legs ached like they'd never hurt before, and once the sun was down, the temperature dropped. His

labor was no longer enough to keep him warm, and his
hands were getting numb.

:*Just one more rise, Bard,*: Yfandes whispered into his
mind. :*Then it's downhill—*:

Suddenly, Vanyel dropped flat, and Stef did the same
without asking why. He crawled up beside the Herald, who
had taken shelter behind a thin screening of scrawny bushes.

Vanyel turned a little and saw him coming; put his finger
to his lips, and pointed down. Stef wriggled up a little farther so he could see, expecting a scouting party or some
such thing below them.

Instead, he saw an army.

They covered the meadow, the snow was black with
them, and they were *not* camped for the night; there were
no bivouacs, no campfires, just rank after rank of men,
lined up like a child's toy soldiers. Stef wondered what they
were waiting for, then saw that there was movement at the
farther edge of the meadow, where the next stretch of the
trail began. More men were pouring into the meadow with
every candlemark, and they were probably waiting for the
last of them to join the rest before making the last push
through the mountains. By night, so that no prying eyes
would see them.

Master Dark was bringing his army into Valdemar, and
there was nothing on the Northern Border that could even
delay them once they came across the pass.

Vanyel wriggled back; Stef followed him.

"What are we—" Stef whispered in a panic. Van placed
his finger gently on Stef's lips, silencing him.

"You're going to alert the Guard post; Yfandes will take
you, and with only you on her back, she'll be able to do
anything but fly. I'll hold them right here until the Guard
comes up."

"But—" Stef protested.

"It's not as stupid an idea as it sounds," Van said, looking
back over his shoulder. "Back there where the old trail
meets the new, one mage can hold off any size army. And
if the Guard can come up quickly enough, one detachment
can *keep* that army bottled up on the trail below the Pass
for as long as it takes for the rest of the army to get here.
But none of that is going to work if *I* don't stop them now,
here."

Stef wanted to object—but he couldn't. Vanyel was right;

even a Bard could see that—this was a classic opportunity
and a classic piece of strategy, and Master Dark couldn't
possibly have anticipated it. "You'd better—just—" Stef
began, fiercely, and couldn't continue for the tears that suddenly welled up. "Dammit, Van! I—"

Vanyel took Stef's face in both hands and kissed him,
with such fierce passion that it shook the Bard to his marrow. "I love you, too. You're absolutely the best friend,
the dearest love I've ever had. I'll love you as long as there's
anything left of me. Now go—quickly. I won't have my
whole attention on what I'm doing if you're not safe."

Stef backed away, then flung himself on Yfandes' back
before he could change his mind.

:Hang on,: she ordered, and he had barely enough time
to get a firm grip on the saddle with hands and legs when
she was off.

Vanyel watched them vanish with the speed only a Companion could manage—just short of flying. Stef weighed far
less than he did, which should improve Yfandes'
progress. . . .

Then he climbed down the sheer slope to the floor of the
new trail. He had to make the best possible time to get to
the end and the bottleneck, and the only way he was going
to be able to *do* that would be to take the easiest way.
Getting down was the hard part—when he got there, he
found that the ground was planed so evenly that he could
run.

First, he began a weather-magic that would bring in the
clouds he sensed just out of sight. Then, run, he did. He
was out of breath by the time he reached his chosen spot,
but he had plenty of leisure time to recover when he got
there. In fact, the worst part was the waiting; he had placed
himself right where the old trail made that sharp turn into
the new, and they wouldn't be able to see him until they
were right on top of him. And *he* couldn't see them, which
made things worse.

He tried not to look around too much; this was the exact
setting of his dreams, and he didn't want to be reminded of
how they had all ended.

ForeSight is just seeing the possible *future,* he reminded
himself, probing beneath the skin of the land for nodes, and
setting up his tap-lines *now,* filtering them through his

mage-focus so that the power would be attuned to him and he wouldn't have to use it raw. *Moondance told me that ages ago, and if anyone would know, the* Tayledras *would. The first dream was almost twenty years ago! Things have to have altered since then. And if I remember what happened in them, I may be able to alter the outcome. Some of those dreams even had 'Lendel in them with me, instead of—*

Stef. Twenty years. 'Lendel had died at seventeen. Van had met Stef when the Bard was seventeen. There was time enough, between 'Lendel's death and now—Stef was exactly the right age to have been born about that time.

More things sprang to mind. The Dreamtime encounter with 'Lendel—the things he had said—the way the *Tayledras* treated Stef and the way Savil had taken the Bard under her wing after that—it was all beginning to make a pattern.

The way he called me ashke *without ever knowing the word. No. Yes. What other answer is there? He came back to me, 'Lendel came back as Stef, somehow—and Savil and the Hawkbrothers knew—*

But there was no opportunity to think about this revelation, for the first of Master Dark's forces had just begun to round the bend in the trail, and it was time to put his plans into motion.

As little bloodshed as I can manage, particularly with the fighters. They could be spell-bound, ignorant—whatever.

The clouds he had been calling loomed above the mountains, hiding the peaks, and full of lightning-crackles just waiting to be released. Vanyel was happy to oblige them; he called lightnings down out of them to lash the ground just ahead of the first rank, as he simultaneously illuminated himself with a blinding blue glare of mage-light.

The lightning exploded the trail in front of him, the ice-covered rocks screaming as the powerful force lashed them, heating them enough to turn the ice into steam in an eye-blink. Vanyel kept his eyes sheltered by his forearm, so that he alone was not blinded. The first ranks of the forces were, however; black-armored men stumbled blindly forward, pushed by the ranks behind them, shouting in fear and anger.

All right, that's one point of difference from the dreams, already. I fought them magic-against-weaponry, I didn't intimidate them right off.

The chaos calmed, as Vanyel stood, ready, energies making his mage-focus glow the same blue as the light behind him, his hands tingling with power. The ranks of armed men and strange beasts stirred restively, the fighters watching him through the slits in their helms. In this much, too, the dreams had been right. Under the armor, they were a motley lot, and only half of them looked human; but they were armed and armored with weapons and protection made of some dull black stuff, and carried identical round, unornamented black shields. And the stumbling chaos he had caused had been righted in short order; that argued for a great deal of training together. This *was* the army he had taken it for.

The ranks in front parted, as in the dreams, and a wizard stepped through. There was no doubt of *what* he was, he was unarmed and unarmored, and the Power sat heavily in him, making him glow sullenly to Mage-Sight. But it was the power of blood-magic—

As was the power of the second, the third, and the fourth.

Four-to-one, then Master Dark to follow. Vanyel flexed his fingers, and hoped Yfandes had gotten Stef to safety by now. *Let's see if these lads know how to work together, or if I can divide them—*

Stefen hung on and closed his eyes, fighting his own panic. He'd never been on—or even near!—anything going this fast before. The ground rushing by his feet and the violent lurching as Yfandes leapt obstacles were making him sick and frightened, with the kind of fear that no rational thought was going to overcome.

They had already covered the same amount of ground that had taken the three of them a day, and now Stef was quite lost.

:I'm doing a kind of Fetching, Bard, only I'm doing it with us. That's why we seem to be jumping a great deal, and why you're sick. Besides, you two got rather sidetracked. You had to come at the Pass obliquely. I'm going straight back.:

Stef gulped. *She's doing Fetching, only with us. No wonder my stomach thinks it got left behind—it may have. . . .*

Lights showed up ahead, against the dark of the trees. Torches along the top of a wall—the lights of the Guard post. Stef couldn't believe it. It hadn't been *nearly* long enough—

But it was. Yfandes thundered into the lighted area in front of the gate, as sentries came piling down off the walls—

She stopped with all four hooves set, in a shower of snow—and bucked. Violently.

Stefen wasn't expecting that. He flew over her head and landed in a snowbank—

He thought he was going to land all right, but his breath was knocked out of him and his head cracked against a buried log and he saw nothing but stars—

—and heard hoofbeats vanishing into the distance, followed by a babble of voices.

Hands hauled him out of the snow; he shook his head to clear his eyes and immediately regretted doing so. His head felt like it was going to explode, and colored lights danced in front of him. But his vision cleared enough for him to see as he looked up that one of the people striding out of the gate was the Commander.

She recognized him immediately. "Great good gods!" she exclaimed. "What in the nine hells are you doing here? Where's the Herald?"

His head was swimming, and his vision blacking out, but he managed to get all of his message out—

The Commander turned white, and barked a series of orders. The alarm bell began ringing. So did Stef's ears. The Commander's aide shoved Stef over to one side, and men and women began pouring out of the barracks, hastily arming and armoring themselves as they ran into their ranks. Stef wasn't sure if he was going to be able to stand much longer; his knees were going weak. The post Healer emerged, took one look at him, and started toward him, arms forward.

And that was all Stef knew, before the ground quietly but violently introduced itself and darkness came over him.

Vanyel trembled with exhaustion—but the nodes were still pouring their power into him, and two of the wizards lay charred and dead on the icy ground in front of him. Of the other two, one had tried to flee and been cut down by his own men, and the other was a mindless, drooling thing

that crawled over to the side of the trail and lay there curled
on its side.

*There's another difference. I didn't defeat the wizards, in
the dream. I fought them to a standstill.* He assessed the
damage to himself, and came up relatively satisfied. There
was a slight wound to his right leg; blood was running down
his leg and into his boot to freeze there. He was a bit
scorched, but really, the damage so far was light.

*Although a young boy who'd never been in combat—as I
was then—would have been convinced that every hurt was
fatal. That may be the reason for that "difference"; it may
not be a difference at all. Well. Now it's time for Master
Dark to appear.*

The front ranks parted again, and a single, elegantly
black-clad figure paced leisurely through, lit by red mage-
light as Vanyel was lit by blue.

Right on cue.

The young man was wearing black armor and clothing
that had to be a conscious parody of Heraldic Whites. He
was absolutely beautiful, with a perfectly sculptured face and
body. Somehow that face looked oddly familiar—

It could just be that the face was so perfect, it looked
like the statue of a god.

*Of course, if I didn't care how I wasted power, I could
look like anything I wanted, too.*

He was a reverse image of Vanyel in every way, from
sable hair to ebony eyes to night-black boots.

"Why do you bother with this nonsense?" he asked,
sweetly, his lips curving in a sensual smile. "You are quite
alone, Herald-Mage Vanyel." His voice was a smooth, silky
tenor; he had learned the same kind of perfect control over
it that he had over his body.

The familiarity of his features bothered Vanyel. At first
he thought it was because he very closely resembled the
Herald himself, but there was more to it than that. A kind
of racial similarity to someone—

"You are," the young man repeated, with finely-honed
emphasis, "quite alone."

Tayledras. He looks Tayledras, *only reversed. Did he
always look that way, or did he tailor himself? Either way,
he's making a statement about himself, the Hawkbrothers,
and the Heralds—*

"You tell me nothing I didn't already know. As I know

you," he heard himself saying. "The *Tayledras* have a name
for you. You are *Leareth*. The name means—"

"Darkness," Leareth laughed. "Oh yes, I quite consciously chose that *Tayledras* name. Hence, 'Master Dark'
as well. A quaint conceit, don't you think? As are—" he
waved at the men behind him, in their sinister panoply, "—
my servants."

"Very clever," Vanyel replied. *This has already deviated
from the dreams—in the dreams, the mages stand behind
him, and this time there were four instead of three. The
fighters stayed out of reach, letting the mages handle me.
Maybe if I can stall the final confrontation long enough, Stef
can get to the Guard and they can get here in time.*

"You need not remain alone, Vanyel," Leareth continued, licking his lips sensuously. "You need only give over
this madness—stretch out your hand to me, join me, take
my Darkness to you. You will never be alone again. Think
how much we could accomplish together! We are so very
similar, we two, in our powers—and in our pleasures."

He paced forward; one swaying step that rippled his
ebony cloak and his raven hair. "Or if you prefer—I could
even bring your long-lost love to you. Think about it,
Vanyel—think of Tylendel, once more alive and at your
side. He could share our life and our power, Vanyel, and
nothing, *nothing* would be able to stand against us."

Vanyel stepped back, and pretended to consider the
offer.

*Dear gods, doesn't he understand us at all? Nothing is
worth having if it comes at the kind of cost he demands.
Can't he understand how much I would be betraying Stef—
'Lendel—if I betrayed Valdemar?*

The cold seemed to gather about him, chilling him and
stiffening his wounded leg.

*He can't know that I know he's lying—either about his
abilities or about the reward if I turn traitor. Or both—
I wonder if I can hold against him. Or even—take him?*

Hope rose in him, and he probed a little around Leareth's
shields.

And hid a shock of dismay. *He's better than I am. Much
better. He's able to tap node-magic through other mages so
that it doesn't burn him out. He's got a half dozen of those
mages feeding him power from the other side of the mountain, from tapped nodes! He's going to kill me—and then*

*he's going to march right through here and take Valdemar.
And I don't have enough left even in the nodes to call the
Final Strike that will take him—*

"Well?" Leareth shifted his weight impatiently.

How can I stall for more time?

Oh, gods—I'm going to die—alone—

And for nothing—

Then—like a gift from the gods, the hoofbeats of a single
creature, behind him.

Yfandes thundered to a halt beside him, and screamed
her defiance at the Dark Mage. He stepped back an involuntary pace or two, his eyes wide with surprise. Yfandes
raised her stump of a tail high and bared her teeth at him
as Vanyel placed one hand on her warm flank.

:*I told you I would never leave you when I Chose you,*:
she said calmly. :*I knew what our bond would come to then,
when I first Chose you—and I don't regret my choice. I love
you, and I am proud to stand beside you. There is not a
single moment together that I would take back.*:

:*Not one?*: he asked, moved to tears.

:*Not one. I will not let you face him alone, beloved. And
I can give my strength to you, for whatever you need.*:

Her strength added to his would be enough—just
enough—to overcome Leareth's protections on a Final
Strike.

Vanyel raised his eyes to meet Leareth's, and with one
smooth motion, mounted and settled into Yfandes' saddle,
and answered the mage's offer with a calm smile and a
single word.

"No."

"Vanyel!"

*Terrible pain—then, nothing. A void where warmth should
be.*

Stefan leapt from the cot, screaming Van's name—the
Healer tried to hold him down, but he fought clear of the
man, throwing the blankets aside in a frenzy of fear and
grief.

*I felt him die—oh, gods. No, no I can't have, it's just
something else, some magic—he's still alive, he has to be—*

He ran, out of the barracks, out into the snow, shoving
people out of the way. He stumbled blindly to the stables

and grabbed the first horse he saw that didn't shy away, saddling it with tack that seemed oddly familiar—

The filly snorted in his hair as he reached up to bridle her—and he recognized her. It was Melody—

But that didn't matter, all that mattered was the ache in his heart, in his soul, the empty place that said *Vanyel*—

He flung himself on Melody's back and spurred her cruelly as soon as he was in the saddle; she squealed in surprise and launched herself out of the stable door, as the Healers and sentries shouted after him, too late to stop him.

Days later, he came upon the battlefield, riding an exhausted horse, himself too spent to speak. The battle was long over; and still the carnage was incredible.

At the edge of camp, one of the Guardsmen stopped Melody with one hand on her bridle, and Stef didn't have the strength to urge her past him. He simply stared dully at the man, until someone else came—a Healer, and then someone in high-rank blue. He ignored the Healer, but the other got him to dismount.

The Commander, her face gray with fatigue, her eyes full of pain.

"I'm sorry, lad," the Commander said, one arm around his shoulders. "I'm sorry. We were all too late to save him. He was—gone—before we ever got here. But . . . I'd guess you know that. I'm sorry."

The dam holding his emotions in check broke inside him, and he turned his face into her shoulder; she held him, as she must often have held others, and let him cry himself out, until he had no more tears, until he could scarcely stand. Then she helped him into her own tent, put him to bed on her own cot, and covered him with her own hands.

"Sleep, laddy," she whispered hoarsely. " 'Tain't a cure, but you need it. He'd tell you the same if—"

She turned away. He slept, though he didn't think he could; the mournful howls of *kyree* filled his thoughts . . . and Vanyel's face, Vanyel's touch. . . .

Candlemarks later, he woke. Another Guardsman sat on a stool next to the cot, keeping watch beside him.

He blinked, confused by his surroundings—then remembered.

"I want to see him," he said, sitting up.

"Sir—" the Guardsman said hesitantly, "There ain't

nothin' to see. We couldn't find a thing. Just—them. Lots
of them."

"Then I want to see where he was," Stef insisted. "I have
to—please—"

The Guardsman looked uncomfortable, but helped him
up, led him out and supported him as he climbed back up
the pass. Bodies were being collected and piled up to be
burned; the stench and black smoke were making Stef sick,
and there was blood everywhere. And at the narrowest
point of the pass, where the mortuary crews hadn't even
reached, it was even worse.

Stefen's escort tightened his grip suddenly and yelped, as
a white-furred shape appeared beside them. Hyrryl's blue
eyes spoke her sympathy wordlessly to Stefen, and he heard
himself saying, "It's all right . . . they're friends," as
another fell in on his left—Aroon. The Guardsman swallowed, and they resumed their walk.

Blackened, burned, and mangled bodies were piled as
many as three and four deep, and all of them wore ebony
armor or robes. The carnage centered around one spot, a
place clean of snow and dirt, scoured right down to the
rock, with the stone itself polished black and shining. Hyrryl
and Aroon took up positions on either side of the pass, and
sat on their haunches, almost at attention, watching over
the Bard. The Guardsman bowed and retreated wordlessly,
and no one else came near.

Stef stumbled tear-blinded through the heaped bodies,
looking for one—one White-clad amid all the black—

There was nothing, just as the Guardsman had told him.
Stef shook his head, frantically, then began looking for anything, a scrap of white, anything at all.

Finally, after candlemarks of searching, a glint of silver
caught his eye. He bent—and found a thin wisp of blood-
soaked, white horsehair. And beside it, the mage-focus he
had given Vanyel; the chain gone, the silver setting half-
melted and tarnished, the stone blackened, burned, cracked
in two.

He clutched his finds to his chest; his knees gave way,
and he fell to the stone, his grief so all-encompassing that
he could not even weep—only whisper Vanyel's name, as if
it were an incantation that would bring him back.

The trees were a scarlet glory behind the dull brown of

the Guard post. "You're the Bard, ain't you? Stefen? The one that was with—" awe made the boy's eyes widen, his voice drop to a whisper "—Herald Vanyel."

Stef tried unsuccessfully to smile at the young Guardsman. "Yes. I'd heard about what's happening up here and I came to see for myself."

That got a reaction; the boy started, and his eyes widened with fear. Then the youngster straightened and tried to look less frightened than he was. " 'Tis true, Bard Stefen. Anybody comes into that Forest as has bad intentions, they don't come out again. Fact is, it looks like it started the night Herald Vanyel died. We found lots of them fellahs in the black armor as had run off inta the Forest, and ev' one of 'em was cold meat."

"I'd heard that," Stefen said, dismounting carefully. "But I'd also heard some tales that were pretty wild." The autumn wind tossed his hair and Melody's mane as he handed her reins to the Guardsman.

"They ain't wild, m'lord Bard. The men as we found— stuck right through with branches, or even icicles, up t' their waists in frozen ground—they was spooky enough. But Lor' an' Lady! There was some tore t'little *bits* by somethin', and more just—dead. No mark on, 'em, just dead—and the awfullest looks on their faces—" The boy shivered. "Been like that ever since. Once in a while we go in there, have a look around, sure enough, we'll find some bandit or other th' same way."

"They say the Forest is cursed," Stef said absently, shading his eyes with his hand, and peering into the shadows beneath the trees beyond the Guard barracks. "It sounds more like a blessing to me."

"Blessed or cursed, 'tis a good thing for Valdemar, an' we reckon Herald Vanyel done it."

Stefen slung his gittern-bag over one shoulder, his near-empty pack over the other, and headed, not for the Guard post, but the Forest.

"Hey!" the boy protested. Stef ignored him, ignored the shouts behind him, and began his solitary trek into the Forest they now called "Sorrows."

Near sunset he finally stopped. *Near enough,* he thought, looking around. *I don't need to be in the Pass to do this. And this is where we were last happy together. This, or a place very like this.*

He was at the foot of a very tall hill—or small mountain; the sun was setting to his left, the moon rising to his right, and there was no sign of any living person. Just the hill, with a shallow cave under it, the trees, and the birds.

He gathered enough wood for a small fire, started it, and took out his gittern. He played until the sun just touched the horizon; all of Van's favorites, all the music he'd composed since—even the melody of the song for the *kyree*, and the song he'd left a copy of back at Bardic Collegium, the one he'd never performed in public—the one he had written for Vanyel, that he called "Magic's Price."

And then he put the gittern down, carefully. He'd thought about breaking it, but it was a sweet little instrument, and didn't deserve destruction for sake of an unwitnessed dramatic scene. He settled on wrapping it carefully and stowing it in the back of the cave. Perhaps someone would find it.

The ache in his soul had not eased in all these months. People kept telling him that time would heal the loss, but it hadn't. They'd kept a close watch on him for months after he returned from the Pass, but lately they hadn't been quite as careful.

But then, lately there had been other things to think about than one young Bard with a broken heart.

He'd taken the opportunity offered by the confusion of King Randale's death and King Treven's coronation to escape them and make his way up here.

It hadn't been easy to get that vial of argonel, and finally he'd had to buy it from a thief. He took it out of the bottom of his pack, and weighed the heavy porcelain vial in his hand.

A lethal dose for ten or so he said. Should be enough for one skinny Bard.

He set it down in front of him, staring at it in the fading, crimson light. *You drift into sleep. Not so bad. Easier death than he had. Easier than Randi's. A lot easier than Shavri's—*

Finally he reached for it—

A shower of stone fragments shook themselves loose from the roof of the cave, and one struck the bottle of poison. It tipped over and rolled out of his reach, then the cork popped out and it capriciously poured its contents into the dust. He scrambled after it with a cry of dismay, glancing worriedly at the ceiling of the cave—

:Go through with it, you idiot,: said a cheerful voice in his mind, *:and I'll never forgive you.:*

That voice— Stef froze, then turned his head, very slowly. Something stood there, between him and the forest.

Van.

A much younger-looking Vanyel. And a very transparent Vanyel. Stef could see the bushes behind him quite clearly—

Before he had a chance to feel even a hint of fear, Van smiled—the all-too-rare, sweet smile Stef had come to cherish in their time together—a smile of pure love, and real, unshadowed happiness.

"Van?" he said, hesitantly. *It can't be—I'm going mad— oh, dear gods, please let it be—*

Tears began to well up, and he shook them out of his eyes as he reached out with a trembling hand. "Van? Is that really—"

Van reached out at the same time; his hand—and just his hand—grew solid momentarily. Solid enough that Stef was able to touch it before it faded to transparency again.

It was real; real, and solid and warm.

It is. Oh, gods, it is—

"How?" Stef asked, through the tears. "What happened?"

Vanyel shrugged—a completely Van-like shrug. *:Something happened, after I took Leareth out with Final Strike. I had a choice. Most Heralds have a couple of choices; they can go on to the Havens, or come back, like the* Tayledras *say people come back—I was given another option.:*

"Another option? *This?*"

:I know it doesn't look like much—: Vanyel smiled again, then sobered. *:The problem is that I was the* last *Herald-Mage. Valdemar needs a guardian on this Border, a magical one—Master Dark wasn't alone, and he left apprentices. So— that was my choice, to stay and guard. Yfandes, too. 'Fandes and I are part of the Forest now—:*

He hesitated a moment. *:Stef—I asked for something before I agreed, and you get the same choice. You can join me—but—:*

"But?" Stefen cried, leaping to his feet, stirring the dust from the now-forgotten pebble attack. "But what? Anything, *ashke*—whatever I have to do to be with you—"

Vanyel moved closer, and made as if to touch his cheek. *:You can join me, but there are conditions. You can only*

*come when it's time. There are things I can't tell you about,
but you have to earn your place. There's something that
needs to be done, and you are uniquely suited to do it. I
won't lie to you, beloved—it's going to take years.:*

"What is it?" Stef demanded, his heart pounding, his
throat tight. "Tell me—"

*:You remember how worried I was, about people thinking
that Heralds were somehow less than Herald-Mages?:*

Stef nodded. "It's gotten worse since you—I mean, you
were the last. There's no one to replace you, no one to
train new ones, no way to *find* new ones. I mean, now
you're a legend, Van, and the people tend to think of leg-
ends as being flawless. . . ."

*:That's where you come in. You have to use your Gift to
convince the people of Valdemar that the Gifts of Heralds
are enough to keep them safe. You, and every Bard in the
Circle. Which means that first you have to convince the other
Bards, then the Circle has to convince the rest of the realm.:*
Vanyel held out both hands in a gesture of pleading. *:The
Bards are the only ones that have a hope of pulling this off,
Stef. And you are the only one that has a hope of convincing
the Bards.:*

"But that could take a lifetime!" Stefen cried involun-
tarily, dismayed by the magnitude of the task. Then, as
Vanyel nodded, he realized what that meant in terms of
"earning his place."

:Exactly,: Van said, his eyes mournful. *:Exactly. Do you
still love me enough to spend a lifetime doing the work I've
left to you? A lifetime alone? I wouldn't blame you if—:*

"Van—" Stef whispered, looking deeply into those
beloved silver eyes, "Van—I love you enough to die for
you—I still do. I always will. I guess—"

He hesitated a moment more, then swallowed down his
tears. "I guess," he finished, managing to dredge up a
shaky, tear-edged smile, "if I love you enough to die for
you, it kind of follows that I love you enough to *live* for
you. And there are worse ways to die for somebody than
by old age—"

:Tell me about it:. For one moment, all the starlight, the
moonlight, seemed to collect in one place, then feed into
Vanyel. The figure of the Herald glowed as bright as the
full moon for a heartbeat, and he solidified long enough to
take Stefen into his arms—

:Oh, ashke—*:* he murmured, and smiled lovingly.

Then he was gone. Completely. And without the evidence of the spilled bottle and the dust in his hair, Stef would never have known Vanyel was there except in his mind.

The Bard looked around frantically, but there was no sign of him. "Van, wait!" he shouted into the still air, "Wait! How will I know when I've earned my place?"

:You'll know,: came the whisper in his mind. *:We'll call you.:*

Epilogue

Herald Andros leaned back in his saddle, and stretched, enjoying the warm spring sunshine on his back. He looked behind him to make sure his fellow traveler was keeping up all right.

The old Bard was nodding off again; it was a good thing that Ashkevron palfrey had easy paces, or the poor old man would have fallen off a half dozen times.

:Why on earth do you suppose he wants to visit Sorrows?: he asked Toril.

His Companion shook her head. *:Damned if I know,:* she replied, amusement in her mind-voice. *:The very old get pretty peculiar. He should be glad there's been peace long enough that someone could be spared to ferry him up here.:*

:It still wouldn't have happened if I wasn't on my way to the Temple in the first place,: he said. *:Poor old man. Not that anyone is going to miss him—all of his old cronies are gone, and hardly anyone even knows he's at Court anymore.:*

Toril tested the breeze for a moment. *:Maybe he's making a kind of memorial trip. Did you know he's the Stefen? Vanyel's lifebonded?:*

:No!: He turned in his saddle to stare back at the frail, slight old man, dozing behind him. *:I thought Stefen was dead a long time ago! Well, I guess he deserves a little humoring. He's certainly earned it.:*

She shook her head in silent agreement, and slowed until they were even with the Bard. "Bard Stefen?" he said, softly. The Bard's hearing was perfectly good—and he didn't want to startle the old man.

The Bard opened his eyes, slowly. "Dozed off again, did I?" he asked, with a hint of a smile. "Good thing this old man has you to watch out for him, son."

"Do you have any idea of where you're going?" Andros

asked. "We've been inside the border of Sorrows for the last couple of candlemarks."

The Bard looked around himself with increased interest. "Have we now? Well—could be why I felt comfortable enough to go on sleeping. I wish you'd told me, I could have saved you a little riding."

He pulled his old mare to a halt, and slowly dismounted, then pointed at a little grove of goldenoak at the foot of a rocky hillside. "That'll do, lad. All I want is to be left alone for a bit, eh? I know that sounds a bit touched, but the old get pretty peculiar sometimes."

Andros blushed at this echoing of his own thoughts, and obediently turned Toril away.

:Well, my lady,: he said, :Where would you like to go?:

:I'd like a good long drink of spring water,: she replied firmly, :And I can smell running water just over that ridge.:

The water not only tasted good—it felt good. Andros became very much aware of how dusty and sweaty the trip had made him, and Toril allowed that she wouldn't object to a bath, either. By the time the two of them were dry, it was late afternoon, and Andros figured the old man would be ready to continue his journey.

When he returned to the grove, the old man was gone.

The gittern was there, though, and the mare—so Andros just sighed, and assumed he'd gone off for a walk. He began a search for the Bard, growing more and more frantic when not even a footprint turned up—

Toril imposed herself in front of him, waiting for him to mount. He blinked at her, wondering what on earth he was doing, wandering around in the woods like this.

:I must have had sun-stroke,: he told her, shaking his head in confusion. :What am—what was I doing?:

:I wondered,: she replied with concern, :You wanted to see the battle site, and I tried to tell you it wasn't here, but you insisted it was. Don't you remember?:

:No,: he replied ruefully. :Next time knock me into a stream or something, would you?:

He caught a twinkle in her eye, but she replied demurely enough, :If it's necessary. It's just that now we're late, and they really need a Herald out here for relay work. Every moment we're not there is trouble for the Healers. It's just a good thing there's a full moon tonight.:

"Oh, horseturds," Andros groaned aloud. "You don't expect me to ride all night, do you?"

:Why not? I'm the one doing all the work. Now get the packmare and let's get going.:

"Why is there a saddle on this mare?" he asked, frowning, as he approached the palfrey. "And why isn't she fastened to your saddle already?"

:The second—because you *unfastened her. You'd better have the Healers look at you when you get there.:* Her mind-voice was dense with concern. *:I think you really must have had a serious sunstroke. She's got a saddle because she's a present from Joserlyn Ashkevron to his sister, and saddles don't grow on trees, not even this close to the Pelagirs.:*

"You're right," Andros said, rubbing his head, then mounting. "I'd better talk to them. Well, let's get going."

They rode off, leaving a gittern behind them, propped up against a tree. When they were quite out of sight—and hearing-distance—the strings quivered for a moment.

A knowledgeable listener might have recognized a ballad popular sixty or seventy years earlier—a love-song called "My Lady's Eyes."

And a very keen-eared listener might have heard laughter among the trees; young male laughter, tenor and baritone, making a joyful music of their own.

* * *

To this day, that gittern is grown into the tree it leaned against then, the goldenoak's roots entwined around its strings in a gentle embrace, and there are bright days, when the winds whispers through the trees, that the Forest of Sorrows seems the most inappropriate name possible.

APPENDIX

Songs of Vanyel's Time

For more information about these songs, contact:
      Firebird Arts and Music
      P.O. Box 14785
      Portland, OR 97214-9998

NIGHTBLADES

*They come creeping out of darkness, and to darkness they
  return.*
*In their wake they leave destruction; where they go, no one
  can learn*
*For they leave no trace in passing, as if all who watched were
  blind*
Like a dream of evil sending,
Nightblades passing, nightblades rending,
Into darkness once more blending
Leaving only dead behind.

*First a threat—and then a death comes in the darkness of the
  night*
And a dozen would-be allies have begun to show their fright.
*When the nightblades strike unhindered, and can take a life
  at will,*
There's no safety in alliance
And much peril in defiance
It is best to show compliance
And the Karsite ranks to fill.

*The chief envoy summons Vanyel, for one ally still seems
  brave*
And the treaty may be salvaged if Vanyel this life can save.
*Herald Vanyel feigns refusal, senses one would play him
  fool;*
Thinks of treachery in hiding,
Lets his instincts be his guiding.
His own counsel he is biding
He'll be no unwitting tool.

*Garbed in black slips Herald Vanyel to their last lone ally's
  keep;*
*Over wall and into window, past all gates and guards to
  creep.*
*Past all gates and guards—no magic has them wrapped in
  deadly spell—*
They are drugged, and they are dreaming.
Some foe strikes in friendly seeming—
See—a metal dart there gleaming!
Vanyel knows the symptoms well.

Now he hears another's footstep soft before him in the dark
And he hastes to lay an ambush while the nightblade seeks
  his mark.
Now he waits beside the doorway of the ally's very room
And the nightblade, all unknowing,
With a single lamp-beam showing
To a confrontation going
Not to fill another tomb.

Out of shadow Vanyel rises and he bars the nightblade's way.
He has only that slim warning—Vanyel has him soon at bay.
When the guards have all awakened, then he bares the night-
  blade's face—
And all minds but his are reeling
When he tears off the concealing—
And the envoy's face revealing—
Brings the traitor to disgrace.

MY LADY'S EYES

(This is drivel. It's *supposed* to be. It's Vanyel's mother's
favorite song. Van puts up with it because he can show off
his fingering.)

My Lady's eyes are like the skies
A soft and sunlit blue
No other fair could half compare
In sweet midsummer hue
My Lady's eyes cannot disguise
Her tender, gentle heart
She cannot feign, she feels my pain
Whenever we must part.
  (Instrumental)
Now while I live I needs must give
Her all my love and more
That she may know I worship so
This one that I adore.
And while away, I long and pray
The days may speed, and then,
I heartward hie, I flee, I fly,
To see her eyes again.
  (Instrumental)
My Lady's eyes, each glance I prize,
As gentle as a dove,
And would that I could tell her why
I dare not speak my love.
Too high, as far as any star
Her station is to mine,
Too wide that space to e'er embrace,
Beneath her I repine.
  (Instrumental)

SHADOW STALKER

It was just a week till Sovven, and the nights were turning
  chill
And the battle turned to stalemate, double-bluff, and feint
  and drill
When a shadow drifted northward, just a shadow, nothing
  more.
No one noticed that the shadows all grew darker than
  before.
No one noticed, while the shadows seemed to creep into the
  heart,
But from then the fight for freedom seemed a fool's quest
  from the start.
All the hopes that they had cherished seemed unreasoned and
  naive
Nothing worth the strength to pray for, or to strive for, or to
  believe.

And the shadows stole the sunlight from the brightest autumn
  day,
As they sang a song of bleakness that touched every heart
  that heard
As they whispered words of hopelessness, all courage fled
  away,
And they wove a smothering blanket over all that lived and
  stirred.

Herald Vanyel came upon them, and he sensed a subtle
  wrong,
And there was some magic working; deeply hidden, yes, but
  strong.
And it moved and worked in secret, like a poison in the vein
Like a poison meant to weaken, this was magic meant to
  drain.
Herald Vanyel saw the Shadows, and they turned their wiles
  on him
For one moment even he began to feel his spirit dim—
But he saw their secret evil, and he swore e'er he was done
He would stalk and slay these Shadows, and destroy them,
  one by one.

Herald Vanyel, Shadow Stalker, hunted Shadows to their
doom
They turned all their powers upon him, turned away from
other men
And although they strove to take him, he unwove their web
of gloom.
So the Shadows fled his anger, their creator sought again.

Herald Vanyel faced the Singer who had sung them into life
And she sang to him of grief and loss that cut him like a
knife.
And she sang to him of self-hate, and she wove a net of pain
With her songs of woe and hopelessness bent to be Vanyel's
bane.
"So now what is there to strive for?" was the song she sang
to him.
And the shadow came upon his heart, the world grew gray
and dim.
But the Singer Of The Shadow did not know the foe she
fought,
Nor how dear he held his duty, nor by what pain power was
bought.

Herald Vanyel looked upon her, and he saw through her
disguise
And she strove then to seduce him into death or madness
sweet.
Herald Vanyel looked within him, and he saw her songs were
lies,
And he gathered up his magic then, her powers to defeat.

Herald Vanyel raised his golden voice and sang of life and
light,
Of the first cry of a baby, of the silver stars of night.
Herald Vanyel sang of wisdom, sang of courage, sang of
love,
Of the earth's sweet soil beneath him, of the vaulting sky
above,
Sang of healing, sang of growing, sang of joy and hope and
dreams,
And the Singer Of The Shadows felt the death of all her
schemes.

It was then she tried to flee him, but his song and magic spell
Struck her down and held her pinioned and she faltered, and
    she fell.

Then the Singer Of the Shadows saw her Shadows shatter
    there,
Saw her lies unmade before her, saw her darkness turned to
    day
And how empty and how petty was the spirit then laid bare—
Like her Shadows then she shattered, and in silence passed
    away.

WINDRIDER UNCHAINED

Windrider, fettered, imprisoned, and pinioned
Wing-clipped by magic, his power full drained,
Valdemar's Heir is defeated and captive,
With his Companion by Darklord enchained.

Darklord of shadows his fetters is weaving
Binds him in darkness as deep as despair,
Mocks at his anger and laughs at his weeping,
"Where is your strength now, oh Valdemar's Heir?"

Darklord has left them by shadows encumbered,
Darshay and Windrider trapped in his gloom,
Deep in his prisons, past hope, past believing,
Heir and Companion, will this be your tomb?

Out of the shadows another draws nearer,
Out of the twilight steals one furtive light.
Shadows dance pain, while the Light sings despairing,
Drawn here by Darshay and Windrider's plight.

Power new-won have the Singer and Dancer,
Power to shatter their curses at last—
Power that also could free the sad captives;
Power to break the bonds holding them fast.

Heart speaks to heart in the depths of the darkness
Grief calls to grief, and they falter, afraid—
Why should they sacrifice all for these strangers?
Then new-won compassion sends them on to aid.

Dancer in Shadows, she weeps as she dances,
Dancing, unmaking the shadow-born bands.
Sunsinger now through tears gives up his power—
Sings back the magic to Windrider's hands.

Spent now, the twain unseen fall into shadow
Gifted to strangers all that they had gained.
Darklord returns, and by fear is confounded—
Flees the avenger, Windrider unchained!

DEMONSBANE

Along a road in Hardorn, the place called Stony Tor
A fearful band of farmers flees Karsite Border war.
A frightened band of farmers, their children, and their wives,
*Seeks refuge from a tyrant, who wants more than their
lives.*

*Now up rides Herald Vanyel. "Why then such haste?" says
he.*
"Now who is it pursuing, whose anger do you flee?
For you are all of Hardorn, why seek you Valdemar?
Is Festil no protection? Bide all his men too far?"

"Oh, Vanyel, Herald Vanyel, we flee now for our lives,
Lord Nedran would enslave us, our children and our wives—
He'd give our souls to demons, our bodies to his men.
King Festil has not heeded, or our peril does not ken."

Now up speaks Herald Vanyel. "The Border is not far—
But you are all of Hardorn, and not of Valdemar.
You are not Randale's people—can call not on his throne—
But damned if I will see you left helpless on your own!"

So forth goes Herald Vanyel, and onward does he ride.
On Stony Tor he waits then, Yfandes at his side.
*With Nedran's men approaching, he calls out from on
high,*
"You shall not pass, Lord Nedran! I shall not let you by!"

Now Herald Vanyel only stands blocking Nedran's way
*"Now who are you, fool nothing, that you dare to tell me
nay?"*
Now up speaks Herald Vanyel in a voice like brittle glass;
*"The Herald-Mage called Vanyel—and I say you shall not
pass!"*

*Now there stands great Lord Nedran, and behind him forty
men,*
Beside him is his wizard—but he pales, and speaks again—
"So you are Herald Vanyel—but this place is not your land.
So heed me, Herald Vanyel; turn aside and hold your hand."

"Let be; I'll give you silver, and I shall give you gold,
And I shall give you jewels fair that sparkle bright and bold,
And I shall give you pearls, all the treasures of the sea,
If you will step aside here, and leave these fools to me."

"What need have I of silver more than sweet Yfandes here?
And all the gold I cherish is sunlight bright and clear.
The only jewel I treasure's a bright and shining star,
And I will protect the helpless even outside Valdemar."

"Now I shall give you beauty, slaves of women and of men,
And I shall give you power as you'll never see again,
And I shall give you mansions and I shall give you land,
If you will turn aside here, turn aside and hold your hand."

"Now beauty held in bondage is beauty that is lost.
And land and mansions blood-bought come at too high a
  cost.
And power I have already—all power is a jade—
So turn you back, Lord Nedran if of me you are afraid!"

Lord Nedran backs his stallion, the wizard he comes nigh.
"Prepare yourself, bold Vanyel, for you shall surely die!"
The wizard calls his demons, the demons he commands,
And Vanyel, Herald Vanyel, only raises empty hands.

The wizard calls his demons, the sky above turns black.
The demons strike at Vanyel, he stands and holds them back.
The demons strike at Vanyel, they strike and hurt him sore,
But Vanyel stands defiant, to raise his hands once more.

The sky itself descending upon bare Stony Tor
Now hides the awful battle. The watchers see no more.
The wizard shouts in triumph—too soon he vents his mirth.
For Vanyel calls the lightning, and smites him to the earth!

The clouds of black have lifted; upon the barren ground
Stands Vanyel hurt, but victor, the demons tied and bound.
He looks down on Lord Nedran; his eyes grow cold and
  bleak—
"Now shall I give you, Nedran, the power that you seek—"

*Now Vanyel frees the demons, and Nedran screams with
    fear,*
*He sets them on the Karsites, who had first brought them
    here.*
He sets them on the Karsites, and on the Karsite land.
*They look down on Lord Nedran. They do not stay their
    hand.*

Now Vanyel calls the farmers. "Go tell you near and far,
How thus are served the tyrants who would take Valdemar.
I am the bane of demons, who flees them I defend.
Thus Heralds serve a foeman—thus Heralds save a friend!"

THE SHADOW-LOVER

Shadow-Lover, never seen by day,
Only deep in dreams do you appear.
Wisdom tells me I should turn away,
Love of mist and shadows, all unclear—
Nothing can I hold of you but thought
Shadow-Lover, mist and twilight wrought.

Shadow-Lover, comfort me in pain.
Love, although I never see your face,
All who'd have me fear you speak in vain—
Never would I shrink from your embrace
Shadow-Lover, gentle is your hand
Never could another understand.

Shadow-Lover, soothe me when I mourn
Mourn for all who left me here alone,
When my grief is too much to be borne,
When my burdens crushing-great have grown,
Shadow-Lover, I cannot forget—
Help me bear the burdens I have yet.

Shadow-Lover, you alone can know
How I long to reach a point of peace
How I fade with weariness and woe
How I long for you to bring release.
Shadow-Lover, court me in my dreams
Bring the peace that suffering redeems.

Shadow-Lover, from the Shadows made,
Lead me into Shadows once again.
Where you lead I cannot be afraid,
For with you I shall come home again—
In your arms I shall not fear the night.
Shadow-Lover, lead me into light.

MAGIC'S PRICE

Every year Companions Choose, as they have done before,
The Chosen come with shining hopes to learn the Herald's
  lore.
And every year the Heralds sigh, and give the same advice—
"All those who would hold Magic's Power must then pay
  Magic's Price."

Oh there was danger in the North—that's all that Vanyel
  knew.
An enemy of power dark sought Heralds out—then slew.
But only those with Magic's Gift were slain by silent rage—
Till Vanyel of them all was left the only Herald-Mage.

Yes, from the North the danger came, beyond the Border
  far—
The Forest did not stay Dark Death, nor did the mountains
  bar.
And Vanyel cried—"We die, my liege, and know not why
  nor where!
So send me North my King, that I may find the answers
  there!"

Then North went Vanyel—not alone, though 'twas of little
  aid
A Bard was like to be to him; and Stefen was afraid—
He feared that he would fail the quest, a burden prove to
  be—
Dared not let Vanyel go alone to face dark sorcery.

So out beyond the Border there, beyond the forest tall,
Into the mountains deep they went that stood an icy wall—
To find the wall had cracked and found there was a passage
  new,
A path clean cut that winding ran a level course and true.

This path was wrought by magecraft; Vanyel knew that when
  he saw
The mountains hewn by power alone, a power he felt with
  awe—
But to what purpose? Something moved beyond them on the
  trail;

They watched and hid—and what they found there turned
  them cold and pale.

An army moved in single file, by magic cloaked and hid—
An army moved on Valdemar that marched as they were
  bid—
A darker force than weaponry controlled the men and place,
For Vanyel looked—and Vanyel knew an ancient evil's face.

Then Vanyel turned to Stefen, and he told the Bard to ride
To warn the folk of Valdemar—"They call me 'Magic's
  Pride.'
It's time I earned the name—now go! I'll hold this army back
Until the arms of Valdemar can counter their attack."

So Stefen rode, and so it is no living tongue can tell
How Vanyel fought, nor what he wrought, nor how the Her-
  ald fell.
The Army came—but not in time to save the Herald-Mage,
Although the pass was scorched and cracked by magic pow-
  er's rage.

They fought the Dark Ones back although they came on
  wave by wave.
No trace they found of Vanyel, nor of his Companion
  brave—
They only found the focus-stone, the gift of Stefen's hand—
Now blackened, burned, and shattered by the power that
  saved their land.

They only found the foemen who into the woods had fled
And each one by unseen, uncanny powers now lay dead.
As if the Forest had somehow bestirred itself that day—
Had Vanyel with his dying breath commanded trees to slay?

And still the forest of the North guards Valdemar from
  harm—
For Vanyel's dying curse is stronger far than mortal arm.
And every year the Chosen come, despite the old advice—
"All those who would be Magic's Pride must then pay Mag-
  ic's Price."

**Exploring New Realms
in Science Fiction/Fantasy Adventure**

The Last Herald-Mage
by Mercedes Lackey

Volumes one and two of this epic trilogy

Book One: Magic's Pawn

Born with the power to work both Herald and Mage magic, Vanyel seeks instead to become a Bard. But his is a talent too dangerous to be left untrained, and so his aunt Savil, a famed Herald-Mage of Valdemar, is entrusted with his instruction.

A headstrong, wilful boy, Vanyel's abuse of his raw magical powers soon unleashes terrifying wry-hunters on the land. Savil asks a Shin'a' in Adept for help, but the boy's wild talent is already beyond control — and Valdemar itself is in desperate peril . . .

Book Two: Magic's Promise

The Wild Magic is taking its toll on the land of Valdemar. Even Vanyel, the most powerful of the Herald-Mages, has almost been destroyed by the twin banes of war and dark magic.

But when his Companion Yfandes is summoned by a desperate cry for help from a neighbouring kingdom, the exhausted Vanyel is drawn into a maelstrom of magic and deception of which the young Prince Tashir is both victim and cause . . .